Dugan yanked the wheel to the left to avoid crashing into the other vehicle, then swung the SUV to the side of the road and threw it in Park.

?e jumped out and ran toward the burning vehicle.

?he driver had shot at them. Tried to kill them.

?hy? Because she was asking questions about her ?on?

?he jerked herself from her immobilized state ?nd climbed out. Dugan circled the car, peering ?nto the window as if looking for a way to get the ?river out. But the gas tank blew, another explosion ?ounded and flames engulfed the vehicle.

?weat beaded on her forehead, the heat scalding ?her. She backed away, hugging the side of the SUV ?s she watched Dugan. He must have realized ?t was impossible to save the driver because he ?strode back toward her, his expression grim.

'Someone doesn't like us asking questions, Sage. But that means we might be on the right track to finding some answers.'

COLD CASE
AT COBRA CREEK

BY
RITA HERRON

MILLS
BOON

Published in Great Britain 2014
by Mills & Boon, an imprint of Harlequin (UK) Limited,
Eton House, 18-24 Paradise Road, Richmond, Surrey, TW9 1SR

© 2014 Rita Herron

ISBN: 978-0-263-91375-0

46-1114

Harlequin (UK) Limited's policy is to use papers that are natural, renewable and recyclable products and made from wood grown in sustainable forests. The logging and manufacturing processes conform to the legal environmental regulations of the country of origin.

Printed and bound in Spain
by CPI, Barcelona

Award-winning author **Rita Herron** wrote her first book when she was twelve, but didn't think real people grew up to be writers. Now she writes so she doesn't have to get a *real* job. A former kindergarten teacher and workshop leader, she traded storytelling to kids for writing romance, and now she writes romantic comedies and romantic suspense. She lives in Georgia with her own romance hero and three kids. She loves to hear from readers, so please write her at PO Box 921225, Norcross, GA 30092-1225, USA, or visit her website, www.ritaherron.com.

To all the Harlequin Intrigue fans
—thanks for reading me all these years!

Prologue

Sage Freeport vowed never to trust a man again.

Not after the way Trace Lanier had treated her. Promises of love and happily ever after—until she'd gotten pregnant.

Then those promises had evaporated, like rain on a strip of scorching-hot pavement.

Her three-year-old Benji had never met his father. She'd worried about him not having a man in his life and done her best to be two parents in one. Still, she couldn't throw a softball worth a darn, and baiting her own hook to go fishing at the pond literally made her feel faint.

Then Ron Lewis had come along a few months ago and swept her off her feet with his kindness and intelligence—and treated Benji like his own son.

Her gaze strayed to the tabletop tree she and Benji had decorated just yesterday. Together they'd made ornaments to hang on the tree, and when he was asleep last night, she'd wrapped his gift. He was going to be ecstatic on Christmas morning to find the softball and glove he'd asked for.

She pulled a pan of homemade cinnamon rolls from the oven to let them cool before her guests at the B and B she owned surfaced for breakfast, then went upstairs to check on her son.

Benji was normally up by now, underfoot in the kitchen when she was cooking—chatting and asking questions and sneaking bacon as soon as she took it off the pan.

But when she opened Benji's door, he wasn't in bed. A few toys were scattered around the floor, a sign he'd gotten up to play after she'd tucked him in the night before.

Figuring he was playing some imaginary game, she darted into his bathroom.

But he wasn't there, either.

She checked under his bed and frowned. "Benji? Where are you, honey?"

No answer.

Her heartbeat stuttered for a moment, but she told herself not to panic. The inn was a big house. The B and B held eight rooms, although most of them were empty at the time. With the holidays approaching, most people were staying home, going to visit family or flying to some exotic location for a winter vacation, not visiting small-town Texas.

She peeked inside Benji's closet but didn't see him. Yet the dresser drawer stood open, and his clothes looked as if he'd pawed through them.

Probably to dress himself. He was three and starting to vie for independence that way. She just had to teach him how to match colors now.

Then she noticed his backpack was missing.

Her heart suddenly racing, she turned and looked at his room again. The big bear he normally slept with wasn't in his bed. Not on the floor or in the room at all. Neither was the whistle he liked or his favorite red hat.

But his blanket was there. He'd never go anywhere without that blue blanket.

Fear seized her, but she fought it off.

Surely Benji was just pretending he was on a camping trip. He and Ron had been talking about hiking the other night. Ron had even asked Benji which one of his special friends/toys he would carry with him if he was going on a long trip.

The bear, whistle and red cap were on his list.

Her hands shaking as other scenarios taunted her, she raced down the hall to the empty rooms and searched inside. No Benji.

Hating to disturb the two guests she did have but panicked now, she knocked on the door to the Ellises', an elderly couple on an anniversary trip. The gray-haired man opened the door dressed in a robe. "Yeah?"

"I'm sorry, Mr. Ellis, but have you seen my son, Benji?"

"No, ma'am. Me and Henrietta been sleeping."

"Would you mind checking your room in case he snuck in? He's only three and mischievous at times."

He scratched his head, sending his wiry hair askew. "Sure." He left the door open, and Sage watched as he checked under the bed, the closet and adjoining bathroom. "Sorry, Ms. Freeport, he's not in here."

Sage's stomach knotted. If—no, *when*—she found Benji, she would explain that hiding from her was not okay.

She climbed the steps to the third-floor attic room. A woman named Elvira had chosen it, saying she needed solace and to be alone. The poor woman had lost a child, and Sage had given her privacy to mourn.

But Elvira didn't answer. Sage let herself in and found a note from the lady saying she'd decided to leave early and didn't want to disturb Sage.

Benji liked this room because the window offered a view of the creek behind the house.

But the room was empty.

Nerves on edge, she ran downstairs, once again checking each room and shouting Benji's name. She rushed outside, wind beating at her as she searched the yard, the garden out back, the swing set, the fort and the tree house.

Benji was nowhere to be found.

Terrified, she ran back inside to call the sheriff. But the phone was ringing as she entered the kitchen. Maybe a neighbor had found Benji.

She grabbed the phone, determined to get rid of the caller so she could phone the sheriff. But his voice echoed back.

"Ms. Freeport, it's Sheriff Gandt."

Her stomach pitched. "Yes, I was just about to call you. My little boy, Benji… He's gone."

"I was afraid of that," Sheriff Gandt muttered.

Icy fear seized Sage.

"I think you'd better come down to River Road Crossing at Cobra Creek."

"Why?" She had to swallow to make her voice work. "Is Benji there?"

"Just meet me there."

He hung up, and Sage's knees buckled. She grabbed the kitchen counter to keep from hitting the floor.

No…Benji was fine. He had to be…

She grabbed her keys and ran outside. The minivan took three tries to crank, but she threw it in gear and tore down the road toward the river crossing.

As soon as she rounded the bend, she spotted flames shooting into the air. Smoke curled upward, clogging the sky in a thick, gray blanket.

Tires squealed as she swung the van to the shoulder of the road, jumped out and ran toward the burning car.

Sheriff Gandt stood by while firemen worked to extinguish the blaze. But even with the flames and smoke, she could tell that the car was a black Jeep.

Ron drove a black Jeep.

"Do you recognize this vehicle?" the sheriff asked.

A cold sweat broke out on Sage's body. "It's Ron's. My fiancé."

Sheriff Gandt's expression looked harsh in the morning light. Then she saw what he was holding in his hands.

Benji's teddy bear and red hat.

No… Dear God. Had Benji been in the car with Ron when it crashed and caught on fire?

Chapter One

Two years later

Dugan Graystone did not trust Sheriff Billy Gandt worth a damn.

Gandt thought he owned the town and the people in it and made no bones about the fact that men like Dugan, men who weren't white, weren't fit for office and should stay out of his way.

Gandt had even tried to stop Dugan from taking on this search-and-rescue mission, saying he could use his own men. But the families of the two lost hikers had heard about Dugan's reputation as an expert tracker and insisted he spearhead the efforts to find the young men.

Dugan rode his stallion across the wilderness, scrutinizing every bush and tree, along with the soil, for footprints and other signs that someone had come this way. A team of searchers had spread across the miles of forests looking for the missing men, but Dugan had a sixth sense, and it had led him over to Cobra Creek, miles from where Gandt had set up base camp for the volunteer workers involved in the search.

Dammit, he hated Gandt. He'd run against him for sheriff and lost—mainly because Gandt bought votes. But one day he'd put the bastard in his place and prove that beneath that good-old-boy act, Gandt was nothing but a lying, cheating coward.

Born on the reservation near Cobra Creek, Dugan had Native American blood running through his veins. Dugan fought for what was right.

And nothing about Gandt was right.

Money, power and women were Gandt's for the taking. And crime—if it benefited Billy—could be overlooked for a price.

Though Dugan owned his own spread, on the side, he worked as a P.I. His friend, Texas Ranger Jaxon Ward, was looking into Gandt's financials, determined to catch the man at his own game.

The recent flooding of the creek had uprooted bushes and trees, and washed up debris from the river that connected to the creek. Dugan noted an area that looked trampled, as if a path had been cut through the woods.

He guided his horse to a tree and dismounted, then knelt to examine the still-damp earth. A footprint in the mud?

Was it recent?

He noticed another, then some brush flattened, leading toward the creek. Dugan's instincts kicked in, and he shone his flashlight on the ground and followed the indentations.

Several feet away, he saw another area of ground that looked disturbed. Mud and sticks and…something else.

Bones.

Maybe an animal's?

He hurried over to examine them, his pulse pounding. No…that was a human femur. And a finger.

Human bones.

And judging from the decomp, they had been there too long to belong to one of the two teenagers who'd gone missing.

The radio at his belt buzzed and crackled, and he hit the button to connect.

"We found the boys," Jaxon said. "A little dehydrated, but they're fine."

Dugan removed his Stetson and wiped sweat from his forehead. "Good. But I need the coroner over here at Cobra Creek."

"What?"

"I found bones," Dugan said. "Looks like they've been here a couple of years."

A foreboding washed over Dugan. Two years ago, a man named Ron Lewis had supposedly died in a car crash near here. Sage Freeport's son had been with him at the time.

The man's body and her son's had never been found.

Could these bones belong to Ron Lewis, the man who'd taken her son?

SAGE SET A PLACE at the breakfast bar for Benji, then slid a pancake onto the plate and doused it with powdered sugar, just the way her son liked it. His chocolate milk came next.

The tabletop Christmas tree she kept year-round still held the tiny ornaments Benji had made and hung on it. And the present she'd had for him the year he'd gone missing still sat wrapped, waiting for his small hands to tear it open.

It was a glove and ball, something Benji had asked Santa for that year.

Would the glove still fit when she finally found him and he came home?

Two of her guests, a couple named Dannon, who'd come to Cobra Creek to celebrate their twentieth anniversary, gave her pitying looks, but she ignored them.

She knew people thought she was crazy. Mrs. Krandall, the owner of the diner in town, had even warned her that perpetuating the fantasy that her son was still alive by keeping a place set for him was dangerous for her and downright creepy.

She also suggested that it would hurt Sage's business.

A business Sage needed to pay the bills—and to keep her sanity.

But she couldn't accept that her son was dead.

Not without answers as to why Ron had taken Benji from the house and where they'd been headed.

Not without definite proof that he wasn't alive out there somewhere, needing her.

Of course, Benji's hat and bear had been found at the scene, but his bones had never been recovered.

Sheriff Gandt theorized that Lewis and Benji probably had been injured and tried to escape the fire by going into the creek. But storms created a strong current that night, and their bodies must have washed downstream, then into the river where they'd never be found.

She should never have trusted Ron with her son. It was her fault he was gone....

She refused to believe that he wouldn't be back. She had to cling to hope.

Without it, the guilt would eat her alive.

DUGAN GRITTED HIS TEETH as Sheriff Gandt studied the bones.

"Could have been a stranger wandering through," Gandt said. "Miles of wilderness out here. I'll check the databases for wanted men. Criminals have been known to hide out here off the grid."

The medical examiner, Dr. Liam Longmire, narrowed his eyes as he examined the body they unearthed when they'd swept the debris from the bones. Most of the skeleton was intact. Of course, the bones had decayed and been mauled by animals, but there were enough that they'd be able to identify him. That is, if they had medical records to compare to.

"What about Ron Lewis?" Dugan asked. "It could be him."

Sheriff Gandt adjusted the waistband of his uniform pants and chewed on a blade of grass, his silence surprising. The man usually had an answer for everything.

Dr. Longmire looked up at Dugan, then Gandt. "I can't say who he is yet, but this man didn't die from a fire or from the elements."

"What was the cause of death?" Dugan asked.

Longmire pointed to the rib cage and thoracic cavity. "See the markings of a bullet? It shattered one of his ribs. I can tell more when I get him on the table, but judging from the angle, it appears the bullet probably pierced his heart."

Dugan glanced at Gandt, who made a harrumph sound.

"Guess you've got a murder to investigate, Sheriff," Dugan said.

Gandt met his gaze with stone-cold, gray eyes, then glanced at the M.E. "How long has he been dead?"

"My guess is a couple of years." Dr. Longmire paused. "That'd be about the time that Lewis man ran off with Sage Freeport's kid."

Gandt nodded, his mouth still working that blade of grass. But his grim expression told Dugan this body was more of a nuisance than a case he wanted to work.

"I'll request Lewis's dental records," Dr. Longmire said. "If they match, we'll know who our victim is."

Gandt started to walk away, but Dugan cleared his throat. "Sheriff, aren't you going to get a crime unit to comb the area and look for evidence?"

"Don't see no reason for that," Gandt muttered. "If the man's been dead two years, probably ain't nothin' to find. Besides, the flood last week would have washed away any evidence." He gestured to the south. "That said, Lewis's car was found farther downstream. If his body got in the water, it would have floated further downstream, not up here."

"Not if his body was dumped in a different place from where he died."

"You're grasping at straws." Gandt directed his comment to the M.E. "ID him and then we'll go from there."

The sheriff could be right. The victim could have been a drifter. Or a man from another town. Hell, he could have been one of the two prisoners who'd escaped jail a couple years back, ones who'd never been caught.

But the sheriff should at least be looking for evidence near where the body was found.

Gandt strode toward his squad car, and Dugan used his phone to take photographs of the bones. Dr. Longmire offered a commentary on other injuries he noted the body had sustained, and Dugan made a note of them.

Then Longmire directed the medics to load the body into the van to transport to the morgue, making sure they were careful to keep the skeleton intact and preserve any forensic evidence on the bones.

Dugan combed the area, scrutinizing the grass and embankment near where the bones had washed up. He also searched the brush for clues. He plucked a small scrap of fabric from a briar and found a metal button in the mud a few feet from the place where he'd first discovered the bones. He bagged the items for the lab to analyze, then conducted another sweep of the property, spanning out a half mile in both directions.

Unfortunately, Gandt was right. With time, weather and the animals foraging in the wilderness, he couldn't pinpoint if the body had gone into the river here or some other point.

Frustrated, he finally packed up and headed back to town.

But a bad feeling tightened his gut. Gandt had closed the case involving Sage Freeport's missing son and Lewis too quickly for his taste.

How would he handle this one?

BY LATE AFTERNOON, news of the bones found at Cobra Creek reached Sage through the grapevine in the small Texas town. She was gathering groceries to bake her famous coconut cream pie when she overheard two women talking about the hikers that had been recovered safely.

The checkout lady, Lorraine Hersher, the cousin of the M.E., broke in. "A body was found out at the creek. Nothing but the bones left."

Sage inched her way up near the register.

"Who was it?" one of the women asked.

"Don't think they know yet. Liam said he was checking dental records. But he said the man had been dead about two years."

Sage's stomach clenched. Two years? About the time Ron's car had crashed.

Could it possibly be…?

Desperate for answers, she pushed her cart to the side, leaving her groceries inside it, then hurried toward the door. The sheriff's office was across the square, and she tugged her jacket around her, battling a stiff breeze as she crossed the street.

Sheriff Gandt had been less than helpful when Benji had gone missing. He wouldn't want her bugging him now.

But she'd long ago decided she didn't care what he thought.

She charged inside the office, surprised to see Dugan Graystone standing inside at the front desk. She'd seen the big man in town a few times, but he kept to himself. With his intense, dark brown eyes and brooding manner, some said he was a loner but that he was the best tracker in Texas. Tall, broad shoulders, sharp cheekbones—the package was handsome. Half the women in town thought he was sexy, while the other half were afraid of him.

Dr. Longmire stood next to him, the sheriff on the opposite side of the desk.

All three men turned to look at her as she entered, looking like they'd been caught doing something wrong.

Sage lifted her chin in a show of bravado. "I heard about the body you found at Cobra Creek."

Dugan's brown eyes met hers, turmoil darkening the depths, while Gandt shot her one of his condescending looks. She couldn't believe the man had ever been married and understood why he wasn't anymore.

She had heard that he'd taken in his ailing mother, that the elderly woman was wheelchair-bound, difficult and demanding. Even though she disliked Gandt, she had to admit his loyalty to his mother was admirable.

"Who was it?" Sage asked.

Dr. Longmire adjusted his hat, acknowledging her with a politeness bred from a different era. "The body belonged to Ron Lewis."

Sage gasped. "You're sure?"

"Dental and medical records confirm it," the M.E. said.

Sage's legs threatened to give way. She caught herself by dropping onto a chair across from the desk. Tears clogged her throat as panic and fear seized her.

But she'd been in the dark for two years, and she had to know the truth.

Even if it killed her.

"Was Benji with him?"

Chapter Two

Sage held her breath. "Sheriff, did you find Benji?"

Sheriff Gandt shook his head. "No. Just Lewis's body."

Relief spilled through Sage. "Then my son… He may still be out there. He may be alive."

Dugan and the medical examiner traded questioning looks, but the sheriff's frown made her flinch. Did he know something he wasn't telling her? Was that the reason he'd closed the case so quickly after Benji disappeared?

"Ms. Freeport," Sheriff Gandt said in a tone he might use with a child, "Dr. Longmire believes Ron Lewis has been dead since the day of that crash. That means that your son has been, too. We just haven't found his body yet. Probably because of the elements—"

"That's enough, Sheriff," Dugan said sharply.

Sheriff Gandt shot Dugan an irritated look. "I believe your part is done here, Graystone."

Sage gripped the edge of the desk. "How did Ron die, Sheriff?"

"Ms. Freeport, why don't you go home and calm down—"

"He died of a gunshot wound," Dugan said, cutting off the sheriff.

Sage barely stifled a gasp. "Then the car crash…? That didn't kill him."

"No," Dr. Longmire said, "he most likely bled out."

Sage's mind raced. Who had shot Ron? And why? "The shot caused the crash," she said, piecing together a scenario in her head.

"That would be my guess," Dr. Longmire said.

"Was there a bullet hole in the car?" Dugan asked Gandt.

Sheriff Gandt shrugged. "I don't know. The fire destroyed most of it."

Sage folded her arms and stared at the sheriff. "But that bullet proves Ron Lewis's death was no accident. He was murdered."

DUGAN WORKED TO rein in his anger toward Gandt. The weasel should be comforting Sage and reassuring her he'd do everything humanly possible to find the truth about what happened to her son.

That was what he'd do if he was sheriff.

But he lacked the power and money the Gandts had, and in this small town, that seemed to mean everything.

"It appears that way," Sheriff Gandt told Sage. "And I will be investigating the matter. But—" he lifted a warning hand to Sage "—if your son had survived, we would have found him by now, Ms. Freeport. Odds are that the shooter fired at Lewis, he crashed and managed to get out of the car and fled. Maybe your son was with him, maybe not. But if he made it to the water with Lewis, he couldn't have survived the frigid temperature or the current. He would have been swept downstream and drowned."

"Sheriff," Dugan snarled, hating the man's cold bluntness.

The M.E. gave Sage a sympathetic look, then excused himself and hurried out the door.

Sheriff Gandt tugged at his pants. Damn man needed a belt to keep the things up. That or lose thirty pounds around his belly so he didn't have to wear them so low.

"I know you want me to sugarcoat things, Graystone, but I'm the sheriff, not a damn counselor. I tell it like it is. Good or bad."

Still, he could consider Sage's feelings. She'd lost a child. "Part of your job is to protect innocent citizens and to find out the truth when something happens to one of them. Benji Freeport was three. He was certainly innocent." Dugan squared off with the sheriff. "But you haven't done a damn thing to give his mother closure or find the answers she needs."

"You think bringing her a mangled bunch of bones is going to make her feel better?" Sheriff Gandt said.

"That would hurt, but at least I'd know the truth," Sage said. "And now that we know Ron was murdered, there is a chance that whoever shot him took Benji." Sage's voice cracked. "That means that Benji may be out there, alone, in trouble, needing me. That he's been waiting for us to find him all this time."

Dugan's chest tightened at the emotions in her voice. Emotions she had every right to feel, because she'd spoken the truth.

Sheriff Gandt swung a crooked finger toward the door. "I don't need either of you telling me how to do my job. Now, leave so I can get to it."

"Then let me know what you find." Sage clutched her shoulder bag, turned and walked out the door.

Dugan stared at the sheriff. "She deserves to know what happened to her son. And if he's alive, she deserves to bring him home."

"She's deluding herself if she thinks she'll find him alive," Sheriff Gandt said. "She needs to accept that he's gone and move on with her life."

Dugan had never had a child, but if he did and that child disappeared, he'd move heaven and earth to find him. "You are going to investigate Lewis's murder, aren't you? After all, you owe it to the people in the town to make sure that his killer isn't still among them."

Gandt tapped his badge. "In case you've forgotten, Graystone, the people elected me, so they obviously have confidence in my abilities. Now, get out of my office."

Dugan shot him a go-to-hell look, turned and stormed out the door. The man might make a token gesture to solve Lewis's murder.

But he doubted he would put forth any effort to hunt for Benji Freeport.

Dugan spotted Sage sitting on a park bench in the square, her face buried in her hands, her body trembling.

He headed across the square to join her. If Gandt wouldn't find Sage's son for her, he would.

SAGE WAS SO ANGRY she was shaking all over. Sheriff Gandt had stonewalled her before.

But how could he dismiss her so easily now that they knew that Ron Lewis had been murdered?

Ron's face flashed in her mind, and her stomach revolted. She'd been such a fool to trust him. Why had he taken her son with him that day? Where was he going?

And who had killed him?

The questions ate at her. None of it made sense.

Ron had waltzed into her life and charmed her with his good looks, his business sense and his talk of giving the town a face-lift and bringing in tourism. Tourists would have greatly impacted her income, so she'd been on board from the beginning.

Maybe that was the one reason he'd warmed up to her. Had he thought she could influence the town council with his plans for putting Cobra Creek on the map?

Footsteps crunched on gravel, and she suddenly felt someone beside her. A hand on her shoulder.

She jerked her head up, wiping at the tears streaming

down her face, and stared into Dugan Graystone's dark eyes. The man was a rebel of sorts and was the only person she'd ever known to go up against the sheriff.

High cheekbones sculpted an angular face, evidence of his Native American roots. His chiseled face was bronzed from work on the ranch, his hands were broad and strong looking, his big body made for ranching and working the land.

Or for a woman.

She silently chided herself. Just because she felt vulnerable and needy, and Dugan was strong and powerful looking, didn't mean she'd fall prey to his charms.

No man would ever get close to her again.

"What do you want?" Sage asked, a little more harshly than she'd intended.

Dugan's eyes flared at her tone. "Gandt is a first-class jerk."

His comment deflated her anger, and a nervous laugh escaped her. "Yes, he is."

"He said he'd look into Lewis's murder."

"Sure he will." Sage brushed her hands together. "Like he looked into the crash two years ago."

Dugan sank his big body onto the bench beside her. "I know you were engaged to Lewis and want answers about who killed him."

Anger shot through Sage. "We may have been engaged, but that was obviously a mistake. The minute he took my son from my house without my permission, any feelings I had for him died." She swallowed the lump in her throat. "I don't care why he was murdered. In fact, I would have killed him myself for taking Benji if I'd found him."

A tense second passed. "I understand," Dugan said in a gruff voice.

"Do you? That man took everything from me."

The anguish in her tone made his chest squeeze. "I'll help you," he said. "I'll find out why Lewis was murdered."

Sage studied his face. He seemed so sincere. Earnest. As if he actually cared.

But she wouldn't buy in to that, not ever again.

On the other hand, Dugan had run for sheriff and Gandt had beaten him, so he probably had his own personal agenda. He wanted to show Gandt up and prove to the town that they'd elected the wrong man.

She really didn't care about his motive. "All right. But understand this—the only reason I want to know who killed Ron is that it might lead me to my son. Whatever dirt you dig up on Ron is fine with me. I don't care about his reputation or even my own, for that matter."

Dugan studied her in silence for a few minutes. Sage felt the wind ruffle her hair, felt the heat from his body, felt the silence thick with the unknown.

"I'll do everything I can to help you," Dugan said gruffly. "But I may not find the answers you want."

Sage understood the implications of his statement. "I know that." She gripped her hands together. "All I want is the truth…no matter what it is."

"Even if it's not pretty?"

Sage nodded. "The truth can't be any worse than what I've already imagined."

DUGAN HOPED THAT was true. But there was the possibility that they'd find out her little boy had been burned in the fire. Or that he'd been kidnapped by a cold-blooded murderer.

The scenarios that came to mind sent a shot of fear through him. For all they knew, the shooter could have abducted Benji and sold him or handed him off to a group trafficking kids. Hell, he could have been a pedophile.

In fact, kidnapping the boy could have been the end-game all along.

Someone could have hired Lewis to get the boy.

But if so, why?

He had to ask questions, questions Sage might not like.

"You've done investigative work before?" Sage asked.

Dugan nodded. "I've been called in as a consultant on some cold cases. I have a friend, Texas Ranger Jaxon Ward, who I work with."

"How do you know him?"

"We go way back," Dugan said, remembering the foster home where they'd met.

Sage arched an eyebrow in question, but Dugan let the moment pass. They weren't here to talk about him and his shady upbringing. "In light of the fact that Lewis's body has been found, I'm going to enter your son's picture into the system for missing children."

Emotions darkened Sage's soft green eyes, but she nodded. "Of course. I tried to get Sheriff Gandt to do that two years ago, but he was certain Benji died in the crash or drowned, and said it was a waste of time."

That sounded like shoddy police work to him.

"If you want to stop by the inn, I can give you one of the latest pictures I took."

"I'll walk with you over there now."

Sage stood, one hand clutching her shoulder bag. "Why don't you meet me there in half an hour? I have an errand to run first."

"Half an hour," Dugan agreed.

Sage hesitated a moment, her breath shaky in the heart-beat of silence that stretched between them. "Thank you, Dugan. I can't tell you what it means to have someone listen to me. I…know some people think I'm nuts. That I just can't let go."

He had heard rumors that she set the table for her son at every meal, as if he was coming home for dinner. Hell, was that crazy, or was she simply trying to keep hope alive?

"I don't blame you for not giving up," Dugan said gruffly. "At least not without the facts or proof that your son is really gone."

He let the words linger between them, well aware she understood the meaning underscoring his comment. If he found proof Benji was dead, she'd have to accept that.

But if there was a chance the boy was out there somewhere, he'd find him and bring him back to her where he belonged.

SAGE UNLOADED THE GROCERIES, grateful the couple staying at the inn had taken a day trip and wouldn't be back until bedtime. Breakfast came with the room rental, but lunch and dinner were optional. In addition, she provided coffee and tea and snacks midmorning and afternoon, including fruit, cookies and an assortment of freshly baked pastries and desserts. She usually conferred with the guests on check-in and planned accordingly.

The doorbell rang; then the front bell tinkled that someone had entered. She rushed to the entryway and found Dugan standing beneath the chandelier, studying the rustic farm tools and pictures of horses on the wall.

People who visited Texas wanted rustic charm, and she tried to give it to them.

"I came for that picture." Dugan tipped his Stetson out of politeness, his rugged features stark in the evening light.

"Come this way." She led him through the swinging double doors to the kitchen. His gaze caught on the tabletop Christmas tree, and she bit back a comment, refusing to explain herself.

Maybe Benji would never come back.

But if he did, his present would be waiting. And they would celebrate all the days and holidays they'd missed spending together the past two years.

Chapter Three

Sage opened a photo album on the breakfast bar and began to flip through it. Dugan watched pain etch itself on her face as she stared at the pictures chronicling Benji's young life.

A baby picture of him swaddled in a blue blanket while he lay nestled in Sage's arms. A photo of the little boy sleeping in a crib, another of him as an infant in the bathtub playing with a rubber ducky, pictures of him learning to crawl, then walk.

Photos of Benji tearing open presents at his first birthday party, riding a rocking horse at Christmas, playing in the sprinkler out back, cuddled on the couch in monster pajamas and cradling his blanket.

Sage paused to trace her finger over a small envelope. "I kept a lock of Benji's hair from his first haircut."

Dugan offered a smile, tolerating her trip down memory lane because he understood her emotions played into this case and he couldn't ignore them.

He shifted uncomfortably. He had a hard time relating to family; he had never been part of one and didn't know how families worked. At least, not normal, loving ones. If they existed.

He'd grown up between foster care and the rez, never really wanted in either place.

She brushed at a tear, then removed a picture of Benji posed by the Christmas tree. "I took that the day before he went missing."

Dugan glanced at the tabletop tree and realized the same present still lay beneath the tree's base. Dammit. She'd kept the tree up all this time waiting on her son to return to open it.

"Can I get the photograph back?" Sage asked. "As you can see, this is all I have left…."

The crack in her voice tore at him. "Of course. I'll take good care of it, Sage." And maybe he'd bring back the real thing instead of just a picture.

But he refrained from making that promise.

"Sage, before I get started, we need to talk. There are some questions I need you to answer."

Sage closed the photo album and laid a hand on top of it. He noticed her nails were short, slightly jagged, as if she'd been biting them.

"What do you want to know?"

"Do you have any idea why Ron Lewis had Benji in the car with him that day?"

"No." Sage threaded her fingers through the long, tangled tresses of her hair, hair that was streaked with red, brown and gold. "Sheriff Gandt suggested that he was taking Benji Christmas shopping to buy me a present."

A possibility. "What do you think?"

"Ron knew how protective I was of my son. I don't understand why he would have left without telling me or leaving me a note. He knew that Benji was all I had, and that I would panic when I woke up and discovered they were gone."

"What about other family?" Dugan asked.

Sage sighed wearily. "I never knew my father. My mother died the year before I had Benji. A car accident."

He knew this could get touchy. "And Benji's father?"

Resignation settled in her eyes. "Trace Lanier. I met him right after my mother died." She traced a finger along the edge of the photo album. "I was grieving and vulnerable. Not that that's an excuse, but we dated a few times. When I discovered the pregnancy, he bailed."

"Where is he now?"

"I have no clue. He worked the rodeos, traveling town to town."

"Did he express any interest in seeing his son?"

Sage laughed, a bitter sound. "No. He didn't even want to acknowledge that Benji was his. In fact, he accused me of lying, of coming after him for money."

Dugan waited, his pulse hammering. Sage didn't strike him as that type at all.

"I was furious," Sage said. "I told him that my mother was a single mother and that she'd raised me on her own, and that I would do the same. I didn't want his money. And I didn't care if I ever saw him again or if he ever met his son."

"And that was that?"

Sage brushed her hands together. "That was that. I never heard from him again."

Dugan contemplated her story. "Do you think that he might have changed his mind and decided he wanted to see Benji?"

Sage shook her head. "No. I think he's doing pretty well in the rodeo circuit now. Making a name bronco riding. That brings the rodeo groupies. The last thing he'd want is to have a child get in the way of that."

Dugan had never met the bastard, but he didn't like him.

Still, he'd verify that information. Perhaps Lanier's manager had suggested that having a little boy could improve his popularity. It was a long shot, but Dugan didn't intend to ignore any possibility.

SAGE HATED ADMITTING that she had fallen for Trace Lanier's sexy rodeo looks, but she had. Even worse, she'd believed Ron Lewis was different.

Could he have simply been taking Benji Christmas shopping and gotten killed before he could bring her son back?

And why would someone kill Ron?

Or had Ron taken Benji for another reason?

But why? She didn't have money to pay a ransom....

"Do you want coffee?" Sage asked.

Dugan nodded, and she poured them both a mug, then placed a slice of homemade pound cake on a plate in front of him. "It's fresh. I baked it last night."

A small smile curved his mouth. "I've heard you're a good cook."

"Really?" Sage blushed. What else had he heard?

"Yes, I'm sure it helps with your business."

"I suppose so," Sage said. "I used to stay with my grandma when I was little, and she taught me everything she knew."

He sipped his coffee. "Tell me about Ron Lewis. How did you two meet?"

"Actually he stayed here when he came to town on business," Sage said. "He was a real estate developer. He wanted to convince the town council to go forward on a new development that would enrich the town, create jobs and tourism and bring us out of the Dark Ages."

"I remember hearing something about that project," Dugan said, although he hadn't exactly been for the development. The group handling it wanted to buy up ranches and farms in the neighboring area, and turn Cobra Creek into a tourist trap with outlet malls, fast-food chains and a dude ranch.

"So you struck up a friendship?"

Sage nodded. "I was reluctant at first, but he was persistent. And he took an interest in Benji."

"Benji liked him?"

"Yes."

"He would have gone with him, without being afraid?"

"Yes," Sage said, her voice cracking. "Ron stayed in Cobra Creek most of that summer, so we went on several family outings together." She'd thought she'd finally found a man who loved her and her son.

Fool.

Dugan broke off a chunk of cake and put it in his mouth. Sage watched a smile flicker in his eyes, one that pleased her more than it should.

"Did the town council approve his plans?"

Sage gave a noncommittal shrug. "They were going back and forth on things, discussing it." She frowned at Dugan. "Do you think his murder had something to do with the development?"

"I don't know," Dugan said. "But it's worth looking into."

Sage contemplated his suggestion. She should have asked more questions about Ron's business, about the investors he said he had lined up, about *him*.

And now it was too late. If something had gone wrong with his business, something that had gotten him killed, he might have taken that secret with him to the grave.

DUGAN NEEDED TO ask around, find out more about how the locals felt about Lewis's proposal. What had happened to the development after his death? Had anyone profited?

But Sage's comment about Ron's interest in Benji made him pause. "You said he showed an interest in Benji?"

Sage stirred sweetener in her coffee. "Yes, some men

don't like kids. Others don't know how to talk to them, but Ron seemed…comfortable with Benji."

"Hmm," Dugan mumbled. "Did he come from a big family?"

Sage frowned. "No, I asked him that. And he actually looked kind of sad. He said he was an only child and lost his parents when he was young."

"Was he married before? Maybe he had a child."

"No, at least he said he'd never married," Sage said. "But at this point, I don't know what to believe. Everything he told me could have been a lie."

True. In fact, he could have planned to kidnap Benji all along. He'd warmed up to the boy so he'd go with him willingly.

But why?

For money? Maybe someone had paid him to take Benji, then killed Ron Lewis to get rid of any witnesses.

But why would anyone want to kidnap Benji?

Sage wasn't wealthy, and she had no family that could offer a big reward. Kidnappers had been known to abduct a child to force a parent into doing something for them, but if swaying the town council to vote for the development had been the issue, it wouldn't have worked. Sage had no power or influence in the town.

Then again, Dugan had no proof that Ron Lewis had done anything wrong. That the man hadn't been sincerely in love with Sage, that he hadn't come to the town to help it prosper, that he was an innocent who had been shot to death for some reason.

And that he might have died trying to save Sage's son.

"DID LEWIS LEAVE anything of his here at the inn? A calendar? Computer?"

"No, I don't think so," Sage said.

"I know it's been two years, but what room did he stay in?"

"The Cross-ties Room."

He arched an eyebrow.

"I named each room based on a theme. People who come to Cobra Creek want the atmosphere, the feel of the quaint western town."

"Can I see that room, or is someone staying in it?"

"You can see it," Sage said. "I have only one couple staying here now. They're in the Water Tower Room."

Sage led Dugan up the stairs to the second floor. She unlocked the room, then stood back and watched as he studied the room.

"Have you rented this room since he was here?"

"Yes, a couple of times," she said. "I was full capacity during the art festival both years."

He walked over and looked inside the dresser, checking each drawer, but they were empty. Next he searched the drawers in the oak desk in the corner. Again, nothing.

"What are you looking for?" Sage asked.

Dugan shrugged. "If Lewis was killed because he was into something illegal, there might be evidence he left behind." He opened the closet door and looked inside. "Did he take everything with him that day when he left?"

Sage nodded. "His suitcase and computer were gone. That was what freaked me out."

"If he'd simply been taking Benji shopping, he wouldn't have taken those things with him."

"Exactly." Sage's heart stuttered as she remembered the blind panic that had assaulted her.

"Did he mention that he was leaving town to you?" Dugan asked.

"The day before, he said he might have to go away for a business meeting, but that he'd be back before Christmas."

"Did he say where the meeting was?"

Sage pushed a strand of hair away from her face. "No... but then, I didn't bother to ask." Guilt hit her again. "I was so distracted, so caught up in the holidays, in making a stupid grocery list for Christmas dinner and finishing my shopping, that I didn't pay much attention." Her voice broke. "If I had, maybe I would have picked up on something."

Dugan's boots clicked on the floor as he strode over to the doorway, where she stood. "Sage, this is not your fault."

"Yes, it is," Sage said, her heart breaking all over again. "I was Benji's mother. I was supposed to protect him."

"You did everything you could."

"Then, why is he missing?" Sage asked. "Why isn't he here with me this year, wrapping presents and making sugar cookies?"

"I don't know," Dugan said in a low voice. "But I promise you that I'll find out."

Sage latched on to the hope Dugan offered. But the same terrifying images that haunted her at night flashed behind her eyes now.

If the person who'd shot Ron had abducted Benji, what had he done with him? Where was he? And what had happened to him over the past two years?

Was he taken care of or had he been abused? Was he hungry? Alone?

Would he remember her when they found him?

"They found Lewis's body."

"Dammit. How did that happen?"

"Floods washed the body up. That Indian uncovered his bones in the bushes when he was looking for those hikers that got lost."

"After two years, they identified Lewis?"

"Yes. Damn dental records. I should have extracted all his teeth."

A tense second passed. "Hell, you should have burned the bastard's body in that car."

"I thought it was taken care of."

"Yeah, well, it wasn't. And Sage Freeport is asking questions again. Knowing her, she'll be pushing to get the case reopened. She's like a bloodhound."

"If she doesn't settle down, I'll take care of her."

"This time make sure nothing can come back to haunt us."

"No problem. When she disappears, it'll be for good."

Chapter Four

"Did Lewis always stay in this same room?" Dugan asked.

"Yes."

"How long was he here?"

Sage rubbed her temple. "The first time he came, he stayed a couple of weeks. Then he left for a month. When he returned, he stayed about six months."

"Where did he go when he left?"

"He was traveling around Texas. Said he worked with this company that looked for property across the state, small towns that were in need of rebuilding. Part of his job was to scout out the country and make suggestions to them."

"Where was his home?"

Sage straightened a pillow on top of the homemade quilt, which had imprints of horses on the squares. "He said he was from South Texas, I think. That he grew up in a little town not too far from Laredo."

Dugan made a mental note to check out his story. Maybe someone in that town knew more about Lewis.

He walked through the room again, the boards creaking beneath his boots as he stepped inside the closet. His toe caught on something and when he looked down, he realized a plank was loose.

He knelt and ran his finger along the wooden slat, his senses prickling. Was something beneath the board?

He yanked at it several times, and it finally gave way. He pulled it free, laid it to the side and felt the one next to it. It was loose, too, so he tugged it free, as well.

His curiosity spiking, he peered beneath the flooring. Something yellow caught his eye. He slid his hand below and felt inside the hole. His fingers connected with a small manila envelope.

"What are you doing?" Sage asked over his shoulder.

"Something's under here." He wiggled his fingers until he snagged the envelope, then removed it from the hole.

"What is that?" Sage asked.

"I don't know, but we'll find out." Dugan felt again just to make sure there wasn't anything else lodged beneath the floor, but the space was empty. Standing, he walked back to the corner desk, opened the envelope and dumped it upside down.

Sage gasped as the contents spilled out. "What in the world?"

Dugan picked up a driver's license and flipped it open. A picture of Ron Lewis stared back at him.

But the name on the license read Mike Martin.

"That's a fake driver's license," Sage said.

Dugan raked his hand over the lot of them, spreading a half dozen different licenses across the bed. "Each one of these has a different name."

"My God, Dugan," Sage whispered. "Ron Lewis wasn't his real name."

"No." Dugan met her gaze. Aliases indicated the man might have been a professional con man. "And if he lied about who he was, no telling what else he lied about."

SAGE SANK ONTO the bed, in shock. "I can't believe he lied to me, that he had all these other identities." She felt like such a fool. "Why would he do that, Dugan? Why come here and make me think he was someone else? Just to make me fall for him?"

Dugan's mouth flattened. "Do you have a lot of money, Sage?"

"No." She gestured around the room. "I put everything into remodeling this house as a bed and breakfast."

"You don't have a trust fund somewhere?"

"God, no," Sage said, embarrassed to admit the truth, "I'm in debt up to my eyeballs."

"Then he didn't fabricate his lies to swindle you out of money," Dugan said. "My guess is that this business of a land development was some kind of sham. You just happened to get caught in the middle."

"So, he never really cared for me," Sage said. She'd asked herself that a thousand times the past two years, but facing the truth was humiliating. It also meant she'd endangered her son by falling for Ron Lewis's lies.

Dugan's apologetic look made her feel even more like an idiot.

"Even if he was running a con, maybe he really did fall in love with you and Benji," Dugan suggested.

"Yeah," Sage said wryly. "Maybe he was going to change for me." She picked up one of the fake IDs, read the name, then threw it against the wall. "More like, he took me for a moron and used me." She studied another name, her mind racing. "But why take Benji that day?"

"I don't know." Dugan shrugged. "Did he know about your debt?"

Sage nodded. "He told me not to worry, that when this deal came through, my B and B would be overflowing with business and we'd make a fortune."

"Maybe he meant that," Dugan said. "Maybe he really wanted to make things better for you and your son."

Sage made a sound of disgust. "Like you said before,

Dugan, he lied about his name. What else was he lying about?" She scattered the IDs around, trying to recall if he'd mentioned any of the other names he'd used. "I can't believe I fell for everything he said." Because she'd been lonely. Vulnerable.

Had liked the idea of having a father for her son.

Never again would she let down her guard.

Not for any man, no matter what.

DUGAN GATHERED THE fake IDs to investigate them. As much as he wanted to assure her that Lewis had been sincere about his intentions with her, the phony IDs said otherwise.

A liar was a liar, and Dugan hadn't found just one alias. The man had a string of them.

Meaning he probably had a rap sheet, as well, and maybe had committed numerous crimes.

It also opened up a Pandora's box. Any one of the persons he'd conned or lied to might have wanted revenge against him.

The fact that he'd lied to Sage suggested he might have lied to other women. Hell, he might have a slew of girlfriends or wives scattered across Texas. Maybe one in each city where he'd worked or visited.

All with motive, as well.

"Do you know who Lewis met with in town about the new development?"

"George Bates, from the bank," Sage said. "He also met with the town council and talked to several landowners, but I'm not certain which ones or how far he got with them."

"I'll start with Bates." Dugan stuck the envelope of IDs inside his rawhide jacket.

Sage followed him to the door. "Are you going to the sheriff with this?"

Dugan shook his head. "I don't think he'd like me nosing into this, and I don't trust him to find the truth."

"I agree." Sage rubbed her hands up and down her arms, as if to warm herself. The temptation to comfort her pulled at Dugan.

God, she was beautiful. He'd admired her from afar ever since the first time he laid eyes on her. But he'd known then that she was too good for a jaded man like him. She and her little boy deserved a good man who'd take care of them.

And that man wasn't him.

But just because he couldn't have her for himself didn't mean that he wouldn't do right by her. He would take this case.

Because there was the possibility that Benji was alive.

Dugan wouldn't rest until he found him and Sage knew the truth about what had happened two years ago.

Sage caught his arm as he started to leave the room. "Dugan, promise me one thing."

He studied her solemn face. Hated the pain in her eyes. "What?"

"That you won't keep things from me. No matter what you find, I want—I need—to know the truth. I've been lied to too many times already."

He cradled her hand in his and squeezed it, ignoring the heat that shot through him at her touch. "I promise, Sage."

Hell, he wanted to promise more.

But he hurried down the steps to keep himself from becoming like Lewis and telling her what she wanted to hear instead of the truth.

Because the truth was that he had no idea what answers he would find.

SAGE WATCHED DUGAN LEAVE, a sense of trepidation filling her.

At least he was willing to help her look for the answers. But the phony drivers' licenses had shocked her to the core.

How could she have been so gullible when Ron was obviously a professional liar? And now that she knew Ron Lewis wasn't his real name, who was he?

Had he planned to marry her and take care of her and Benji?

No…everything about the man was probably false. He'd obviously fabricated a story to fit his agenda.

But why use her? To worm his way into the town and make residents believe he cared about them, that he was part of them?

Devious. But it made sense in a twisted kind of way.

She straightened the flooring in the closet, then went to Benji's room. Benji had loved jungle animals, so she'd painted a mural of a jungle scene on one wall and painted the other walls a bright blue. She walked over to the shelf above his bed and ran her finger over each of his stuffed animals. *His friends,* he'd called them.

At night he'd pile them all in bed around him, so she could barely find him when she went to tuck him in. His blankie, the one she'd crocheted before he was born, was folded neatly on his pillow, still waiting for his return.

Where was her son? If he'd survived, was he being taken care of? Had someone given him a blanket to sleep with at night and animal *friends* to comfort him in bed?

She thought she'd cried all her tears, but more slipped down her cheeks, her emotions as raw as they were the day she'd discovered that Benji was gone.

The news usually ran stories about missing children. For a few weeks after the car crash, they carried the story about Ron and her son. Although the implication was that both had died in the fire, a request had been made for any information regarding the accident. They'd hoped to find a witness who'd seen the wreck, someone who could tell them if another car had been involved.

But no word had come and eventually other stories had

replaced Benji's on the front page. With this new development, maybe she could arouse the media's interest again.

She hurried downstairs to the kitchen and retrieved the scrapbook with clippings she'd morbidly kept of the crash and the coverage afterward. Why she'd kept them, she didn't know. Maybe she'd hoped one day she'd find something in them that might explain what had happened to Benji.

The small town of Cobra Creek wasn't big enough for a newspaper, but a reporter from Laredo had interviewed her and covered the investigation. At least, what little investigation Sheriff Gandt had instigated.

She noted the reporter's name on the story. Ashlynn Fontaine.

Hoping that the reporter might revive the story and the public's interest, now that Ron's body had been found and that his death was considered a homicide, she decided to call the paper the next morning and speak to Ashlynn.

DUGAN DROVE TO the bank the next day to speak with George Bates, the president. One woman sat at a desk to the left, and a teller was perched behind her station, at a computer.

He paused by the first woman and asked for Bates, and she escorted him to an office down a hallway. A tall, middle-aged man with wiry hair and a suit that looked ten years old shook his hand. "George Bates. You here to open an account?"

Dugan shook his head. "No, sir, I need to ask you some questions about Ron Lewis."

Bates's pudgy face broke into a scowl. "What about him? He's been dead for two years."

"True," Dugan said. "I don't know if you heard, but his body was discovered this morning at Cobra Creek.

It turns out he didn't die in that car crash or fire. He was murdered."

Bates's eyes widened. "What?"

"Yes, he was shot."

Bates rolled his shoulders back in a defensive gesture. "You think I know something about that?"

"That's not what I meant to imply," Dugan said, using a low voice to calm the man. "But the fact that Ms. Freeport's little boy wasn't with him raises questions about where he is. Ms. Freeport asked me to look into his disappearance. Learning who killed Lewis might lead us to that innocent little boy." Dugan paused. "You do want to help find that child, don't you?"

His comment seemed to steal the wind out of Bates's sails. "Well, yes, of course."

"Then tell me everything you can about Ron Lewis."

Bates tugged at his suit jacket, then motioned for Dugan to take a seat.

"Lewis came in here with all kinds of plans for the town," Bates said. "He had sketches of how he wanted to renovate the downtown area, parks that would be added, housing developments, a giant equestrian center and a dude ranch, along with an outlet mall and new storefronts for the downtown area."

"Did he have backing?" Dugan asked.

Bates scratched his chin. "Well, that was the sketchy part. At first he said he did. Then, when it got down to it, he approached me to invest. I think he may have hit on some others around town. Especially Lloyd Riley and Ken Canter. They own a lot of land in the prime spots for the equestrian center and dude ranch."

"He made them offers?"

"You'd have to talk to them about it," Bates said. "Neither one wanted to tell me any specifics. But I think Riley signed something with him and so did Canter."

So, what had happened to those deals?

"Were most of the people in town in favor of the project?"

"A few of the store owners thought it would be good for business. But some old-timers didn't want that dude ranch or the mall."

"When he asked you to invest, did you check out Lewis's financial background?"

Bates frowned. "I was going to, but then he had that crash and I figured there wasn't no need."

"Was he working with a partner? Another contact to deal with on the project?"

"If he was, he didn't tell me."

Probably because he was running a scam. Lewis had never had backing and was going to swindle the locals into investing, then run off with their money.

Had one of them discovered Lewis's plans to cheat him and killed Lewis because of it?

Chapter Five

Dugan stopped by his ranch before heading out to talk to the ranchers Lewis had approached.

He'd worked hard as a kid and teen on other spreads, doing odd jobs and then learning to ride and train horses, and had vowed years ago that he would one day own his own land.

Growing up on the reservation had been tough. His mother was Native American and had barely been able to put food on the table. Like little Benji's, his father had skipped out. He had no idea where the man was now and couldn't care less if he ever met him.

Any man who abandoned his family wasn't worth spit.

Then he'd lost his mother when he was five and had been tossed around for years afterward, in foster care, never really wanted by anyone, never belonging anywhere. It was the one reason he'd wanted his own land, his own place. A home.

He'd hired a young man, Hiram, to help him on the ranch in exchange for a place to live. Hiram was another orphan on the rez who needed a break. He also employed three other teens to help groom and exercise the horses and clean the stalls. Keeping the boys busy and teaching them the satisfaction of hard work would hopefully help them stay out of trouble. He'd also set up college scholarships if they decided to further their education.

Everything at the ranch looked in order, and he spotted Hiram at the stables. He showered and changed into a clean shirt and jeans, then retreated to his home office.

He booted up his computer and researched Trace Lanier. Seconds after he entered the man's name, dozens of articles appeared, all showcasing Lanier's rise in success in the rodeo. Other photos revealed a line of beautiful rodeo groupies on his arm. For the past two years, he'd been traveling the rodeo circuit, enjoying fame and success.

He had no motive for trying to get his son back. He had plenty of money. And now fame. And judging from the pictures of him at honky-tonks, parties and casinos, he enjoyed his single life.

At the time of Benji's disappearance, he was actually competing in Tucson.

Dugan struck Lanier off the suspect list, then phoned his buddy Jaxon and explained about finding Lewis's corpse and the phony identities.

"Sounds like a professional con artist," Jaxon said. "Send me a list of all his IDs and I'll run them."

Dugan typed in the list and emailed it to Jaxon. He could use all the help he could get.

"I'm plugging them in, along with his picture," Jaxon said. "Now, tell me what you know about this man."

"He came to Cobra Creek on the pretense of saving the town. Said he had a developer wanting to rebuild the downtown, and expand with an equestrian center, dude ranch, shopping mall and new storefronts. The banker in town said he approached him to invest and that he solicited locals to, as well. I'm going to question them next. But I'm anxious to learn more about his background. Does he have an arrest record?"

"Jeez. He was a pro."

"What did you find?"

"He stole the name Lewis from a dead man in Corpus Christi."

"A murder victim?"

"No, he was eighty and died of cancer."

"So he stole his identity because it was easy."

"Yeah, Lewis was an outstanding citizen, had no priors. His son died in Afghanistan."

"What else?"

"Three of the names—Joel Bremmer, Mike Martin and Seth Handleman—have rap sheets."

"What for?"

"Bremmer for theft, Martin for fraud and embezzlement and Handleman for similar charges."

"Did he do time for any of the crimes?"

"Not a day. Managed to avoid a trial by jumping bail."

"Then he took on a new identity," Dugan filled in.

"Like I said, he's a pro."

"Who bailed him out?"

"Hang on. Let me see if I can access those records."

"While you're at it, see if you can get a hold of Sheriff Gandt's police report on Lewis's car accident. I want to know if Lewis was shot before the accident or afterward."

"The sheriff doesn't know?"

"According to Gandt, he thought the man died in the car fire. Now we have a body, the M.E. pointed out the gunshot wound. When I asked Gandt if he saw a bullethole in the car, he sidestepped the question, and said the car was burned pretty badly. But all that tells me is that he didn't examine it."

"Shoddy work."

"You could say that."

Dugan drummed his fingers on the desk while he waited. Seconds later, Jaxon returned.

"Each time, a woman bailed him out. The first time, the lady claimed to be his wife. The second, his girlfriend."

"Their names?"

"Eloise Bremmer," Jaxon said. "After Bremmer disappeared, the police went to question her, but she was gone, too. Same thing with Martin's girlfriend, Carol Sue Tinsley."

"Hmm, wonder if they're one and the same."

"That's possible."

"How about the other names?"

"One more popped. Seth Handleman. He was charged with fraud, but the charges were dropped. Says here his wife, Maude, lives in Laredo."

"Give me that address," Dugan said. "Maybe she's still there."

She also might be the same woman who'd bailed out Bremmer and Martin.

SAGE RUBBED HER FINGER over the locket she wore as she parked at the coffee shop where Ashlynn Fontaine had agreed to meet her. After Benji had disappeared, she'd placed his picture inside the necklace and sworn she wouldn't take it off until she found her son.

It was a constant reminder that he was close to her heart even if she had no idea if he was alive or…gone forever.

Clinging to hope, she hurried inside, ordered a latte and found a small corner table to wait. Five minutes later, Ashlynn entered, finding Sage and offering her a small smile. Ashlynn ordered coffee, then joined her, shook off her jacket and dropped a pad and pen on the table.

"Hi, Ms. Freeport. I'm glad you called."

"Call me Sage."

"All right, Sage. You said there's been a new development in the case."

Sage nodded. "I take it you haven't heard about Ron Lewis's body being found."

The reporter's eyes flickered with surprise. "No, but that is news. Who found him?"

"Dugan Graystone, a local tracker, was searching for some missing hikers and discovered his body at Cobra Creek."

"I see. And the sheriff was called?"

Sage nodded. "Sheriff Gandt said he would investigate, but he didn't do much the first go-around."

"How did Lewis die?" Ashlynn asked.

"He was shot."

"Murdered?" Another flicker of surprise. "So he didn't die from an accident?"

"No." Sage ran a hand through her hair. "He died of a gunshot wound. At this point it's unclear if he was shot before the accident, causing him to crash, or after it, when he tried to escape the burning vehicle."

"Interesting."

"The important thing is that they found Lewis's body but not my son's. So Benji might be alive."

Ashlynn gave her a sympathetic look. "Did they find any evidence that he survived?"

"No," Sage admitted. "But they also didn't find any proof that he didn't."

"Fair enough."

"Think about it," Sage said. "The shooter may have wanted to kill Ron. But maybe he didn't realize Ron had Benji with him. When he killed Ron and discovered Benji, he may have taken my son."

A tense heartbeat passed between them, fraught with questions.

"That's possible," Ashlynn said. "But it's also possible that he didn't."

Sage's stomach revolted. "You mean that he got rid of Benji."

"I'm sorry," Ashlynn said. "I don't want to believe that, but if he murdered Lewis, he might not have wanted any witnesses left behind."

Sage desperately clung to hope that Ron's killer hadn't been that inhumane. Killing a grown man for revenge, if that was the case, was a far cry from killing an innocent child.

Ashlynn traced a finger along the rim of her coffee cup. "I hate to suggest this, but did the police search the area for a grave, in case the killer buried your son?"

Sage's throat closed. She clutched her purse, ready to leave. "I didn't call you so you'd convince me that Benji is dead. I hoped you'd run another story, this time focus on the fact that Lewis's body was found but that Benji might still be out there."

She pulled a picture of her son from her shoulder bag. "Please print his picture and remind people that he's still missing. That I'm still looking for him." Desperation tinged her voice. "Maybe someone's seen him and will call in."

Ashlynn reached over and squeezed her hand. "Of course I can do that, Sage. I'll do whatever I can to help you get closure."

Sage heard the doubt in the reporter's voice. She didn't think Benji would be found.

But Sage didn't care what she thought. "I know you have your doubts about him being alive, but I'm his mother." Sage stroked the locket where it lay against her heart. "I can't give up until I know for sure."

Ashlynn nodded and took the picture. "Did Benji have any defining characteristics? A birthmark, scar or mole? Anything that might stand out?"

"As a matter of fact, he does," Sage said. "He was born with an extra piece of cartilage in his right ear. It's not very noticeable, but if you look closely, it almost looks like he has two eardrums."

"Do you have a photo where it's visible?"

Sage had actually avoided photographing it. But it was obvious in his first baby picture. She removed it from her wallet and showed it to Ashlynn.

"This might help," the reporter told her. "I'll enhance it for the news story. And I'll run the story today." Ashlynn finished her coffee. "As a matter of fact, I have a friend who works for the local TV station. I'll give her a heads-up and have her add it to their broadcast. The more people looking for Benji, the better."

Sage thanked her, although Ashlynn's comment about searching for a grave troubled her.

As much as she didn't want to face that possibility, she'd have to ask Dugan about it.

DUGAN ENTERED THE ADDRESS for Maude Handleman into the note section on his phone, then drove toward Lloyd Riley's farm, a few miles outside town.

He'd heard about the tough times some of the landowners had fallen upon in the past few years. Weather affected farming and crops, the organic craze had caused some to rethink their methods and make costly changes, and the beef industry had suffered.

Farmers and ranchers had to be progressive and competitive. He noted the broken fencing along Riley's property, the parched pastures and the lack of crops in the fields.

He drove down the mile drive to the farmhouse, which was run-down, the porch rotting, the paint peeling. A tractor was abandoned in the field, the stables were empty and a battered black pickup truck was parked sideways by the house.

It certainly appeared as if Riley might have been in trouble.

Dugan parked and walked up the porch steps, then knocked. He waited a few minutes, then knocked again, and the sound of man's voice boomed, "Coming!"

Footsteps shuffled, then the door opened and a tall, rangy cowboy pushed the screen door open.

"Lloyd Riley?"

The man tipped his hat back on his head. "You're that Indian who found the hikers?"

"I was looking for them, but another rescue worker actually found them," Dugan said. He offered his hand and Riley shook it.

"Name's Dugan Graystone."

"What are you doing out here?" Riley asked.

Dugan chose his words carefully. Tough cowboys were wary of admitting they had money problems. "I spoke with George Bates at the bank about that development Ron Lewis had planned around Cobra Creek."

Riley stiffened. "What about it?"

"Bates said he asked him to invest before he died. He also mentioned that he talked to some of the locals about investing, as well."

"So?" Riley folded his arms. "He held meetings with the town council and talked to most everyone in town about it. Didn't he approach you?"

Dugan shook his head. "No, he probably meant to, but he didn't get around to me before he died."

Riley pulled at his chin. "Yeah, too bad about that."

The man sounded less than sincere. And Bates had said that he thought Riley made a deal with Lewis. "I heard Lewis offered to buy up some of the property in the area and made offers to landowners. Did he want to buy your farm?"

Riley's eyes flickered with anger. "He offered, but I told him no. This land belonged to my daddy and his daddy.

I'll be damned if I was going to let him turn it into some kind of shopping mall or dude ranch."

"So you refused his offer?"

"Yeah. Damn glad I did. Heard he cheated a couple of the old-timers."

"How so?"

"Offered them a loan to get them out of trouble, supposedly through the backer of this rich development. But fine print told a different story."

"What was in the fine print?"

"I don't know the details, but when it came time to pay up and the guys couldn't make the payments, he foreclosed and stole the property right out from under them."

Riley reached for the door, as if he realized he'd said too much. "Why'd you say you wanted to know about all this?"

"Just curious," Dugan said.

Riley shot him a look of disbelief, so he decided to offer a bone of information.

"Lewis was a con artist," Dugan said. "The day of his so-called accident, I suspect he was running away with the town's money."

Riley made a sound of disgust. "Sounds like it."

"Who was it he swindled?"

"Don't matter now. Lewis is dead."

"Why do you think that?"

"I figured the deal was void when he died. Haven't seen anyone else from that development come around."

That was true. But if they'd signed legal papers, the deal would still be in effect. Unless the paperwork hadn't been completed or whoever killed Lewis had him tear up the papers before Lewis died. "Can you give me a name or two so I can follow up?"

"Listen," Riley said. "These are proud men, Graystone. You know about being proud?"

His comment sounded like a challenge, a reminder

that Riley knew where Dugan had come from and that he should be grateful he'd gotten as far as he had. "Yes, I do."

"Then, they don't want anyone to know they got gypped. Maybe that accident was a blessing."

"I guess it was for some people," Dugan said. "But, Riley, the body I found earlier was Ron Lewis's. He didn't die in an accident."

Riley's sharp angular face went stone-cold. "He didn't?"

"No, he was murdered." Dugan paused a second to let that statement sink in. "And odds are that someone Lewis cheated killed him." Anger hardened Riley's eyes as he realized the implication of Dugan's questions. "What about Ken Canter? Was he one of those Lewis cheated?"

"Canter didn't care about the money. He was just happy to unload his place. He wanted to move near his daughter and took off as soon as he signed with Lewis." Riley made a low sound in his throat. "We're done here."

Riley reached for the door to slam it, but Dugan caught it with the toe of his boot. "I know you want to protect your buddies, but Sage Freeport's three-year-old son disappeared the day Lewis was murdered." He hissed a breath. "Lewis was a con artist, there's no doubt about that. And I'm not particularly interested in catching the person who killed him, *except*—" he emphasized the last word "—except that person may know where Benji is. And if he's alive, Sage Freeport deserves to have her little boy back."

Chapter Six

Sage had slept, curled up with Benji's blanket the night before. Just the scent of him lingering on it gave her comfort.

But Ashlynn's comment about a grave haunted her.

After she arrived back at the B and B, she called Dugan. She explained about her visit with Ashlynn and her suggestion that the sheriff should have looked for a grave where the killer might have buried her son.

"According to the report my friend got for me, the sheriff arrived at the scene shortly after the explosion. I don't think the killer would have had time to dig a hole and bury Benji, but if it'll make you feel better, I'll check it out."

His words soothed her worries, but she couldn't leave any questions unanswered. "Thank you, Dugan. It *would* make me feel better."

"All right. I'll head over there now."

"I'll meet you at the crash site."

She hung up, poured a thermos of coffee to take with her, yanked her unruly hair into a ponytail, then rushed outside to her van.

By the time she arrived, Dugan was waiting. "You didn't have to come, Sage. I could handle this."

"This search should have been done a long time ago."

"Actually, the police report said that searchers did comb the area for Benji after the crash."

She studied Dugan. "Were you part of that team?"

He shook his head, the overly long strands of his dark hair brushing his collar. "I was out of town, working another case."

"I understand it's a long shot, and I hope there isn't a grave," Sage said, "but ever since that reporter suggested it, I can't get the idea out of my head."

"All right." He squeezed her hand, sending a tingle of warmth through her.

She followed him to the spot where the car had crashed and burned. He pulled a flashlight from his pocket and began scanning the ground near the site, looking for anything the police might have missed.

Sage followed behind him, the images of the fire taunting her. She'd imagined them finding Benji's burned body so many times that she felt sick inside.

But they hadn't found him, and that fact gave her the will to keep going.

The next two hours, she and Dugan walked the scene, searching shrubs and bushes, behind rocks, the woods by the creek and along the river and creek bank.

Finally, Dugan turned to her. "He's not here, Sage. If he was, we would have found something by now."

Relief surged through her. "What now?"

"Maybe the news story will trigger someone to call in."

She nodded, and they walked back to their vehicles. "I have a couple of leads to check out," Dugan said. "I found some information on the fake IDs and discovered that at least one of Lewis's aliases was married. I'm driving to Laredo to see if I can talk to the woman."

Sage's stomach lurched. So Ron had not only lied to her but proposed to her when he'd already had a wife.

DUGAN WAS RELIEVED when he didn't discover a grave. Knowing there had been a search team after the crash had suggested the area was clean, but Gandt had led the team and Dugan didn't trust him.

The sheriff had obviously taken the accident at face value and hadn't had forensics study the car, or he might have found a bullet hole and realized the accident wasn't an accident at all. Unless Lewis was shot after he left the burning vehicle...

"Let me go with you to see the woman," Sage said.

Dugan frowned. "If she's covering for her husband, she might not want to talk to us."

"You think she knew what he was doing? That he had other women?"

Dugan shrugged. "Who knows? If he's run the same scam in other cities, she might be his accomplice. Or... she could have been a victim like you were."

"Just a dumb target he used."

"You aren't dumb, Sage," Dugan said. "Judging from the number of aliases this man had, he was a professional, meaning he's fooled a lot of people."

"He also could have made a lot of enemies."

"That, too." More than one person definitely had motive to want him dead.

Sage's keys jangled in her hand. "Follow me back to the inn and then let me ride with you. If she was a victim, then she might talk to me more easily than you."

Dugan couldn't argue with that. "All right."

Ten minutes later, she parked and joined him in his SUV, and he drove toward Laredo. "How did you find out about her?" Sage asked.

"My buddy with the rangers plugged the aliases into the police databases. Lewis had a rap sheet for fraud, money laundering and embezzlement."

"He did time?"

"No. In each instance, a woman bailed him out. Then he disappeared under a new name."

"It sounds like a pattern."

"Yes, it does," Dugan agreed.

Sage leaned her head against her hand. "I still can't believe I was so gullible."

"Let it go, Sage," Dugan said gently.

"How can I? If I hadn't allowed Ron—or whatever his name was—into our lives, Benji wouldn't be gone." Her breath rattled out. "What kind of mother am I?"

Dugan's chest tightened, and he automatically reached for her hand and squeezed it. "You were—are—a wonderful mother. You loved your son and raised him on your own. And my guess is that you never once considered doing anything without thinking of him first."

Sage sighed. "But it wasn't enough. I let Ron get close to us, and he took Benji from me…."

Dugan reminded himself not to let emotions affect him, but he couldn't listen to her berate herself. "I promise you we'll find him, Sage."

Of course, he couldn't promise that Benji would be alive.

Tears glittered in Sage's eyes, but she averted her gaze and turned to stare out the window.

Dugan hated to see her suffering. Still, he gripped the steering wheel and focused on the road, anything to keep himself from pulling over and dragging her up against him to comfort her.

Sage latched on to Dugan's strong, confident voice and his promise. He seemed to be the kind of man who kept his word.

But she'd been wrong about men before. Her track record proved that. First Benji's father and then Ron.

No, she was obviously a terrible judge of character.

But this was different. Dugan was known for being

honest and fair and good at what he did. Taking on her case was nothing personal, just a job to him.

She studied the signs and business fronts as they neared Laredo. Dugan veered onto a side street before they entered town and wound through a small modest neighborhood. He checked the GPS and turned right at a corner, then followed the road until it came to a dead end.

A small, wood house with green shutters faced the street. Weeds choked the yard, and a rusted sedan sat in the drive.

"This woman's name is Maude Handleman," Dugan said as they walked up to the front door. He knocked, and she studied the neighboring houses while they waited. If Ron had made money conning people, what had he done with it? He certainly hadn't spent it on this property.

Dugan knocked again, and footsteps pounded, then the sound of a latch turning. The door opened, revealing a short woman with muddy brown hair pulled back by a scarf.

"Mrs. Handleman?" Dugan said.

Her eyes narrowed as she scrutinized them through the screen. "If you're selling something, I don't want it."

"We aren't selling anything," Dugan said. "Please let us come in and we'll explain."

"Explain what?"

Sage offered her a smile. "Please, Maude. It's important. It's about your husband."

The woman's face paled, but she opened the door and let them in. "What has he done now?"

Sage followed Maude inside, with Dugan close behind her. The woman led them into a small den. Sage glanced around in search of family pictures, her pulse hammering when she spotted a photograph of Maude and the man she called Ron Lewis, sitting on the side table.

"All right," Maude said impatiently. "What's this about?"

Dugan glanced at her, and Sage began, "Your husband, what was his name?"

"Seth," Maude said. "Except I haven't seen him since I bailed his butt out of jail nearly four years ago."

"Mrs. Handleman, did you know that Seth has other names that he goes by?"

Surprise flickered in the woman's eyes. "Other names?"

"Yes." Dugan explained about finding the various drivers' licenses. "He has been arrested under at least three assumed names. That's how we found you."

She studied them for a minute. "Who are you—the police come to take him back to jail?"

Sage inhaled a deep breath. "Actually, no. Seth came to Cobra Creek where I live, but he told me and everyone in the town that his name was Ron Lewis."

Maude twisted a piece of hair around one finger.

"He posed as a real estate developer who had big plans for Cobra Creek," Sage continued.

"He did do some real estate work," Maude said.

"He was arrested for fraud and embezzlement," Dugan cut in. "And I believe he was trying to swindle landowners around Cobra Creek."

Maude crossed her arms, her look belligerent. "Look, you can accuse him all you want, but if you want me to pay back whatever he took from folks, I don't have any money." She gestured around the room. "Just look at this. He left me high and dry."

"We don't want your money," Dugan said.

"Then, what do you want?"

Sage sighed softly. "Maude, the day Ron Lewis left Cobra Creek, he took my three-year-old little boy with him."

"He kidnapped your son?" Shock flashed red on Maude's face. "He might have been a cheat, but I find that hard to believe."

Sage nodded. "It's true. He took him from my house. My son's name is Benji." She pulled a photo from her purse and handed it to the woman. "That was taken two years ago. I haven't seen him since."

Maude's alarmed gaze met hers. "I don't understand. Seth…he cheated people out of money, but he wasn't no kidnapper."

Sage's stomach knotted. "I don't know why he took Benji," she said. "But I know that he lied to me. He asked me to marry him, and he warmed up to Benji from the start. Did the two of you have children?"

She shook her head. "I had a miscarriage right after we got married. After that, I was scared to try again."

"Did he talk about children a lot? Did he want a family?"

Maude's lip curled into a scowl. "No."

"What about his own family?" Dugan asked. "Did he tell you anything about them? Did you ever meet his mother or father?"

"No, he said his parents were dead and he didn't have any brothers or sisters."

"When was the last time you saw or talked to him?"

"I told you, right after I bailed him out of jail about four years ago."

"Did he come home with you that night?" Dugan asked.

"Yeah. He spent the night, then said he was going to make things right, that he had to talk to someone about a job and that he'd be back when he got things worked out."

Sage lowered her voice. "Did you have any idea that he'd been arrested before?"

Maude shook her head no.

"How about that he used different names?"

"I told you I didn't know what he was up to."

"He didn't call you and tell you about being in Cobra Creek?" Sage asked.

"No. I… When I didn't hear from him, I was afraid something bad happened to him. That the law caught up with him and he was back in jail."

"So you didn't look for him?" Sage asked.

"I called his cell phone, but it was dead."

"You haven't heard the news, then?" Sage asked.

She crossed her arms, irritation tightening her face. "No, what the hell is going on?"

Sage glanced at Dugan, and he cleared his throat. "I'm sorry to have to tell you, Mrs. Handleman, but Ron Lewis…aka Seth Handleman…was murdered."

Maude gasped and twisted the afghan between her fingers. "What? Who killed him?"

"That's the reason we're here," Dugan said. "I'm investigating his murder."

Sage studied Maude's reaction. She seemed sincerely shocked. And she'd given no indication that she'd killed him or that she wanted him dead.

"Please, Maude, if you can think of a place Seth would have gone or someone he would have contacted, tell me. I'm afraid that whoever killed him took my little boy, and that Benji's in danger."

MAUDE'S FACE PALED. "I…just can't see my Seth kidnapping your boy. If he did, someone must've forced him to."

Dugan had considered that. "But Ms. Freeport didn't receive a ransom note."

Maude threw her hands up. "I don't know what to say except I'm sorry, Ms. Freeport. But I don't know anything."

"Do you recognize the names Mike Martin or Joel Bremmer?" Dugan asked.

"No, should I?"

"They're two of Lewis's other aliases."

Maude dropped her face into her hands. "You think someone he conned killed him?"

"That's possible," Dugan said. "Or it could have been one of the other women in his life."

Maude made a strangled sound. "I shoulda known he wasn't faithful when he left me. Why do I always fall for the losers?"

Sage patted her back with compassion. "I know just how you feel, Maude."

He laid a business card on the table beside her. "Call us if you think of anything."

Sage sighed as they walked outside to the SUV and got inside. "What do we do now?"

"There were two other women on the list I want to question."

"Other wives?"

"One was a wife, one a girlfriend." He fastened his seat belt. "Maybe one of them can shed some light on Lewis. If he lied to Maude about having a family, one of them might know."

"You think if he had family, they might have Benji?"

"I don't know, but there might be some answers in his past that will tell us who killed him."

Chapter Seven

Sage laid her head against the back of the seat and dozed while Dugan drove to the address he had for Mike Martin. According to Jaxon, his girlfriend was named Carol Sue Tinsley. She volunteered at a local women's shelter.

The small town was south of Laredo and took him an hour to reach. Just as he neared the outskirts, Sage cried out, "No, please don't take him...."

Dugan gritted his teeth and realized she was in the throes of a nightmare. How many nights had she actually slept in the past two years without suffering from bad dreams?

"Please..." She choked on a sob.

Dugan gently reached over and pulled her hand into his. "Sage, shh, you're dreaming."

She jerked her eyes open with a start.

"It's okay," he said softly. "A nightmare?"

She blinked as if to focus and straightened as if to shake off the dream, although the remnants of fear and sorrow glittered in her green irises.

He turned into an apartment complex that had seen better days, checking the numbers on the buildings until he reached 10G, Martin's last known address.

A few cars and pickups filled the parking spaces, although there were more empty spaces than those occupied, indicating that the building wasn't filled to capacity. The patios looked unkempt, and overlooked parched land, and the roof of the building needed repairs.

He parked and turned to Sage. "Do you want to wait here?"

"No, let's go."

Together they walked up to the building, then climbed the stairs to the second-floor unit. The cinder-block walls needed painting, and someone had painted graffiti on the doorway to the stairs.

"Ron liked money. He always wore designer suits and drove a nice car." Sage wrapped her arms around her waist. "I can't imagine him living in a place like this."

Dugan silently agreed. Although Mrs. Handleman's home hadn't been in great shape and her house wasn't filled with expensive furnishings, it was upscale compared to these apartments.

"Maybe he and Carol Sue were lying low until he made the big score." And his fancy suits and car were a show to make the ranchers believe he was big, important. That he could save them financially.

It was dark inside.

"No one is here," Sage said.

Dugan tried the door, but it was locked. He removed a small tool from his pocket and picked the lock. The door screeched open, revealing a deserted living area with stained carpet and faded gray walls.

"Stay behind me," Dugan said as he inched inside. He glanced left at the kitchen, then spotted a narrow hallway and paused to listen for sounds that someone was inside. Something skittered across the floor, and Sage clutched his arm. "It sounds like rats."

Dugan nodded, senses alert as he crept closer. There were two bedrooms, both empty. He stepped inside the first one, crossed the room and checked the closet. Nothing.

He and Sage moved to the next one, but when he opened the door, a bird flew across the room, banged into the window and then flew back.

"It's trapped," Sage said.

Dugan closed the distance to the window and opened it, giving the bird a way to escape.

"It looks like whoever lived here has been gone awhile."

Judging from the bird droppings and the musty odor, he agreed. "After I search the apartment, I want to speak to the landlord and find out if they left a forwarding address."

"I saw an office when we first drove in."

Dugan checked the closets, but they were empty. Then he led the way back to the living area. He stepped into the kitchen and searched the drawers and cabinets. "Nothing. And no sign of where she went."

They walked outside and Dugan locked the door. Then they drove to the rental office. Dugan carried a photo of Lewis inside, and a receptionist with big hair and turquoise glasses greeted them. "You folks looking for an apartment?"

If he was, he sure as hell wouldn't spend money at this dump. "No, just some information. Is the landlord here?"

She shook her head. "It's his day off."

Dugan checked her name tag—Rayanne—and faked a smile. "Then maybe you can help us, Rayanne."

She batted blue-shadowed eyes at him. "I'll sure try."

"How long have you worked here?"

She laughed, a flirty sound. "Feels like half my life."

He laid the picture of Ron Lewis on the desk. "Do you recognize this man? He lived in 10G."

She adjusted her glasses and studied the picture. "Well, that looks sort of like Mike Martin. Except he had sandy brown hair and a mustache."

Dugan glanced at Sage, then laid the phony license with Martin's picture on it. "This was him?"

"Yeah, that was Mike." She looked up at him with questioning eyes. "He was a real charmer, although that girlfriend of his was a piece of work."

"How so?" Dugan asked.

"She always ragged on him about this place. Didn't think it was good enough for her."

"Did you know them very well?"

"Naw, he was kind of a flirt. Kept telling me he was gonna make it big one day and then he'd show Carol Sue he was important. That she was wrong about him." She fiddled with her glasses again. "But they've been gone from here a long time. What's this about?"

"Did you know Mike was arrested?" Dugan asked.

Rayanne averted her gaze, a guilty look. "Why are you asking about that?"

"Because he tried to con the people in my town, and he conned me," Sage said. "He also ran off with my little boy and then he was murdered. I'm looking for my son now."

Rayanne's expression went flat. "Well, damn."

"What?" Dugan asked.

"I did hear he was arrested, but I didn't know what it was all about."

"Carol Sue bailed him out of jail after his arrest," Dugan said.

"Yeah," Rayanne muttered. "But the next day, both of them packed up and ran. Skipped out on the rent and left the place in a mess. Mr. Hinley had to hire someone to haul out all their junk."

"What did he do with it?" Dugan asked.

"Took it to that landfill," Rayanne said. "Wasn't anything worth keeping or selling."

Another dead end. "Did Mike ever mention anything about a family? His parents or a sibling?"

Rayanne shook her head.

"How about a friend he might have gone to when he needed a place to stay or hide out?"

Rayanne looked sheepish. "Well…"

"Give us a name," Dugan said.

"He had another woman on the side. Carol Sue didn't know about her, but she lived in 2D. Beverly Vance. She's a hairstylist down at Big Beautiful Hair."

"Does she still live in the complex?" Sage asked.

Rayanne nodded. "But I'd appreciate it if you didn't tell her that I sent you."

"Why not? Don't you two get along?"

Rayanne frowned. "Tarnation, that woman was as jealous as they come. She hated Carol Sue and told me to stay out of her way. Declared she was going to have Mike to herself, one way or the other."

Dugan grimaced. So, he could add Beverly Vance to the growing suspect list.

In fact, any one of the women Lewis had conned and scorned could have killed him.

SAGE SILENTLY PRAYED that Beverly Vance knew something about her son as they walked up to the woman's apartment and knocked. "If Beverly killed Ron…Mike…maybe she took Benji," Sage said.

"That's possible. But Rayanne didn't mention anything about a child living with her."

Sage's mind raced. "Maybe she dropped him at a church or hospital, somewhere where he'd be safe."

"That's possible," Dugan said. "Although when the story aired about Benji being taken by Lewis, if he had been dropped off, someone would have probably notified the authorities."

"Maybe," Sage said. "But maybe not. Especially if they took Benji to another state. And Gandt didn't issue an Amber alert."

Dugan's dark look made Sage's stomach knot.

"Oh, God…what if whoever took him carried him to Mexico?" Then she might never know what happened to him or get him back.

"We can't jump to conclusions," Dugan said. "Let's follow the pieces of the puzzle and see where they lead us."

Sage just hoped they didn't lead to Mexico. Finding Benji in the United States would be difficult enough, but crossing into another country where the legal system was less than satisfactory would complicate matters more.

Dugan knocked again, but no answer, so they walked back to his SUV and drove to the hair salon where Beverly worked.

Big Beautiful Hair was housed in a trailer on the edge of the small town, across from a convenience store called Gas & Go and a liquor store called Last Stop. Several cars were parked out front, a sign painted in neon pink-and-green advertising the big hair Texas women were famous for.

Sage hurried up the steps to the trailer, anxious to speak to Beverly. When she entered, the whir of hair dryers and blow-dryers filled the air, the scent of perm solution and hair dye nearly overwhelming.

There were three workstations, with patrons in various stages of coloring, cutting, highlighting and dying scattered through the long, narrow room. A half dozen bracelets jangled on the arm of the buxom brunette who approached her.

"Can I help you, miss?" She started to examine Sage's unruly hair, but Sage took a step back.

"I need to see Beverly."

The woman shrugged, then turned and called for Beverly. The platinum blonde at the second station glanced over, her sparkling eye shadow glittering beneath the lights. "Yeah?"

Sage crossed the distance to her, while Dugan hung

back. On the ride over, they'd decided Beverly might open up to her before she would to someone investigating the man Beverly apparently loved. "Can we talk for a minute, Beverly?" Sage said in a low voice.

"You don't want a cut and color today?"

"No, I need to ask you some questions about Mike Martin."

Beverly dropped the curling iron she was using and hurried over to Sage. "Mike, good Lord… Now, there's a blast from the past."

"When was the last time you saw him?" Sage asked.

Beverly chewed her bottom lip for a moment before she answered, "About four and a half years ago."

"How was he?" Sage asked.

Beverly tapped one of her three-inch high heels. "Agitated."

"Did he tell you that he'd been arrested?"

Beverly coaxed Sage to the back by the hair dryers. "Yes, but that was a mistake. He said he was going to get it all worked out and then he'd come back for me."

Sage forced a calm to her voice when she wanted to scream at the woman that she'd been a fool to believe anything Mike Martin had said.

Just as *she'd* been a fool to believe Ron Lewis.

"So you knew he was leaving town?"

Beverly nodded. "He said he was due to make a small fortune and then the two of us would get married and buy a house. Maybe even a ranch of our own."

Disgust filled Sage. Ron certainly could be convincing. "Did he say where he was going to make this fortune?"

Beverly leaned in close. "Said he was into a real estate deal with this developer and he was buying up property left and right. He'd already picked out some land for us." She batted her eyes. "I always dreamed about having a big place in the country. Waking up to the sun."

Clearly Beverly had been snowed by Ron's charm. "Then what happened?"

An odd look glimmered in Beverly's eyes. "Then he just disappeared. I tried calling the phone number I had for him but got a recording, saying it was disconnected. I haven't heard from him since."

"What did you think happened to him?" Sage asked.

Tears moistened Beverly's big blue eyes. "I don't know, but I've been scared to death that something bad happened. That his old girlfriend Carol Sue found out our plans and did something crazy."

"What do you mean, crazy?"

Beverly's voice choked. "I mean, like kill him. She was always jealous of me."

"Did Carol Sue own a gun?"

Beverly nodded. "A .38. She was good at shooting, too. Mike said her daddy took her to the shooting range every week when she was a kid. That she won the skeet-shooting contest at the county fair three years in a row."

Sage dug her nails into the palms of her hands. They had to find Carol Sue. If she'd shot Lewis, maybe she knew where Benji was.

DUGAN SAW THE FRUSTRATION on Sage's face as they left Big Beautiful Hair and drove toward Cobra Creek. Beverly had been completely in love with Mike Martin, aka Ron Lewis.

Dammit, he needed the man's real name. Learning the truth about his upbringing might explain what had shaped him into a con artist. A man who not only swindled people out of their money, but charmed women into believing and trusting him when he told them nothing but lies.

Sage lapsed into silence until they neared the outskirts of Cobra Creek.

"I almost feel sorry for Beverly," Sage said. "She really thought he was coming back to her."

Dugan winced. "He fooled her like he did everyone else."

"Like he did me." Sage's tone reeked of self-disgust. "The minute I realized he took Benji with him, without asking me, I was done with the man. He knew how protective I was of my son. Even if he had simply gone shopping, like I thought at first, I would have been furious." Her voice gained momentum. "You just don't do that to a mother."

Dugan agreed.

"If Beverly was right about Carol Sue, and she shot Ron, what did she do with Benji?"

"I'm going to call Jaxon and ask him to search hospital and church records nationwide for any child who might have been abandoned or dropped off around that time."

"That should have been done two years ago."

"I agree," Dugan said, his opinion of the sheriff growing lower by the minute. Gandt should have explored every avenue to find Benji.

"But if Carol Sue dropped him off, surely Benji would have told someone his name."

A dozen different scenarios ran through Dugan's mind. Not if he was injured, confused, or traumatized. Or if she'd threatened him.

But he tempered his response so as not to panic Sage. "If Carol Sue did leave him, she might have given false information, signed him in using a different name."

"You're right," Sage said. "The woman could have claimed he was her child, given a fake name and said she was coming back for him."

Dugan nodded. "I'll call Jaxon now."

His phone buzzed just as he reached for it, but suddenly

a car raced up behind them and a gunshot blasted the air, shattering the back window.

Sage screamed, and he swerved and pushed her head down, then checked his rearview mirror as the car sped up and slammed into their side.

Chapter Eight

Sage screamed as a bullet pinged off the back of the SUV. Dugan swerved sideways and sped up, but the car behind them roared up on their tail.

"Stay down!" Dugan shouted.

Sage ducked, clutching the seat edge as Dugan veered to the right on a side road. The SUV bounced over ruts in the asphalt, swaying as he accelerated. Suddenly he spun the car around in the opposite direction, tires squealing as he raced back onto the main road.

"What's happening?" Sage cried.

"I'm chasing the bastard now."

Sage lifted her head and spotted a black sedan peeling off and getting farther and farther way. "Who is it?"

"I didn't see his face." He pressed the gas to the floor and tried to catch the car, but they rounded a curve and the driver began to weave.

Dugan closed the distance, pulled his gun and shot at the sedan's tires. The car screeched to the right, skidded and spun, then flipped over and rolled. Metal scrunched and glass shattered as it skated into a boulder.

A second later, the car burst into flames.

Dugan yanked the wheel to the left to avoid crashing into it, then swung the SUV to the side of the road and threw it into Park.

Then he jumped out and ran toward the burning vehicle. Déjà vu struck Sage, images of flames shooting from Ron's car two years ago pummeling her.

That night she'd been terrified Benji had been inside the car.

Today...the driver had shot at them. Tried to kill them. Why? Because she was asking questions about Benji?

She jerked herself from her immobilized state and climbed out. Dugan circled the car, peering in the window as if looking for a way to get the driver out. But the gas tank blew, another explosion sounded and flames engulfed the vehicle.

Sweat beaded on her forehead, the heat scalding her. She backed away, hugging the side of the SUV as she watched Dugan. He must have realized it was impossible to save the driver, because he strode back toward her, his expression grim.

"Did you see who it was?"

"A man. I didn't recognize him." Dugan punched a number into his phone. "Jaxon, it's Dugan. I want you to run a plate for me."

Dugan recited the license number, then ran a hand through his hair while he waited.

"Who?" A pause. "No, send a crime team. He's dead, but maybe they can find some evidence from the car."

When he hung up, Sage asked, "Who did the car belong to?"

"Registered to a man named Joel Bremmer."

"Bremmer?"

Dugan nodded. "One of Ron Lewis's aliases."

Sage gasped. "But Ron is dead, so he couldn't have been driving the car."

Questions darkened Dugan's eyes. "I know. The M.E. will work on ID once he gets him to the morgue."

Sage gritted her teeth. "Do you think he was working with Ron?"

"That's possible." Dugan traced his thumb under her chin. "Are you okay?"

She nodded, although she was trembling. Heat reddened his face, the scent of smoke and hot metal permeating him.

"Someone doesn't like us asking questions, Sage. But that means we might be on the right track to finding some answers."

Dugan's gruff voice wrapped around her just as his arms did, and for the first time in two years, she allowed herself to lean on another man.

DUGAN STROKED SAGE'S BACK, soothing her with soft, non-sensical words.

Whoever the bastard was driving the car—he had almost killed them. An inch or two to the right, and that bullet would have pierced Sage's skull.

Cold fear and rage made him burn as hot as the fire consuming the shooter's car.

If Sage had died...

No, she was fine. So was he. And he wasn't going to stop until he unearthed the truth. The fact that someone had shot at them meant he was on the right path. That someone was afraid he'd find Lewis's killer and Benji.

A siren wailed, and Dugan released Sage. "Are you all right now?"

She nodded and tucked a strand of hair behind her ear. "Yes, thanks, Dugan."

Blue lights twirled as the sheriff's car and a fire engine careened toward them. The fire truck screeched to a stop, three firemen jumping down along with a female firefighter who'd been driving.

They rushed to extinguish the blaze while Sheriff Gandt lumbered toward them. "What happened?"

Dugan explained, "The car ran up on us, and the driver shot at us." He pointed out the bullet hole in the back of his SUV. "I swerved to avoid him and he sped past. Then I turned around and tried to catch him, but he lost control and crashed."

Gandt scowled as he looked from Dugan to Sage. "He just come up and shot at you, out of the blue?"

Dugan choked back an obscenity. Gandt was the sheriff and he had to cooperate. If he didn't, the jerk would probably lock him up and then he couldn't find the truth. But he didn't like it. "Yes."

"You've been asking questions about Lewis?"

Dugan nodded. "Turns out Ron Lewis had a few other names he went by," he said. "Then again, I'm sure you already know that."

A cutting look deepened the sheriff's eyes. "Of course. I am the sheriff."

"Right. Have you made any progress on solving his murder?"

"I'm working on it," Sheriff Gandt said, "which means you need to stay out of my investigation."

Sage spoke up. "We're just trying to find my son."

"Right." This time Sheriff Gandt's tone was sarcastic.

A crime van rolled up, interrupting them, and Gandt's mouth twitched with irritation.

"You called them?"

Dugan nodded. "I figured I'd save you the time."

The van parked, and two CSIs exited the vehicle and approached them.

Gandt crossed his beefy arms. "If you know something, spit it out, Dugan. Because if I find out you're holding back, I'll haul your butt in for interfering with a homicide investigation."

Dugan gritted his teeth. The hell he would. "I've told you all I know." He gestured toward the charred remains of the sedan. "Tell me when you identify the driver. I'd like to know who tried to kill me."

Gandt's steely gaze met Dugan's, a challenge in his expression. "Sure thing. After all, I was elected to serve and protect."

Dugan bit back a surly remark, took Sage's arm and they walked back to his SUV. He had a feeling Gandt would have handed the shooter a gun if it meant getting Dugan out of his hair.

But he'd survived a rough childhood, taunts about being a half-breed, other taunts about being a bastard kid. And then the fights as a teenager, when he'd defended himself.

Gandt couldn't intimidate him into doing anything. In fact, his obstinacy only fueled Dugan's drive to get to the bottom of Ron Lewis's murder.

His phone buzzed, and he checked the number. George Bates at the bank.

Sage slipped into the passenger seat, her expression troubled as she watched the firefighters finishing up.

He took the call. "Dugan Graystone."

"Listen, Mr. Graystone, after you left the other day, I got to thinking about Lewis and that development and looked back into some foreclosures. Worst part of my job, but sometimes I don't have a choice."

"Go on."

"There were two that troubled me. Two ranchers I threatened foreclosure on, but they paid me off at the last minute. When I asked how they came up with the money, neither one wanted to tell me. They just said they'd had a streak of luck."

"How so?"

"In both cases, the ranchers were in bad trouble financially. I think they worked out some kind of deal with Lewis, that he offered to pay off their debt by loaning them money from his own company."

Money that he might have earned through another scam.

"What happened?"

"One of the men came to me complaining that when he got behind on the payments, Lewis took over his property. Said something about he hadn't read the fine print."

Dammit. That fit with what Lloyd Riley had told him. If Lewis had a large party interested in paying big bucks for the property once he took control of it, Lewis could have turned a big profit by picking it up at foreclosure prices and then reselling.

And Lewis would have given the men he'd conned motive for wanting him dead.

"When Lewis disappeared, the ranchers asked me to keep it quiet that they'd been cheated."

A strong motive to convince Bates not to go public, to void the deal. Although technically, they would have had to go through legal channels, fill out paperwork, and look at Lewis's will, if he had one.

"Which ranchers wanted the deal covered up?"

"I don't want my name mentioned," Bates said. "Bank transactions are supposed to be confidential. If folks think I talk about their private business, they'll quit coming to me."

"I understand. Just give me the names."

"Donnell Earnest," Bates said. "And the other man was Wilbur Rankins."

"Where are they now?"

"Both are still here. When Lewis died, they refused to move, said had reason to believe the deals weren't legal. That they had a ninety day window that hadn't passed. And so far no one has come forward to uphold the contracts they signed."

Suspicious in itself. If Lewis had investors or a legitimate corporation, someone would follow up on the deals.

Dugan thanked Bates, then made a mental note to talk to both Earnest and Rankins.

He punched Jaxon's number as he started the engine and pulled back onto the road. He asked Jaxon to research children, specifically three-year-old boys, who were left at churches, orphanages, hospitals or women's shelters around the date Benji disappeared.

"Also find out everything you can on these names. Martin's girlfriend, Carol Sue Tinsley. Handleman's wife, Maude. And a woman named Beverly Vance. Any one of them could have killed Lewis."

Jaxon agreed to call him with whatever he learned and then Dugan headed toward Donnell Earnest's ranch outside Cobra Creek.

SAGE'S NERVES FLUTTERED. "You know, Carol Sue could have just run off with Benji. Or since she volunteered at a shelter, what if she faked spousal abuse to get help, then left Benji at one of those women's shelters. From there, they could have disappeared and we may never find them. Carol Sue could have changed their names a dozen times by now."

"Those groups do have underground organizations to help women escape abusive relationships," Dugan agreed. "But we have no real reason to suspect that Carol Sue took him. She may have just freaked out when Martin was arrested and decided to skip town in case she was collared as an accomplice."

"Or she could be dead, too," Sage suggested.

"Maybe. Hopefully Jaxon will find something on her."

Another frightening scenario hit Sage. "What if Benji was hurt or in shock? If he was in that crash or witnessed the shooting, he could have been too traumatized or terrified to talk." Or the shooter could have killed him so there would be no witness left behind.

God…

Dugan squeezed her hand. "I know it's hard not to imagine the worst that could happen, but Benji's age could have worked to his advantage. Toddlers and young children don't make reliable witnesses. And killing a child takes a certain brand of cold-bloodedness that most people don't possess."

"You sound like you have a trusting nature," Sage said wryly.

Dugan made a low sound in his throat. "Not hardly. But I think the fact that we haven't found Benji may be a good sign that he's alive."

Sage tried to mentally hang on to his words.

It was all she had. Besides, she wasn't ready to give up. She never would be.

DUGAN REFUSED TO SPECULATE with Sage, because all the scenarios she mentioned were possible and dwelling on them wouldn't do anything but frighten her more. God knows he'd seen his share of bad outcomes. He'd even met a couple of men he'd called sociopaths.

But intentionally taking the life of a toddler… That was a different breed. A sociopath, maybe.

He was banking on the fact that Lewis's killer wasn't one of them.

Sage's comment about Carol Sue triggered questions.

What if the woman had abducted Benji? If she was aware of Ron's various identities, she might have adopted another name and be living somewhere, raising Benji as her own son.

He phoned Jaxon and asked him to look into that angle and to talk to the people at the shelter where Carol Sue volunteered.

Meanwhile he wanted to check out some of Ron's

aliases. Maybe he'd get lucky and find one of them was still active.

He reached the drive for Donnell Earnest's ranch, the Wagonwheel. Dugan turned the SUV down the dirt drive and drove past several barns and a horse stable. Donnell raised beef cattle, but Dugan saw very few cattle grazing in the pasture.

He parked in front of an ancient farmhouse. Live oaks spread across the dry lawn.

"What's his story?" Sage asked as they climbed out.

"Apparently Donnell Earnest was in trouble financially. Lewis offered the man a loan to help him pay off his bills, but when he fell behind, Lewis took ownership of his ranch. Bates said that no one has come forward from Lewis's company about the deal, and that there was a ninety day window that hadn't passed before Lewis died, so the ranchers think the deal wasn't legal." He paused. "Of course, with Lewis's phony ID, they would have had reason to question the legality anyway."

"*If* they'd discovered he was using an alias," Sage pointed out.

True.

A scrawny beagle greeted them by sniffing his boots and Sage's leg. She bent to pet him, and Dugan walked up the rickety stairs.

Before he could knock, a heavyset guy with a thick dark beard appeared at the screened door, a shotgun in his hand.

"Get off my property or I'll shoot!" Donnell shouted.

"THE HIT WAS BOTCHED. Graystone and the Freeport woman are still alive."

"Dammit to hell and back. That body washing up at the creek was a big mistake."

"You don't have to tell me that. But the guy deserved to die."

"That's not the point. The point is that I don't want to go to jail."

"Don't worry. They'll never know what happened that day."

"You swear. Because that Freeport woman is about the most persistent woman I've ever known."

"I told you not to sweat it." He'd take care of her if he had to.

They'd come too far to get caught now.

Chapter Nine

"Listen, Mr. Earnest," Dugan said. "I need to ask you some questions about the deal you made with Ron Lewis."

"That's none of your business," Earnest growled.

Dugan gently eased Sage behind him. "I know he cheated you and I don't care. I'm trying to help Ms. Freeport find her little boy. He disappeared the day Lewis did, and his mother misses him."

"I do." Sage stepped up beside Dugan. "I just want to find him, Mr. Earnest. He's probably scared, and he doesn't understand what happened to him."

Donnell waved the gun in front of the screen door. "What makes you think I know something about your kid?"

Sage started to walk forward, but Dugan caught her arm. "Careful. Stay back."

But Sage ignored him. "I know you don't have Benji," Sage said. "But I know Ron Lewis conned you out of your property."

"This land is mine!" Donnell bellowed.

"Yes, it is. Ron Lewis was not the man's real name," Dugan said. "He had several aliases and used them to swindle others besides you."

"You mean that deal was no good?"

"It's not legal," Dugan said, hoping to gain the man's trust. "The lawyers and bank will have to sort out the details."

The big man seemed to relax and lowered his gun. "That's good news, then."

"Except that Ron Lewis's body was found at Cobra Creek. He's dead. In fact, he died the same day of that car crash."

A moment of silence stretched between them. Then Earnest raised the gun again. "So you're here 'cause you think I killed Lewis?"

"I didn't say that. I'm talking to everyone who knew Lewis in hopes that someone Lewis knew or something Lewis said might lead us to Benji."

"I don't know anything and I didn't kill him," Donnell said. "But I'm not sorry the guy's dead."

Dugan started to speak, but Sage cut him off. "I understand, Mr. Earnest. All I want is to find my son. Did Ron mention someone he might meet up with once he left Cobra Creek? Or maybe he had a partner?"

The man lowered the gun, opened the screen and stepped onto the porch. "Naw. He talked about that developer that was going to make Cobra Creek big on the map."

"Was there a contact person or address on any of the papers you signed?"

Donnell scratched his head, sending hanks of hair askew. "Don't recall one." His voice cracked. "I can't believe I was such a damn fool. My mama always said if something was too good to be true, it probably was."

"He fooled a lot of us, Donnell," Sage said sympathetically.

A blush stained his cheeks. "Downright embarrassing to know I was stupid enough to let that jerk steal my land out from under me. Hell, if a man don't have land, he don't have anything."

"Did Ron ever talk about a family?" Dugan pressed. "Did he have parents?"

"Don't remember no folks." The big man rubbed the back of his neck. "Seems like he said he grew up near San Antonio. Or maybe it was Laredo. I think he mentioned a sister once."

"Did he mention her name?"

The dog nuzzled up to his leg, and Donnell scratched him behind the ears. "Janet or Janelle, something like that."

"Thanks," Dugan said. "That might be helpful."

In fact, he'd have Jaxon run the name through the system, along with all of his aliases. Maybe one of them would pop.

"DO YOU THINK Mr. Earnest killed Ron?" Sage asked as they left the ranch.

"It's too soon to say. He seems to be telling the truth, but he has motive."

"So do some of the other ranchers." Sage studied the withered grass in the empty pastures, and the stable that looked empty. "But he did seem surprised that Ron was murdered."

"People can fake reactions," Dugan said. "Maybe he was just surprised that we found the body. After two years, whoever killed Lewis had probably gotten complacent. Thought he'd gotten away with murder."

Sage fought despair. Two years a murderer had gone free.

Two years Benji had been gone.

Children changed every day. He would have lost any baby fat from his toddler shape, would have grown taller, more agile. Had the person who'd abducted him been good to him? Was he eating right?

Who tucked him in at night and chased the bogey-man away?

Benji had been afraid of the dark. She'd bought a cartoon-figure night-light and plugged it in before he went to bed. Still, he'd been scared of monsters, so they'd played a game where she checked under the bed and the closets in a big show that she'd chased them away before she kissed him good-night.

Tears pricked her eyes.

At five, he would have started kindergarten this year. She would have already taught him to recognize the letters of the alphabet, and he could count to twenty. Was he learning to read now? Could he write his name?

A dozen more questions nagged at her, but the idea of Benji being in school kept returning. "Dugan, Benji would be five now. He might be in school somewhere. In kindergarten."

Dugan slanted her a sideways look. "That would be risky for the person he's with."

"I suppose you're right. The kidnapper could be home-schooling him." Or locking him in a room and leaving him there alone and afraid.

"Then again, you made a good point. If the person who has Benji is working, he might need for him to be in day care or school." Dugan reached for his phone again. "And it's another place to check out."

He punched in a number and spoke to his friend Jaxon, then asked him to hunt for a Janet or Janelle who might be Lewis's sister. "Make sure the photo of Benji Freeport is circulated to all the school systems in Texas and the surrounding states. Also try day cares."

Sage's heart pounded as Dugan hung up. "Thank you, Dugan."

"I haven't done anything yet," he said in a self-deprecating voice.

"Yes, you have." Sage swallowed the knot in her throat. "You're looking for him and exploring avenues the sheriff never did."

Dugan's gaze met hers, a guarded look in his eyes. "He should have done all this two years ago."

"I know. But he just assumed Benji was dead and told me to accept it and move on." She twisted her fingers in her lap. "But I couldn't do that, Dugan. Not without knowing for sure."

And maybe not even then. Because Benji had been her life. And if he was dead, it was her fault for getting involved with Ron Lewis.

An image of Benji writing his name flashed behind her eyes, and she battled another onslaught of despair as stories of other kidnappings on the news blared in her mind.

Stories where children had been brainwashed, told that their real parents didn't want them, that they'd given them away. Stories where a boy was forced to dress like a girl or vice versa. Stories where children were abducted at such a young age that they adapted to the kidnapper and accepted, even believed, that that person was their real parent.

She couldn't fight the reality that whoever had taken her son had most likely changed his name. That they weren't even calling him Benji anymore.

That the name he might be writing wasn't his own, which would make it even more difficult for a teacher or caretaker to realize that he'd been abducted.

That even if someone asked Benji his name, he might not remember it.

He might not remember her, either, or that she'd once held him in her arms as a baby and rocked him to sleep. That she'd sung him lullabies and chased the bogeyman away and promised to protect him forever.

That she'd dreamed about what he'd become when he grew up.

God…she'd jeopardized her son's life by trusting Ron. And now she might never see him again.

DUGAN DROVE TO Wilbur Rankins's ranch next. Both Rankins and Earnest had reasons to want Lewis dead.

And they were the only two that Dugan knew of at this point. There could be others. People he'd swindled, along with ex-wives and girlfriends.

The man had been a real class act.

Sage had lapsed into silence. No telling what she was imagining. He wished he could keep her mind from going to the dark places, but that was impossible.

He couldn't even keep his own mind from traveling down those roads.

Rankins's property was fifteen miles outside town and just as run-down as Donnell Earnest's. Both ranchers had probably been desperate and had fallen for Lewis's easy way out.

Dugan pulled up in front of the sprawling ranch house, bracing himself for another hostile encounter. "Stay here until I see if this guy is armed."

Sage nodded. "Okay, but I want to talk to him."

"Sure, once I make sure it's safe." He'd be foolish to let her go in without assessing the situation first. If Donnell had wanted, he could have blown their heads off before they'd even made it onto the porch.

He checked his weapon, then strode up the stone path to the front door. A rusted pickup sat to the left of the house, beneath a makeshift carport. He spotted a teenage boy out back, chopping wood.

Smoke curled from the chimney, and a Christmas tree stood in view, in the front window. He knocked, scanning the property and noting a few head of cattle in the west pasture. Maybe Rankins was getting back on top of his business.

He knocked again, and the door was finally opened. A man who looked to be mid-forties stood on the other side, his craggy face crunched into a frown. "Yeah?"

"Are you Wilbur Rankins?"

"Naw, that'd be my daddy. I'm Junior."

"Is your father here?"

"He's not feeling too good." The man crossed his arms, his tattered T-shirt stretching across his belly. "Who are you and what do you want with him?"

He heard the SUV door open and glanced back to see Sage emerge from the passenger side. He motioned that it was okay for her to join him.

"What's going on?"

Dugan explained who he was and introduced Sage.

"We know that Ron Lewis swindled you," Dugan said. "That you're not the only one."

"I heard he was murdered," Junior Rankins said. "But if you think I did it, think again. I didn't know he'd conned my daddy out of his ranch until after the creep had that car crash."

"Did you meet him yourself?" Sage asked.

Junior shook his head no. "My boy out there and I lived in Corpus Christi at the time. We came down a few months ago when my father took ill."

"I'm sorry," Sage said. "Is it serious?"

"Cancer. He's been fighting it about three years. That's when he started letting things go around here."

"And Lewis popped in to save the day," Dugan guessed.

A disgusted look darkened the man's eyes. "Yeah, damn vulture if you ask me."

Footsteps sounded behind the man, and Dugan saw an older man in a robe appear. *Must be the father.*

"What's going on?" the man bellowed.

Junior turned to his father. "Everything's under control, Dad."

"Mr. Rankins," Dugan said. "Can we talk for a minute?"

The old man shuffled up beside his son and motioned for them to come in. "What the hell's going on? A man can't get any rest."

"I'm sorry," Junior said. "I was trying to take care of it."

The older man looked hollow-eyed, pale, and he'd lost his hair. "Take care of what?"

Dugan cleared his throat and introduced himself and Sage again.

"Mr. Rankins," Sage interjected. "We know that Ron Lewis tried to con you out of your land. But the morning he was leaving town, he took my little boy with him. If you know anything about where he might have been going or who he was working with, please tell me. It might help me find my son."

"I don't know a damned thing." The man broke into a coughing spell. "But I'm glad that bastard's dead so he can't cheat anyone else."

"Where were you the morning he disappeared two years ago?" Dugan asked.

Junior stepped in front of his father. "You don't have to answer that, Dad." Junior shot daggers at Dugan with his eyes. "Now, I suggest you leave before I call the sheriff and tell him you're harassing us."

Dugan was about to make a retort, but his phone buzzed. Surprisingly, Sheriff Gandt's name flashed on his caller ID display. "Graystone speaking."

"Is Sage Freeport with you?"

Dugan said yes through gritted teeth. "Why?"

"Bring her to my office. I have something to show her."

"What?"

"Something that got overlooked after the crime scene workers searched the crash site."

"We'll be right there."

Dugan ended the call, an anxious feeling in his gut. Did Gandt have bad news about Benji?

SAGE'S HANDS FELT clammy as she and Dugan parked at the sheriff's office. Dugan said the sheriff was cryptic about the reason he'd asked them to stop by.

But it couldn't be good news or else he would have told Dugan over the phone.

She reminded herself that she had survived the past two years living in the dark, that she needed closure, no matter what the outcome was.

But she'd be lying if she didn't admit that finding Ron's body and not Benji's had rekindled her hope.

Dugan opened the door to the sheriff's office and gestured for her to enter first. She did, her insides trembling as the sheriff looked up at them from the front desk, his expression grim.

"Sheriff?" Dugan said as they approached.

Sheriff Gandt stood. "After we found Lewis's body, I decided to look back at the evidence box we collected two years ago after the original accident."

"You found something?" Sage asked, her voice a painful whisper.

He nodded. "This envelope was in the bottom of the box stuck under the flap." He opened it and removed a blue whistle.

Sage gasped. The whistle was Benji's.

And it had blood on it.

Chapter Ten

Sage sagged against the desk, then stumbled into a nearby chair. "That was my son's."

"Did you test the blood to see if it belonged to Benji?" Dugan asked.

"Not yet. I wanted to show it to Ms. Freeport first and see if she recognized it."

Sage struggled to pull herself together.

"Get it tested," Dugan said firmly. "It may be Benji's blood. But blood from the person who shot Lewis might also be on it."

"Did you find anything else?" Sage said in a choked voice.

"That's it," Gandt said.

"What about on the man who tried to shoot us?"

"M.E. has him at the morgue now." He gave Dugan a warning look. "Why don't you take Ms. Freeport home and let me do my job? I've got this investigation under control."

Sage bit her tongue to keep from lashing out and telling him that Dugan had already accomplished more in two days on the case than Gandt had in two years.

But arguing with the sheriff was pointless.

She gestured toward the whistle. "After you finish with that, I'd like to have it back."

"Of course."

"You'll let me know what you find?" Sage asked.

His eyes narrowed, but he offered her a saccharine smile. "Sure. And know this, Ms. Freeport, I'm doing everything I can to find Lewis's killer and your son."

"I appreciate that," Sage said, grateful her voice didn't crack. She wanted out of the room, away from Sheriff Gandt.

Away from that whistle with the blood on it, blood that might belong to her son.

DUGAN DROVE SAGE back to the B and B, well aware she'd hit an emotional wall that could crumble any second.

The big question was if she would be able to put herself back together again if she received bad news.

So far, she had held it together. Shown amazing strength and fortitude. But she also had held on to hope.

Damn. She was stubborn, beautiful and fragile and in need of something to turn the nightmare she'd been stuck in the past two years into a distant dream where her son emerged at the end, safe and back at home with her where he belonged.

Dugan walked her up to the door of the inn. "Sage, even if that whistle has Benji's blood on it, it doesn't mean that he's dead."

She winced, and he berated himself for being so blunt. But she had made him promise to be honest with her.

"I know. And I appreciate all you're doing." Her phone beeped that she had a text, and she pulled it from her purse.

"What is it?"

"I talked to that reporter, Ashlynn Fontaine. Not only is she running the story in the newspaper, but she said the story is airing on the news."

Dugan gritted his teeth. The media could be a double-edged sword.

"You think I shouldn't have contacted her?"

He hadn't realized his expression was so transparent. "I didn't say that."

"But?"

Dugan squeezed her arm, aching to do more. To pull her in his arms and promise her he'd fix all her problems and make her happy again.

But the only way to do that was to bring her son home.

"The more exposure Benji's story receives, the more chances are that someone might recognize him."

"That's what I thought."

Dugan lowered his voice. "But be prepared, Sage. It also may bring false leads. And letting everyone know the case has been reopened could be dangerous."

"Someone already shot at us," Sage said. "And just because it's dangerous doesn't mean I'll stop looking." She gripped his hands. "Dugan, I will never give up, not as long as I know there's a chance Benji's out there."

Dugan had heard of kidnapping cases and missing children that spanned decades. He honestly didn't know how the parents survived. They had to live hollow shells of their lives, going through each day on empty hope, like a car running on gas fumes.

"Call me if you hear from your contacts," Sage said. "I'm going inside now."

Dugan nodded, his chest constricting. He hated to leave her alone. But he had work to do.

He needed to track down that woman named Janet or Janelle, Lewis's alleged sister.

Perhaps Lewis had planned to make his fortune in Cobra Creek and then convince Sage to disappear with him. If so, he might have told a sibling about her.

And he might have asked her to watch Benji until he could clean up the mess and return for Sage.

It was a long shot, but Dugan couldn't dismiss any theory at this point.

SAGE WALKED THROUGH the empty B and B, hating the silence. The couple renting from her had gone home to be with their family for the holidays.

Just where they should be.

But the quiet only reminded her that she would spend another Christmas in this house by herself. When she first bought the place and renovated it, she'd imagined a constant barrage of people in and out, filling the rooms with laughter and chatter. She'd spend her days baking her specialty pastries and pies, with Benji helping her, stirring and measuring ingredients and licking icing from the bowl, his favorite part.

Ron must have picked up on that dream and played her. Although she'd wanted a houseful of people because she'd been without family for so long, he'd obviously thought she'd wanted the place to be a success so she could make money.

She glanced in the fridge and pulled out a platter of leftover turkey and made herself a sandwich. Although she had no appetite, she'd forced herself to eat at least one meal a day for the past two years, telling herself that she had to keep up her strength for when she brought her son home.

Would that ever happen?

She poured a glass of milk and took it and the sandwich to the table and turned on the TV to watch the news report.

An attractive blonde reporter, who identified herself as March Williams, introduced the story by showing a picture of Ron Lewis. She recapped the details of the accident two years ago.

"Police now know that Lewis was an alias, and that he was wanted on other charges across the state. They also know he was murdered and are searching for his killer." She paused for dramatic effect. "But another important question remains—where is little Benji Freeport?" A photograph of Benji appeared, making Sage's heart melt.

"Three-year-old Benji Freeport lived with his mother, Sage Freeport, who owns a bed and breakfast in Cobra Creek. The morning Lewis disappeared, he took Benji with him. Police have no leads at this time but are hopeful that Benji is safe and still alive. If you have any information regarding this case or the whereabouts of Benji Freeport, please call the tip line listed on the screen."

Sage glanced at the Christmas tree and Benji's present waiting for him. Each year she'd added another present. How big would the pile get before he came back to open them?

The treetop star lay in the box to the side, taunting her. She had opted not to hang the star, because that was Benji's job.

Battling tears, she folded her hands, closed her eyes and said a prayer that someone would recognize Benji and call the police.

That this year he could hang the star for Christmas and they'd celebrate his homecoming together.

DUGAN STOPPED AT the diner and ordered the meat loaf special. He'd learned to cook on the open fire as a boy on the rez, but he'd never quite mastered the oven or grocery shopping.

Food was meant for sustenance, a necessity to give him the energy to tackle his job. Manning the ranch meant early mornings and manual labor, both of which he liked. It helped him pass the days and kept him busy enough not to think about being alone.

Not that being alone had ever bothered him before. But seeing Sage and the way she loved her son reminded him of the way his mother had loved him before she died.

And the way he'd felt when he was shuffled from foster home to foster home where no one really wanted him.

What had Lewis told Benji the day he abducted him? Where was he now?

He knew the questions Sage was asking herself, because they nagged at him.

Two old-timers loped in, grumbling about the weather and their crops. An elderly man and woman held hands as they slid into a booth.

Sheriff Gandt sat in a back booth, chowing down on a blood-red steak.

Donnell Earnest loped in, claimed a bar stool, removed his hat and ordered a beer.

Nadine, the waitress behind the counter, grinned at him. "Hey, Donnie, you all right?"

"Hell, no, that Indian guy was out asking questions about my business."

Nadine glanced at Dugan over Donnell's shoulder. "I heard he's looking for Sage Freeport's kid."

"Yeah, and Ron Lewis's killer. Son of a bitch deserved what he got."

"I hear you there," Nadine murmured.

Donnell rubbed a hand across his head. "Rankins called me, said Graystone was out there bothering him. That guy starts trying to pin Lewis's murder on one of us, we gotta teach him a lesson."

Dugan rolled his hands into fists to control his temper. The jerk was just venting. God knows, he'd heard worse.

Still, the names and prejudice stung.

The one woman he'd been involved with years ago had received the brunt of more than one attack on him by idiots and their prejudice. She'd broken it off, saying he wasn't worth it.

His daddy had obviously felt the same way.

He'd decided that day that his land and work were all that mattered.

A cell phone rang from the back. Then the sheriff

jumped up from his booth and lumbered toward the door. "I'll be right there."

Anger flared on Gandt's face as he spotted Dugan. "What the hell were you doing out at the Rankins ranch?"

Dugan squared his shoulders. "I just asked him some questions."

"That's my job." Sheriff Gandt poked Dugan in the belly. "Because of you nosing around, Wilbur Rankins just killed himself."

"What?"

"He shot himself, you bastard."

Dugan's mind raced. "Wilbur Rankins was dying of cancer. Why would he kill himself?" To end his pain?

"His son said he was upset about that news broadcast about Ron Lewis swindling folks in Cobra Creek. Said his daddy was too humiliated to live with people knowing he'd been foolish enough to lose his land."

Dugan silently cursed. The story hadn't revealed any names, though. "You going out there now?"

"Yeah, I'm meeting the M.E."

"I'll go with you."

"Hell, no," Gandt said. "You've done enough damage. You're the last person Junior Rankins wants to see."

Dugan held his tongue. But as Gandt strode from the diner, doubts set in. Had Rankins really killed himself?

Or had someone murdered him because he'd talked to Dugan? Because they thought Rankins knew more about Lewis's death than he'd told them?

SAGE CLEANED THE ROOM the couple had stayed in, needing to expend some energy before she tried to sleep.

That bloody whistle kept taunting her.

She stripped the bed, dusted the furniture and scrubbed the bathroom, then put fresh linens on the bed and carried the dirty sheets downstairs to the laundry room. Benji's room with the jungle theme and his stuffed animals and trains beckoned her. After she started the wash, she went back to his room and traced her finger lovingly over his bedding and the blanket he'd been so attached to.

She lay back on the bed and hugged it to her, then studied the ceiling where she'd glued stars that lit up in the dark. Benji had been fascinated with the night sky. She could still hear him singing, *Twinkle, twinkle, little star,* as he watched them glittering on his ceiling.

Did he dream about her, or did he have nightmares of that car crash? Had he felt safe with Ron or frightened?

A sob tore from her throat. Where was he, dammit?

She gave in to the tears for a few minutes, then cut herself off as she'd done the past two years.

She could not give up hope.

Taking a deep breath to calm herself, she tucked the bear beneath Benji's blanket, then whispered good-night. One day she would bring Benji back here and he'd know that she'd never forgotten him. That not a day had gone by that she hadn't thought of him, wanted to see him, loved him.

She turned off the light and closed the door, then walked to her room and slipped on her pajamas, latching on to the hope that the news report would trigger someone's memory, or a stranger would see Benji in a crowd or at school and call in.

Exhausted, she crawled into bed and turned off the lights. Dugan's face flashed behind her eyes, the memory of his comforting voice soothing. Dugan was working the case.

If anyone could find her son, he could.

Outside, the wind rattled the windowpanes, jarring her just as she was about to fall asleep. A noise sounded in the hall. Or was it downstairs?

She pushed the blanket away to go check, but suddenly the sound of someone breathing echoed in the room.

Fear seized her.

Someone was inside her bedroom.

She needed a weapon, but she didn't have a gun. If she could reach her phone...

She moved her hand to try to grab it off the nightstand, but suddenly the figure pounced on top of her, and a cold hard hand clamped down over her mouth.

"Lewis is dead. If you don't stop asking questions, you'll be next."

Chapter Eleven

A cold chill engulfed Sage.

"Did you do something to my son?" she whispered.

"Just let it go," he hissed against her ear.

The fear that seized Sage turned to anger. She would never let it go.

Determined to see the man's face, she shoved an elbow backward into his chest. He bellowed, slid his hands around her throat and squeezed her neck.

Sage tried to scream, but he pushed her face down into the pillow, crawled on top of her and jammed his knee into her back, using his weight to hold her down.

"I warned you."

Sage struggled against him and clawed at the bedding, but he squeezed her neck so hard that he was cutting off the oxygen. She gasped and fought, but she couldn't breathe, and the room spun into darkness.

DUGAN PLUGGED ALL the aliases Ron had used into the computer, then entered the name Janet to see if he could find a match.

The computer scrolled through all the names but didn't locate anyone named Janet associated with any of the aliases. The name Janelle popped, though.

Janelle Dougasville lived in a small town outside

Crystal City, one of the addresses listed for Mike Martin. Dugan checked records and discovered she had a rap sheet for petty crimes and was currently on parole for drug charges. He jotted down the address. He'd pay her a visit first thing in the morning.

If she'd been in contact with Lewis around the time he'd disappeared, she might have known his plans and the reason he'd taken Benji with him.

If he'd known he was in trouble, why take a child with him? A child that would slow him down and bring more heat down on him?

It didn't make sense.

What if he'd left Benji with someone before the accident? Was it possible he'd dropped him off with an accomplice? Maybe with Janelle?

His phone buzzed, and he checked the number. Not one he recognized, but he pressed Answer. It might be a tip about Benji. "Dugan Graystone."

"Mr. Graystone, this is D. J. Rankins."

Dugan frowned. "D.J.?"

"Wilbur's grandson. I saw you at the house before, when you came and talked to my dad."

"Right. I'm sorry to hear about your grandfather."

A labored breath rattled over the line. "That's why I'm calling. You came asking him about his land, and he was real upset. He and Daddy got in a big fight after you and that lady left."

What was the boy trying to tell him? "What happened?"

"Daddy called Grandpa an old fool for falling for that Lewis man's scheme, and Grandpa yelled at Daddy to get out, accused Daddy of waitin' on Grandpa to kick the bucket so he could get his land. Then Daddy grabbed his rifle and stalked off."

"Was that when your grandfather killed himself?"

A tense minute passed. Then Dugan thought he heard a sniffle.

"D.J.?"

"Yeah, I'm here. I...probably ought not to be callin'. My dad is gonna be real mad."

But still the kid had called. "D.J., you called because you thought it was the right thing to do. Now, tell me what's on your mind."

Another sniffle. "I don't think Grandpa killed himself."

SAGE SLOWLY ROUSED back to consciousness. The room was dark, and she couldn't breathe. The musty odor of sweat and another smell...cigarette smoke? A cigar? Shoe polish?

Dizzy and disoriented, she rolled to her side and searched the room.

What had happened?

She gasped, her hand automatically going to her throat and rubbing her tender skin as the memory of the intruder surfaced. The man...big...heavy...on top of her, holding her down. Strangling her...

Those threatening words. "Lewis is dead. If you don't stop asking questions, you'll be next."

God... Was he still in the inn?

·She froze, listening for his voice. His breathing?

But only the sound of the furnace rumbling echoed back.

The wind rattling the panes had woken her. He must have broken a window downstairs and snuck in.

Trembling, she slid from bed, grabbed the phone and punched Dugan's number. She hurried to look out the window, searching for her attacker outside, but clouds obscured the moon, painting the backyard a dismal gray.

The phone rang a second time as she hurried to her bedroom door and peered into the hallway. Downstairs seemed quiet, but what if he was still in the house?

The phone clicked. "Sage?"

"Dugan, someone broke into the inn. He…threatened me."

"Is he still there?"

"I don't think so," Sage said.

"Where are you?"

"In my bedroom."

"Lock yourself inside and don't come out. I'll call you when I arrive."

Sage stepped back inside the room, closed the door and locked it. She flipped on the light, then looked into the mirror above her vanity. Her hair looked wild, her eyes puffy, the imprint of a man's fingers embedded into her neck.

She tried to recall the details of her attack. How big her attacker was, how tall… Had she felt his beard stubble against her cheek when he'd whispered that threat in her ear?

Fear clouded her memory, but she heard his voice playing over and over in her head. A gruff, deep voice. Definitely male.

But who was he?

DUGAN SPED FROM his ranch toward Cobra Creek, his heart hammering. Sage had sounded shaken, but she was all right.

Unless the intruder was still there….

His tires squealed as he swerved down Main Street, then hung a right into the drive for the B and B. The drive was empty, but he spotted Sage's car in the detached garage. He scanned the street and property, searching for someone lurking around.

A dog roamed the street but took off running when his headlights startled him. A trash can lid rolled across the neighboring drive, clanging. Down the street, a truck rumbled, heading out of town.

Could it be the intruder's?

He hesitated, considered following it, but what if Sage's attacker was still in the house?

He flipped off his lights, parked and cut the engine. Pulling his weapon from the holster inside his jacket, he texted Sage that he was outside. Then he slowly approached the inn.

The front door was locked, and no one was around, so he eased his way to the fence, unlatched the gate and stepped inside, scanning the property. At least two miles of wooded land backed up to the creek. A walking trail wove through the woods, and park benches were situated by the water for guests to lounge and relax.

Sage didn't have enough land for horseback riding, but a ranch close by catered to guests craving the western experience. That ranch belonged to Helen Wiley, a middle-aged woman who loved kids and families and offered riding lessons to locals and tourists.

The silhouette of an animal combing the woods caught his eye, and he stepped nearer the woods to check it out. Deciding it was a deer, he turned and glanced at the back of the inn.

A rustic deck spanned the entire back side, with seating areas for guests to relax and enjoy the scenery. The deck was empty now, although one of the windows was open, a curtain flapping in the wind.

The intruder must have broken in through the window.

He kept his gun trained as he climbed the steps to the deck, then he checked the open window. The glass was broken. He'd come back and look for prints.

Right now he wanted to see Sage, make sure she was safe.

His phone buzzed with a text, and he glanced at it. Sage wanted to know where he was.

He texted, Back door.

He turned the doorknob and it opened easily. The intruder had obviously snuck in through the window but exited the back door, leaving it unlocked.

Didn't Sage have a damn alarm?

He inched inside the kitchen, tensing at the sound of footsteps on the stairs. Keeping his gun braced at the ready, he crept through the kitchen to the hallway and waited.

Seconds later, Sage came running down the stairs. Pale and terrified, she threw herself into his arms.

SAGE HAD BEEN alone with her grief and fears and the terrifying questions in her head for so long that she couldn't drag herself away from Dugan.

How long had it been since someone had held her? Taken care of her?

Two years…but any affection Ron had had for her had been an act.

Dugan stroked her back, soothing her. "It's okay now, Sage."

She nodded against him, but she couldn't stop trembling. "He choked me until I passed out."

His big body went so still that she felt the anxiety coiled in his muscles. "God, Sage."

He pulled away just enough to tilt her face up so he could examine her. Rage darkened his eyes when he spotted the bruises.

"Did you get a look at him?" Dugan asked, his voice low. Lethal.

She shook her head, her heart fluttering with awareness as he traced a finger along her throat. "It was too dark. And he threw me facedown on the bed and shoved my head into the pillows."

"What else do you remember?"

"He smelled like sweat and something else—maybe

cigarette smoke? He said Lewis was dead and that if I didn't stop asking questions, I'd be next."

"Damn," Dugan muttered.

Her gaze locked with his, the fierceness of a warrior in his eyes. Eyes the color of a Texas sunset.

Eyes full of dark emotion—anger, bitterness, maybe distrust.

And hunger. Hunger followed by a wariness that made her realize that he felt the sexual chemistry between them just as she did.

"Stay here. Let me search the rest of the inn."

She nodded and hugged the wall as he inched up the stairs to the second floor. His footsteps pounded above her as he moved from room to room. Seconds stretched into minutes, a moment of silence making her catch her breath in fear that her attacker had been hiding in one of the other rooms to ambush Dugan.

Finally, he appeared at the top of the staircase. "It's clear." He tucked his gun back into his holster and strode down the steps.

Sage's heart was beating so frantically that she reached for him.

Emotions clogged her throat as he tilted her chin up again.

But this time instead of examining her bruises, he closed his mouth over hers.

Sage gave in to the moment and savored the feel of his passion. She parted her lips in invitation, relishing the way he played his tongue along her mouth and growled low in his throat.

Hunger emanated from him, in the way his hands stroked her back, and the way his body hardened and melded against hers.

A warmth spread through her, sparking arousal and titillating sensations, earth-shattering in their intensity.

Dugan splayed his hands over her hips, drawing her closer, and she felt his thick erection press into her belly.

She wanted him.

Wanted to forget all the sadness and grief that had consumed her the past two years. Wanted to feel pleasure for a few brief moments before reality yanked her back to the ugly truth.

That her son was still missing.

Those very words made her pull away. What was wrong with her? Was she so weak that she'd fall into any man's arms?

She certainly had made that mistake with Ron.

She looked into Dugan's eyes and saw the same restless hunger that she felt. She also saw his turmoil.

He hadn't expected her to react like that to him.

It couldn't happen again.

DUGAN CURSED HIMSELF for his weakness. But one look into Sage's vulnerable eyes and he couldn't not kiss her.

Pain radiated from her in waves. For the first time, he'd forgotten about his resolve to keep his hands off her. She'd needed him.

And he'd needed to hold her and know that that bastard who'd tried to choke her hadn't succeeded.

Why had her attacker let her live? Did he really think he'd scare her so badly she'd stop looking for her son?

Chapter Twelve

Dugan adopted his professional mask, relieved she'd donned a robe over her long pajamas before he'd arrived. If he'd seen a sliver of her delicate skin, he might lose control, change his mind and take her to bed. "I'll check your room for prints."

"He wore gloves," Sage said. "Leather."

"Figures. Still, I'll look around in case he dropped something or left a stray hair."

She led the way, and he spent the next half hour searching her room. When he spotted the bed where she'd been sleeping when she was attacked, images of the man shoving her facedown assaulted him.

He was going to catch this jerk and made him suffer.

Sage excused herself to go to the bathroom while he searched the room. Grateful for the reprieve, he forced his mind on the task and checked the sheets. He ran his hands over the bedding but found nothing, so he stooped down to the floor and shone a small flashlight across the braided rug.

A piece of leather caught his attention. A strip, like part of a tassel to a boot or glove or jacket. Sage had said her attacker had worn gloves.

Hoping to find forensic evidence on it, he dragged on gloves and picked it up.

Sage emerged from the bathroom, her hair brushed, her robe cinched tight. "Did you find anything?"

He dangled the leather strip in front of her. "Do you recognize this?"

Sage shook her head no. "It's not mine."

"You struggled with the man?"

She shivered. "Yes."

"I'll bag this and send it to the lab." He strode toward the door. "Go back to bed, Sage. I'll stay downstairs and keep watch."

"I don't think I can sleep," Sage said, her voice as forlorn as the expression on her face.

Hell, he knew he wouldn't sleep. Not while worrying about Sage's attacker returning to make good on that threat.

And not while thinking about that damn kiss.

"Then just rest. I'm going to find something to fix that broken window."

She tugged at the top of her robe, pulling it together. "There's some plywood in the garage."

"That'll work." He forced his gaze away from her. "You need a security system."

"That's hard to do with guests."

"You can arrange a key system."

"Won't that be expensive?"

"It'll be worth it for you and your guests."

"I'll look into it," Sage agreed.

He turned to go down to the garage.

"Thank you for coming tonight, Dugan."

He paused, shoulders squared. "I'm going to catch this bastard and find Benji."

The soft whisper of her breath echoed between them. "I know you will."

Her confidence sent a warmth through him. Other than Jaxon, he'd never had anyone believe in him.

Especially a woman.

He didn't want to disappoint her.

Shaken by the thought, he rushed outside to the garage, found a toolbox and some plywood in the corner.

It took him less than ten minutes to cover the broken glass. When he'd finished, he walked around the other rooms, checking locks and windows and looking for other evidence the intruder might have left behind.

Then he made a pot of coffee and kept watch over the house until morning. But Sage's Christmas tree haunted him as the first strains of sunlight poured through the window.

More than anything, he wanted to bring Benji back to Sage for Christmas.

SAGE DIDN'T THINK she would sleep, but exhaustion, stress and worry had taken their toll, and she drifted off. She dreamed about Benji and the holidays and the attack. She felt the man's fingers closing around her neck, his knee jamming into her back, his weight on her. She was suffocating, couldn't breathe…

She jerked awake, disoriented for a moment. She scanned the room, searching the corners as reality returned. She was safe. The intruder was gone.

Knowing Dugan was downstairs watching out for her, she closed her eyes again. This time after she drifted off, she dreamed that Dugan was in bed with her, kissing her, stripping her clothes, making love to her…

When she stirred from sleep, her body felt achy and languid, content yet yearning for something more. More of Dugan's touches.

But sleeping with him would be a mistake. She wasn't the kind of woman who could crawl in bed with a man and walk away. She was too old-fashioned. Making love meant more to her than just a warm body.

Still, she craved his arms and hands on her.

Frustrated, she jumped in the shower. One blast of the cold water and she woke to reality. She adjusted the nozzle to warm and washed her hair, letting the soothing spray of water pulse against her skin until she felt calmer.

Finally she dried off, dressed and hurried down the stairs. Dugan had cooked eggs and bacon, and poured her a cup of coffee as soon as she entered. With remnants of the dream still playing through her head, the scene seemed cozy. Intimate.

What in the world was she thinking?

She and men didn't work.

"Last night before you called, I looked for Lewis's sister."

Sage blew on her coffee to cool it. "You found her?"

"I discovered a woman named Janelle Dougasville who lived near one of the addresses for Mike Martin."

"Have you talked to her?"

"Not yet. I'm planning to pay her a visit after breakfast."

"Then let's go."

"Eat something first."

"Dugan—"

He gestured toward the plate. "Humor me. I need food in the morning."

She agreed only because he made himself an egg sandwich using the toast he'd buttered, and wolfed it down. Her stomach growled, and she joined him at the table and devoured the meal.

"Thank you," she said. "I'm not accustomed to anyone cooking me breakfast. Usually that's my job."

Dugan shrugged. "Breakfast is the only meal I make."

She smiled, grateful for the small talk as they cleaned up the dishes.

"Where does this woman live?" Sage asked as they walked outside and settled in his SUV.

"Near Crystal City." He drove onto the main street. "I'll drop that leather strip at the lab on the way."

She glanced at the holiday decorations as they wove through town. Wreaths and bows adorned the storefronts. A special twelve-foot tree had been decorated and lit in the town square, and a life-size sleigh for families and children to pose for pictures sat at the entrance to the park where Santa visited twice a day.

Signs for a last-minute sale on toys covered the windows of the toy store. The bakery was running a special on fruit cakes and rum cakes, with no charge for shipping.

Soon Christmas would be here. Kids would be waking up to find the presents Santa had left under the tree. Families would be gathering to exchange gifts and share turkey and the trimmings.

The children's Christmas pageant at church was tonight.

Tears blurred her eyes. If Benji was here, they would go. But she couldn't bear it…not without him.

"I stopped by the diner for dinner after I left your place, and ran into Sheriff Gandt."

Thoughts of holiday celebrations and family vanished. "What did he have to say?"

"Wilbur Rankins killed himself last night after we left him."

Sage gasped. "Because of our questions?"

"His son claims he was ashamed over being swindled," Dugan said.

"Oh, my God." She twisted her hands together. "But the news story didn't name names."

"There's more," Dugan said. "D. J. Rankins, Wilbur's grandson, called me. He thinks his grandfather didn't commit suicide."

"What?"

"Apparently his father and grandfather argued after we left."

The implications in Dugan's voice disturbed her. "You think Junior Rankins killed his father?"

"I don't know," Dugan said. "But if he didn't, someone else might have."

Because they were asking questions. Because of the news story.

She'd been threatened, too.

Which meant she and Dugan were both in danger.

Two hours later, Dugan parked at the address he found for Janelle Dougasville. The woman lived in a small older home, with neighboring houses in similar disrepair.

According to the information he'd accessed, she didn't have a job. A sedan that had once been red but had turned a rusted orange sat in the drive.

"If Ron had made money on other scams, he certainly didn't share it with the other women in his life."

"True. And if one of those women discovered he was lying about who he was, that he had other women, or that he was hoarding his money for himself, it would be motive for murder."

That meant Carol Sue Tinsley and Maude Handleman were both viable suspects. So was Beverly Vance.

Dugan knocked, his gaze perusing the property. The cookie-cutter houses had probably looked nice when new, but age and weather had dulled the siding, and the yards desperately needed landscaping.

Inside, the house was dark, making him wonder if Janelle was home. He knocked again, and seconds later, a light flickered on.

Beside him, Sage fidgeted.

The sound of the lock turning echoed and then the door opened. A short woman with dirty blond hair stared up at them, her nose wrinkled.

"Yeah?"

"Ms. Dougasville," Dugan said. "We'd like to talk to you."

The woman snorted. "You the law?"

"No." Dugan started to explain, but Sage spoke up.

"We're looking for my little boy. His name is Benji Freeport. You may have seen the news story about him. He disappeared two years ago."

The woman hunched inside her terry-cloth robe, her eyes squinting. "What's that got to do with me?"

"Probably nothing," Dugan said. "But if you'll let us in, we'll explain."

"Please," Sage said softly.

A second passed, then the woman waved them into the entryway. Dugan noted the scent of booze on her breath, confirmed by the near-empty bottle of whiskey sitting on the coffee table in the den.

Janelle gestured toward the sofa, and he and Sage took seats while she poured herself another drink. Her hand shook as she turned up the glass. "All right. What do you want?"

Dugan explained about Ron Lewis, his scams and phony identities.

"I don't understand why Ron took my little boy with him that day," Sage said, "but I've been looking for him ever since."

Janelle lit a cigarette, took a drag and blew smoke through her nose. "I don't know anything about your kid."

Sage sagged with disappointment.

"What can you tell us about Ron Lewis? He was your brother?" Dugan asked.

Janelle sipped her whiskey. "Not by birth. We grew up in the foster system together."

"Do you know his real name?"

She snorted. "I'm not sure he knows it."

"What was he called as a boy?"

"Lewis was his first name."

"So that's why he chose it this last time," Sage said. Had he planned to keep it? "Tell us more about his childhood."

"He was a quiet kid. His folks beat him till he was black-and-blue. First time I got put in the same foster with him, he told me they were dirt poor. He was half-starved, had one of them bloated bellies like you see on the kids on those commercials."

"Go on," Dugan said when she paused to take another drag on the cigarette.

"We was about the same age, you know. My story was just about like his, except I never had a daddy, just a whore for a mama. So we connected, you know."

"When was the last time you saw him?"

She tapped ashes into a soda can on the table. "About three years ago. He showed up one day out of the blue, said he was on to something big and that he was finally going to make all those things we dreamed about come true." A melancholy look softened the harsh lines fanning from her eyes. "When we got sent to the second foster home to-gether, we made a pact that one day we'd get out and make something of ourselves."

Judging from her situation, Dugan doubted Janelle had succeeded.

"We used to go down to the creek and skip rocks and dream about being rich. I used to dream about us getting married and having a real family."

"Did Ron…I mean, Lewis, share that dream?" Sage asked.

Janelle shrugged. "He said he wanted all that, but he also lied a lot. Every time we got moved to a new foster, he took on the people's names."

That fit with his ability to assume different identities. He'd learned early on to switch names and lives.

Dugan would have felt sorry for him if he hadn't de-stroyed lives and hurt Sage so much.

"Tell me more about his real parents," Sage said.

"His daddy blew all he made on the races, and his mama liked meth."

"Do you know what happened to them?"

"Last we talked, he said his mama died. Don't know about his old man. Seems like I heard he got killed, probably by one of the bookies he owed money to."

Sage sighed, a frustrated sound. "Was there anyone else he might go to if he was in trouble? Another girlfriend?"

Janelle stubbed out her cigarette and tossed down the rest of her whiskey. "There was one girl he had a thing for bad. A real thing, I mean, like he wasn't just using her. He was young when it happened, but they talked about getting married."

"What was her name?"

"Sandra Peyton," Janelle said bitterly. "He knocked her up, but she lost the baby, and things fell apart."

Dugan made a mental note of the woman's name. If Sandra was the love of Lewis's life and he thought he'd finally made the fortune he wanted, maybe he had been going to see her, to win her back again.

Another thought nagged at Dugan—what if he was taking Benji to replace the child they'd lost?

Chapter Thirteen

Dugan stopped for lunch at a barbecue place called The Pig Pit, but Sage's appetite had vanished. She kept replaying the story Janelle Dougasville had told her about Ron Lewis…rather Lewis, the foster kid.

His upbringing had definitely affected him, had motivated him to want more from life, especially material things. He was trying to make up for what he hadn't had as a child.

Being shuffled from one foster family to another had turned him into a chameleon. A man who could deftly switch names, lives and stories with no qualms or hesitation.

A man who had learned to manipulate people to get what he wanted.

One who played the part but remained detached, because getting attached to a family or person was painful when you were forced to leave that family or person behind.

That, Dugan could relate to.

"I almost feel sorry for him," Sage said, thinking out loud.

"Don't." Dugan finished his barbecue sandwich. "Sure, he had some hard knocks in life, but a lot of people have crappy childhoods and don't turn out to be liars and con artists."

"You're right. He could just as easily have turned that trauma into motivation for really making something of himself."

"You mean something respectful," Dugan clarified. "Because he was something. A liar and a master manipulator."

"Yes, he was." Sage sighed. "If he really loved this woman, Sandra Peyton, do you think he might have tried to reconnect with her?"

"Anything is possible."

Sage contemplated that scenario. If Sandra Peyton had Benji, at least she was probably taking care of him and he was safe.

But where was she?

DUGAN SNATCHED HIS PHONE and punched in a number as they left the restaurant and got in the car. "Jaxon, it's Dugan. Did you learn anything about that women's shelter where Carol Sue volunteered?"

"Women there are hush-hush," Jaxon said. "But when I explained that Benji might have been kidnapped they were cooperative. That said, no one saw him, and the lady who runs the house denied that Carol Sue brought Benji there."

A dead end.

"See if you can locate a woman named Sandra Peyton."

"Who is she?"

"Lewis's foster sister, Janelle Dougasville, claims that he was involved with Sandra Peyton years ago, so he might have reconnected with her."

"I'm on it."

Dugan's other line was buzzing, so he thanked Jaxon and answered the call. "Graystone."

"Mr. Graystone, this is Ashlynn Fontaine. I ran the story

for Ms. Freeport about her son in the paper, and my friend covered it on the news."

"Yes."

"Ms. Freeport gave me your number to contact in case any leads came in regarding her son."

His pulse spiked. "You have something?"

"I received a call from an anonymous source who said that a woman and a little boy Benji's age moved in next to her about a month after Ms. Freeport's son went missing. She's not certain the child is Benji, but she said the woman was very secretive and kept to herself. Thought you might want to check it out."

"Text me her name and address."

A second later, the text came through. Dugan headed toward the address. It might be a false lead.

Then again, maybe they'd get lucky and this child might be Sage's missing son.

SAGE CLENCHED HER HANDS together as Dugan explained about the call.

"I hope this pans out, Sage," Dugan said. "But normally when a tip line is set up, it triggers a lot of false leads."

Sage nodded. She knew he was trying to prepare her for the possibility that this child might not be her son, but still, a seed of hope sprouted. Even if it wasn't Benji, maybe the tip line would work and someone would spot him.

Worry mounted inside her, though, as he drove. The half hour drive felt like years, and by the time they arrived, she'd twisted the locket around her neck a hundred times. Her neck still felt sore from the attack, the bruises darkening to an ugly purple.

A stark reminder that someone wanted her dead.

The woman lived in a small ranch-style house with a giant blow-up Santa Claus in front and a Christmas tree with blinking, colored lights visible through the front window.

Sage's heart squeezed. If Benji was here, at least the woman was taking care of him and decorated for the holidays.

Although resentment followed. Those precious moments had been stolen from her.

Dugan parked on the curb a few feet down from the house. The front door opened and a woman wearing a black coat stepped out, one hand clutching a leash attached to a black Lab, the other hand holding a small child's.

Sage pressed her face against the glass to see the boy more clearly, but he wore a hooded navy jacket. He looked about five, which was the correct age, but she couldn't see his eyes.

Sorrow and fear clogged Sage's throat. Children changed in appearance every day. What if Benji had changed so much she didn't recognize him?

Sage started to reach for the door to get out of the SUV, but he laid his hand over hers. "Wait. Let's just watch for a few minutes. We don't want to spook her."

As much as Sage wanted to run to the boy, Dugan was right. If this woman had her son and knew Sage was searching for them, she might run.

Dugan pulled a pair of binoculars from beneath his seat and handed them to her, then retrieved a camera from the back, adjusted the lens and snapped some photographs. She peered through the binoculars, focusing on the little boy and the woman.

The woman kept a tight hold on the child's hand. A natural, protective gesture? Or was she afraid he might try to get away?

Stories of other kidnappings where the victims identified with their kidnapper nagged at her. Benji had been only three when he was abducted.

Did he even remember her?

Or had he bonded with whoever had him? If it was a woman, did he think she was his mother?

A pang shot through her. Did he call her Mom?

DUGAN SENSED THE TENSION radiating from Sage. Hell, he couldn't blame her. She hadn't seen her son in two years—she was probably wondering what he looked like now. If he would even recognize her.

If he was alive and had been living with another woman or a family, he might have developed Stockholm syndrome.

He studied the body language of the woman and child as she spoke to the little boy. They seemed completely at ease with each other. The boy was saying something, and she tilted her head toward him with a smile. They swung hands as they rounded the corner, then paused while the dog sniffed the grass in a neighboring yard.

"I can't really see his face," Sage said.

"I don't have a good shot of it, either," Dugan admitted. "When they reach the house, and he takes his coat off, maybe we'll get a better look."

The dog nuzzled up to the little boy, and the kid laughed. Then the woman looked up and scanned the streets, as if nervous. A second later, he swore her gaze latched with his.

Dugan lowered the camera to the seat. "I think she spotted us," Dugan said. "Drop the binoculars, Sage."

Dugan pulled a map from the side pocket of the car and pretended he was looking at it. But he continued to watch the woman and boy out of the corner of his eye.

"He looks happy and well taken care of," Sage said in a voice laced with a mixture of pain and relief.

Dugan gave her a sympathetic look. The woman suddenly turned and ushered the boy and dog back toward the house. This time, instead of walking leisurely, she picked up her pace and looked harried. Even frightened.

Sage sat up straighter. "She looks scared. Maybe we should go talk to her."

Dugan shook his head. "Wait. Let's watch and see what she does."

Sage's frustrated sigh echoed through the SUV. "What if she runs?"

"Then we'll follow her."

Panic streaked Sage's voice. "But if it's Benji, I don't want to lose him again."

Dugan wanted to promise her she wouldn't, but he bit back the words. They didn't know for certain that this was Benji.

When the woman reached the walkway to her house, she broke into a jog, half dragging the dog and the boy. She ushered them both inside, then shut the door.

But not before glancing over at them again. Fear had flashed in her eyes.

Dugan's pulse pounded.

What was she running from?

SAGE DUG HER FINGERNAILS into her palms to keep from opening the SUV door and bolting toward the house. She desperately wanted to see the little boy's face.

And the woman was definitely afraid.

Memories of Benji smiling up at her as a baby with his gap-toothed grin taunted her. His curly blond hair, the light in his green eyes, his chubby baby cheeks... Then he'd turned from a pudgy toddler to a three-year-old overnight.

More memories flooded her—his first words, the way he loved blueberries and called them BBs, his attachment to a pair of cartoon pajamas and the yellow rubber boots he'd worn to play in the rain.

The side door to the house opened, and the boy and dog spilled out. The dog barked and raced across the fenced-in yard, and the boy ran over to the swing set and climbed the jungle gym. She needed to see his ear, that piece of cartilage....

The hood to his jacket slipped down, and she stared at the mop of blond hair. Her breath caught, lungs straining for air.

Could it be her son?

Suddenly a siren wailed, and Dugan cursed. She looked over her shoulder and spotted the sheriff's car rolling up behind them.

"Damn. She must have called the law," Dugan said.

Sage bit her tongue. Would she have done that if she was hiding out with a child that the police were searching for?

Dugan shoved the camera to the floor, and she slid the binoculars into her purse. The sheriff's car door slammed, and then he hitched up his pants and strode toward them, a sour look pinching his face.

He tapped on the driver's window, and Dugan powered the window down. "Sheriff," Dugan muttered.

Sheriff Gandt leaned forward, pinning her and Dugan with his scowl. "What are you two doing here?"

Dugan indicated the map. "Just stopped, looking for directions."

"Don't lie to me," Sheriff Gandt growled. "Get out of the car."

Sage clenched the door handle. Was he going to arrest them?

Dugan opened the door, climbed out and leaned against the side of the SUV. She walked around the front of the vehicle and joined him.

Sheriff Gandt hooked a thumb toward the house. "The woman that lives inside there called, freaked out, said a couple was stalking her and her child."

Sage's stomach knotted. "We weren't stalking them."

"But you were watching them," Sheriff Gandt said, one bushy eyebrow raised.

Dugan cleared his throat. "We had a tip we were following up on."

"What kind of tip?"

"From the news story that aired about Benji," Sage explained. "Someone called with suspicions that the woman who lives here might have Benji."

Sheriff Gandt mumbled an ugly word. "Then you should have called me."

Why would she call him when he hadn't helped her before? When she didn't trust him?

DUGAN BARELY RESISTED slugging the imbecile. He should be following up on leads, searching for Benji, but so far he'd either been incompetent or just didn't care. "We assumed you were busy investigating Rankins's supposed suicide."

Gandt's eyebrows crinkled together. "What the hell does that mean?"

"Are you sure it was a suicide?" Dugan asked.

"Of course it was. His own son called me. Said he heard his daddy pull the trigger."

"Did you check Junior for gunshot residue?" Dugan asked.

Anger reddened Sheriff Gandt's cheeks. "Wasn't no need. His daddy was upset about your visit and he was dying of cancer and decided to end his misery. End of story." Gandt planted his fists on his hips. "Besides, I'm not the one breaking the law here. You are."

"We didn't break the law," Sage said.

"You scared that poor woman to death," Gandt said. "She thought you were child predators, here to steal her son."

Sage stiffened. Those words hit too close to home. "Maybe she's afraid because she's the one who stole Benji,

and now that the story aired about him again, she's terrified someone will recognize Benji and call the police."

Which was exactly what had happened.

Gandt looked exasperated, but Dugan didn't intend to
let him off the hook. If the kid inside was Benji, once they
left, the woman would take him and run.

Then they might never find him again.

"There's one way we can settle this," Dugan said. "Let's
go talk to her."

Sheriff Gandt huffed. "That could be considered ha-
rassment."

"Then go with us," Sage suggested. "You can explain
the circumstances. If she has nothing to hide, she'll talk
to us. And if that little boy isn't Benji, then we'll go on
our way and she won't ever see or hear from us again."

Gandt looked annoyed and frustrated, but he heaved
a weary breath. "All right. But if she insists on pressing
charges against you, I won't stop her."

Dugan nodded and pressed his hand to the small of
Sage's back as they followed the sheriff up to the door.

He could feel Sage trembling beneath his touch as Gandt
rang the doorbell.

Chapter Fourteen

Sage held her breath as they waited on the woman inside to open the door.

When she did, her wary look made Sage's heart pound.

"Ms. Walton," Sheriff Gandt said. "I came as soon as I got your call."

Dark hair framed an angular face that might have been pretty had it not been for the severe scowl pulling at her mouth and the jagged scar that ran down her left cheek. A scar Sage hadn't noticed from a distance because of the coat and scarf the woman had been wearing.

Ms. Walton glanced back and forth between Sage and Dugan, her eyes angry. "Why were you two watching me?"

"Can we please come in and explain?" Sage said, grateful her voice didn't quiver and betray her.

Ms. Walton looked at the sheriff, who rolled his shoulders. "They're not stalkers," he said, although his tone indicated they were barely a notch above it.

"I'm a private investigator," Dugan said. "And this woman is Sage Freeport. You may have seen the recent news story that aired about her missing son, Benji Freeport."

The woman clenched the door in a death grip as if she was ready to slam it in their faces and flee. "I don't see what that has to do with me."

"Maybe nothing," Sage said. "But we received an anonymous tip that you might know something about my little boy."

"Me?" Shock strained the woman's voice. "I don't know anything." She angled her head toward the sheriff. "Now, are you going to make them leave me alone?"

"Yes, ma'am, I'm sorry—"

"We're not leaving until you answer some questions," Dugan said.

Gandt shot him a warning look.

"I told you I don't know anything about your little boy, Ms. Freeport. But I am sorry about what happened to you, and I hope you find him."

Sage swallowed hard. The woman sounded sincere.

But if she was innocent, why was she so nervous?

DUGAN STUDIED MS. WALTON'S body language. She was definitely scared and hiding something.

But what?

"Did you know a man named Ron Lewis?"

"No." A noise sounded behind them, and Dugan realized it was the back door shutting. The little boy was coming back inside.

"How about Mike Martin or Seth Handleman or Joel Bremmer?"

"No, who are those people?"

"Aliases of Ron Lewis, the man who abducted Benji Freeport."

"I told you, I don't know any of them." She started to shut the door, but Sage caught it this time.

"How old is your little boy?" Sage asked.

A dark look crossed the woman's face. "He'll be six next week."

Sage's sigh fluttered in the tension-laden air. "What's his name?"

Ms. Walton's eyes widened with alarm, as if she realized the implications of Sage's question. A second later, anger sparked. "I named him Barry after my father." Her tone grew sharp. "He is not your son, Ms. Freeport."

"Then, you have his birth certificate?" Dugan asked.

Panic flared in her expression. "I don't have to prove anything to you."

Sheriff Gandt made a low sound in his throat. "No, you don't, Ms. Walton." Sage opened her mouth to argue, but Gandt continued. "But if you have it, please get it and we'll clear this matter up. Then these folks will be on their way and I'll make sure they never bother you again."

"I…actually I don't have it here," she said shrilly. "It's in a safe-deposit box at the bank."

Dugan cleared his throat. "Then you won't mind bringing the boy to the door so we can meet him." Not that they still wouldn't need DNA if Sage recognized the child.

The fear that had earlier pervaded Ms. Walton's eyes deepened, but she looked directly at Sage. "He's not your son. He's mine."

Dugan gritted his teeth. Was that her way of telling Sage the truth? Or could she be mentally and emotionally unstable?

If she'd wanted a child and had lost one or hadn't been able to have a baby, she might have taken Benji and now perceived him as her own.

SAGE FORCED HERSELF not to react to Ms. Walton's possessive, defensive tone. Was she defensive because she was an honest, loving mother who had to defend herself?

Or because she was a kidnapper, afraid of getting caught?

"Just introduce us to the little boy," Dugan said.

Ms. Walton glanced at the sheriff, who managed a grunt. "Do it, ma'am. Then we'll be out of your hair."

Ms. Walton shot Sage a wary look. But she turned and yelled for Barry to come to her. A minute later, the child ran to the front door and slipped up beside his mother.

Sage soaked in his features. The wavy blond hair. The cherub face. The wide eyes that looked distrustful and full of fear.

Eyes that were brown, not green like her son's. And his ears…no extra piece of cartilage.

Disappointment engulfed her, and she released a pained breath. Dugan had warned her about getting up her hopes, but still she had latched on to the possibility.

He looked at her for a response, and Sage shook her head. She'd feared she wouldn't recognize her son, but she immediately knew that this precious little boy was not hers.

"Hi, Barry," Dugan said. "We saw you walking your dog. He's pretty cool."

Sage tried to speak, but her voice refused to come out.

"Well?" Sheriff Gandt said bluntly.

"No," Sage finally managed to say.

"I'm sorry we bothered you," Dugan said.

Relief softened the harsh lines of Ms. Walton's face, and she stooped down and kissed Barry. "Honey, why don't you get the spaghetti out of the pantry and we'll start dinner?"

Barry nodded eagerly and raced to the pantry. Ms. Walton squared her shoulders. "I'm sorry for you, Ms. Freeport. I didn't mean to overreact."

"But you were afraid," Sage said, still confused.

"I was. I am…" Her voice cracked. "My husband was abusive. He did this." She rubbed the scar along her cheek. "I had him arrested, but he keeps getting out of jail and looking for us. Barry and I went into a program and changed our names so he wouldn't find us."

"Why didn't you just tell us that when we first arrived?"

"I…when I saw you watching me, I was afraid he'd hired you to find us."

"You have a restraining order against him?" Sheriff Gandt asked.

"Yes," she said in a low voice, "but that didn't stop him before."

That explained the reason the caller said the woman stayed to herself and seemed nervous.

"I'm sorry," Sage said. "We honestly didn't mean to frighten you or your son." She reached inside her purse and handed the woman a card with her name and number. "I own the B and B in Cobra Creek. If you ever need anything, even just a friend to talk to, I'm there."

"I haven't made many friends 'cause I've been on the run. Thanks." Tears blurred the other woman's eyes as she gripped the card between her fingers. "I'll pray that you find your son."

Sage battled tears of her own. Tears for the woman whose little boy had to be afraid of his own father.

Tears for her child, who could be safe somewhere—or in danger from whomever had stolen him.

COMPASSION FOR SAGE filled Dugan as they walked back to his SUV. Gandt escorted them, his disapproval evident.

"You two need to go home and let me do my job. You can't be scaring women and children like this."

"We didn't mean to frighten them," Sage said.

Gandt's nostrils flared. "But you did."

"Only because she had something to hide," Dugan said, refusing to let Gandt intimidate him. If the man had done his job as he should have, Dugan wouldn't have jumped in to help Sage.

Gandt folded his beefy arms. "Hear me and hear me good. If I receive another call like this one, I'll lock both of you up just to get you off the street so that I *can* do my job."

With a deep grunt, he turned and strode back to his car.

Dugan slid behind the steering wheel, irritated that

Gandt waited until Sage climbed in his SUV and he pulled away from the curb before he started his squad car.

The sound of Sage's breathing rattled between them.

He turned onto the main road, then sped back toward Cobra Creek, but his mind kept replaying that phone call from Junior Rankins's son.

Had Rankins killed himself because of the cancer or because he was embarrassed that he'd been duped by Lewis?

Or had someone killed Rankins because he'd talked to them? Because they feared he knew something that would lead them to Lewis's killer?

SAGE STRUGGLED TO hold herself together. If she fell apart, Dugan might drop her case.

But Benji's innocent face flashed in her mind, and she closed her eyes, vying for courage. A mother was supposed to protect her child. Keep him safe and guide him through life. Comfort him when he was scared, chase the monsters away and sacrifice everything to give him a good life.

She had failed at all of those.

She wrapped her arms around her middle, counting the minutes until they reached the B and B. Anxious to be alone and vent her emotions, she opened the SUV door as soon as Dugan parked.

The Christmas lights mocked her, twinkling along the street and the fence in front of the B and B. A blow-up Santa waved to her from across the street at the children's clothing shop, making her throat thick with unshed tears.

She wrestled with her keys, fumbling, then dropping them on the front porch. Dugan's footsteps pounded behind her. Then suddenly he was there, retrieving her keys and unlocking the door for her.

He caught her arm before she could rush inside. "Let me check the inn first."

God… She'd forgotten about the break-in and the attack.

He gestured for her to wait on the porch swing, and she sank onto it and knotted her hands together, looking out at the twinkling Christmas lights and the darkness as he pulled his gun and inched inside.

It felt like hours but was probably only minutes before he returned, holstering his gun as he approached. "It's clear."

She nodded, too upset to speak. If she lost it, he'd probably stop helping her and then she'd be all alone again, with no one looking for her son.

DUGAN KNEW HE should walk away. Leave Sage to deal with the fallout of the day.

Focus on the case.

He wanted to see the original file on the investigation into Benji's disappearance and Lewis's automobile accident.

But he'd made an enemy of Gandt, and the sheriff probably wouldn't hand over the file. So how could he get it?

Maybe the deputy? If he refused, he'd sneak in and steal it....

Sage looked up at him, her eyes luminous with unshed tears, then she stood and stepped toward the door.

"Thanks, Dugan."

Dammit, she was trying to be so strong. Holding herself together when he knew she was hurting inside.

He'd be a damn, cold-hearted bastard to walk away right now.

"I'm going to review the notes in the original file when Benji first disappeared," he said in a feeble attempt to soothe her.

She nodded, her back to him, clenching her purse strap with a white-knuckled grip. "You're not giving up?"

"No."

Hell, he wished he could. But he wanted answers now himself. Not just for her.

But for that innocent little boy out there who might be suffering God knows what. Who might not even know that his amazing mother missed him every day.

A mother who would sacrifice anything for her son.

Sage was strong and gutsy and tenderhearted and beautiful, both inside and out.

He stepped inside with her, so close he inhaled her scent. Some kind of floral fragrance that smelled natural, like a spring garden before the Texas summer heat robbed it of life.

She shivered, totally unaware of the effect she had on him.

Needing to touch her and reassure her that she wasn't alone, he rubbed her arms with his hands. "I made you a promise, and I intend to keep it. I won't stop until we know what happened to your son."

Sage turned toward him then, her face so angelic and tortured that it broke his heart. "No one keeps promises anymore," she whispered.

Dugan had let people down before. Hell, he'd let himself down.

But he would not let down this strong, loving woman who needed someone on her side.

"I do," he said simply.

But there was nothing simple about it. He just couldn't walk away.

Her gaze met his, and his heart clenched. A second later, he pulled her into his arms and kissed her, his lips telling her all the things that his heart couldn't say.

Chapter Fifteen

Sage felt as if she was unraveling from the inside out.

Dugan's arms around her gave her strength, and she leaned into him, grateful not to be alone.

His kiss set her on fire and aroused long-forgotten needs. Desperate for more, to be even closer to him, she parted her lips in invitation. Dugan made a low sound in his throat, a passionate sound that made her heart flutter.

He deepened the kiss, teasing her with his tongue as his hands raked down her back. Her nipples budded to hard peaks, aching for attention, and she threaded her fingers in his hair and moaned.

Titillating sensations tingled through her as he splayed his hands across her hips and pulled her closer. His thick length rubbed against her belly, stirring her passion.

He ended the kiss, then trailed his lips down her neck and teased the sensitive skin behind her ear. She moaned softly and unfastened the top button of his shirt. He lowered his head, his tongue dancing down her neck, and then he used his teeth to tug at the neckline of her sweater.

Sage wanted more.

She made quick work of his buttons, then pushed his shirt aside and kissed his neck and chest. His chest was rock solid, bronzed, muscles corded and hard. She traced his nipple with her tongue, then sucked it gently.

Dugan groaned, gripped her arms and pulled away. "We should stop."

"No," Sage said. "Please, Dugan. I don't want to be alone right now."

"And I don't want to take advantage of you," he said gruffly.

"You aren't." She raised her head and brushed her lips across his neck, a seductive maneuver that seemed to trigger his passion, then led him to her bedroom.

With a low groan, he tugged her sweater over her head. She lifted her arms, eager to be closer, for skin to touch skin. She pushed his shirt off and dropped it to the floor.

His dark gaze devoured her, his look hungry and appreciative. He gently eased her bra strap over her shoulder, then the other, and heat curled in her abdomen.

"You are beautiful," he said in a low, husky murmur.

Sage started to shake her head no. She didn't want words, didn't know if she believed them.

She simply wanted to feel tonight. To forget that he was with her only because she'd asked him to help her find Benji.

God…Benji…what was she doing?

Dugan must have realized her train of thought, because he tilted her chin up, forcing her to look into his eyes. The heat and hunger burning there sparked her own raw need.

"It's okay to feel, to take comfort," he said. "That doesn't mean you've forgotten your son. That you're a bad mother for needing someone."

Tears threatened, but his forgiving words soothed her nerves. The past two years, she had experienced guilt on a daily basis. Guilt for being alive when her little boy might not be.

"Shh, don't think," Dugan murmured against her ear.

She nodded and shut out the turmoil raging inside her as he kissed her again. He brushed his fingers across her nipples, teasing them again to stiff peaks, then he lowered his mouth and closed his lips over one nipple, sucking her gently and stirring sensations in her womb.

Sage reached for his belt buckle, her body burning with the need to have him inside her.

DUGAN CALLED HIMSELF all kinds of fool for letting things go as far as they had with Sage. But she'd looked too forlorn, defeated and disappointed for him to leave her alone tonight.

Her fingers skated over his chest, eliciting white-hot heat on his skin. Touched and honored that she wanted to be with him, he paused for a moment to drink in her beauty. Her breasts were high, round, firm.

One touch of his lips to her nipples and she clutched at him with a groan. He tugged the turgid peak between his teeth and suckled her, his own body on fire, with hunger for more.

The hiss of his zipper rasping on his jeans as she lowered it sounded erotic, and made him reach for hers, as well. He peeled them down her legs. A pair of the sheerest black lacy panties he'd ever seen accentuated her curves and hinted at the secrets that lay below.

His mouth watered.

She blushed at his perusal, and he threaded one hand into her hair while he trailed kisses along her neck and throat. She moaned and ran her hands down his chest, then over his hips, and his body jerked as sensations splintered through him.

She shoved his boxers down his thighs, and his sex sprang free, pulsing with need. Full, hard, thick. Then her hand closed around him, and he hissed between his teeth at the pure pleasure rippling through him.

But he had to slow things down. Tonight wasn't about him but about pleasing her. Giving her comfort. Reassuring her that it was okay for her to feel alive when she still had questions about her son.

Sometimes you had to feel that life in order to move past the darkness and survive.

He gently eased her down on the bed, his gaze raking in her feminine curves. She arched her back, like a contented cat, and he smiled, then tugged her lacy panties down over her hips. Cool air hardened her nipples again, making heat flood him as he rose above her and kissed her again.

Their tongues danced, mated, played a game of seduction, then he ripped his mouth from hers and trailed his tongue down her body again. He made love to her with his mouth, suckling each breast until she threw back her head and groaned. Then his tongue played down her torso, circled her belly button, and dipped lower to taste her sweet essence.

He eased her legs farther apart, lifted her hips and drove his mouth over her heat, tasting, teasing, devouring her as a starving man would his last meal.

Seconds later, her release trembled through her. He savored her sweetness as she cried out his name and gave herself to him.

SAGE SHIVERED WITH mindless pleasure. She closed her eyes, clawing at the covers as sensation after sensation rippled through her.

Dugan didn't pull away, though, as Ron had done. He consumed her with his mouth.

She groaned his name and reached for him, wanting more. Needing more.

Craving all of him.

The muscles in his arms bunched and flexed as he finally rose above her. He had an athlete's muscular body, broad shoulders, corded muscles. And hints of his Native American heritage in his slick dark chest.

The fierceness of a warrior in his dark, endlessly sexy, bedroom eyes touched her soul.

Eyes that had once seemed distant and unbending but now flickered with stark, raw passion.

She lowered her hand, cradled his thick length in her palm and stroked him. He threw back his head on a guttural moan, and feminine power raged through her.

"I want you, Sage," he said between clenched teeth.

She stroked him again, guiding him to her core. "I want you, too."

His breath rattled in the air as he left her for a moment, and she twisted, achy and missing him. He dug a condom from the pocket of his jeans on the floor, and started to roll it on.

She held out her hand and urged him to come to her. His eyes flared with unadulterated lust as she slipped the condom over his erection.

With one quick thrust, he entered her. Sage's body exploded with need and pleasure. He pulled out and thrust back inside her again, filling her to the depths of her soul with his rawness.

She gripped his hips, angling hers so he could reach deeper, and he rasped her name, his movements growing faster and harder as he plunged inside her. She wrapped her legs around his waist and clutched his back, their skin gliding together as they built a frantic rhythm and another orgasm began to spike.

A deep animal-like sound erupted from his throat, his release triggering her own, and together they rode the waves of pleasure.

Dugan's labored breathing echoed in the air as they lay entwined in the aftermath of their lovemaking. But he pulled away too quickly and strode to her bathroom.

A minute later, he returned. His expression looked troubled, his body tense.

Naked, he was so sexy and masculine that she reached for him again. The familiar guilt threatened, but she shut it out and pulled him back in bed with her.

He wrapped his arms around her, and she curled against him. "Sage?"

"Don't say anything," she said softly. She especially didn't want an apology or promises that he couldn't keep.

She trusted him to help her find her son, but she'd vowed never to chance losing her heart again.

All she wanted tonight was to have him comfort her and keep her warm and chase away the nightmares.

Those would be waiting in the morning, just as they had been for the past two years.

DUGAN WAITED UNTIL Sage fell asleep, then slid from beneath the covers and dressed. He walked downstairs and outside to the back deck overlooking the creek.

Dammit, he shouldn't have taken Sage to bed.

Normally he considered himself a love-'em-and-leave-'em kind of guy. Sex was sex. No attachments. No emotional ties.

He was not the kind of man to stick around or to belong to a family. Hell, he'd never been part of a real one and figured he'd screw it up just as his old man had.

The old man he'd never known.

Besides, letting emotions get in the way caused him to lose focus. And right now he needed to focus on finding Benji.

That one lead hadn't panned out, but the little boy's picture was all over the news, so hopefully if he was still alive, someone would spot him.

Yeah, right. If whoever had Benji had kept his identity a secret for two years, they certainly wouldn't want to be found now. Worse, the story might cause the person to panic and flee the state, even the country.

To take on another name, go into hiding somewhere completely off the grid.

He texted Jaxon and asked him to be sure to alert airports, train stations, bus stations and border patrols to look for Benji.

Somewhere in the woods, leaves rustled. The wind whipped them into a frenzy. An animal howled.

He stepped closer to the end of the porch, searching the darkness. Was that a shadow near the creek?

Senses on alert, he studied the trees and creek edge, hunting for a predator.

Another noise, and he spotted a figure slipping behind a boulder.

Dugan pulled his gun from his holster, descended the porch steps and crept through the woods. The figure moved again, tree branches crackling. Something darted across the dark…the figure running?

He hunkered low, using the trees as cover as he moved closer. A noise to the right startled him, and he glanced toward it. A flicker of a light. A thin stream of smoke.

Hadn't Sage mentioned that her attacker smelled like cigarette smoke?

Had he returned to make good on his threat?

"THEY'VE GOT HALF the country looking for that little boy. You have to do something. No one can ever know what we did."

"Dammit, I'm doing the best I can."

"Kill the woman if you have to. She's getting too close. She went to see Janelle Dougasville today."

"What did that woman tell them?"

"She told them about Sandra Peyton."

Hell. The Dougasville woman should have kept her trap shut.

Now Sandra Peyton had to die.

Chapter Sixteen

Dugan rounded the corner of the oak, his gun drawn. "Hold it or I'll shoot."

A shriek echoed in the air, and then the silhouette of a man filled his vision. A thin young man with his hands up in surrender. "Please, don't shoot, mister."

Dugan frowned, then pulled a penlight from his pocket and aimed it at the guy. Damn. He was a teenager. A big guy who looked as though he might play football.

And he was shielding the girl behind him, who was frantically rebuttoning her blouse.

"A little cold to be out here in the woods this time of night, don't you think?" Dugan asked.

The boy shrugged, his leather jacket straining his linebacker shoulders. "We weren't doing anything wrong."

The girl yanked on a jacket, then inched up behind the guy, her eyes wide with fear. "Please don't hurt us, mister."

"I'm not here to hurt anyone," Dugan said, irritated they'd drawn him away from Sage's. What if someone really was watching her house, and Dugan was chasing two randy teenagers and that person got to Sage?

"I thought you were stalking the inn, here to cause trouble for the owner."

The boy said a dirty word that Dugan didn't even use

himself. "We came here 'cause Joy's mama won't let me come to the house."

"I can't say as I blame her," Dugan said, "considering you're mauling her daughter and cussing like a sailor."

"He wasn't mauling me," the girl said, her tone stronger now. "I'm seventeen. I make my own choices."

These teenagers weren't his problem. When he was the boy's age, he was probably doing the same thing.

Dugan tucked his gun back in his holster, then gestured for them to settle down. "Go on, get out of here." He gave the boy a warning look. "And don't come back to these woods again."

"No, sir, we won't." The boy grabbed the girl's hand, and they hurried back toward the wide part of the creek where they'd crossed in a small boat from the other side.

Something about seeing that boat nagged at Dugan. The creek ran wide and deep in certain areas and eventually emptied into the river that kayakers, rafters and boaters frequented. People could park in one area and boat to the other. In fact, rafters or boaters often parked cars in two areas, one where they put in and the other where they got out.

He remembered glancing at the report showing the location of Lewis's crash.

He wanted to see that report again. And he wanted to go back and walk the search grid, as well. Maybe the sheriff and his team had missed something.

THE NEXT MORNING Sage rolled over, sated and more rested than she had been in ages.

Memories of making love with Dugan the night before floated back in a euphoric haze.

But the bed beside her was empty. Not just empty but cold, as if Dugan hadn't slept there.

She'd been so deep in slumber that she hadn't even known when he'd left her bed.

Two years of exhausting, sleepless nights had finally caught up with her.

But morning sunlight poured through the window, slanting rays of light across the wood floors and reminding her that today was one more in a long list where Benji wasn't home.

One more day closer to another Christmas she would spend alone.

God, she was so tired of being alone.

Her heart clenched as if in a vise. What if she never found him? Could she go on day after day without knowing? Would the fear and anxiety eventually destroy her?

Throwing off the covers, she slid from bed. Muscles she hadn't used in forever ached, but with a sweet kind of throb that had eased the tension from her body and chased the nightmares away. At least for a little while.

She hurried into the shower, regretting the fact that the inn was empty of guests. At least having to cook breakfast for guests gave her something to do to start the day. Some sense of normalcy when nothing in her life for the past two years had been normal.

Dugan…was he still here?

She quickly showered and threw on some clothes, then dried her hair and pulled it back at the nape of her neck with a clip. Last night had sent them hunting down a false lead.

But today might provide another lead to pursue. She firmly tacked her mental resolve into place.

Rejuvenated by the night of mind-blowing sex, she pulled on boots and hurried to the kitchen. A pot of coffee was half-full and still warm. She poured herself a cup, then searched the living area for Dugan, but he wasn't inside.

Had he left? Why hadn't he told her?

She took her coffee to the back porch and found him there in one of the rocking chairs. He looked rumpled, his beard growth from the day before rough and thick, his eyes shadowed from lack of sleep.

"Have you been out here all night?"

"Off and on."

She sipped her coffee and sank onto the porch swing, using her feet to launch it into a gentle sway. "Why did you leave the bed?"

Silence, thick and filled with regret, stretched between them for a full minute before he spoke. "I offered to do a job, Sage. I shouldn't have slept with you."

True. But his words stung. Still, she sucked up her pride and lifted her chin. "So, what do we do today?"

"Last night I saw a shadow in the woods and came out to check it. Turned out it was a couple of teenagers necking in the woods."

Why was he telling her this? "So?"

"I ran them off, but it started me thinking about the day Lewis crashed."

"I don't get the connection."

"The teenagers tied a boat downstream. They took it back across the creek where they'd probably left a car."

Sage sipped her coffee again, the caffeine finally kick-starting her brain and dragging her mind away from memories of bedding Dugan again.

That was obviously the last thing on his mind.

"Anyway, after the crash, no bodies were found in the fire or anywhere around the area. Which made me start thinking—if Benji is alive and he didn't die with Lewis, who we now know was murdered—how did the shooter escape? As far as I know, the police report didn't mention another car. No skid marks nearby or evidence anyone else had stopped until the accident was called in."

Slowly, Sage began to grasp where he was headed.

"You're thinking that whoever killed Ron escaped on a boat across the creek?"

Dugan shrugged. "It's possible." He stood. "It's also possible that Lewis was meeting someone else. It's just a theory, but let's say that he had reconnected with his first love, Sandra Peyton."

"The woman who'd been pregnant and lost his child."

"Exactly." Dugan stood. "What if she was meeting him and he planned to take Benji to her so they could have the family they'd lost?"

Hope sprouted in Sage's head again.

They had to find Sandra Peyton. But if she had Benji, she probably didn't want to be found.

DUGAN WANTED TO look at that report again, and see the area for himself, so he drove to the sheriff's office.

Sage insisted on accompanying him. Luckily Gandt was out, but the deputy was in. Once Dugan explained that he was helping Sage look for her son, the deputy pulled the file, handed it over and allowed Dugan to make a copy while he returned some phone calls.

"Was there any mention of a boat?" Sage asked as she looked over his shoulder.

"I'm looking." Dugan skimmed the report. The accident had happened at approximately six-forty. A motorist had called it in when she saw the fire shooting up from the bushes.

Sheriff Gandt had arrived along with the fire department, but the car was already burned beyond saving. Once the fire had died down and the rescue workers found no evidence of anyone inside, Gandt organized a search party to comb the area.

During that two-hour interval, Lewis's shooter had escaped.

Dugan spread the photos of the area across the desk

in the front office. Sage made a low, troubled sound as she studied the pictures. The land looked deserted. The weather had been cold that day, patches of dead brush and desolate-looking cacti.

"No boat," Sage said.

"The shooter could have been following Lewis. He caused the crash, then shot Lewis…or he shot him first, causing Lewis to crash."

"If he shot him first, why not let the fire take care of destroying evidence and his body?" Sage asked.

"Because finding the body proves Lewis was murdered, that he didn't die in an accident."

Sage shivered. "If the shooter dragged him out, he must have been bleeding. But I don't see blood in the pictures."

"You're right." Dugan analyzed each one, looking for signs that a body had been dragged from the car, but saw nothing.

He tried to piece together another possibility. What if Lewis had planned to meet someone and fake his death with the car crash? Perhaps whoever it was he'd met had turned on him and shot him.

But why not leave Benji?

Maybe the shooter took Lewis and Benji at gunpoint, shot Lewis, then dumped his body? But again, why take Benji? Because he was a witness?

"Sage, I'd like to go back to the scene and walk the area."

"If you think it'll help."

"Sometimes I work with a dog named Gus. He's an expert tracker dog. Do you have something of Benji's that carries his scent, for Gus to follow?"

Another pained look twisted Sage's face. "Yes."

The deputy was still on the phone, so Dugan mouthed his thanks and they left. He drove to the inn, and Sage hurried inside to get something that had belonged to her son.

SAGE CLUTCHED BENJI'S BLANKET to her and inhaled his sweet scent. Even after two years, it still lingered. She hadn't washed it, and had held on to it for his return, the memory of him cuddling up to it so vivid that it still brought tears to her eyes.

She blinked them back, though, and carried the blanket to Dugan, who was waiting in his SUV.

"He slept with this all the time," Sage said. "I…don't know how he made it the past two years without it."

Dugan squeezed her hand as she laid it in her lap. "Hang in there, Sage."

That was the problem. She was hanging on to the hope of finding him alive and bringing him home.

As strong as she pretended to be on the surface, she didn't know if she could handle it if that hope was crushed.

Her mind traveled down that terrifying path that had opened up to her two years ago, to the possibility that he was dead and that they might find his body lying out in the wilderness somewhere. She'd seen the stories on the news and had no idea how parents survived something so horrible.

Dugan drove to his place, a ranch with horses running in the pasture and cattle grazing in the fields, and she forced herself to banish those terrifying images.

"I didn't know you had a working ranch."

Dugan shrugged. "I have a small herd, and I train quarter horses in my spare time."

"And you still have time to consult on cases?"

"Search-and-rescue missions mostly. I have a couple of hired hands, teens from the rez, who help out here."

They climbed out, and she noted the big ranch house. It was a sprawling, rustic log house with a front porch, a house that looked homey and inviting.

A large chocolate Lab raced up and rubbed up against

Dugan's leg. He stooped down and scratched the dog behind his ears. "Hey, Gus. I've got a job for you."

The dog looked up at him as if he understood.

"Did you train him?" Sage asked.

Dugan nodded. "I need to grab a quick shower and change clothes."

Memories of the two of them making love the night before teased her mind, but she reminded herself that he'd stayed with her because someone had tried to kill them, not because he was in love with her.

"Gus, come." Dugan instructed the dog to stay at the front door when they entered, and she noted the Native American artifacts and paintings of nature and horses on the wall. Dark leather furniture, rich pine floors and a floor-to-ceiling stone fireplace made the den feel like a haven.

Dugan disappeared into a back room, and she heard the shower water kick on. She tried not to imagine him naked again, but she couldn't help herself.

Trace and Ron had been good-looking men, but more business types than the rugged, outdoorsy rancher Dugan was.

She spotted a collection of arrowheads on one wall and handwoven baskets on another. But there were no personal touches, no photographs of family or a woman in the house.

She couldn't imagine why a sexy, strong, virile man like Dugan didn't have a woman in his life.

He probably has dozens.

She dismissed the thought. She had to concentrate on finding Benji. When she brought him home, he would need time to acclimate. Like Humpty Dumpty, she'd have to put the pieces of her family back together again.

Dugan appeared, freshly shaven and wearing a clean

shirt and jeans, and nearly took her breath away. Lord help her.

He attached his holster and gun, then settled his Stetson on his head and called for Gus. "Are you ready?" he asked.

She nodded and pushed images of Dugan's sexy body from her mind.

Finding Benji and rebuilding her family was all that mattered.

DUGAN PARKED AT the site of the crash, and they climbed out. He knelt and held Benji's blanket up to the dog to sniff. Gus was the best dog he'd ever had. He had personally trained him, and so far the dog had never let him down. Although with two years having passed, it was doubtful he'd pick up Benji's scent.

Gus took a good sniff, then lowered his nose to the ground and started toward the creek. Dugan followed him, Sage trailing him as Gus sniffed behind bushes and trees and along the creek bank.

But Gus ran up and down the creek, then stopped as if he'd couldn't detect Benji's odor.

Dugan wasn't giving up. He began to comb the area, pushing aside bushes and bramble. Sage followed his cue.

Weeds choked the ground, the dirt dry and hard along the bank. Dugan leaned down to see something in the brush.

A second later, he pulled a tennis shoe from the weeds.

The devastation in Sage's eyes told him the shoe had belonged to her son.

Chapter Seventeen

"That's Benji's shoe." Sage stepped closer. "How did it get in the bushes?"

Dugan didn't want to frighten her with speculations, so he tried to put a positive spin on it. "He could have lost it near the car and an animal found it and carried it here."

Gus sniffed the ground again, and Dugan searched the bushes for the other shoe or any signs of Benji.

Grateful when he didn't find bones, he released a breath. Gus turned the opposite direction and sniffed again, then followed the creek, heading closer to the town and the inn. But again, the time and elements made it impossible to track.

However, they did find an area used for putting boats in and out.

Sage wrung her hands together as she looked across the creek. "Maybe Ron realized he was in trouble, that someone was on to his scam, and he planned to meet that woman Sandra here. Or Carol Sue, one of his other girl-friends or wives?"

Dugan knew she was grasping at straws, but he didn't stop her. "Sounds feasible."

"Maybe he handed Benji off to this woman before he was shot," Sage said.

Dugan shrugged. He doubted that was the case, but he'd be damned if he destroyed Sage's hopes without proof.

They spent another hour coaxing Gus with the blanket and shoe, but they turned up nothing, and Gus kept returning to the site where Dugan thought a boat had been.

The fact that they didn't find Benji's other shoe meant he could have still had it on or that it had floated downstream.

His phone buzzed, and he checked it. Jaxon.

He connected the call. "Yeah?"

"I have an address for Martin's girlfriend, Carol Sue."

"Text it to me."

They hung up and the text came through. Carol Sue lived about forty miles from Cobra Creek.

With no traffic, he could make it there in thirty minutes.

But as he and Sage and Gus headed back to his SUV, he spotted something shiny in the grass. He paused, bent down and brushed a few blades away, then plucked a bullet casing from the ground.

"What is it?" Sage asked.

He held it up to the light. "A bullet. I'll send it to the lab for analysis."

If it was the same one that had shot Lewis, identifying the bullet could lead them to the gun that had shot the man.

And to his killer.

SAGE FOLLOWED DUGAN into the lab, where he dropped off the bullet casing he'd found in the weeds by the creek. He introduced her to Jim Lionheart, who ran the lab.

"It's bent, but it looks like it's from a .38," Lionheart said. "I'll run it. Lots of .38s out there, though. If you bring me a specific gun, I can match it."

"I'm working on it," Dugan said. "Did you see the M.E.'s report on Wilbur Rankins's death?"

Lionheart shook his head no. "You want me to pull it up?"

"I'd appreciate it."

Dugan followed Lionheart to the computer. "Why are you interested in his autopsy?"

"Rankins's grandson called me and said he heard his father and grandfather arguing before he heard the shot."

"You mean his grandson thinks his own father killed his grandfather?" Sage asked.

"He was suspicious. Of course, Gandt didn't even question it."

Lionheart accessed the report, a scowl stretching across his face. "Hmm, odd. Rankins was shot with a handgun. But most of the ranchers around here use rifles or shotguns."

Sage saw the wheels turning in Dugan's head.

"Find out if the bullet I brought in is the same kind that killed Rankins."

"Will do."

"Didn't they do an autopsy?" Sage asked.

"It's standard in a shooting, but I don't think they've ordered one. Since Junior's daddy was dying of cancer anyway and was humiliated by the questions I was asking about the land deals, Junior figured his father just wanted to end the pain."

"I'll call you when I get something."

Dugan thanked him, and Sage walked with him back to his vehicle. "But why would Junior kill Wilbur?" Sage asked. "If he wanted his land, he'd eventually get it."

"Good question," Dugan said. "And one I intend to find the answer to."

QUESTIONS NAGGED AT DUGAN as he drove toward the address he had for Carol Sue. There were too many random pieces to the puzzle, but they had to fit somehow.

If Junior had killed his father, had he also killed Lewis? And why kill his old man if he was going to die and leave him his property, anyway?

The motive for Lewis's murder was clear. Someone— either a woman or a man Lewis had deceived—had gotten revenge by murdering him. If a female had shot him, she'd probably wanted to lash out against him for his lies and betrayal. She might have seen Benji and decided to take him as her own.

On the other hand, if one of the ranchers Lewis had swindled killed him, he wouldn't have wanted the kid. And he certainly couldn't have kept him in Cobra Creek.

There was always the possibility that someone from Lewis's past, another identity Dugan knew nothing about yet, had traced him to Cobra Creek under his new name and shot him.

A half hour later, he turned into a pricey condo development that featured its own stable, tennis courts and country club.

"Carol Sue lives here?" Sage asked.

"That's the address I have. Either she has her own money or Lewis did well when they were together and she benefited."

"Maybe she's just a hardworking woman Ron tried to con."

Dugan stopped at security and identified himself. The guard let him in, and Dugan checked the numbers for the buildings until he found Carol Sue's condo, an end unit at the rear of the complex.

Designated spots were marked for visitors, but each

condo had a built-in garage. He parked, and he and Sage walked up to the door. Dugan punched the doorbell and glanced around, noting that the small lawns were well tended, each unit painted to create a unified feel.

When no one answered, he rang the doorbell again, then stepped to the side to peer in the front window. There was no furniture inside.

"Looks like she's moved out," Dugan said.

Sage sighed. "Are you sure?"

"There's no furniture in the living room. Let me check around back." He descended the brick steps, then walked around the side of the condo. A small fenced-in yard offered privacy, and when he checked the gate, it was unlocked.

Sage followed on his heels as he entered the backyard. The stone patio held no outdoor furniture. He crossed the lawn to the back but the door was locked.

Damn.

He removed a small tool from his pocket, picked the lock, then pushed the door open. The back opened to a narrow entryway with a laundry and mudroom to the left. Sage trailed him as he stepped into a modern kitchen with granite counters and stainless steel appliances.

"There's no table." Sage opened a few cabinet doors. "No food or dishes, either. You're right. She's gone."

A noise sounded upstairs. Footsteps?

Dugan pulled his weapon and motioned for Sage to move behind him. Then he crept through the hallway. He checked the living and dining area. Both empty.

The footsteps sounded again. Then a woman appeared on the stairs. She threw up her hands and screamed when she saw them.

She was dressed in heels and a dress and wasn't armed, so he lowered his gun.

"Sorry, ma'am. Are you Carol Sue?"

The woman fluttered her hand over her heart, visibly shaken. "No, I'm Tanya Willis, the real estate broker for the development. Who are you?"

Dugan identified himself and introduced Sage. "We're looking for Carol Sue."

"I have no idea where she is," the woman said. "Why do you want to see her?"

"We think she was connected to a man, Ron Lewis, whose body was recently found in Cobra Creek. Carol Sue knew him by another name, though, Mike Martin."

Tanya gasped and gripped the stair rail. "You said Mike was murdered?"

"Yes, ma'am," Dugan replied.

Sage stepped up beside him. "He also took my little boy, Benji, with him the day he was killed. You may have seen the story on the news."

"Oh, my God, yes." Tanya swept one hand over her chest. "You think Carol Sue had something to do with that man's murder and your little boy's disappearance?"

"That's what we're trying to discern." Dugan paused. "Does Carol Sue own the condo?"

"Yes," Tanya said. "She was so excited when she first bought the place and moved in. Told me she'd never had a nice home before, and that her boyfriend had a windfall and they were planning to get married and live here together."

"When was that?"

"A little over three years ago," Tanya said. "I stopped to see her a couple of times after that, thought I'd meet her fiancé since he sounded so wonderful, but both times she said he was out of town."

"Her boyfriend's windfall was due to the fact that he was a con artist," Dugan said.

Again, the real estate broker looked shocked.

"When did Carol Sue move out?" Sage asked.

"Just a couple of days ago," Tanya said. "That was weird, too. She called me and said she had to relocate and wanted me to handle putting the unit on the market."

Dugan traded looks with Sage. Had the discovery of Lewis's body prompted her quick departure?

"Did she say why she had to relocate?" Sage asked.

Tanya shook her head, her lower lip trembling. "No, but she definitely sounded upset. Like she might be afraid of something."

Dugan considered that comment. Had Carol Sue been upset because she'd learned Lewis was dead and feared his killer might come after her? Or because she'd killed him and didn't want to get caught?

Or had the publicity about the murder and Benji's disappearance made her run because she had Sage's son?

SAGE TWISTED HER HANDS together as they left the condo complex. Dugan phoned his friend Jaxon, with the rangers, and relayed what they'd learned about Carol Sue.

Sage's cell phone buzzed, and she checked the number. An unknown.

Curious, she hit Answer. "Hello."

"You need to stop nosing around."

A chill swept up her spine. It was a woman's voice this time. "Who is this?"

"It doesn't matter who it is. If you don't stop, you're going to end up dead."

The phone clicked silent.

Sage's hand trembled as she lowered the phone to her lap.

"Who was that?" Dugan asked.

"I don't know," Sage said, shaken and angry at the same time. "A woman. She warned me to stop nosing around or I'd end up dead."

Dugan checked her phone. An unknown number. Probably a burner phone, but he called Jaxon to get a trace put on Sage's phone in case the caller phoned again.

When he hung up, he turned to Sage, trying to make sense of everything. "First, a man breaks in and threatens you. And now a woman calls with threats. They must be working together."

"Do you think it was Carol Sue?"

"Could be. Or it could have been Sandra Peyton."

"But if Sandra met up with Ron before he died and took Benji, who is the man?"

"I don't know," Dugan said. "As far as we know, Sandra had nothing to do with the land scams in Cobra Creek."

What if Sandra had reconnected with Ron and they'd planned to con the people in Cobra Creek, then disappear with the money?

If so, did she have Benji with her?

HE WAS CLOSE on Carol Sue's tail. The damn woman thought she'd get away, but she was wrong.

He had to tie up all loose ends.

He held back in his car, following her at a safe distance, careful not to tip her off. She'd been hiding out since Lewis disappeared.

But she'd tried to blackmail him first.

He didn't kowtow to blackmail from anyone.

Not that she had understood what was going on, but she knew enough.

Too much.

She swerved the little sedan into the motel, parked at the front and rushed inside, scanning the parking lot and checking over her shoulder as if she sensed she was being followed.

Stupid broad. She'd gotten greedy.

Now she would pay.

He parked to the side and waited until she rushed out

with the key. She moved her car down the row of rooms to the last one at the end.

He grinned as she grabbed her bag and hurried inside the room.

Laughter bubbled in his chest.

Night was falling, but it wasn't dark enough to strike just yet. The motel backed up to a vacant warehouse parking lot. There he might stick out.

Better to blend in with the crowd, so he parked a few spaces down in front of a room with no lights on, indicating it was vacant. Satisfied she'd tucked in for the evening, he walked across the street to the bar/diner.

He slid into a back booth and ordered a burger and beer but kept a low profile as he enjoyed his meal. Night had descended by the time he finished, but he wanted to wait another half hour to give the bar time to fill up so no one would notice him leaving.

So he ordered a piece of apple pie and coffee and took his time.

His belly full, he paid the bill in cash, then stepped outside for a smoke. The first drag gave him a nicotine buzz, and he stayed in the shadows of the bar until he finished and tossed the cigarette butt to the ground. He stomped it in the dirt with his boot, then walked back across the street.

Still, he waited, watching her room until she flipped off the lights. He gave her time to get to sleep, then slid from his car and eased down the row of rooms until he reached hers.

He quickly picked the lock, then inched inside. The soles of his shoes barely made any noise as he walked toward the bed. She lay curled beneath the blanket on her side, one hand resting beneath her face.

He grabbed a pillow from the chair, then leaned over her. Her eyes popped open, and she started to scream when she saw him.

But he shoved the pillow over her face and held it down, pressing it over her nose and mouth. She struggled, kicked and clawed at him, but he was stronger and used his weight to smother the life out of her.

Even after her limbs went still and her body limp, he kept the pillow on her for another two minutes to make sure she was dead.

He didn't want her returning to haunt him and ruin all he'd done to get where he was.

In fact, he'd kill anyone who got in his way.

Including Sage Freeport and that damn Indian, who were asking questions all over Cobra Creek.

Chapter Eighteen

Dugan's phone buzzed as he drove back to Cobra Creek.

"Mr. Graystone," Donnell said, his voice hesitant.

"Yes. What can I do for you, Mr. Earnest?"

"I've been thinking about what you said that day, about my ranch and that Lewis jerk."

"Go on."

"I heard Wilbur Rankins is dead."

"That's true. The sheriff said he shot himself because of the truth about the scam coming out."

A tense moment passed. Earnest cleared his throat. "Listen to me, mister. I don't know what the hell's going on, but I do know Wilbur. That man was the most prideful man I've ever known. Sure, he would have hated being showed up by some bigwig stranger that duped him out of his land, but he would never kill himself. *Never.*"

"What makes you so sure?"

"First of all, he loved his grandson too damn much. He always said suicide was a coward's way out. His daddy took his own life, and Wilbur hated him for it."

Interesting. "What about his cancer? If he was in a lot of pain, maybe he committed suicide to keep his family from watching him suffer or to keep them from paying medical bills."

Earnest mumbled a crude remark. "He might have been

worried about money and bills, but he just got a report saying he was doing better. He thought he was going to beat that cancer after all."

Dugan stifled a surprised response. That wasn't the impression he'd gotten. "Do you know who his doctor was?"

"Doc Moser sent him to some specialist oncologist in San Antonio."

"What is it you want me to do?" Dugan asked.

A long sigh echoed back. "Find out the truth. If Wilbur didn't kill himself, then someone murdered him. And if it has to do with the land, I'm worried they're gonna come after me."

Dugan scrubbed his hand over his neck. That was a possibility. "Thanks for calling, Mr. Earnest. I'll let you know what I find."

When he hung up, Sage was watching him, so he relayed the conversation. Then he turned the SUV in the direction of the doctor's office in Cobra Creek.

BY THE TIME they reached Cobra Creek, the doctor's office was closed.

"Do you know where he lives?" Dugan asked.

"Two houses down from the inn."

She pointed out Dr. Moser's house, and Dugan parked. "Do you know him?"

Sage nodded. "He's the only doctor around. He treated me and Benji."

Dr. Moser's house was a two story with flower boxes in front and a garden surrounded by a wrought-iron fence in back. His wife apparently spent hours tending her flowers.

Sage rang the bell while Dugan glanced up and down the street. A moment later, Mrs. Moser, graying hair and a kind smile, opened the door and greeted them.

Sage introduced Dugan and explained that he was helping her look for her son. "Can we come in?" Sage asked. "We need to talk to Dr. Moser."

The doctor appeared behind her, adjusting his bifocals. "Hello, Sage. Is something wrong?"

"Please let us come in and we'll explain," she said.

Mrs. Moser waved them in and offered coffee, but they declined. The doctor gestured toward the living room, and they seated themselves.

Dugan began. "I suppose you heard that Ron Lewis's body was found by the creek."

Dr. Moser nodded. "I did hear that. Saw Dr. Longmire yesterday, and he told me that Lewis was shot."

"Yes, he was," Dugan said.

Dr. Moser gave Sage a sympathetic look. "I'm sorry. I heard they still haven't found Benji."

Sage folded her hands and acknowledged his comment with a small nod.

"So what brought you here?" Dr. Moser asked.

Dugan explained about Lewis's scam. "I have reason to suspect that Wilbur Rankins might not have killed himself."

Dr. Moser pulled a hand down his chin. "I don't understand. I'm not the medical examiner."

"No, but you can answer one question. Sheriff Gandt said that Rankins shot himself because he was ashamed that he'd been duped by Lewis and because he was dying of cancer."

Dr. Moser looked back and forth between them. "He did have cancer. But you know the HIPAA law prevents me from discussing his medical condition."

"Dr. Moser," Dugan said bluntly. "The man is dead. In fact, he may have been murdered. All I need to know is if his condition was terminal or if he was going to get better."

Indecision warred in the doctor's eyes for a moment,

then he leaned forward in his chair. "I do believe he'd just learned that the chemo was working."

Sage sucked in a sharp breath. If he'd just received a good prognosis, it didn't make sense that he'd take his own life.

DUGAN THANKED THE DOCTOR, Donnell Earnest's suspicions echoing in his head. Was Earnest right? Had someone murdered Rankins?

Someone who'd partnered with Lewis?

He drove toward the bank, wondering if Bates had any insight. "When Lewis was with you, did he ever mention a partner?"

Sage rubbed her temple. "Not that I remember."

"How about the name of the developer?"

She closed her eyes as if in thought. "It was something like Woodard or Woodfield. No, Woodsman. I remember thinking that it suited the business."

"We need to research it." Dugan parked at the bank, and he and Sage entered together.

"While you talk to Mr. Bates, I'm going to talk to Delores," Sage said. "She's the loan officer here. Maybe she knows something."

"Good idea." Dugan strode toward Bates's office while Sage veered to the right to speak to her friend.

When he knocked, Bates called for him to come in. The man looked slightly surprised to see him but gestured for him to sit down.

"What can I do for you today, Mr. Graystone?" Bates asked.

"Who was this developer working with Lewis?"

Bates tugged at his tie, nervous. "The company name was Woodsman."

"What about Junior? Does he know this?"

"Yes. Junior is irate. He was furious with his father for signing with Lewis in the first place."

So Junior might have killed his father...

Or someone from the company could have killed Rankins to keep him from challenging the legitimacy of the deal.

Dugan thanked him and phoned Jaxon as he left the man's office. He had to find the person behind Woodsman.

SAGE KNEW DELORES from the bank and church. In fact, Delores had helped her with her loan for the renovations with the inn when she first decided to buy and refurbish it. They had become friendly enough for an occasional lunch and social gathering.

Until Benji disappeared. Then she'd shut down and kept to herself.

Delores waved to her from her desk. "Hey, Sage. How are you?"

"Can we talk in private?" Sage asked.

Delores's eyebrows shot up, but she gestured toward the door to her office. Jingle bells tinkled on it as Sage closed it. She sank into one of the chairs opposite her friend's desk, noting a Christmas tin full of cookies and candy canes.

"What's going on?" Delores asked. "I heard that Dugan Graystone found Ron Lewis's body."

Sage knew some of the residents in town weren't as friendly to the people from the reservation as they should be, an archaic attitude that she had no tolerance for. Dugan seemed to travel between both worlds fairly well. Most of the single women in town were intrigued by his dark, sexy physique and those haunted bedroom eyes.

But the men were standoffish.

Normally she didn't listen to gossip, but occasionally, a grain of truth could be found beneath the murk. "What are they saying?"

"That he was murdered," Delores said in a low voice as if she thought someone might be listening.

"He was shot," Sage said.

"Do they know who did it?"

"No, but Dugan Graystone is investigating."

Delores thumbed her auburn hair over her shoulder. "That's why he's here?"

"Yes," Sage said. "He's also helping me look for Benji."

"Yes, that's what they said on the news." Delores sighed. "You don't think…?" She cut herself off as she realized the ugly implications. "I'm sorry, Sage. I know this must be horrible for you."

"It has been," Sade admitted. "That's why I want to talk to you. Ron Lewis wasn't really who he said he was. He was a fraud who conned people out of their land. Ron said that he worked for this developer by the name of Woodsman. Do you know anything about that company?"

Delores wrinkled her nose. "No. Although that name sounds familiar." She turned and tapped some keys on the computer, her frown deepening. "I shouldn't be telling you this, but that name does show up on an account here."

Sage leaned forward. "Do you have any more information about the person who opened the account?"

Delores tapped a few more keys, a look of frustration tightening the lines around her eyes. "Hmm."

"What is it?"

"Let me look into something."

Sage drummed her fingers on her leg as she waited while Delores worked her magic. Her friend had confided once that she was somewhat of a hacker.

Delores sighed, long and meaningful, into the silence. "Oh, this is interesting."

"What?"

"I think Woodsman might be a dummy corporation."

"One Ron Lewis set up so he could personally hide money he was stealing from landowners."

Delores nodded, although her face paled as she looked at Sage. "That's not all. There's one other person who has access to the money in that account."

Sage's mind raced. It had to be someone at the bank who'd figured out what was going on. "You mean Mr. Bates?"

Delores shook her head no. "Sheriff Gandt."

DUGAN'S PHONE BUZZED as he left Bates's office. "Graystone."

"It's Jaxon. Meet me at the motel outside Cobra Creek."

"What's going on?"

"The cleaning staff found a body in one of the rooms."

"I'll be there ASAP."

He waited outside Delores's office for Sage. Her complexion looked a pasty-gray as she exited the office.

"Sage?"

She motioned for him to walk with her, and they left the bank. She didn't speak until they'd settled into his SUV.

"What did your friend say?"

Sage heaved a wary breath. "Delores looked up the account for Woodsman."

"And?"

"There was another person attached to the account." She turned to him, her expression etched in turmoil. "You won't believe who it was."

Dugan's patience was stretched thin. "Who?"

"The sheriff."

Dugan muttered a curse. "So Gandt was working with Lewis?"

Sage shrugged. "It looks like that. I guess the question is whether or not Gandt knew Ron was running a con, and if he was in on it."

Chapter Nineteen

Dugan should have been shocked at the fact that Gandt's name was associated with the account, but he'd never liked the bastard, so shock wasn't a factor.

But he drove to the motel, furious at the idea that the man who was supposed to be protecting and taking care of the town might be dirty. And that he might have taken advantage of the very people who'd trusted him and voted him into office.

"Do you think the sheriff knew what Ron was up to?" Sage asked, almost as if she was struggling to face the fact that Gandt might have lied to her.

"That arrogant SOB thinks he owns this town. I wouldn't put it past him to join in on a scheme that would garner him a bigger part of the pie."

Dugan spotted Jaxon's car in front of the motel room at the far end, room eight, swung his SUV into the lot and parked.

"What are we doing here?"

"Jaxon called. A body was found here."

Sage's mouth twitched downward. "Oh, God. Who is it?"

"We'll find out." Dugan reached for the door and opened it, then walked around to Sage's door, but she was already out. He was amazed at the strength she emanated.

When they reached the motel room, a uniformed officer met them where he stood guard. Dugan identified himself, and Jaxon walked up.

"Wait outside, Sage," Dugan told her.

He followed Jaxon across the room where Sheriff Gandt stood by the body of a woman on the bed. The M.E. was stooped beside her, conducting an exam.

"Have you identified her?" Dugan asked Jaxon.

Jaxon nodded. "Found a wallet in her car outside, with her license. Her name is Carol Sue Tinsley. That's why I thought you'd be interested."

"Damn." He'd halfway hoped they would find her and Benji together.

Sheriff Gandt glared at him. "What are you doing here?"

"I phoned him," Jaxon said. "This woman had a prior relationship with the man you knew as Ron Lewis."

Gandt's thick eyebrows shot up. "How do you know that?"

"I'm a Texas Ranger," Jaxon said, a sharp bite to his tone. "It's my job to investigate murders and kidnappings."

Dugan almost grinned. He knew Jaxon well enough to understand the implied message, that it was his job to step in when incompetence reigned.

"What was cause of death?" Dugan asked.

The M.E. was conducting a liver temp test. "The petechial hemorrhaging in the eyes suggests asphyxiation." He used his fingers to lift her eyelids, one at a time.

Dugan glanced at the pillow on the floor by the bed. Probably the murder weapon.

No bullet this time.

Was she murdered by the same perp who'd shot Lewis? If so, why a different MO?

To throw off the police?

"Have you found any forensics evidence?" Dugan asked.

Gandt shook his head. "I searched the room, but no signs of who did this."

"Any sexual assault?" Dugan asked.

Dr. Longmire shook his head. "None." He pulled the sheet back to reveal that she was still clothed in flannel pajamas. "My guess is she was sleeping when she was attacked."

"Was anyone with her when she checked in?" Dugan asked.

"No." Jaxon rubbed his chin. "Her car was registered to the name on her driver's license. But at the registration desk, she signed in as Camilla Anthony."

"So she was hiding from someone."

"Or meeting a lover," Sheriff Gandt said.

Dugan scoffed. "Most women don't wear flannel pj's to a romantic rendezvous."

Jaxon murmured agreement. "I'm going to canvass the other rooms in case another guest saw something."

The M.E. lifted one of her hands, indicating a broken nail. "It looks like she put up a fight. I'll see if I can get DNA."

"Even a thread of her attacker's clothing could help," Dugan added.

The sheriff shifted, walked over and bent to study the body. "I still think she was probably running from an ex-boyfriend. Maybe he followed her here, waited till she went to bed, then slipped in and choked her."

"What about the lock?" Dugan asked.

"It was picked," Jaxon said. "So far, no prints."

"And her belongings?" Dugan asked.

"We found a suitcase," Jaxon said. "Clothing, shoes, toiletries. I searched her purse, but no indication where she was headed. No map or papers with any kind of address on it."

"Money?"

"She did have a stash of cash, nearly a thousand dollars," Jaxon said.

"So robbery was not a motive." Dugan chewed over that information, then turned to Gandt. "Did you know this woman, Sheriff?"

Gandt hitched up his pants. "No, why would I?"

Dugan studied the way the man's mouth twitched. "Because she was Lewis's girlfriend when he went by the name of Mike Martin."

"That so?"

"Yes," Dugan said. "He had a string of names he used for his other scams."

Gandt crossed his beefy arms. "What else have you found out about Lewis?"

"He has a rap sheet for arrests under three different names for fraud and embezzlement. And he conned some local ranchers in Cobra Creek." Dugan glanced at Jaxon. "Did you find a cell phone in her purse or car?"

Jaxon shook his head no. "If she had one, the killer must have taken it."

To cover his tracks.

Dugan turned and scrutinized the room. The neon lights of a dive bar flickered against the night sky. "While you sweep the room for forensics, I may take a walk over there." Dugan turned to the sheriff. "Like you said, if the killer was watching her, he might have gone inside to wait until he thought she was asleep."

The sheriff tugged at his pants. "I'll do that," he said in a tone that brooked no argument. "I'm the law around here, Graystone, and don't you forget it."

He was the law. But Dugan didn't trust him worth a damn, especially now that he knew Gandt's name was associated with the account related to the land deals.

Could Gandt have killed Lewis so he could gain access

to the property and money for himself? So he really could own Cobra Creek?

And what about Carol Sue? Maybe she'd traced Lewis to Cobra Creek and come looking for Lewis or her share of whatever money she thought he owed her.

Sage paced outside the motel room, anxious to know what was going on inside.

Finally Dugan stepped out with a tall muscular man in a Stetson wearing a Texas Ranger badge on his shirt. Dugan introduced him as his friend Jaxon, and Sage thanked him for his help.

"Who was the woman?" Sage asked.

"Carol Sue," Dugan said with an apologetic look.

Disappointment ripped through Sage. If Carol Sue had any information about Benji, she couldn't tell them now.

"She was smothered," Dugan continued. "She put up a fight, though, so hopefully the M.E. can extract DNA from underneath her fingernails."

"I'm going to talk to the other guests at the motel," Jaxon said. "Maybe we'll find a witness."

"Let's divide up and it'll go faster." Dugan touched Sage's elbow. "Will you be okay here?"

"Sure, go ahead."

Jaxon headed to the first unit while Dugan took the one next to the room where the woman lay dead.

Sheriff Gandt stepped outside. "Did you know the woman in there, Ms. Freeport?"

"No," Sage said. "Did you?"

The sheriff's eyebrows drew together, creating frown lines across his forehead. "No. She's not from Cobra Creek."

"What do you think she was doing here?" Sage asked.

Sheriff Gandt shrugged and made a noncommittal

sound. "Looks like she was probably meeting a lover. They had a quarrel and he killed her."

"Still, it seems odd that she was in Cobra Creek," Sage countered. "Especially so soon after Ron Lewis's body was found."

"You think she came here looking for his killer?" Gandt asked in a skeptical tone. "Hell, it's been two years since he disappeared."

"She probably saw the news of his death and wanted to talk to you about it," Sage suggested.

The sheriff's mouth twitched. "I guess that's possible."

"You also had connections to the land deal Ron had put together."

Shock widened Gandt's eyes. "Who the hell told you that?"

"It doesn't matter who told me," Sage said curtly. "What matters is that you were in cahoots with Ron to buy up the land around Cobra Creek. You were swindling your own people."

A dark rage flashed in the sheriff's eyes. "You don't know what you're talking about, Ms. Freeport."

"I know that you never really tried to find my son." Sage was spitting mad. "And that your name is associated with the developer Ron was working with." She planted her hands on her hips. "And that you could have killed him so you'd get all the money and land yourself."

"I'd be really careful about making accusations, Ms. Freeport," he said with a growl. "I'd hate to see you end up like that woman in there."

Sage's heart hammered in her chest. Was he threatening her?

THE MOTEL HELD twelve rooms, but only half of them were occupied.

The first door Dugan knocked on held an elderly couple

who claimed they hadn't seen or heard anything because they'd retreated to bed as soon as it got dark. Apparently they'd both grown up on a farm, and they rose with the roosters and went to bed with the sun.

He moved to the next room and knocked on the door. A minute later, a young man in jeans and a cowboy hat opened the door. He pulled off headphones from his ears. "Yeah?"

"I'm sorry to bother you, but there was a woman murdered in room eight. We're asking everyone in the motel if they saw or heard anything."

The guy gestured toward his guitar, which was propped against the bed. Two young guys in their twenties also sat in a circle with a banjo and fiddle, and a brunette was strumming chords on her own guitar.

"Afraid not. We were jamming, working on some new material."

"Are you guys from around here?"

"North Texas. We're on our way to Nashville for a gig."

Dugan gestured toward the others. "Did any of you see someone near room eight?"

A chorus of nos rumbled through the room. "I thought I heard some banging," the girl said. "But I figured it was someone getting it on."

This group was no help. Dugan didn't see any reason to collect their contact information, but he laid a card on the dresser. "Call me if you remember anything. Maybe a car or person lurking around."

He tried the door next to them, but a family with twin toddlers answered the door. "Sorry, we went to dinner and drove around to see the Christmas lights," the father said. "By the time we returned, the sheriff's car was already outside."

Dugan thanked them, then moved down the row of rooms. But it was futile. Barring the cars and trucks in the lot, which were all accounted for by guests, no one had witnessed anything.

His phone buzzed against his hip, and he checked the number. Unknown.

He quickly connected the call. "Dugan Graystone."

"I have some information about Ron Lewis."

Dugan clenched the phone and looked around the parking lot in case the caller was nearby. "Who is this?"

"Meet me at Hangman's Bridge. An hour."

The voice was blurred, low, hoarse. Disguised.

"I'll be there." He hung up and checked his watch for the time. It could be a setup.

But it could be the tip he needed to end the case and find Benji.

Nerves knotted Sage's shoulders as she and Dugan walked across the street to the bar.

"The canvass of the motel turned up nothing."

Sage sighed. "The sheriff warned me not to go around making accusations against him."

Dugan's eyes flared with anger. "Bastard. He's in this. I just need to prove it."

Sage still couldn't believe it. She had turned to Sheriff Gandt two years ago and even trusted him at first. Sure, she'd been frustrated that he hadn't found Benji, but it had never occurred to her that he might have been involved in her son's disappearance.

Even if he had killed Ron, why would he do something to Benji? As sheriff, he could have covered up the murder, then returned Benji to her and looked like a hero.

The bar was dark and smoky as they entered. Dugan had snapped a picture of Carol Sue and showed it to the hostess. "Do you recognize this woman?"

She shook her head. "What's going on?"

Dugan relayed the fact that Carol Sue had been murdered in the room across the street. "Was she in here earlier?"

"I didn't see her," the hostess said. She waved the bartender over. "Lou, was this woman in here earlier tonight?"

Lou dried his hands on a towel. "Naw. She ain't been in."

Dugan explained about the murder. "It's possible that her killer came in," Dugan said. "Did you notice anyone suspicious? Maybe someone who seemed nervous? He might have watched the door or checked the time."

"All that's been in tonight is the regulars," Lou said. "Well, 'cept for this group of young folks, said they was in a band."

"We talked to them." Dugan handed them each a card. "If you think of anything, no matter how small, please give me a call."

Sage and Dugan walked back outside to the SUV. An ambulance had arrived to transport Carol Sue's body back to the morgue for an autopsy. Sage looked up and saw Sheriff Gandt lift his head and pin her with his intimidating stare.

Dugan's expression was grim as he drove her back to the inn. Night had set in long ago and exhaustion pulled at her limbs. And it was another day closer to Christmas.

And still no Benji.

The memory of Dugan's arms around her taunted her, making her yearn to have him make love to her again. To comfort her and chase her nightmarish fears away for a few more hours.

But after he searched the inn, he paused at the door.

"An anonymous caller phoned that he has information about Lewis," Dugan said. "Lock the doors, Sage, and stay inside until I get back."

She nodded, then watched him leave. Too antsy to sleep, she combed the inn.

A knock sounded at the door, and she rushed to answer it. The sheriff stood on the other side.

"Sheriff?"

"Come with me, Ms. Freeport. I may have a lead on your son."

Sage's heart stuttered. After the visit at the bank, she didn't know whether or not to trust him.

"Let me call Dugan to go with us."

"That's not necessary," Sheriff Gandt said.

"But—"

Her words were cut off as he raised his gun and slammed it against her skull.

Pain ricocheted through her temple, and then the world went black.

Chapter Twenty

Dugan parked in the woods by Hangman's Bridge, his instincts on alert. The fact that the anonymous caller had chosen this area to meet aroused his suspicions.

It was called Hangman's Bridge for a reason—two teenagers had died in a suicide pact by hanging themselves from the old metal bridge.

He pulled his gun, surveying the trees and area surrounding the bridge, looking for movement. An animal howled from somewhere close by, and the sound of leaves crunching crackled in the air.

He spun to the right at the sharp sound of twigs snapping. Then a gunshot blasted. Dugan ducked and darted behind an oak to avoid being hit.

Another shot pinged off the tree, shattering bark. He opened fire in the direction from where the bullet had come from, searching the darkness.

The silhouette of a man lurked by the bridge, the shadow of his hat catching Dugan's eye. Dugan crept behind another tree, careful to keep his footfalls light so as not to alert the man that he'd spotted him.

Another shot flew toward him, and he darted beneath the rusted metal rungs of the bridge and returned fire. His bullet sailed into the bushes near the man, then leaves rustled as the gunman shifted to run.

Dugan raced from one hiding spot to another, quickly closing the distance, and snuck up behind the man just before he ran for his truck in a small clearing to the left.

Dugan tackled the guy from behind, slamming him down into the brush. The man struggled, but his gun slipped from his hand and fell into a patch of dried leaves and branches.

They wrestled on the ground as the bastard tried to retrieve it, and the man managed to knock Dugan off him for a second. Dugan scrambled back to his feet as the shooter jumped up to run. But Dugan lunged toward him, caught him around the shoulders and spun him around.

Lloyd Riley.

"Riley," Dugan said. "Give it up."

But Lloyd swung a fist toward Dugan and connected with his jaw. A hard right.

Dugan grunted and returned a blow, the two of them trading one after the other until Dugan kicked Riley in the kneecap and sent him collapsing to the ground with a bellow of pain.

Dugan kicked him again, this time a sharp foot to the solar plexus, rendering him helpless.

Riley curled into a ball, hugging his leg. "You broke my damn kneecap!"

"You're lucky you're alive." Dugan flipped the big man over, pressed one foot into Riley's lower back to hold him still while he jerked his arms behind him, yanked a piece of rope from his pocket and tied his wrists together.

Riley growled an obscenity into the dirt. Dugan rolled him over and shoved his gun into his face.

"Why the hell were you shooting at me?"

Riley's lips curled into a hiss. "I had to," he muttered.

Dugan gripped Riley's shirt collar, yanking it tightly to choke the man. "What does that mean?"

Blood trickled down Riley's forehead near his left eye,

another line seeping from the corner of his mouth. Then Dugan noticed the leather tassel on Riley's gloves. One was missing.

"You damn bastard, you broke into Sage Freeport's bedroom and tried to strangle her."

"I'm not talking till I get a lawyer."

Dugan laughed, a bitter sound. "You will talk to me. I'm not the law, Riley." He shoved the gun deeper into the man's cheek. "Now, why were you trying to kill me?"

Riley's Adam's apple bobbed as he swallowed hard.

"Spit it out," Dugan snarled.

"Gandt told me to."

Dugan's stomach knotted. "What?"

"That Freeport broad found out he was in cahoots with Lewis, and he knew you were on to him."

"So it's true, Gandt and Lewis were working together?"

"Not at first," Riley said. "But Gandt figured out Lewis was a con man and wanted in."

"Then he got greedy and killed Lewis so he could have the land to himself."

Riley nodded. "He told me I could keep my ranch if I helped cover for him."

"If you killed me?" Dugan asked.

Riley spit blood from his mouth. "He said he'd frame me for killing Lewis. Then I'd lose my ranch and go to jail."

"What about the driver of that car that ran me and Sage off the road?"

Riley's face twisted with pain. "He was one of my hired hands."

Dugan gripped the man's collar tighter. "Where is Gandt now?"

Riley averted his eyes, and Dugan cursed. "Where is he?"

"He went after the Freeport woman. Said if I took care of you, he'd take care of her."

Dugan went stone-cold still. He had to get to Sage.

SAGE STIRRED FROM unconsciousness, the world a dark blur. What had happened? Where was she?

Gandt... God, the sheriff had been in on the scam. And now he had her....

And he was going to kill her.

She had to find a way out, call Dugan. Make the sheriff confess what he'd done with Benji.

She blinked to clear her vision, then realized she was tied to a chair, her hands bound behind her back, her feet bound at the ankles. She struggled to untie the knot at her wrists as she searched the darkness.

The scent of hay and horses suffused the air. She must be in a barn. But whose?

The sheriff didn't own a ranch...did he?

Maybe it was one of the properties he'd confiscated through the phony land deals.

But which one? And where was he now?

The squeak of the barn door startled her, and she whipped her head to the side and saw a shadowy figure in the doorway.

"What are you going to do, kill me, too?" Sage shouted.

His footsteps crushed the hay on the floor as he walked toward her. A sliver of moonlight seeped through the barn door where it was cracked, painting his face a murky gray.

"I warned you not to keep poking around," Gandt said in a menacing tone. "You should have listened."

Still struggling with the ropes behind her back, Sage clenched her teeth. "Where is my son?"

Gandt lumbered toward her, tugging at his pants. His gun glinted in the dark as he trained it on her. "I don't know."

Sage's heart raced. "What do you mean, you don't know?"

His scowl deepened, a muscle ticking in his jaw. "When I got to Lewis that night, he was alone."

Sage's head throbbed from where he'd slammed the butt

of the gun against her temple, but she gritted her teeth at the nausea. "You're lying. We found Benji's shoe by the creek near the crash site."

Gandt waved the gun around. "I'm telling you the kid was already gone when I met up with Lewis."

Fear engulfed Sage. He had to be lying. "I don't believe you. Benji had to be with Ron."

Gandt cursed. "Listen, Ms. Freeport, I'm telling you, he wasn't. Lewis must have dropped him off before he came to meet me."

"You were going to meet him about the land?"

"Yeah," Gandt said with a smirk. "You think I'm not smart enough to figure out what he was doing?" He paced in front of her, his jowls jiggling. "Well, I am. Once I talked to a couple of locals and they told me he'd offered to buy up their property, I started looking into him. Ain't nobody messin' with my town."

Sage almost had one end of the rope through the back loop. "So you blackmailed him for a cut of the money?"

"I wanted that land," Gandt said. "First off, he said no way, but I can be convincing."

"You killed him, didn't you?" Sage's stomach rolled. "Then you forged papers so you could take over the rancher's properties."

"Hell, they'd rather be beholden to me than let some stranger turn their ranches into shopping malls and those damn coffee shops."

He lit a cigarette, then lifted it and took a drag. The ashes sparkled against the dark.

"Then that Indian friend of yours had to find Lewis's body, and you started nosing around."

Panic seized Sage. "All I want is my son. Just tell me where he is, and I promise I won't tell anyone what you did to Ron."

A dark laugh rumbled from Gandt. "Sure you won't.

You talked to people at the bank. You went to the stinking press."

Tears burned the backs of Sage's eyes. "Please, just tell me. Is Benji all right?"

Gandt blew smoke through his nostrils, smoke rings floating in the air between them. "I told you the truth. I don't know what happened to the boy."

Sage struggled to understand. Could he have been in the car when they crashed and ran when he saw Gandt? "What happened?"

"I set fire to the car to cover up the murder. And it would have worked if you hadn't come along asking questions."

Sage's mind tried to piece together the facts. Had Ron left Benji with someone else when he went to meet the sheriff? Maybe one of the women from his past?

Not Carol Sue—she was dead.

Sandra Peyton…

Her conversation with Maude Handleman, then Janelle Dougasville echoed in her head. Sandra had lost Ron's baby, and so had Maude. And Janelle said he'd never had a real family.

Was that what Ron was chasing? The reason he'd chosen her in the first place, so he could take Benji and raise him with Sandra, his first love?

Frantically she worried with the ropes, but the sheriff inhaled another drag from his cigarette, then dropped it onto the floor of the barn. She gasped as the embers sparked and a blade of hay caught fire.

Gandt leered at her and backed toward the door, and fear paralyzed her. He was going to burn down the barn with her in it.

DUGAN CALLED SAGE, panicked that Gandt had hurt her. Her phone trilled and trilled, his heart hammering as he waited to hear her voice.

But on the fifth ring, it rolled to voice mail. "Sage, the sheriff is dirty. If he shows up, don't open the door. And call me so I know you're okay."

He ended the call, then punched her number again, but once more he got her machine.

Dugan jerked Riley up and hauled him to his SUV. "Where would Gandt take Sage?"

Riley's eyes bulged. "I don't know."

Dugan shook him hard. "Tell me, dammit. If he hurts her, you're going down for it, too."

"I told you I don't know," Riley bellowed. "He ordered me to take care of you and said he'd handle her."

Dugan wanted to kill him on the spot. But he had to find Sage.

He searched Riley for another weapon, but he was clean, so he shoved him into the backseat. For a brief moment, he considered calling the deputy, but the deputy might be in cahoots with Gandt.

Jaxon was the only one he trusted.

He reached for his phone and started to shut Riley's door, but Riley's phone buzzed from his pocket.

Maybe it was Gandt, checking in.

Riley frowned as Dugan retrieved the rancher's phone from his shirt pocket.

Dammit, not Gandt.

He flipped it around to show Riley the name on the caller ID display. Whalen.

"Who is that?" Dugan asked.

"The only ranch hand I have left," Riley said.

On the off chance that Gandt was at Riley's, Dugan punched Connect and held the phone up to Riley, tilting it so he could hear the conversation.

"Riley?"

"Yeah, what is it?"

"The barn on the south side of the property is on fire!"

"Good God," Riley shouted. "Call the fire department."

The man yelled that he would, and Dugan took the phone, fear riddling him.

He'd wondered where Gandt would take Sage....

What if he'd taken her to Riley's? He could have planned to kill her there, then frame Riley for her murder.

Heart hammering, Dugan jumped in the SUV and tore down the dirt road, slinging gravel and dust in his wake.

"Take me to my place," Riley yelled.

"That's where we're going," Dugan snapped. Although Riley would be going to jail when this was over. "I have a bad feeling Gandt is there with Sage, and that he's behind the fire."

A litany of four-letter words spewed from Riley's mouth. "He was going to set me up."

"Yeah, and probably frame you for it." Dugan couldn't help himself. He enjoyed the terror on Riley's face.

He pressed the pedal to the floor, speeding over the potholes and bumps in the road. The ten miles felt like an eternity, but finally he veered down the drive onto Riley's ranch.

"Turn left up there to go to the south barn," Riley said.

Dugan yanked the steering wheel to the left and careened down the dirt path. Pastureland and trees flew by. He passed a pond and saw flames shooting into the air in the distance.

"Holy hell," Riley said. "If that spreads, my pasture will be ruined."

Dugan didn't give a damn about the man's property.

He phoned the deputy to meet him at Riley's property to arrest the rancher as he zoomed down the narrow road. He wished the fire engine was here, but he'd beat them to it. An old beat-up pickup truck was parked by a shed, and he spotted an elderly man pacing by the fence.

His tires screeched as he slammed on the brakes and

came to a stop. He jumped out and ran toward the burning building.

"Did you see anyone inside?" Dugan shouted.

"I didn't go in," the old man said with a puzzled look on his craggy face. "We didn't have any livestock in there."

But Sage…what about Sage?

The old man hadn't checked because he had no reason to think she'd be inside.

Panic streaked through Dugan. But he didn't hesitate.

"Don't bother to try and get away," he told Riley. He grabbed a blanket from the back of his SUV, wrapped it around himself and ran into the blaze.

Chapter Twenty-One

Sage struggled against the ropes as the fire began to eat the floor and rippled up the walls. The smoke was thick, curling through the air and clogging her lungs.

She was going to die.

And then she'd never know where her son was.

No…she couldn't leave him behind. He needed her.

She kicked the chair over, searching blindly for a sliver of wood to use as a knife. She managed to grab a rough piece that had splintered from one of the rails and clutched it between her fingers. Then she angled and twisted her wrists and hands to get a better stab at the ropes.

Heat seared her body and scalded her back, and she used her feet to push herself away from the burning floor to a clear patch. Her eyes stung from the smoke, and each breath took a mountain of effort. She curled her chin into her chest, breathing out through her mouth and focusing on sawing away at the ropes.

Wood crackled around her, the stall next to her collapsing. Sparks flew as the flames climbed the walls toward the ceiling. The building was so old, places were rotting, and it was going to be engulfed in seconds.

The sliver of wood jabbed her palm, and she winced and dropped it. Panicked, she fumbled to retrieve it and felt heat burn her fingers.

Tears trickled down her cheeks as pain rippled through her, then a piece of the barn loft suddenly crackled and popped, debris flying down to the floor around her.

DUGAN RACED THROUGH the flames to the inside, where the fire blazed in patches across the barn. The raw scent of burning wood and leather swirled in an acrid haze around him. He scrutinized the interior, searching as best he could with the limited visibility.

Tack room to the left, completely engulfed in flames.

Three stalls to the right. Two were ablaze.

Flames inched toward the third.

Smoke clogged the air like a thick gray curtain, forcing him to cover his nose with a handkerchief.

"Sage! Sage, where are you?" Maybe he was wrong, and she wasn't here.

He hoped to hell he *was* wrong.

Wood splintered and crashed from the back. He dodged another patch as he ran toward the last stall. Fire sizzled and licked at the stall door.

"Sage!"

He touched the wooden latch. It was hot. Using the blanket to protect his hand, he pushed it open.

Sage was lying on the floor, her hands and feet tied to a chair. She wasn't moving.

Terror gripped him, and he beat at the flames creeping toward her, slapping out the fire nipping at his boots. His feet were growing hot, but he ripped his knife from his back pocket, sliced through the ropes, then quickly picked Sage up in his arms.

She was so still and limp that fear chased at his calm. But he had to get them out.

"Sage, baby, I've got you." She didn't make a sound, but he thought he detected a breath. Slow and shallow, but she was alive.

He wrapped the blanket around his shoulders, tucked her close to him and covered her with it, then darted from the stall. The front of the barn was sizzling and totally engulfed.

He scanned the interior, searching for a way out. An opening near the back door. Just enough to escape.

He clutched Sage to him, securing her head against his chest and tugging the blanket over her face as he ran through the patches of burning debris and out the back door. Flames crawled up his legs, but he continued running until he was a safe distance away. Then he dropped to the ground, still holding Sage as he beat the flames out with the blanket.

A siren wailed and lights twirled in the night sky as the fire engine raced down the dirt road toward them. They were too late to save the barn.

He hoped to hell they weren't too late to save the woman in his arms.

SAGE STIRRED FROM UNCONSCIOUSNESS, disoriented and choking for a breath.

"Here, miss, you need oxygen." A blurry-looking young woman pushed a mask over her face, and someone squeezed her hand.

"You're okay, Sage. Just relax."

Exhaustion and fatigue claimed her, and she closed her eyes, giving in to it. But her mind refused to shut down. Questions screamed in her head.

What had happened? Where was she? Where was Dugan?

Then reality seeped in, crashing against her, and she jerked and tried to sit up.

"Shh, it's okay, you're safe," Dugan murmured.

She rasped the sheriff's name, then looked through the

haze and saw Dugan looking down at her, his forehead furrowed with worry.

"I called Jaxon. I'll find Gandt, Sage, I promise."

She wanted to believe him, to trust him, but Gandt had gotten away. And…he didn't know where Benji was.

Tears clogged her eyes. If that was true, finding the sheriff didn't matter. She still wouldn't have her son.

She clawed at Dugan's hand, silently begging him to move closer. A strangled sound came from her throat as she tried to say his name.

"Don't try to talk," Dugan whispered. "You need rest."

She shook her head, frantic that he hear her, then shoved at her mask.

The medic tried to adjust it, but she pushed her hand away.

"Dugan…"

Dugan finally realized she needed to tell him something and leaned closer. "What? Do you know where he went?"

She shook her head, her eyes tearing from emotions or smoke, she didn't know which. "Said…Benji…" She broke into a coughing spell.

Dugan clung to her hand. "Did he tell you where Benji is?"

She shook her head again, choking out the words between coughs. "Gandt killed Ron."

"I know, and he sent Lloyd Riley to kill me."

Sage's face paled even more. "Said Benji not with Ron…."

"What?" Dugan sighed deeply. "You're sure?"

She nodded, tears running down her cheeks, like a river.

He wiped them away and pressed a kiss to her lips. "Don't give up. I will find him, Sage, I promise."

Despair threatened to consume her, and she gave in to the fatigue and closed her eyes. She felt Dugan's hand closing around hers, heard his voice whispering to her to hang on, and the paramedics lifted her into the ambulance.

Dugan squeezed her arm. "I'll meet you at the hospital."

She nodded. At least she thought she did. But she was too tired to tell.

Then the ambulance jerked, a siren rent the air and she bounced as the driver raced off toward the hospital and away from the burning barn.

DUGAN HATED THE FEAR in Sage's eyes because it mirrored his own. If he'd been five minutes later, she would have died.

He shut out the thought. She hadn't died, and the medics would take care of her.

He had to find Gandt.

But if Benji wasn't with Lewis, and Gandt didn't know his whereabouts, where was he?

He'd already phoned Jaxon while waiting on the ambulance, and Jaxon agreed to put out a statewide hunt for Gandt.

What the hell should he do now?

Gandt was missing. Lewis dead. Rankins dead. Carol Sue dead.

Who had Benji? Sandra Peyton?

He jumped in his SUV and followed the deputy to the sheriff's office to make sure that he locked Riley up. He half expected Gandt to be cocky enough to be sitting in his office, with his feet propped up.

Did the sheriff know that Sage had survived? That Riley hadn't killed Dugan?

Did he think he'd gotten away?

Itching to know, Dugan decided to check the man's house. If he thought he'd gotten off scot-free, Gandt might be celebrating his good fortune. Or if he was afraid he was about to be caught, he might be packing to run.

Dugan knew where the man lived. Out on the river, by the gorge.

He whipped his SUV in that direction, eager to check it out.

Traffic was nonexistent on the country highway, the wilderness surrounding him as he veered off the main road and drove into the wooded property where Gandt lived.

The driveway was miles long, farm and ranch land sprawling for acres and acres.

Why Gandt was so greedy when he had all this, Dugan would never know.

When he neared the clearing for the house, he slowed and cut his lights.

He rolled up behind a tree and parked, pulled his gun and slipped through the bushes along the edge of the property. The sheriff's car was parked in front of the house, one car door open.

Dugan slowly approached it, bracing for an ambush. But as he crept near the car and looked inside, he saw it was empty.

Breathing out in relief, he ducked low and walked along the fence until he reached the side of the porch, which ran the length of the front of the house.

The door screeched opened, and Gandt appeared. Dugan ducked low and watched, surprised at the sight of Gandt pushing a gray-haired woman in a wheelchair out the door.

"I don't understand why I have to leave," the woman said shrilly.

"Because I'm going away for a few days and can't take care of you, Mother," Gandt said, his tone contrite.

"Can't you hire a nurse like you did before?"

"No, that costs a fortune. Gwen said you can come and stay with her."

The woman laid a hand on Gandt's arm. "But her husband doesn't like me."

"Mother," Gandt said, his patience wearing thin in his voice, "just please try to get along with them. When I straighten things out, I'll come back for you."

He pushed her down a ramp attached to the opposite side of the porch.

"What do you have to get straightened out?" she cried.

Dugan stepped from the shadows, his gun drawn. The woman gasped, and Gandt reached for his weapon.

"Don't," Dugan said. "I'd hate to have to shoot you in front of your mother."

The woman shrieked again. "Please don't hurt us." She clutched Gandt's arm. "Who is this man?"

"My name is Dugan Graystone," Dugan said. "I hate to tell you this, ma'am, but your son is not all you think he is."

Her sharp, angry eyes pierced Dugan like lasers. "You have no right talking to me about my son. What are you, some criminal on the loose?"

"Mother, be quiet," Gandt said through gritted teeth.

"I'm not the criminal here," Dugan said. "Mrs. Gandt, your son tried to have me killed, and he tied Sage Freeport—"

"Shut up," Gandt snarled.

"You don't want your mother to know what kind of man her son really is?"

"My son is a wonderful man. He takes care of this town."

"Mother—"

"He stole land from the ranchers and conned them. Then he shot Ron Lewis." Dugan paused. "Did you kill Wilbur Rankins, too?"

The woman turned shocked, troubled eyes toward Gandt. "Son, tell him that's not so...."

"It is true." Dugan waved his gun toward Gandt. "Now I want to know where Sage Freeport's little boy is."

Gandt walked toward Dugan, his eyes oozing steam as if he refused to admit to any wrongdoing. "You have a lot of nerve coming to my house, carrying a gun and making accusations." He handed his mother his phone. "Call my deputy and tell him to get over here right now."

Dugan stepped forward, unrelenting. Did Gandt really think he could get away with all this? "Fine, tell him to come, Mrs. Gandt. Also tell him he'll be arresting your son for murder."

The older woman gasped and clutched at her chest.

Dugan dug the gun barrel into Gandt's belly. "Now, where is Benji Freeport?"

Chapter Twenty-Two

A siren wailed, headlights lighting a path on the house as Jaxon roared up in his Texas Ranger truck.

Gandt cursed. "Let me take my mother back inside," he said to Dugan. "Then we'll talk."

Dugan felt sorry for the older woman, but he shook his head. No way did he intend to let Gandt out of his sight. Not even for a minute.

Mrs. Gandt curled her arthritic hands in her lap, around the phone, fear mingling with doubt in her expression now. Had she suspected her son was helping to swindle the town? Or that he was capable of murder?

Jaxon's car door slammed, and he strode toward them.

"Sheriff Gandt," Jaxon said. "You are under arrest for the murder of Ron Lewis and for the attempted murder of Sage Freeport." He read the sheriff his rights.

Gandt reared his head, shock on his face. He hadn't known Sage had survived. "You have no evidence of any crime I've committed. I'm the law around here."

"As a matter of fact, Sage Freeport is alive and she will testify that you tied her into the barn and set fire to it."

Gandt's mother gasped, her expression reeking of shock. "No, no…tell them, son, you didn't do those awful things."

"Lloyd Riley also claims that you blackmailed him into helping and ordered him to kill me," Dugan added.

"And speaking of evidence," Jaxon said, "I just got confirmation from ballistics that the bullet that killed Wilbur Rankins is the same caliber you use, so add on another murder charge." Jaxon took handcuffs from inside his jacket. "Put your hands behind you, Gandt."

Gandt shifted to the balls of his feet, jerking his hands as Jaxon grabbed his arms. "Mother, call Sherman, my lawyer," he snarled.

"No one is going to get you off," Dugan said. "Because you're going to pay for what you've done to Sage and to the people in this town."

Jaxon snapped the handcuffs around Gandt's wrists, then spun him back around. "Do you know what happened to Benji Freeport? Did you kill him, too?"

Gandt shook his head. "I told that woman he wasn't with Lewis. I have no idea where he is."

Dugan ground his molars. Gandt was already facing murder and attempted murder charges, along with fraud charges.

Why wouldn't he tell them where the boy was?

Because he really didn't know. Which meant they might never find Benji.

SAGE WOKE IN the hospital to find Dugan sitting by her bed. He looked worn out, his face thick with beard stubble, his eyes blurry from lack of sleep, his expression grim.

She broke into another coughing spell, and Dugan handed her a glass of water and held the straw for her to drink. "What time is it?"

"About four in the morning. You okay?"

Was she? She'd nearly died. And she still didn't have her son back. "I'll live," she said softly.

A pained smile twisted at his lips. "I got Gandt. He's in jail."

Sage sighed and took another sip of water.

"He blackmailed Lloyd Riley into helping him and or-dered him to kill me."

Sage's eyes flared with shock. "Did he tell you where Benji is?"

A darkness fell over Dugan's face, making her stomach tighten with nerves. "Dugan?"

"He claims he has no idea, that Benji wasn't with Lewis when he killed him."

Sage closed her eyes, hating the despair overwhelm-ing her. She'd thought for certain that finding Ron's killer would lead them to her son.

"I won't give up," Dugan said in a gruff voice.

"But Carol Sue, the woman we thought might have Benji, is dead."

"True, but Sandra Peyton is still unaccounted for."

"I know. Thanks, Dugan." Her earlier ordeal weighed her down. Or maybe it was defeat.

Sage closed her eyes, willing sleep to take her away from the memory of Gandt leaving her in that burning barn.

And the reality that she still had to face another Christ-mas without her little boy.

DUGAN SETTLED ONTO the recliner beside Sage and watched her sleep. Although the danger was over for her, he couldn't bear to leave her alone tonight.

Not with knowing he'd failed to find Benji.

And not with images of her lying in that blazing fire, nearly dead, tormenting him. He could have lost her to-night.

Lost her? He'd never had her....

The realization that he cared so damn much that it hurt made him stand and pace to the window. Cobra Creek was quiet tonight.

The deputy would temporarily take over for Sheriff

Gandt. Once the red tape was handled, the ranchers who'd been duped would get their land back.

But Sage was right back where she was when he'd decided to help her.

Making matters worse, Christmas was almost here. The image of that pitiful little Christmas tree with the unopened package under it taunted him.

Sage should have a full-size tree with dozens of gifts beneath it, and her little boy should be home making cookies with her and opening presents Christmas morning.

He considered buying her a gift, but nothing he could buy would make up for the void in her life that losing Benji had left.

She stirred, restless, and made a mewling sound in her throat, then thrashed at the covers. He soothed her with soft words, gently stroking her hair with one hand, until she calmed.

More than anything, he wanted to bring Benji back to her.

He'd never felt this emotional attachment before. This intense drive to please someone.

God…he was falling for her. Maybe he had been from the moment she'd looked up at him with those trusting, green eyes.

But what was he going to do about it?

He couldn't tell her or pressure her. Sage had already suffered too much. And she was vulnerable.

Besides, why would she want him when he'd failed her?

He finally fell asleep in the chair but woke a couple of hours later when the nurse returned to take Sage's vitals. He stepped out for coffee and to grab some breakfast while they helped her dress.

By the time he returned, the doctor was dismissing her.

"I'll drive you home, Sage."

She thanked him but remained silent as the nurse

wheeled her to the exit and on the drive home. When they arrived at the inn, the Christmas lights mocked him.

"Thank you, Dugan. I have to go shower and get out of these clothes. They stink like smoke."

She was right. Worse, they were probably a reminder of her near-death experience. He climbed out and walked her to the door.

"I can stay with you for a while if you want."

Sage shook her head, fumbling with the key as she tried to unlock the door. "I need to be alone."

Dugan took the keys from her and unlocked the door, not ready to leave her. He needed to hold her, to know that she was still alive and safe. That there might be hope for the two of them.

But she stepped inside and blocked the doorway. "Good night, Dugan."

Dugan reached up to take her hand, but she pulled it away and clenched the door edge.

"I'm not giving up, I will find Benji," Dugan said earnestly. Sandra Peyton might be the key.

She gave a small nod of acceptance, yet the light he'd seen in her eyes had faded. Damn, she'd lost hope.

The hope that had helped her survive the past two years.

She closed the door in his face, and Dugan cursed.

Maybe she didn't return the feelings he'd developed for her. But he'd be damned if he'd let her give up on her son.

SAGE WAITED UNTIL Dugan left, then walked to the kitchen for a glass of water. The Christmas tree with Benji's present sat on the table, looking as bare and lonely as she felt.

Dugan said he wasn't giving up.

But she was smart enough to realize that they'd reached a dead end. If Gandt didn't know where Benji was, who did?

Sandra Peyton.

The woman could be anywhere by now. If she'd taken Benji knowing Ron abducted him, she had probably gone into hiding.

Angry and frustrated and full of despair, she took the water to her bedroom and jumped in the shower. The hot spray felt heavenly as it washed away the stench of the smoke.

But the memory of Gandt coldly leaving her to die couldn't be erased so easily.

The silence in the house echoed around her, eerie and lonely, as she dried off, pulled on a pair of pajamas and collapsed onto her bed.

Dugan's scent lingered, teasing her senses and making her body ache for his comforting arms and touch.

But she couldn't allow herself to need him. She had to stand on her own.

The only thing she wanted right now was the little boy who'd stolen her heart the day he was born.

She had nothing to give to a man like Dugan. A man who deserved so much more than a broken woman like her.

Chapter Twenty-Three

Christmas Eve

Dugan had called Sage several times the past two days, but she had cut him off. Not that she hadn't been polite. She'd made it clear that if he learned anything new about her son, he should call her.

But she obviously didn't want a personal relationship with him.

Because he'd let her down. He'd promised to bring her son home and he hadn't, and she would never forgive him.

He let Hiram and his other two hands go early so they could spend Christmas Eve with their families.

Dugan would spend another one alone.

Normally the holidays meant nothing. Being alone didn't bother him. He loved his land and his work and his freedom.

He didn't know how to be part of a family.

So why did his chest have a sharp pain to it because he wasn't spending the night with Sage? Why couldn't he stop thinking about her, wondering what she was doing, if she was baking for Christmas dinner, if the inn smelled like cinnamon, if she was lighting a candle for her son, in hopes that it would bring him back to her?

Dammit.

He rode back to the stables, dismounted and brushed down his favorite horse, then stowed him in his stall. Just as he walked across the pasture toward his house, his cell phone buzzed.

Hoping it was Sage, he snatched it up, but Jaxon's voice echoed back.

"Dugan here."

"That reporter, Ashlynn Fontaine, called. Said she got another tip from that tip line."

Dugan's pulse jackknifed. "Tell me about it."

"This woman claims she thinks she's seen Benji, that she works with this waitress named Sandy Lewis, who has a little boy named Jordan. When she saw the news report, she realized Jordan was the spittin' image of Benji."

Sandy Lewis—Sandra Peyton Lewis? "What's the address?"

"I'm texting it to you now."

Dugan ended the call and referred to the text. He had to check this lead out. But the last time he'd taken Sage with him, it had been nearly devastating for her.

This time he'd go alone.

If Jordan turned out to be Benji and he recovered the little boy, he'd surprise her. If not, she would never know.

SAGE FORCED HERSELF out of bed each day, but the depression that seized her was nearly as paralyzing as it was the first few weeks after Benji disappeared.

She had to face the fact that she might never see her son again.

Could she bear to go on without him?

The women's group at church surprised her by stopping by with baked goods Christmas Eve morning. She had joined the group two months after Benji disappeared because she'd woken up one day with no desire to live.

It had scared her to think that she might do something

crazy like take her own life. Worse, if she did and Benji was found, she wouldn't be around to take care of him.

That day had driven her to ask for help, and she'd gone to the church seeking solace and prayer. She had found it, both with the pastor and the women who'd embraced her and revitalized her spirit with their positive thinking and compassion.

Today she felt as if she'd regressed. They must have sensed it, because the coffee and goodies were simply a backdrop to let her talk.

She hugged them all goodbye and thanked them for coming, then waved as they hurried to their cars. Five women with five different backgrounds and lives. Families of all sorts. Troubles of their own.

But they had come to her when she needed emotional support the most.

Wiping at tears, she cleaned up the kitchen and stored the tins of cookies on the kitchen bar, setting them out as she would for Benji. The Christmas plate with reindeer on it awaited the cookies and milk they would have left for Santa.

The women had reminded her of the candlelight service at six, and she had promised she would attend. Determined to keep herself from spiraling downward, she spent the afternoon wrapping the presents she'd bought for the children's hospital and the women's shelter, then stacked them all in her car to carry to the church.

A group would disperse them in the morning to make sure that children in need had Christmas, like all the other kids in the world.

She had volunteered last year. Maybe she'd go this year, as well.

Anything to help her get through the long, lonely day.

Her mind turned to Dugan and the numerous calls he'd

made. She wanted to see him, missed him in a way she'd never expected to.

And not just because he'd been helping her.

Because he'd stood by, solid and strong. He was handsome, sexy, protective, honorable. He owned and worked his own ranch, but he also worked search-and-rescue missions for strangers.

All qualities Ron and Trace had never possessed.

But Dugan deserved someone who could love and take care of him, not an empty shell of a woman who had to force herself to get out of bed to face the day.

DUGAN FOUND SANDY'S HOUSE fifty miles from Cobra Creek. It was a nondescript wooden house with a fenced yard, a swing set in the back and a gray minivan in the drive.

At first glance, it appeared to be homey. Christmas lights twinkled from the awnings, a handmade wreath garnished the front door and a tree complete with trimmings was visible through a picture window. A bike with training wheels sat in the front yard, and a soccer ball had been left in the driveway.

Was this woman simply a mother or a kidnapper?

He was just about to climb out when the front door opened, and a woman stepped outside, pulling a rolling suitcase. She wore sunglasses and a scarf and seemed to be in a hurry. She glanced up and down the street, opened the back of the minivan and tossed her suitcase inside, then shut the door.

She rushed back to the house and seconds later, emerged with a little boy in tow, a jungle backpack slung over his shoulder. Dugan sat up straighter to get a better look. The kid was the right size, but he was wearing a baseball cap, and Dugan couldn't see his face.

She tugged the boy's hand, but he drew back, and she

stooped down and appeared to be reprimanding him. The boy dropped his head, allowing her to lead him to the van.

Dugan almost interceded then. It looked as though Sandy was getting ready to take a trip. Had Gandt's arrest spooked her enough to run?

Deciding she might be meeting up with an accomplice, he waited until she backed from the drive, then followed her. He kept his distance, and maintained a steady speed so as not to alarm her.

A half hour later, she turned into the bus station. Dugan parked a couple of spaces from her and watched to see if she was meeting someone. She climbed out, looking over her shoulder and all around the parking lot as if she feared someone was after her.

Seemingly satisfied, she retrieved her suitcase, then pushed open the boy's door and helped him from the van. After kneeling to speak to him, she took his hand and ushered him toward the bus station.

Dugan didn't intend to let her get away.

He strode toward the entrance and caught up with her just as she stepped up to the ticket counter. The boy kept his head down, and she had a death grip on his hand.

"I need one adult and one child's ticket to New Mexico." She fished out ID and a wad of cash.

"You're not going anywhere, Miss Peyton," Dugan said in a low voice near her ear. "Not until you answer some questions."

She gasped and turned around, wide-eyed. "Who are you?"

"A friend of Sage Freeport."

Her face paled, and she tried to tug her arm from his grip, but he held her firmly. "Now, unless you want me to pull my gun and make a scene here, do as I say."

She stilled, and he saw her glance at the boy in panic.

The little guy made a frightened sound, which ripped at Dugan's heart.

"It's okay, son. I'm not here to hurt you." He hated to scare him, but if the child was Sage's son, he was saving the boy. He nudged the woman. "Walk back outside to your van."

She darted furtive looks around her as if she was debating whether or not to scream for help, but he opened his jacket enough to reveal his gun, and she sucked in a breath and headed toward the van. When they reached it, he ordered her up against the door.

"Please don't hurt my son," she cried.

"I'm not here to hurt him," Dugan said, intentionally lowering his voice to calm the kid, who looked as if he might bolt any second.

"Then what do you want? I have some cash—"

"This is not a robbery." Dugan gestured toward the boy, who had huddled up against her with his head buried in her stomach. "I'm here because of Benji."

Her eyes flared with panic, and the boy suddenly whipped his head around.

Dugan stooped down to his eye level and reached for the boy's hat. "Are you Benji Freeport?"

"His name is Jordan," the woman cried. "He's my son."

The hat slid off to reveal a head of choppy, blondish hair and eyes that looked familiar.

Sage's deep green eyes.

Remembering Sage said he had an extra piece of cartilage in his ear, he lifted the boy's hat. Yes. Just like the picture.

"You are Benji, aren't you, son?"

The boy fidgeted but didn't respond.

Dugan removed a photo that Sage had given him of the two of them from his pocket and showed it to him. "This woman, Sage, she's my friend. She wanted me to find you.

She's your real mother, and she's been looking for you ever since you disappeared two years ago."

The boy's face crumpled. "Mama?"

"Yes," Dugan said softly. "Your mama loves you, and she misses you and wants you to come home."

Benji angled his head toward Sandra Peyton, his look sharp with accusations. "You said she didn't want me anymore."

Dugan's pulse hammered.

"She didn't, but I wanted you." Sandra's chin quivered, and she began to cry. "I love you, Jordan. I'm your mama now."

The boy looked confused, his gaze turning back to Dugan. "Sage is your mother," Dugan said. "And she never gave you up, never told this woman she could have you." He kept his voice gentle. "She loves you so much. She's kept your Christmas tree up with your presents under it, just waiting on you to come back and open them."

Benji's little face contorted with anguish.

"Do you remember what happened, Benji? A man named Ron Lewis took you one morning…."

Tears pooled in his eyes, but Benji nodded as if the memory was slowly returning.

A strangled sound came from Benji's throat. "He took me to the river and told me to go with her."

Dugan glared at Sandra. "You and Lewis were a couple. You planned the kidnapping together."

Sandra broke down in tears. "I loved Ron and he loved me. We hadn't seen each other since I had that miscarriage. But he called me one day and said he was about to make a big windfall, and that he wanted us to be a family." Her voice broke. "But I couldn't get pregnant again."

Disgust churned inside Dugan. "So Lewis cozied up to Sage so he could get to know Benji?"

She wiped at tears. "He didn't want Benji to be afraid when he left with him, so he got to know him. And it would have worked, too. We would have all been together if someone hadn't killed Ron."

Dugan punched Jaxon's number. "I have Sandra Peyton and Benji Freeport at the bus station. I need backup."

As soon as Jaxon arrested Sandra, he'd take Benji home to Sage, where he belonged.

SAGE LET HERSELF into the inn, grateful for her friends who'd convinced her to attend the service. Of course, when they'd lit candles, turned off the church lights and sung "Silent Night" in the candlelight, she remembered the joy on Benji's face as he'd held his candle up, and she nearly collapsed in tears.

The Christmas lights twinkled as she flipped on the light switch, and the scent of cinnamon and apples swirled toward her from her earlier baking.

Maybe she'd take the baked goods to the seniors' center in the morning. She couldn't stand the thought of eating cinnamon rolls by herself. She twisted the locket, her heart thumping. She thought she'd gotten accustomed to being alone, but tonight she ached for Benji.

Dugan's face flashed in her mind, and she wondered where he was tonight. He hadn't mentioned any family.

Was he still looking for Benji, or had he given up?

She dropped her keys in the ceramic pot on the table by the door, then decided to light the candles in the kitchen and living room.

She had just poured herself a glass of wine and started to play her collection of Christmas music when a knock sounded at the door. Probably someone else from church, checking on her.

She hurried to the front door, prepared to assure her visitor that she was fine, but Dugan stood on the other side.

He looked so utterly handsome that her knees nearly buckled.

"Sage, I had to see you."

The urgency in his tone sent a streak of panic through her. "Is something wrong?"

"No." A small smile tugged at his mouth, and his eyes were sparkling, making him look even more handsome. Come to think of it, she'd never seen him smile. "I have a present for you," he said gruffly.

Sage twisted the locket again. "You didn't need to get me anything."

"Yes, I did. I made you a promise, and I keep my promises." Then he stepped to the side, and Sage's heart went wild as she saw the little boy beside him.

Emotions choked her. After two years, she'd been afraid she wouldn't recognize her son when she saw him again, but she instantly knew him.

Dugan had kept his promise. He had found Benji.

She dropped to her knees, soaking in the sight of him, desperate to pull him into her arms. But he looked hesitant, frightened, wary.

"Benji?"

She glanced up at Dugan, needing answers.

"Lewis took him to Sandra Peyton. He's been living with her for the past two years."

Sage wiped at the tears streaming down her face.

"She told him that you gave him up," Dugan said almost apologetically, "that you didn't want him anymore."

"Oh, God…" Pain rocked through Sage. Her poor little boy thought she'd abandoned him.

She took Benji's hands in hers and gave him a smile. She had to convince him she'd always loved him. "Benji, I never gave you up. I would never do that." She brushed at a tear. "One morning I got up, and Ron had taken you without telling me. I called the police, I called the news station, we put the story on TV, I did everything I could to find you."

He had grown taller and lost some of his chubby baby fat, but his eyes were just as bright and sweet. "I love you so much, Benji. I prayed every day that I'd find you."

He lifted his chin, big tears in his eyes. "Mommy?"

"Yes, sweet boy. I'm your mommy." She nearly sobbed at the feel of his tiny palm in hers. "Come on, I want to show you something."

She led him into the kitchen and showed him the table-top tree, leaving Dugan in the foyer. "Remember when you used to decorate this for your room? It was your own tree."

His eyes widened as he stared at it. Then she pointed out the presents with his name on them. "This one in Santa paper was the gift I bought for you the year you disappeared. Do you remember it? You were only three, but you shook it every day and tried to guess what was in it."

He wrinkled his forehead as if he was trying to recall the memory.

"I bought this one in the snowman paper for you last year," she said as she gestured toward another package. "And this one wrapped in reindeer paper this year, because I was hoping I'd find you and you'd come home."

He looked torn as if he wanted to believe her but was still on the verge. She hated Sandra Peyton for what she'd done to him, for lying to him.

Then she had an idea. "Let me show you your room. I kept it just the way it was."

She led him up the stairs and to his bedroom, the room she hadn't changed since he left. Inside, she walked over to the bed and picked up the special blanket he'd slept with and held it out to him. "See, I saved your blankie. I knew one day that you'd come home."

His little chin wobbled as tears filled his eyes. "Mommy?"

"Yes, baby, I've missed you so much." She opened her arms, and he fell into them, his tears mingling with hers as they savored the reunion.

Chapter Twenty-Four

By the time, Sage and Benji came back downstairs, Dugan was gone. A pang of disappointment tugged at her. He obviously felt as if he'd done his job and had gone home.

But she missed him, anyway.

Still, her son was finally home. It was the day she'd been waiting for. And soothing Benji's fears and rebuilding his trust were the only things that mattered tonight.

They spent the evening making sugar cookies and talking about the past. At times they were both sad, but she tried to help him focus on the fact that they were together again, and he was safe.

Much to her relief, Benji indicated that Sandra had been good to him, had been patient and played with him and read him stories.

Of course, they'd moved around a lot. Sandra had probably known that one day the truth would catch up with her.

Sage fought against the bitterness eating at her. She was grateful Sandra had loved Benji, but the woman had stolen all that time and precious memories from her.

And Benji had suffered the trauma.

But focusing on the past they'd lost would only keep her from enjoying the future, so she vowed to let go of the bitterness.

She read him Christmas stories and tucked him in, then watched him fall asleep, soaking in his features.

When she crawled in bed that night, she was happier than she'd been in ages. She and Benji were a family again.

But there was one thing missing.

Dugan.

She sat up, her heart stuttering. Oh, goodness.

While she'd been guarding her heart and looking for her son, she'd fallen in love with Dugan.

What was she going to do about it?

Did Dugan have feelings for her?

DUGAN MISSED SAGE like crazy. But she needed time to reunite with her son. Not pressure from him.

But when he rose Christmas morning and combed his ranch house, the deafening silence got to him. He couldn't help imagining Benji running down to find Santa's presents and Sage making breakfast for the two of them.

Work and the land had always been his first loves.

But his life felt empty now.

He suddenly felt antsy and had to get out. A ride across his ranch would do him good, help him clear his head, pass some time and take his mind off the woman who'd stolen a piece of his soul the past few days. And her kid, who'd won his heart the minute he laid eyes on him.

He combed the property, examining fences in case they needed mending, then checking livestock. Hiram and his other two hands had done a good job taking care of things while he worked the case. Now it was time for him to get back to it.

By the time he reached the farmhouse, his stomach was growling. He had nothing in the house to cook, certainly no holiday dinner.

Maybe he'd drive into town for a burger. That is, if the diner was open. Most folks were home with family today.

He guided his horse up to the house, slowing when he saw Sage's car. What was she doing here?

His heart began to race. He steered the horse to the rail and dismounted, then saw Sage and Benji sitting in the porch swing. Sage had her arm slung around Benji, and he was leaning into her as they rocked the swing back and forth.

It was the most beautiful sight he'd ever seen.

His heart took a funny leap, his mind roaring down a dangerous path. What would it be like to have a family to come home to?

To have Benji and Sage in his life forever?

Sage looked up at him with a tentative smile, but Benji vaulted up and leaned over the porch rail. "Your horse is cool, Mr. Dugan."

Gone was the traumatized kid from the night before. One night at home with his mother had the boy smiling and at ease.

"Thanks. If your mama agrees, I'll take you riding sometime."

Sage stood, walked to the rail and leaned over it, then looked down at him. "Maybe you can take us both out?"

The subtle question in her eyes made him smile. Was she flirting with him?

"Maybe I will," he said with a wink.

She laughed softly in response, and he realized she *was* flirting.

One night with her son had erased the shadows and pain from her eyes.

Benji ran down the steps. "Can I pet him?"

"Sure." Dugan showed him how to gently rub the horse's mane.

"We brought dinner for you," Sage said. "That is, if you don't have plans."

Dugan met her gaze. "That was real nice of you."

She walked down the steps and rubbed a finger along his arm. "It wasn't nice. I missed you, Dugan."

He liked this side of her. He angled his head, heat sizzling between them. And something more. An attraction that went far beneath the surface. He admired her. Liked her.

Loved her.

"I missed you, too," he said in a gruff voice.

For a brief moment, his breath stalled as he waited on her to make the next move.

Finally she lifted a finger to his lips. "Did you?"

A grin split his face. She was fishing for a compliment? "Yes." He suddenly couldn't help himself. That big rambling farmhouse needed her and Benji in it.

He yanked her up against him. "I'm in love with you, Sage."

Her eyes sparkled as she looped her arms around his neck. "Good, 'cause I'm in love with you, too."

Then she rose on her tiptoes, closed her lips over his and kissed him. Dugan had never felt anything so sweet, so wonderful.

And suddenly he knew what being in a family was like. He would make one with Sage and Benji, and he would never let them go.

* * * * *

Look for award-winning author Rita Herron's next book, COLD CASE IN CHEROKEE CROSSING, on sale in December 2014.

"Want to go for a drive?"

Abby did. Desperately. The intensity scared her. "Aren't you tired of Christmas lights and holiday displays by now?"

"Are you tired of police work?"

"A little," she confessed, startling a laugh out of both of them.

"Take a drive with me. I'll buy you a drink."

"You're a terrible flirt."

"So I've been told." Riley winked, opening the passenger door of his truck for her.

"No, I mean you're really bad at it."

"You want me to up my game?"

Yes. No. Uncertain, she pulled the door shut. When he slid into the driver's seat, she said, "I don't want any games. I want you to be yourself."

"Easy enough." He stared at her for a moment that went on and on, and she realized she was holding her breath. "What you see is what you get, Abby."

THE HUNK
NEXT DOOR

BY
DEBRA WEBB & REGAN BLACK

Published in Great Britain 2014
by Mills & Boon, an imprint of Harlequin (UK) Limited,
Eton House, 18-24 Paradise Road, Richmond, Surrey, TW9 1SR

© 2014 Debra Webb

ISBN: 978-0-263-91375-0

46-1114

Harlequin (UK) Limited's policy is to use papers that are natural, renewable and recyclable products and made from wood grown in sustainable forests. The logging and manufacturing processes conform to the legal environmental regulations of the country of origin.

Printed and bound in Spain
by CPI, Barcelona

Debra Webb, born in Alabama, wrote her first story at age nine and her first romance at thirteen. It wasn't until she spent three years working for the military behind the Iron Curtain—and a five-year stint with NASA—that she realized her true calling. A collision course between suspense and romance was set. Since then the *USA TODAY* bestselling author has penned more than one hundred novels, including her internationally bestselling Colby Agency series.

Regan Black, a *USA TODAY* bestselling author, writes award-winning, action-packed novels featuring kick-butt heroines and the sexy heroes who fall in love with them. Raised in the Midwest and California, she and her family, along with their adopted greyhound, two arrogant cats and a quirky finch, reside in the South Carolina Lowcountry where the rich blend of legend, romance and history fuels her imagination.

For Mark, my personal hero, who always knows
when I need encouraging words, quiet space
or dark chocolate.
And many, many thanks to Deb for inviting me
into this wonderful new adventure!
Regan

To my hero, Nonie! Though four decades have
passed since we first met, you continue to be
the only hero for me!
Debra

Prologue

Washington, D.C.
Friday, November 25, 6:10 p.m.

Thomas Casey, director of the elite team known as the Specialists, leaned back in his chair and watched the footage filling his computer monitor one last time. The woman on the screen stared directly at the camera, her expression one of fearlessness.

"Let this be a clear message to anyone with criminal intent," she announced in a steely tone. "Belclare will not stand for drug activity on our docks or criminal action in our town. We will stand against you and we *will* seize your product, your people and your money at every opportunity. No matter your affiliation or intent, this community will not be used for illicit gain."

The knock on his closed office door was a welcome distraction. Thomas muted the feed. "Come in."

The beautiful face of his wife, Johara di Rossi, peered around the door. "Is it safe to come in?"

He motioned her forward. It was still a thrill to realize they were married, that he had the rest of his life to make up for lost time. No one had ever made him feel that way… no one but Jo.

Her smile wide, she stepped into the office. "If you're sure. Your face tells a different story."

Removing his glasses, he rubbed the bridge of his nose. "Am I running late?" He checked his watch, wishing he had the luxury of forgetting this video in favor of the standing dinner date with his wife. But when the President of the United States issued a directive, department heads were expected to drop everything and act immediately.

"No." She strolled across the room and leaned over his desk to give him a kiss. "I was out this way and thought we could ride to dinner together."

"That's fine. I just have one last meeting to take care of first."

A knock at the door interrupted him. Damn. One of these days very soon he intended to make personal time a priority.

Jo winked at him. "I'll wait for you at reception."

"Thanks." He watched her go, grateful he'd been given a second chance with the one woman who mattered and that she understood the urgency of his work.

Ever the professional, Jo didn't exchange a word with the man in a charcoal-gray suit who walked in as she walked out.

"Close the door," Thomas said to his visitor. "And take a seat."

Specialist Riley O'Brien followed both orders with a quiet "Sir."

Thomas looked from the image of the Belclare police chief on his computer monitor to the man sitting patiently in front of him. "I appreciate your quick response."

"Yes, sir."

Thomas hesitated. One more sign that his decision to retire was the right one. A man in his position couldn't afford to regret the tasks he assigned, but what he needed from O'Brien was extreme even for a Specialist.

He pushed away his own bias, pushed aside the memories of his own career and focused on O'Brien. All of his Specialists excelled in the obvious areas necessary for a successful covert operative, and each of them had a unique set of skills. It was O'Brien's distinctive résumé that made him the perfect fit for this operation.

"O'Brien, you've been selected as the first agent for a new task force. Before you agree, let me assure you, you can turn this assignment down without penalty."

The younger man settled a little deeper into the chair, his eyes intent. "Understood, sir."

Already, they both knew he would agree. Thomas leaned forward, bracing his forearms on his desk. "I'm asking you to take on a deep-cover assignment. We will rework your background accordingly. You'll keep your name, but your new address will be Belclare, Maryland."

"On the Chesapeake Bay?"

"You've heard the latest news out of Belclare." Thomas turned his computer monitor around for O'Brien.

"Kind of hard to miss, sir."

Thomas concurred. "This new team is tasked with embedding agents on long-term assignments where threats are expected."

"And the end date, sir?"

"None." Thomas cleared his throat. "In the short term, you are assigned to keep the Belclare police chief, Abigail Jensen, alive."

"You believe retaliation is imminent?"

"Yes. She's done a hell of a job, but she's made herself a target. They might come after her directly or they may attack another target in town to cause trouble first. It could be next week, or next year, or…"

"A decade down the road," O'Brien finished for him.

"Yes." On a sigh, Thomas leaned back into the supple leather executive chair and studied the agent on the opposite side of his desk. "Based on the intel, I feel confident you'll see some action right away, but this is a lifetime commitment I'm asking for."

"All right." O'Brien shifted forward, propping his elbows on his knees, his gaze on the floor. "Any backup?"

"Not on the ground."

O'Brien lifted his gaze to Thomas's. "Can you be more specific?"

Fair question. "You'll have a way to upload any relative intelligence to our analysts, but I expect you to take action as necessary to protect our nation's interests against terrorism. We can give you anything you need. We just can't be *there* in under an hour."

O'Brien nodded his understanding.

"Belclare is too close to D.C. and other valuable targets," Thomas went on. "We've heard disturbing chatter about a sleeper cell in the area."

"What kind of cause?"

While that wasn't a question he would typically answer, this wasn't a typical assignment. "The drug shipment the chief intercepted was meant to fund a known terrorism splinter group gaining a foothold here in the States. Homeland Security has been monitoring Jensen's email since the speech went viral. Some of the hate mail is too specific for an outsider. Additionally, we've tracked a recent shipment of stolen military detonators to Baltimore."

Throughout his career, Thomas had led by example, never asking more of his agents than he asked of himself. *Until today.* Looking across the desk, he put himself in O'Brien's shoes and wondered how he might have responded if he'd been offered a similar assignment in his early thirties. "Take your time, O'Brien. Think it through."

Normally he wouldn't drop something like this on an agent with limited field experience, but the key to this task force came down to the ability to blend in. To be the guy next door. Raised in an orphanage, O'Brien had been melding with his community and surroundings his whole life. During his two years as a Specialist, he'd worked behind the scenes, offering physical and technical support during various operations. An agent with less field experience meant the tech experts would have less to scrub away and an easier time rebuilding the personal history. Also in his favor for this particular operation, O'Brien had proved to be a natural when it came to managing explosives.

A few more seconds of silence ticked by and then O'Brien nodded, his gaze resolute. "Count me in, sir."

"Good." Especially for the police chief and her town, Thomas mused. "Belclare will be finishing preparations for their annual Christmas Village when you arrive. With your experience in construction, you'll be able to find work easily."

"But you want me to stay on in the area after that's over."

"Yes. You'll need to make yourself at home within the community. Chief Jensen will need you, whether she knows it or not. We'll get the necessary background ready."

"Thank you, sir."

Thomas stood and reached across the desk to shake the agent's hand. "Let me be the first, and quite possibly the only person, to thank you for your service."

Chapter One

Riley measured the span of the double doorway and clipped the tape measure back on his tool belt. He'd picked up work with the company in charge of transforming Belclare into a Christmas extravaganza just as the director suggested. Riley considered his assignment off to a stellar start when he was sent over to decorate the police station.

"She's in a meeting." The young cop working the reception desk behind him was having trouble with one of Belclare's citizens. "May I take a message?"

"She's a young hothead is what she is," the irritated older man replied. "The historical society has never been handcuffed in this manner. I will not stand for it. The tourists expect…"

Riley continued tacking holiday garland around the door frame as the man droned on about tourism, children and intrusive patrols.

"Safety is our utmost priority," the young officer said. "From our chief right down to our newest recruits."

Preach on, kid, Riley thought. Belclare would need every patrol if only half of the chatter about retaliation was true. Chief Jensen was in serious trouble. Via email, the director had kept him in the loop with the most direct threats to help Riley identify the locals who no doubt had to be involved. At the moment, this guy from the historical society was quickly gaining himself a spot at the top of the list.

Riley stepped down the ladder to gather up the next length of evergreen woven with velvet ribbon and colorful ornaments. This town pulled out all the stops for the holiday. He couldn't see why the police station needed decorating, but the work put him close to the chief. At this stage, she didn't have a clue that by doing an excellent job as chief, she'd not only protected her town, she'd also put them in more jeopardy.

Though he hadn't yet seen more than a photo of the lady with the tough-as-nails reputation, Riley admired her efficiency.

The older man with the beef against the chief's new security requirements was turning red in the face as he continued his protest.

Finished with the doorway, Riley decided a break in the tension was needed. "I'm taking a break for hot chocolate," he said to no one particular. "Can I get anyone anything?"

The old man swiveled around, scowling at him. "Who are you?" He turned back to the young cop behind the desk. "Do you know *him*? He might very well be an assassin right here in our midst. Now who isn't being careful enough?"

"Don't worry about me," Riley said, laughing off the accusation. "I just follow the work. Riley O'Brien." He stuck out his hand, but the older man refused to take it.

"Martin Filmore, president of the Belclare Historical Society," he replied, a sour look on his weathered face.

"Pleased to meet you." Riley gave him a big smile and hooked his thumbs into his tool belt. "Can I get you anything from that shop across the street while you wait?"

Filmore rolled his eyes. "The shop is called Sadie's. Owned by the Garrison family, the building has been a landmark in Belclare since the town was founded."

"Good to know." He looked past Filmore to the kid behind the desk. Riley pegged him as early twenties and fresh out of the academy. "How about you, Officer?"

"Call me Danny." The young cop grinned, relief stamped on his face. "I'll take a hot chocolate."

"All right. Marshmallows or whipped cream? Cinnamon on top?"

"Sounds like you've been to Sadie's before," Danny said knowingly.

Riley shrugged into his down vest. "A man who doesn't cook has priorities."

The cop's expression brightened more, making him look even younger. Riley was grateful to gain an ally in town, even a young one. Since getting hired on, he'd learned that people here were a bit edgy around strangers. The guys on the crew who'd worked previous seasons said it wasn't normal for Belclare, but they all agreed the folks had good reason. The national news headlining drug bust marked the first serious crime in their community and they were worried that more would follow.

"I take marshmallows," Danny said. "No cinnamon."

"Good choice," Riley smiled. "How about you?" he asked the older man again. "Last chance."

"No," Filmore snapped. "Thank you. I am capable of fetching my own coffee."

Riley paused, one hand on the door. "The girl at the counter said they were doing some sugar-cookie thing this afternoon. What's that about?"

Danny sighed wistfully. "I asked for the time off but didn't get it."

Filmore glared at the kid. "You cannot convince me the

police department puts safety first when our officers are more concerned with a sugar-cookie party."

"It's a big deal," Danny defended himself.

Filmore launched right into another snobby rant, complaints and insults flying like fists.

Riley was about to intervene with another dumb new-guy-in-town question when a harsh, earsplitting whistle silenced the argument.

All three men in the lobby turned to the woman in the doorway that led back to the bull pen.

The woman of the hour, Riley decided, soaking up his first live view of Police Chief Jensen. Her blond hair was pulled back from her heart-shaped face and her blue eyes were sharp as lasers as she studied each of them.

Unlike the other officers he'd seen coming and going today, she wasn't wearing the dark blue uniform. No, she wore a deep green suit with an ivory shirt, tailored perfectly to her curves. Was it some attempt at a civilian disguise or didn't she lead by example? He took in her slender legs and the high heels and decided he appreciated the view too much to criticize her choice or rationale. Were police chiefs supposed to wear skirts? He knew the formal uniforms for women were that way, but on an average day? He'd seen her on television, had researched the decorated career that led to her current post. None of it accurately portrayed the size of her personal presence. She might be a petite little thing, but without saying a word she had full command of the room.

Her hard gaze moved deliberately from Danny to Filmore to him. He felt it like a touch. After a moment, she settled that tough blue gaze back on Filmore.

"Mr. Filmore, what is the problem here?"

"I need a moment of your time," he began. "The new precautions are an impediment—"

She held up a hand and he stopped talking. Riley put that skill right up there with a superpower. One fact had been immediately clear: the president of the historical society loved the sound of his own voice.

Her cool gaze landed on Riley again, raked him from head to toe and back up. "You are?"

"Not a part of this," he said, holding up his hands. "I'm just on garland detail." He pointed to the ladder.

She eyed the ladder and then stepped forward, holding out a hand. "Name and identification, please."

He hoped this was a stunt for the crotchety Filmore. "Was I hanging garland too fast, ma'am?"

She glared at him.

"I checked his credentials when he came in, Chief," Danny piped up. "He's with the design team."

"Your name," she insisted.

Riley gave her his friendliest lopsided grin. "Riley O'Brien." The grin didn't appear to be any more effective on the police chief than when he'd used it on his teachers in private school.

"You're Irish?"

"That's what my parents tell me." According to his new background courtesy of the Specialists' technology wizards, he was first-generation American, born of Irish immigrants. As he'd memorized his manufactured past it was as if the techs had somehow tapped the childhood fantasy that carried him through his long years at the orphanage.

"What brings you to Belclare?"

"Steady work," he replied as she returned his Maryland driver's license and the work permit.

"And you'll be leaving when?"

"Actually, I'm thinking I'll stay." He looked over to Danny. "Maybe you can point me to a place to rent?"

"The personnel don't typically stay on after the work is done," the chief countered before Danny could reply.

Riley shrugged. "So far, I like what I see."

She examined his progress with the decorations. "Why aren't you done?"

"I was taking my required break, but that got interrupted."

"Well, we won't waste any more of your time."

"Thank you." He returned his wallet to his back pocket and zipped up his vest halfway. With a wave to Danny, he headed out to Sadie's while the chief addressed Mr. Filmore.

The sky was heavy and he smelled snow on the air. Riley didn't need a weather forecast to tell him Belclare's annual Christmas Village would benefit from an idyllic blanket of fluffy white snow for the opening weekend. The most profitable weekend according to the background reports. All he had to do was make sure no one ruined it for them by assassinating their beloved chief of police.

Sadie's was quiet and the hot chocolate orders were ready sooner than he'd hoped. He needed to keep an eye on the chief, but he also wanted a few minutes of distance to gather his thoughts. Whatever he'd expected, she'd been... more. Sure, she was beautiful and she clearly had her finger on the pulse of this town. He didn't like how that made him feel. Uneasy. Turned-on. A potential lifelong assignment out here suddenly took on a new element of risk. And a potential unexpected angle.

What if he asked her out? It would be a valid way to stay close, especially in these early days. He headed back over to the police station, planning how best to get a few details about her out of Danny. Riley knew how to ask questions without giving away his real motives.

Work, he reminded himself. That was his real motive. This wasn't the time to get distracted.

Chapter Two

"You simply must relax the police presence on Main," Mr. Filmore said, not for the first time.

Too bad Abby didn't have any evidence tying him to any illegal activity. Not even a whiff of mental instability or aggression in his background.

As much as Filmore tested her patience, she refused to give in to the temptation to play favorites. All the citizens of Belclare deserved her best effort as their police chief. It was a shame she didn't trust them equally anymore.

Despite the press conference that had gone viral thanks to national news and social media, in recent days her confident speech felt more like a publicity stunt. She knew the value of perception as well as caution. The mail and email that flooded the department and website in the days following the drug bust was mostly positive, but the threats, in an increasing number, had to be assessed and cleared or sent up to the feds, who claimed she was in trouble. They'd even suggested she employ a protective detail, but they hadn't given her the personnel. Besides, with everyone in town watching for her next mistake, she had enough eyes on her already.

The threats monopolized her time, taking her away from other important daily endeavors, though Homeland Security would disagree with that assessment. They were sure she was dealing with a sleeper cell and their insistence, while absurd, had her looking at everyone in town with suspicion. She knew these people. Cared about them—even the hardheaded one glaring at her right now.

Of course, Martin didn't care that she'd drawn that line with his safety in mind. Aesthetics and historical accuracy mattered more than anything else to him. Thankfully, the men and women on the police force agreed with the aggressive line she'd drawn.

"I will not relax the patrols on Main or anywhere else, Mr. Filmore."

"But the problem was out at the docks. Isn't it a better use of resources to keep your patrols focused in that area?"

He wanted her to save resources in the hope that he could divert any funds she didn't spend into his budget at the next council meeting. She knew the tactic far too well. She'd taken this job despite the politics that went with it. Abby felt the tension mounting. Her shoulders were tight, her legs were ready to spring and her toes were cramping in these stupid pumps. She reminded herself she couldn't throw a tantrum. There were better outlets than the blood-curdling scream of frustration trapped in her throat.

A soft tap-tap-tap of a hammer and squeak of boots on the metal ladder told her O'Brien was back to work in the lobby. Talk about an outlet. Wow. Riley O'Brien would certainly qualify as an effective distraction. He was handsome and built. If only she could be sure he wasn't also a threat in contractor's clothing. Had she really just thought that? She gave herself a mental shake. This had to be some universal female fantasy involving a thermal shirt, faded jeans and a tool belt that sparked sudden, inexplicable lust in a stranger under present circumstances.

"Well?" Filmore demanded.

She dragged herself back to the present. Mr. Filmore

deserved a thoughtful reply. "I could have the increased patrols work in their civilian clothes."

"How is that any better?"

She knew it! It wasn't about the official uniform presence hindering anything. His dissatisfaction was about the budget. She was done with Filmore's whining and she had another appointment in just fifteen minutes. Abby squared her shoulders. "My officers will be out there, in uniform. End of discussion. They will not harass anyone, because I've given clear instructions—" based on the most recent threats that she didn't bother explaining "—regarding what they should look for."

Filmore made an unpleasant sound of frustration. "I suppose you expect me to be grateful."

She smiled, remembering he was a decent guy if a bit uptight about historical accuracy. "I expect you to recognize the necessity of the situation. Together is the only way Belclare gets through this rough patch."

His beady eyes locked on to her. "You might have thought of this 'rough patch' before you turned our town into a target."

Before she could respond, he spun on his heel and marched out of her office, his spine ramrod straight.

Abby let him have the last word. Not because he deserved it, but because she refused to be late to her next appointment. She was ready for a bit of solitude in her car and the comfort of coffee and conversation with a friend who didn't have an agenda. She shut down her computer and moved away from her desk. Adjusting the silk scarf at her throat, she slipped into her black wool overcoat.

She was debating the wisdom of ruining her look by switching from her heels to her winter boots when someone knocked on her office door. Again. She turned and the professional smile she'd forced onto her face faded at the sight of Riley O'Brien filling her doorway. "Yes?"

"Danny said I could come on back."

She made a mental note to have a chat with Danny.

"I just wanted you to know I'd finished the lobby as well as the display out front."

"I'm sure your boss will be thrilled with your efficiency."

"Probably so." He gave her a grin that reminded her of the young men she'd pulled over in the past who tried to get off with a warning. "Today's project list filled two pages."

"That's…" Why did he think she cared? "Ambitious," she finished. "If you'll excuse me I have an appointment."

"Oh, sure." He stepped out of the doorway but hovered while she locked up. It was a new procedure and no reflection on her department but—

"Can't be too careful these days," he said, echoing her thoughts.

"Precisely." She maneuvered around him, unable to ignore the enticing scent of evergreen and cinnamon clinging to his clothing. "The garland is scented this year? I didn't approve that."

"I'm not sure it's possible to un-scent fresh pine, ma'am."

"Stop that."

"Stop what?"

"The ma'am thing. I don't like it much." It made her feel old and right now the increased pressure following the drug bust was more than enough to cope with.

"Right." He shoved his hands deep into his pockets. "Danny mentioned that."

She was definitely having a talk with Danny. He needed a reminder about basic security around strangers. "Enjoy your stay in Belclare, Mr. O'Brien."

"Call me Riley."

Abby had no intention of calling him anything at all.

While it wouldn't be a problem under normal circumstances, this wasn't the best time to make new friends. Except when she looked up, his expression was open and there was a humor lurking in his brown eyes. Her earlier thoughts about a stress relief outlet flooded back.

"I'd like that."

"Pardon?" In her fantasy, she'd apparently lost the thread of the conversation. Reaching into her pocket, she gripped her car keys and strode toward the back of the station. He followed her.

"I'd like to enjoy my stay. If you're not doing anything tonight, maybe you could show me around?"

Startled, she stopped, gathered her foolishly scattered wits. "I'm the chief of police, Mr.—" she made the correction before he could "—*Riley*. If you need a map or a tour guide, check with the Visitor's Center."

"I don't get it." He shook his head.

She shouldn't ask. If she let him stall her much longer, she'd be late. "What's the matter?"

He grinned again. "I thought we sort of, well, connected earlier."

"You're joking." The idea was absurd.

"Only a little." His eyes twinkled. "Call it instant hero worship instead of a connection. I didn't think anything could make Mr. Filmore stop talking."

The urge to laugh startled her and she smothered it quickly. "That was more luck than skill." A distaste for Filmore's voice was a connection shared by 90 percent of Belclare's population. "I really need to go."

"Okay." He pushed open the door and held it for her. "If you change your mind or need anything decorated, I'll be around."

His slow smile and the warmth of his body as she brushed by him created a stir low in her belly. Simple lust.

A tempting distraction she couldn't risk at the moment, no matter how genuine he seemed or how efficiently he tacked up decorations. The cold air slipped around her legs and up her knee-length skirt. She was rather grateful for the assist from Mother Nature as parts of her had turned inappropriately warm during this bizarre conversation. "You'll be around? For the month?"

"Longer, I think. I like the views," he added, his gaze holding hers. "Better get going before you catch a chill."

Right. If only her feet weren't rooted to the spot.

As he pulled the door closed, she brought out her key to lock it. "Don't worry. I'll get it from this side. Danny told me all doors had to be locked at all times."

She clamped her lips together. No sense hollering at the new guy for the mistakes of the rookie cop at the desk. "Thank you," she murmured when the door latch clicked. She counted to ten, then tugged the handle, pleased when the lock held.

She hurried to her car. At least the new guy in town kept his word about the little things. Even that small assurance immediately put her in a better frame of mind as she drove out to her meeting with Belclare's most reluctant celebrity, Deke Maynard.

Quiet, reserved and a gifted artist, Deke had become a true friend. Aside from his assistant, she was probably the only person in town he trusted. She appreciated that and after all the recent criticism, she valued the few people like Deke who supported her. Keeping to their weekly routine of coffee and conversation in his elegant home gave her hope things would soon return to normal in Belclare and made her feel like more than just the chief.

Nothing wrong with wanting to feel like a woman now and again. Didn't have to mean anything. She thought of the handsome new stranger in town and shook her head.

The dead last thing she needed was another complication in her life.

Maybe she'd better stick with just being the chief.

Chapter Three

Standing at the wall of windows on the east side of the room he'd converted into a painting studio, Deke Maynard stared out over the sleepy town of Belclare. Three years ago he'd visited during their annual Christmas Village and declared himself enamored with the charm, views and people.

He'd purchased this house and established himself as a recluse during the remodeling. Oh, he wandered out occasionally and spoke with people, but it was all he could do not to laugh in the eager faces of the ignorant citizens of Belclare as they gladly accommodated his every whim and eccentricity.

He should have asked for hazard pay when he'd agreed to create his base of operations here. The day-to-day tedium of Belclare might kill him. Yet there were certain perks, he admitted to himself as the police chief's car turned into his long driveway.

The woman was beautiful and intelligent. If he bothered with regrets, he might have second thoughts about the things he'd set in motion. As it was, he scolded himself for entertaining the idea of keeping her as a trophy. It was a risk the operation could not afford.

"Chief Jensen has arrived, sir," his assistant reported after a quick rap on the studio door.

"Thank you," he said, as though he wasn't watching her approach.

The reports from town annoyed him. She'd doubled patrols everywhere. Quite a feat considering the limits of her staff, but if nothing else, they were a determined and loyal flock of sheep.

He was reluctantly impressed that she'd managed to make the drug bust at all. That had been pure police work. There had been no leaks in the chain of information. When he'd arrived and become acquainted with her, he'd considered her more of a decorative figurehead than a real cop. He'd mistakenly assumed she'd been named police chief out of some misguided attempt to appeal to those who clamored for equality.

Looking back, he was grateful he'd been diligent about his manufactured background or today's meeting might be taking an entirely different and unpleasant turn.

The doorbell rang and Deke smiled to himself. His assistant would manage the door and get her settled with coffee. Then Deke could make his entrance as the eccentric artist she expected.

Appreciating her strengths didn't change the fact that Chief Jensen had become enemy number one. As the town dressed itself for their penultimate tourist season, Deke had been making his own preparations. He weighed the pros and cons of his limited choices.

In a matter of weeks, Chief Jensen had single-handedly wrecked a strategy years in the making. If he didn't act swiftly to rectify the situation, his reputation would be ruined beyond repair.

He examined the landscape on the canvas in front of him. His raw artistic talent would never carry him as far as his other skills. Skills powerful men and organizations paid handsomely for.

Wiping the paint from his hands, he checked his appearance in the mirror at the top of the stairs before he descended to meet the police chief. This would be one of his most critical performances to date. And with all good performances, it would be better for tapping into the truth.

Her drug bust might have cut off a vital money supply line, but that didn't change his base, physical attraction to her. It would be that truth he monopolized today for the greater good of his real career.

Pausing at the landing, he took one last deep breath before rushing the rest of the way down the stairs. "Ah, Abby, hello," he said as he entered the sitting room just off the foyer. "Forgive me for keeping you waiting."

Chief Jensen smiled brightly as she stood to greet him. "You could've rescheduled if you're working."

"Nonsense. Coffee with you is the highlight of my week." That put a rosy glow in her cheeks. He stepped back to admire her. "You are looking as lovely as ever."

"Thank you."

He motioned for her to resume her seat, then he poured a cup of coffee for himself. "So how are the preparations going? From my vantage point it seems everything is on schedule."

"You should come down and take a look for yourself," she suggested, a soft smile on her lips.

He was filled once more with the urge to keep her. He deserved a reward for the nonsense he tolerated day in and day out. "Right now I'd only be in the way. I'll come down after the crush of opening weekend is over."

"I'll look forward to it." She raised the china cup to her full lips and he had to look away. "The mayor came by the station yesterday."

"Oh?" he queried.

"Yes. He wanted me to thank you for the sketches you donated to the silent auction."

"Of course he had you bring me the message." Deke snorted derisively and adjusted his rolled-back sleeves, pleased to see her watching him so closely. "He knew I wouldn't let him past the driveway after the way he spoke to you."

"Probably," she allowed. "Thanks again for defending me."

"You're a hero," he said. "And you're a dear friend," he added quietly. He checked the time, wondering how far he could push her today.

"To be fair, I might have shown a little restraint at the press conference." She held up her hand, thumb and finger close together. "Maybe a smidge less gloating."

"That drug bust was important." Deke leaned forward and laid a hand on her knee. It wasn't the first time he'd touched her, but this time he wanted her to understand it was a romantic advance. "You're a passionate woman." Her eyes widened and he knew he had her on the hook. "Belclare is fortunate that you're putting fear and doubt into the minds of criminals looking to abuse our resources."

He sat back once more, his hand trailing away slowly, giving her the impression that the next move was hers. He'd long ago learned how to manipulate and guide while maintaining the illusion of free will.

She cleared her throat. "I was surprised to see you at the emergency council meeting."

"Should I have stayed home?"

"No." Her brow furrowed for a moment before her expression cleared. "Your defense meant the world to me. Frankly, after the mayor's reprimand, I didn't expect anyone to admit I existed. Your example reminds me I do have allies."

She's made her decision. He could sense victory on the horizon. That moment, when she was his, would be so sweet. His body responded, anticipating the pleasure of using her before he publicly humiliated and destroyed her. In a few days' time her world would come crashing down around her. He glanced at the clock on the mantel. "Then I'm even happier to have made the effort."

"You've been an asset to the entire community." Whatever she intended to say next was cut short by the hum of her phone. "Excuse me, it's the station."

"Of course," he said with a nonchalance he didn't feel. This might be the very call that signaled the beginning of his vengeance.

He refilled his coffee and waited while she took the call in the foyer. He didn't hear much beyond her greeting before his own phone rang. The timing couldn't be worse, but he answered anyway. "Yes?"

"This is a mistake," the caller said with a quaking voice.

"The only mistake is questioning me."

"I was told I had the authority—"

"Enough." Deke checked to be sure Chief Jensen remained distracted. "When you exhibit good judgment your authority will be restored. Are you reneging on our solution?"

"N-n-no," the voice on the other end of the line stuttered.

"Good." Deke ended the call and tucked his phone back into his pocket.

"Deke?"

"Yes, my dear," he said, coming to his feet. "Don't tell me duty calls." She'd already taken her overcoat from the hall tree.

"Something like that." She hesitated, her bold, blue gaze roaming over his face. "Thank you for the coffee, Deke."

He stepped forward, taking her coat to help her into it.

He let his hands brush the soft skin at her nape as he adjusted the collar, smiling to himself when she trembled.

"Let's not wait a week," he said. "Come back for dinner tomorrow night."

She turned, and he took great pleasure watching her face as all of her responsibilities went to war against the desire he'd carefully stoked. "I would like that," she replied.

"But?"

Her mouth tipped down, heavy with regret. "I have a security update tomorrow night."

"Stop by after. I'll show you my latest seascape," he said, hoping she'd laugh.

She did. "I know you better than that."

"I would like you to," he said, raising her hands to his lips.

She took a small step back, her eyes wide.

He cursed himself for pushing too hard, but he had a schedule to keep.

"I'll call you when my meeting is done tomorrow." She paused at the door. "Then you can let me know if I should stop by or if it's too late."

He knew she wasn't referring to the time. Again, she impressed him by understanding the little nuances. If only more of the men he worked with were as astute.

As he closed the door behind her he let himself enjoy another heady rush of anticipation. As angry as he was that she'd busted a drug shipment his clients relied on, she deserved respect. When she came by after her meeting everything would be different. She would be in pain over the blow he was about to inflict on her precious Belclare and he would be the only one able to soothe her. Tomorrow night, his plans would be in full swing and his reputation preserved.

He watched from the sidelight window as she drove

away. She made him angry, yes, but he liked her. He could send a message to others and still preserve the idealism that made her so unique. Silently he vowed that she wouldn't live to know how badly she'd misjudged him.

It was the only courtesy he could afford when it came to Chief Abby Jensen.

Chapter Four

Abby left Deke's house, almost grateful to be called to a vandalism scene at the town limit. When he touched her, she couldn't decide how to feel about it. Maybe because he didn't touch her often enough? She was starting to wonder if anyone would ever touch her enough.

She wasn't sure about the answer, which only annoyed her. When they'd started these weekly coffee meetings it had been a way for her to keep tabs on the enigmatic and cloistered resident of Belclare. Now, though, the truth was far more embarrassing.

For months, she'd been fighting her attraction to the man. He was in his mid-forties, but the gray at his temples and his artistic worldview only made him more distinguished in her eyes. The flawless manners, superb taste and maturity didn't hurt, either.

He treated her as if she was someone special and she liked the idea that at least one person saw beyond her badge and title to the woman underneath. She liked to think of herself as more than a uniform dedicated to maintaining law and order.

"So you've been taking a weekly coffee break for the ego boost," she muttered, drumming her fingertips on her steering wheel. Even in solitude that sounded pretty pathetic.

Except it had felt anything but pathetic when he'd called

her passionate. And that invite to dinner…was he heading where he seemed to be heading?

"You're flattered," she said, coaching herself right out of the potential romance of it. She hadn't had much of a social life since taking the top post in the Belclare police department, hesitant to set herself up for idle gossip. "Get over yourself. The positive attention is nice, but you can't afford the distraction."

As if on cue, her cell phone launched into "I Fought the Law," the ringtone she'd programmed for business calls. She toggled the button on her steering wheel to answer. "Chief Jensen."

"Hi, Chief. It's Danny."

"I'm ten minutes away."

"Right. It's just…"

She waited. He cleared his throat as worst-case scenarios danced at the edge of her mind. She would not entertain those unless and until facts forced her to do so.

Her personal life might be a haze of self-doubt and bad timing, but her career had been marked with success every step of the way. Her work ethic, common sense and focus had served her well and she wasn't about to toss those strengths out the window.

"Spit it out, Danny."

"The responding officers want you to know the media is already on-site."

Damn it. "Thanks for the heads-up." She appreciated the warning. If the media was on-site, then Mayor Scott wouldn't be far behind. Now she was doubly grateful for choosing the suit and heels today. In her opinion, her suits made her more relatable than the uniform, especially after her hard-nosed speech had become a viral internet sensation.

As she approached the scene, she cringed at the growing crowd. Good grief. If she'd just heard, how had a news crew from Baltimore arrived so quickly? Her officers were pushing people back, but that only gave the media a better overall shot for tonight's headlines.

It looked worse in person than it had on her phone. The Welcome to Belclare display had been altered with spray paint. The phrases "Death to Chief Jensen" and "Open season on Belclare" were now blotting out points of town pride.

The threats weren't new, but they'd been out of the public eye. This…*this* was bold and obvious. It was a challenge she couldn't ignore. "Open season on Belclare" required a careful, strategic response. How had whoever was responsible for this pulled it off without getting caught?

A reporter shoved a microphone in front of her as she went to join the responding officers. "Chief, what's your reaction to such personal threats?"

She pushed her clenched fists deeper into her coat pockets. "The childish vandal responsible for this negative display will be found and dealt with."

"Are there any security cameras out here that might have caught the vandal?"

Abby kept walking, refusing to acknowledge the silly question. There was a Christmas tree lot just around the next bend and nothing but trees until the sign. "If you'll excuse me, I need to speak with my officers." She ducked under the tape the responding officers had used to block the immediate area.

Reporters shouted at her back.

"Should the citizens of Belclare be taking more defensive action?"

"Will you shut down the city?"

"Will the Christmas Village be canceled?"

She couldn't let that one go. She turned, ready to answer when the mayor's voice rang out through the crisp winter air.

"This small attempt to interrupt our annual traditions is hardly cause for alarm."

Abby couldn't believe he was taking her side. *About time,* she thought.

"Chief Jensen's—" he hesitated for three seconds "—*enthusiasm* has obviously created a few unpleasant ripples, but Belclare is strong and united, and determined to make this the best holiday season ever. We look forward to seeing all of you this weekend."

Abby found herself fighting a sudden urge to silence Mayor Scott. She banished the compulsion. He was better in the media spotlight and, whether or not he believed her or agreed with her methods, ultimately they were working toward the same goal: a safe community and a safe holiday event.

She let him ramble on giving the proper sound bites that likely included a subtle invitation for other criminal justice professionals to apply for her job.

"Do we have anything?" Abby ignored her chilled feet as she listened to her officers explain what they'd found. Or rather what they hadn't found.

"One of the vendors coming in for the weekend reported it," said Officer Gadsden.

"Did you get a statement?"

"We did, so it helps set a time frame for the vandals."

She stepped closer, pressed her finger to a dripping streak of paint. "Still tacky. Someone had fun during their lunch hour." She looked to the ground. "Any hope for shoe prints?"

"No." Officer Gadsden knelt down and Abby followed suit. "The snow's been trampled by more than one person. Right back to the road."

"Great." Abby wanted to clean this up herself, right this minute. "See what you can get off any traffic cameras between here and Baltimore. And ask around Sadie's and other restaurants. Maybe the vandals came into town for lunch."

"You got it."

She covered her mouth with her hand, unwilling to risk anyone in the media reading her lips. "As you take pictures, get the bystanders." It wasn't unusual for vandals of this sort to hang around to watch the cops scramble for answers.

"Chief Jensen!"

She turned slowly, unable to ignore the mayor's shout. "Yes?" It was a small measure of relief that he remained on the other side of the tape. For her, the shock was seeing him alone. Victor Scott loved his entourage, whether it was his hired staff or an impromptu gathering of media professionals.

He waved her closer and she did her best to hide her distaste at the arrogant summons. Mayor Scott enjoyed the political posturing, but playing along was her least favorite, necessary part of the job. She preferred a straightforward exchange. Less chance for mixed signals or missed goals that way.

"How long until you have this cleaned up?" he demanded with his practiced concerned frown in place.

"The sign or the crime?"

"You can't manage both?"

"Repairing the sign isn't exactly police responsibility," she said, clinging to her last shred of composure. "As for the vandal—" she glanced back at the damage "—we believe there was more than one person involved. There are databases with graffiti signatures and tags—"

"This criminal signed his work?" the mayor exclaimed too loudly.

"We're not sure yet. That's part of the problem. Or the solution," she added, just to give him something else to focus on. "As for the sign itself, once we have our pictures it can be repainted and repaired right away."

"No! Nooo!"

Abby and the mayor swiveled toward the pitiful wail of Mr. Filmore. When Mayor Scott rolled his eyes, she realized they shared a mutual frustration with the historical society president. It was strangely affirming.

"What now, Filmore?" With a hand on Filmore's shoulder, the mayor stopped him from barreling into the crime scene.

"You can't just *paint* that sign."

"We can't just leave it," the mayor shot back.

Abby glanced at her officers, grateful they were snapping pictures of everything and everyone as she'd asked and not laughing aloud at the ridiculous debate.

"This gateway to Belclare has been meticulously maintained for over one hundred and eighty years. It must be cleaned, not merely slapped at with another coat of paint."

The mayor loomed over the skinny frame of Filmore. "I am not allowing those threats to remain visible any longer than necessary. Get a team out here if you must but get it handled immediately."

For once, Abby was grateful for Filmore's presence. The man's shrill insistence about preservation diverted the mayor's attention from her.

She used the time and space to take her own inventory of faces in the crowd. She recognized reporters and television station logos. More than a few people from town had followed the noise and commotion to come take a look. She felt the collective irritation from those business owners whose praise for her drug bust quickly turned to criticism after her speech garnered national attention.

She returned to her officers. "Keep the area secure. Do we have anything to cover it in the short term?"

"I have a tarp in my car."

She nodded. "It's a start." Pointing to the camera Gadsden was using, she asked, "Is anyone standing out to you?"

He shook his head. "No one seems too proud of themselves. Except the mayor."

She chuckled. "I'm sure he has photo evidence of his whereabouts for the entire morning."

"Our chances of catching the vandals and making an arrest are pretty slim."

"All we can do is our best." She pulled her car keys from her pocket. "I'll find someone to babysit the sign." Her department was stretched too thin already, but she refused to allow a repeat performance.

"We could put up a couple of motion-activated cameras," Gadsden offered.

"With this circus watching?" She shook her head. "I like the idea but the vandals would only come back and hit those first." She scanned the faces on the other side of the road again. It was a valid idea, if they could find a window when no one else was around. Too late to contain the media, she knew Belclare residents would be upset with her all over again. "Let's talk about it at the station when we have more than the nothing we have now."

Gadsden agreed and Abby headed back to her car, giving appropriate sound bites to the media on the way. She wanted the quiet of her office and some heat for her freezing feet. Unfortunately, she was blocked in by a dark blue pickup truck she didn't recognize.

It had to belong to one of the temporary workers or vendors. She stifled the urge to look back at the death threat on the sign. She would not let some silly stunt likely staged by a teenager with too much idle time and a bad sense of humor get under her skin. Paranoia was neither professional nor helpful.

"Excuse me, Chief Jensen."

A car door slammed with a bang and, despite her best effort, her body jerked, braced for an attack.

"Didn't mean to startle you."

Abby surveyed the tall stranger who seemed determined to show up in her life today. And he *had* startled her. Denying it would be foolish. "No problem. Mr. O'Brien, isn't it?"

"That would be my father," he said with a softer smile that did strange things to her pulse. "I'm just Riley, remember?" He leaned against the pickup's door. "I heard the breaking news on the way out." His brown eyes were taking in the ugly scene behind her. "Any leads?"

She tucked her hands back into her pockets. "I could have sworn you told me you had steady work. Why are you insinuating yourself into mine?"

"I'll take that as a no. And I'd be working if my next job wasn't taped off."

She gave in and rubbed at the tension in her neck. Hadn't there been a time when Belclare folks had just done their own thing without professional design teams and small armies of temporary workers? She missed those days. Of course, with the way the Christmas Village had grown it was impossible to set up without help. While everyone liked how December brought a wealth of tourists into town, the police department maintained a higher alert for petty crimes.

Since she'd taken over, the worst they'd dealt with had been a string of burglaries and one car theft. The burglaries had been teenagers looking for trouble and all of the stolen items had been recovered and returned. The car theft had been a pair of temporary workers operating under the influence of alcohol and stupidity.

Yeah, those were the days.

This year, she had legitimate concerns about how to protect Belclare effectively. There wasn't enough time or manpower to run background checks on every new person in town. Her meetings with business owners hadn't gone well, most of them siding with the mayor that the additional threats were her problem to solve since she'd brought it on them.

At some point in Belclare's past, the police chief would have been hailed as a hero for that bust for more than a few hours. But despite the public resentment and doubt, she understood the financial importance of the upcoming days and she was doing her best to make sure it all came together without any further tragedy.

The ugly vandalism didn't bode well.

"Until Mr. Filmore decides how to proceed with the cleanup, this area is off-limits."

"I'll let my boss know." He pulled a cell phone out of the pocket of his dark red vest.

She frowned. "Don't you own a real coat?"

"Sure." He gave her a strange look. "It gets in the way when I'm working."

"I see."

"Don't worry. I won't die of frostbite on you."

Based on the way her body reacted to him, frostbite wasn't a concern for her, either, if he was nearby. She'd nearly forgotten about her freezing feet during this unexpected conversation. She glared back at the sign. "No one is going to die of anything around here."

"Glad to hear it," he said, his attention on his phone.

"Could you move your truck, please? I have things to do and you're blocking me in."

"Sure." With the phone to his ear, he settled into the

driver's seat. His voice was a low rumble as he explained the problem to his boss.

Then the engine masked his conversation as he rolled out of the way, giving her a small wave.

In her own car, she cranked up the heat and hit shuffle on her iPod, letting the blast of AC/DC fill the car on her way through town. She needed the loud, demanding beat to blot out her thoughts. There was no point in doubting her course of action. She wouldn't take back the words even if she could. As her thoughts cycled, she spotted Riley's truck about a block behind her.

He wasn't following her. That would be paranoid, fearful thinking and she wouldn't give in to it. She wouldn't sink to the level that gave some rumored local terrorists the advantage. He was headed for one of the warehouses down by the docks and this was the most direct route through town. But he turned when she did, heading north away from Main Street, directly opposite the route to the docks.

She practiced it in her mind, running through her defensive options as he continued to tail her. Preparation wasn't paranoia, she assured herself.

Abby nearly cracked when he was practically on her bumper as she turned onto her street. She debated driving right by her house, but decided her address was no secret and it was time to make a stand. With that thought echoing in her brain, she pulled into her driveway.

But Riley didn't pull in behind her; he pulled into the driveway right beside hers. In fact, the way the two homes were situated, they were now parked side by side.

What the hell? All concept of her attraction to the man vanished instantly. He was like a bad penny turning up everywhere today. The house next door had been vacant for several weeks, since Mr. and Mrs. Hamilton had gone to Florida to visit their grandchildren. He had no business being on her street or in their driveway.

She yanked her purse from the passenger seat and got out of the car. "What do you think you're doing, Mr. O'Brien?"

Chapter Five

"Hey, Chief." Riley tipped his head in greeting, his expression easy. "Call me Riley," he reminded her. He shrugged. "The boss told me to try again first thing tomorrow. No sense unloading tonight just to load it up again in the morning."

She rounded the hood of her car, one hand in her purse on the grip of her gun. "That doesn't explain why you're following me."

"Following you?" He glanced at the two vehicles as if just noticing they were parked next to each other. "No such luck. I just came on home."

"Home?"

"Well, at least home for now. I signed the rental agreement during my lunch break."

"The Hamiltons didn't say anything about renting out their house."

He shrugged. "I wouldn't know. I've never met them."

"Never met?" she echoed. "But that's their house." Exasperated, she stepped forward. "I need some sort of proof of your claim, Mr. O'Brien."

He raised his hands like he was surrendering. "Take it easy. Let me get the paperwork."

This was intolerable. He couldn't be her neighbor. She couldn't cope with having a stranger living so close. Not right now when she saw a potential threat in the faces of people she'd known for years. Okay, so maybe it was more than the easygoing attitude and absolute raw sex appeal. While neither of those traits had ever ranked high on her list of trustworthy features, Riley affected her differently. At precisely the time when she needed to trust herself, life dumped this hunk of handsomeness and doubt right next door.

Frustrated, she hastily flipped through the folder he handed her. The letterhead was familiar, as was the Realtor's name. The lease agreement and signatures all seemed to be in order.

"She should have told me," Abby muttered.

"I told you I liked your town."

"That hardly validates renting a house."

"Are you always this anxious when someone moves in?"

The question seized her attention, forced her to think like a cop rather than a frightened victim trapped in the crosshairs of a rifle she couldn't see. "No. No," she repeated as the day suddenly caught up with her. She handed him the folder. "My apologies. It's been a little dicey around here lately. I'm surprised the realty company didn't warn you off. I thought everyone believed I was a magnet for trouble."

"They did mention it actually."

She laughed. The sound was laced with a bit of weary hysteria, but it felt pretty good anyway. "So you're looking for trouble?"

RILEY TOSSED THE paperwork back into the cab and stuffed his hands into his pockets. He almost felt bad that he couldn't tell the woman the truth, but breaking cover wasn't the answer. "I'm not looking for trouble, just work." He glanced to the house. "And anywhere that isn't a hotel room, really."

"That lease is for a year," she said.

He watched her shifting, rubbing her legs together a bit. She was cold but too stubborn to take care of herself until she knew if he was friend or foe. Based on the threats aimed her way, he figured that showed remarkable determination and a hefty dose of intelligence.

"The Realtor approached me while I was decorating their building. When I learned the owners wanted some work done and ideas for a remodel, I knew this was the right place for me." Again he was grateful for the deep background and work history Director Casey had created for him. The proximity to the chief simplified his surveillance plans.

"Welcome to the neighborhood," she said with obvious reluctance. She stuck out her gloved hand.

He accepted the gesture. Her hand felt small in his, but there was strength in the grip. He wanted to ask what kind of weapon she preferred. The woman oozed tough under the contrasting layers of wariness and the feminine heels and power suit. She was a puzzle he wanted to solve, but he suspected he wouldn't get anywhere by pushing her.

"You'd better get inside and warm up," he said, releasing her hand and closing his truck door. "If you need anything, just come on over."

"Right. Same goes."

"Thanks." When she walked away, he turned for his own front door.

"A word of warning, Riley."

"Yeah?"

"Mrs. Wilks will probably be down with a plate of cookies."

"That doesn't sound so awful."

"Exactly. Her cookies are addictive, you'll see." Her smile changed everything about her face. It chased away the worry and brightened those blue eyes. It gave him a glimpse of what she was like without the cloud of stress over her head. "It's why we all put up with her benign nosiness."

"Got it."

With a nod, she pushed open her front door and disappeared.

He walked around the truck and up the path, entering the front door of his house wondering what the hell to do now. When they'd left the vandalized sign, he'd hoped she'd go to the police station so he could take a quick walk through her house.

Light flirting hadn't worked at the station and just now she'd barely accepted him being neighborly. He had to find a way to keep an eye on her without driving her out of his sight while he searched for an imminent threat. From what he'd heard around town, everyone was at least irritated with her if not outright angry. It made it tough to sort out who was hiding the terrorist tendencies.

He walked straight back to the kitchen and put his vest on the peg by the back door. The simple act had him recalling the chief's concern about his coat. One more piece of the developing picture that was her. Could he use that innate concern to his advantage?

He glanced out the side window, across their mirrored driveways, to her house. Resigned, he pulled a beer from the refrigerator, leaned back against the counter and contemplated the Hamiltons' outdated kitchen.

His tape measure was on his tool belt in the truck, but he paced off the flooring and started mulling over the cost and benefits of tile versus vinyl. Reclaimed hardwood might be an option, too. The space wasn't too big. But the weather could make tracking down those materials a challenge. Per his agreement, any changes beyond basic repair would need to be approved.

Oh, well, he wasn't in a rush. There was plenty of re-modeling to keep him busy and maintain his cover even after he was done with the holiday setup. He rolled some of the ache from his shoulders. The physical work would give his brain time to sort out the people who were ready to act on their anger toward the chief.

He'd only been in town a couple of days and it wasn't a stretch that criminals thought they could slip under the radar in this sleepy little waterside town. Chief Jensen had things under control, but the police force was small, as was the community. The docks did brisk business and the smaller port meant quicker turnaround, which meant shipments didn't linger long enough to get caught.

Riley walked into the den where he'd tucked his laptop into the small writing desk. The Hamiltons' decorating style wasn't exactly his taste, but the privacy and security beat a motel.

He turned on the television and found a music channel for background noise, then sat down to review everything he could find about Belclare, working backward from the most recent news. By now, he'd been over all of the details and press about the drug bust a hundred times and still couldn't pinpoint who might have set it up.

Taking a long draw on his beer, he pulled up files he'd created on key people in town, especially those who'd vo-calized frustration and concern over the chief's victory speech. The hardware store owner had gone public for a Baltimore news station. The mayor, too, more than once. Riley chalked that up to making the most of free publicity for the hardware store and the mayor was leveraging the attention for his political advancement. The well-spoken politician was nearly as irritating as the whiny Mr. Filmore.

Riley was digging deeper into Filmore's background when the doorbell chimed. He quickly closed the windows related to his search and brought up the remodeling sites that fit his cover story. In the hall, he spied visitors at his kitchen door. Chief Jensen and an older lady. Both were smiling, but only the older woman looked like she was truly happy to be there.

He manufactured a smile and answered the door. "Evening, ladies." He flashed the chief a covert smile.

"Excuse us for dropping in without any warning," the older woman said cheerfully. "I'm Matilda Wilks, just two doors down. Abby here offered to join me in welcoming you to the neighborhood."

Abby's cloudy expression told a much different story. He grinned, knowing she'd either been dragged along or had joined Mrs. Wilks solely for the purpose of checking the Hamiltons' property. His money was on the latter.

"We brought cookies." Mrs. Wilks waved the foil-covered plate in her hand. "Fresh from the oven."

"I'd be a fool to turn you away," Riley said, holding the door wide for them. Let Abby look around. She needed to realize he wasn't a threat to her, even if he couldn't tell her outright that he was her best asset.

Mrs. Wilks bustled in and the scent of warm chocolate-chip cookies tickled his nose. But the scent of Abby, as she strolled past him in the narrow hall, brought his entire body to high alert. She'd let down her hair and the glossy blond mane smelled of flowers warmed by sunshine. While he didn't understand the science behind fragrances, he appreciated the effects.

That scent took him back to the garden behind the orphanage, where he'd first discovered the satisfaction of working with his hands.

"Poor Abby here hadn't heard about the Hamiltons, what with everything she's had on her mind," Mrs. Wilks was saying. Making herself right at home, she put the plate on the table and removed the foil, revealing a pile of thick, perfectly browned chocolate-chip cookies. Then she spotted the beer on the counter. "Tell me you have milk? Or even coffee?"

"Both," he said, grinning.

"Good boy." Mrs. Wilks beamed up at him, her steel-gray hair swinging as she turned to the chief. "Which do you prefer, Abby dear?"

"Milk, please."

Mrs. Wilks arched a brow and gave a soft, speculating hum. "Your stomach must be a bother with all this extra stress."

When a blush crept into the chief's cheeks, Riley tried to distract Mrs. Wilks. "Have a seat," he encouraged, pulling out the nearest chair. Mrs. Wilks claimed the seat. Riley reached for the next chair and smiled at the chief.

"No, thanks," she said, obviously in police chief mode. "Mind if I look around?"

"Abby," Mrs. Wilks scolded, "at least have a cookie before you go investigating."

Riley smothered a laugh while he filled three glasses with milk. "Aside from a suitcase and my laptop, I promise you it's just the way the Hamiltons left it."

"I've told her everything they told me," Mrs. Wilks said. She arrowed Abby a knowing look. "She just doesn't know how to relax."

Abby threw up her hands in surrender and took a seat.

Riley joined them, taking the one remaining chair and being careful not to bump Abby's knee with his.

"A body gets tired of the cold," Mrs. Wilks was saying. "If I had family in Florida, I might do the very same thing."

"I'm not sure I could let you do that," Abby said, choosing a cookie. "Who would bake for me?"

"You know your way around a kitchen, young lady, don't

even pretend. What about you?" She turned a sharp eye his
way. "Do you need me to bring over a casserole?"

He grinned at the older woman again. "I can manage.
Thanks."

"More than beer and chips, I hope."

"Yes, ma'am." He broke a cookie in two and stuffed one
half into his mouth. As he chewed, he watched the way
Abby dunked her cookie in her milk glass. Deliberate and
methodical, he found it oddly endearing. "The cookies are
perfect, Mrs. Wilks. Thanks for bringing them by."

"Good company makes everything better." She looked
around the kitchen. "What did the Hamiltons want you to
do here?"

"A little of this and that," he replied. "There's some
minor repair work I'll take care of first."

"That rotted wood under the sink, I hope. Abby, do you
remember what a mess that was?"

Abby bobbed her chin, her mouth full of cookie. Riley
smothered a laugh. "I was just debating tile or vinyl. Any
thoughts, ladies?"

As Mrs. Wilks launched into a full report of which families on the street had made which type of upgrade, Riley
caught the chief watching him.

He arched his eyebrows and her gaze abruptly returned
to the glass of milk in front of her. "Another cookie?" He
nudged the plate her way.

She shook her head and pushed back from the table.

"You don't have a preference on the flooring?" he asked.

The look she sent him was cool at best. "No. You should
go with whatever the owners want," she replied, taking her
glass to the sink and rinsing it.

"True," he admitted. "I'll work up a few ideas for them
to consider. If it were my place I'd go with tile."

"Hard on the knees," Mrs. Wilks interjected. "Then you just end up with rugs and mats everywhere."

He mentioned the reclaimed hardwood and Mrs. Wilks offered an exuberant opinion on the value of that idea. He pretended not to notice Abby slipping away from the kitchen.

Mrs. Wilks had no such problem. She motioned for him to lean in closer. "That girl is suspicious of everyone these days. Don't let it bother you."

"I hear she has cause."

"That she does," Mrs. Wilks agreed. "Go with the reclaimed floor. Better all around."

"All right," he said, listening to the stair treads creak. He grinned at Mrs. Wilks. "I promise I'm not here to cause more trouble."

"Oh, I could tell that first thing," she said. "She'll relax. Personally, I'm glad to have a strapping young man so close. Makes me feel safe." She got up, put her glass in the sink and walked to the door. "She cooks when she's upset. Based on the groceries she hauled in the other day, there's at least one lasagna in her freezer and another in the oven. You could do worse than get yourself invited to dinner."

Startled by the older woman's suggestion, he didn't have a chance to reply before she was gone. The older woman was a matchmaker. He'd stake his skill with a weapon on it.

He was putting the glasses in the dishwasher when the chief reappeared.

"Where's Mrs. Wilks?"

"Home," he replied, drying his hands. "She said something about dinner in the oven."

"I'm the one with dinner baking," she muttered. She'd been watching his hands with an odd expression, but those blue eyes abruptly locked on to his face.

He looped the towel through the bar on the front of

the dishwasher and tucked his hands into his pockets. She tempted him, her dark, snug jeans hugging her curves and her soft gray cable-knit sweater emphasizing the storms in her eyes. "Are you satisfied now?"

She scowled at him. "With what?"

"Your search," he reminded her. "You were kind of obvious. Whatever you think I am, you're wrong." It was one of the few things he could say with absolute certainty.

"You have no idea what I think about you."

He pushed away from the counter, pleased when she held her ground. Maybe she wasn't seeing him as a threat after all. "Enlighten me," he suggested as he covered the plate of cookies.

"I'm still assessing," she said, reaching for the coat she'd draped over the chair back.

He laughed.

"What's so funny?" She paused, her hands going still on the second toggle of her coat.

"Sorry." He held up his hands. "Just the two of us tip-toeing around the facts."

"Which are?"

"We're neighbors. The whole welcome thing reminds me of something my mom used to say."

"Which is?"

"Not really appropriate." And nonexistent. "Is there anything I could do or say to put you at ease?"

"Tell me what your mom said."

"Maybe another time." He grabbed his beer, taking a long pull from the bottle while he watched her.

"You seem legit," she admitted reluctantly.

"Thanks." He returned the beer to the counter. "I could raise a little hell if it would make you feel better."

"I'd feel better if you stayed at one of the long-term hotels like the rest of the crews."

"Ah. But that's not happening."

"What did your mother say?"

He shook his head. She was tenacious, a trait that must serve her well. "It had to do with snooping and gossip, but it doesn't really apply in this case."

A telltale blush crept into her cheeks. "Why not?"

"Because you were checking the closets for bodies or stolen goods, right?"

"Maybe."

He shrugged. "That's your job," he replied. "And why should I get offended if I'm not hiding anything." Not where she could find it, anyway.

She pursed those full, rose-colored lips, pushing his thoughts into dangerous territory. "Coming over here was Mrs. Wilks's idea."

"I believe you," he said with a smile. "And you made the most of the opportunity. Considering recent events, I would've been more concerned if you hadn't taken a look around."

She pushed back her sleeve and checked her watch. "Still haven't seen the basement," she pointed out.

He gave her a mock grimace. "It's musty and more than a little spooky down there."

"Then you can go first."

"That's a big risk. What'll you give me in return?"

"If we survive, you mean?"

He nodded, liking this playful side of her. "Let's assume the positive."

She checked her watch again. "If we survive, I'll share dinner at my house."

"What's on the menu?"

"What a guy question." She rolled her eyes. "It's lasagna—homemade—and more than enough for two."

"Sounds great. Follow me." He led her into the hallway

and opened the door to the basement. "Don't say I didn't warn you."

"Just move," she said at his back.

He hit the switch and the fluorescent light at the bottom of the stairs slowly brightened.

Riley started down, hearing her footsteps on the wooden stairs echo a half beat after his. Reaching the cement floor, he moved aside so she could examine the space.

She hesitated on the last step, studying him closely while she held a brief height advantage.

Wondering how she saw him, he let her look her fill. It gave him time to return the favor. Her wide blue eyes made him hate the threats that had her wary of everyone around her.

He'd done his homework; he knew what she'd looked like before the drug bust. The new, perpetual scowl was a telltale sign of the damage to her confidence. She'd probably always been cautious, but now she didn't trust anyone. Except maybe Mrs. Wilks.

As she finally moved past him, he caught a whiff of her shampoo again. He cleared his throat. "Storage and laundry to the left—"

"Pinball to the right," she finished for him. "Mr. Hamilton's hobby."

"So you have been down here."

"Not recently." She turned a slow circle. "It's like a time capsule."

It was a valid assessment. "Fortunately they left decent appliances."

"That's a plus." She walked over to the first pinball machine on the short wall.

"Want to play a game or two? It works great."

"No, thanks. I'm obsessive. If I start I won't want to quit and dinner will burn."

"In that case, allow me to see you safely up the stairs."

Her smile chased away the shadows haunting his thoughts. "Thanks for indulging my curiosity."

"My pleasure." He gestured for her to go up first, immediately regretting the chivalry as it put the shapely curve of her hips and backside right at eye level. No one could fault her fitness. Thinking of Director Casey's reaction if such an unprofessional observation showed up in his report cooled him right down.

She didn't seem to pick up on his wayward thoughts, waiting patiently while he locked up and followed her across the driveway and into her kitchen. The houses were similar Cape Cod floor plans, but her decor reflected a more modern sense of style. He liked it.

"How are the knees?" He pointed to the large ceramic tiles under her feet.

"Just fine," she replied as the oven timer went off.

So much for asking for a tour of her place.

"My biggest adjustment was the cold," she said, pulling the large pan out of the oven.

"I didn't think of that."

"No one does. Go for the reclaimed hardwood."

He nodded in agreement. The remodeling ideas were coming to him almost as quickly as questions regarding the drug bust. But he hesitated to wreck the momentum by quizzing her about that case. "Man, that smells good."

"It tastes better."

She put him to work tossing a salad while she pulled the lasagna out of the oven, letting it stand while she set the table.

He hadn't been hungry until he'd walked in. The rich aroma of sausage, cheese, tomato sauce and oregano had his mouth watering in anticipation by the time she served.

"Whoa," he said, setting down his fork after the first bite. "That's amazing."

"Thanks. It's the sauce."

"Here I thought it was the company."

She rolled her eyes. "Do you always come on so strong?"

He shrugged, taking another bite and giving himself time to think of a reasonable reply. "Call me a doer," he said, keeping it light. "All my life I've seen people waste time and effort waffling about what they want and how to get it."

"Are you saying you want me?" Her eyebrows arched, silently daring him to reply honestly.

He grinned at her. "I'm saying I decided to live my life differently. Focused on the moment."

"Interesting philosophy."

"It's working so far." They ate in silence for a few minutes more. "Looking at you, Madam Police Chief, I'd say that's pretty close to your philosophy, too."

She raised her water glass in a toast. "Close enough." She sipped, returned the glass to the table. "And my friends call me Abby."

"I've moved up from suspicious stranger to friend?"

She chuckled. "It's a long ladder, but you're on your way. You were nice to Mrs. Wilks."

"That's easy."

"Remember that when she starts asking the personal questions."

"I'm an open book."

She snorted. "I think Danny is infatuated with you, but he's a fair judge of character."

"Danny's impressionable," Riley said with a laugh. "He'll be a good neighborhood cop one day."

"He needs experience. Have you remodeled many old homes?"

He recognized a diversionary topic when he heard one,

but if it kept her at ease, kept him close enough to protect her, it worked for him. "A few. I've been swinging a hammer since I was about eight."

"A calling?"

He thought about those early days in the orphanage garden. "I guess so. A completed job, done well, is a reward in itself," he replied, echoing the teachers who'd raised him.

"Another phrase from your mother?"

He nodded, letting her make the assumptions that supported his cover story. "Do you need help with anything around here?"

"Not today."

"Say the word if you change your mind. What about your calling? Have you always been interested in criminal justice?"

"My uncle was a cop and I thought he was the coolest thing going," she said. "Whenever I got the chance, I'd go down to the station and hang out. Talk about impressionable."

"Doesn't sound like a place for a kid."

"My parents worried, but I've always thought it depends on the kid."

"There's some truth to that," he agreed. "Are you thinking kids trashed the sign?"

"I'd like it to be."

"Meaning?" He leaned back in his chair, debating another serving. He was full, but he wanted to keep her talking. Danny had given him some insight about the community, but Abby would have a better overall picture.

"I've been thinking kids wouldn't have been so careful."

"I'm not following. It looked like a fast and dirty tag to me."

"I think it was supposed to look that way," she agreed.

"But how many kids, moving fast enough to not be seen by traffic, would think to cover their footprints?"

"You're sure they didn't just get lucky?"

"I'm sure the tracks were deliberately concealed." She blotted her lips and set the napkin next to her plate. "I need to think about something else. More lasagna?"

"Twist my arm," he said, reaching for the pan. "What's the secret with the sauce?"

"If I told you, it wouldn't be a secret."

"Tell me anyway. You'll feel better."

"I feel fine now."

"But there's so much more to life than 'fine,'" he teased with a wink.

She opened her mouth but whatever she'd been about to say was cut off by a loud crash outside. They were both on their feet in an instant. He followed her as she raced through the house and out the front door.

Across the street, a man was caught under an extension ladder, a reel of brightly colored Christmas lights still blinking in his hand. Riley swore, reaching for his cell phone to dial 911 while Abby kept running. Mrs. Wilks and others were soon in the street, wondering how to help and speculating on what happened.

ABBY TOLD HERSELF this was only an accident as she ran across the street. Letting her instincts take over, she shouted for blankets and they appeared moments later.

"An ambulance is on the way," Riley said, appearing beside her. "Hang in there," he said to the man under the ladder.

"Well, this is a fine way to meet your neighbors," Abby said briskly. "Riley O'Brien, this is Roy Calder."

"Everyone calls me Calder. Wish I could say it was a pleasure," he added through gritted teeth.

"Does it hurt everywhere?" Riley took the lights out of Calder's grip.

"Yeah."

"Good."

"Riley!" Abby pushed him back. "What are you doing?"

"He's right," Calder said. "Feeling everything means my back's in one piece."

"Oh." She hadn't thought of the injuries in terms of potential paralysis. "That is good." Abby rubbed the chill from her arms, accepting a coat that appeared from somewhere. Mrs. Wilks was cheerfully scolding their neighbor for working without a net.

"I was almost done," he defended. "Anyone see the bastard who pushed the ladder?"

Abby shivered with a chill that had nothing to do with the cold. "What did you say, Calder?"

"I'm not an idiot, Chief, despite the looks of this. Someone brought me down on purpose."

She looked around the scene wondering who might have done such a terrible thing. All she saw were the familiar faces of her neighbors looking as stunned as she felt. "Did you get a look?"

"No more than a glimpse of a dark knit cap when I felt something at the ladder."

"Back everyone up," she said to Riley, hoping he could manage crowd control. She wished she'd remembered to grab her phone. She was going to need someone to help her walk the area and look for evidence. But first things first. She knelt beside Calder again. "What did you hear?"

Calder groaned a little, either thinking about it or just struggling to breathe. "A crunch. Boots on the landscaping."

"Okay. Good." Calder's wife used white rock in the flower beds. Covered in snow, the assailant must have miscalculated. "What else? A car? A bike?"

"No. That's about it. I was falling before I could even shout at him to stop."

She looked at Calder's house. "Did he come from your left or right?"

"The left." Calder groaned again. "Christ. Libby will kill me. I wanted to get this done for her tonight."

"Maybe I should question her," Abby said, teasing him. Libby was known as one of the gentlest people in Belclare. And she was seven months pregnant with their second child.

Calder's laughter turned into a cough. "I'm sure she feels she has cause to do me harm more days than not."

Abby pasted a smile on her face as the paramedics arrived and took over. As she backed out of the way, she hit an immovable wall. Before she could apologize, she felt warm hands on her shoulders, steadying her. "Easy. I've got you."

Riley. His touch was somehow calming. But that didn't last long. Anger, shock and worry spun like a wild tornado in her belly as Calder was moved first to the backboard and then to the ambulance.

When the ambulance was gone, Abby walked toward the landscaping to have a look.

"You should go inside," Riley said from right behind her.

"No." She faced him. This close, she had to tip her head back to meet his gaze. "He thinks someone pushed the ladder. I need to call in some help and check out the scene."

His eyes narrowed and his mouth, usually so quick with that wry grin, turned into a dark frown. He handed her his phone. "Make the call. I'll clear out the spectators."

He managed the task efficiently and politely, turning down offers to help clean up the mess while she explained the situation to the officer on duty at the station.

When Riley returned, the street was eerily quiet.

"Here." He handed her a heavy flashlight. "Figured you'd need that."

"Thanks." She wasn't sure what she hoped to find, but it wasn't the nasty note scrawled on the siding of Calder's house: "One down. Who's next?"

"Not paint. Looks like charcoal," Riley observed.

"Guess Calder was right about being pushed." *Open season on Belclare.* The media would be showing that all night long and as soon as the word got around about this, the rest of the town would know Calder was in the hospital because of her.

Her stomach clutched and she nearly tossed her dinner right there at the scene. Anger jolted her. She'd never come close to contaminating a crime scene in her career. "Damn it. If they want me, they should come at *me*."

"They want you to suffer."

Knowing he was right made her feel worse. "What am I supposed to do, leave town? How would that help anyone?"

"That might be the most important question."

She glared at him, wishing the light was better. "You sound more like a cop than a carpenter."

"From you, I'll take that as a compliment."

"It wasn't meant that way."

"Too bad. I'd think you know from experience that very few people do bad things for the fun of it." He flashed the light on the grim message again. "It's kind of obvious someone is trying to get under your skin."

To her ultimate frustration, it was working.

She didn't know what to make of her new neighbor. He had a presence people responded to, herself included. His easygoing manners didn't quite fit with his critical thinking. And how insensitive of her to think a guy with a tool belt had only one dimension.

She had enough experience with people to know better,

but something about Riley was different. Something more than the way her body went hot when he was close. Whatever else she felt, this was hardly the time to address her physical attraction to him.

"Do you see any footprints?" The beam from the flashlight sliced through the darkness as she searched for anything helpful.

"Too many," he answered.

That new urge to scream returned with a vengeance. She wouldn't give the people behind these hateful acts the satisfaction. Whatever system she'd disrupted with the drug bust, the criminals were playing hardball now. She'd read the emails and threats in chat rooms about retaliation that involved taking out innocent civilians. Until now, she'd thought it was so much smoke and hot air.

They were lucky Calder hadn't been paralyzed or even killed.

When she found the person responsible—and she silently vowed to do just that—she would see them rot behind bars.

When an investigative team arrived, Abby relinquished the scene as soon as she brought them up to speed. With her head spinning, she would only impede their progress. Belclare deserved the best from their police department.

Trudging back across the street, she could almost hear the gossip chasing her. The graffiti on the welcome sign was bad enough. As word spread about Calder she'd be lucky if Mayor Scott didn't fire her at the next town council meeting.

He didn't exactly have the authority, but that wouldn't stop the posturing. And the posturing would weaken her position. Reaching her front door, she glanced back over her shoulder one last time, but the view of Calder's house was blocked by Riley's wide shoulders. "What are you doing?"

"Relax." He rubbed a hand gently across her shoulder,

making her want to lean in for a hug. "I was going to help you clean up the kitchen."

"No, thanks. You've done more than enough to help me tonight." This time she *was* praising him and he shuffled his feet, apparently uncomfortable with the compliment. Interesting.

"Let's try again tomorrow." He signaled to the Hamiltons' house. "At my place."

She sighed. Being around her wasn't smart. The vandals and Calder's attacker proved that. "I can't tell if you're brave or a glutton for punishment."

"A guy could say the same about you," he replied with a grin.

No. Most men said different things about her. Aside from Deke, Riley was the first man who seemed to see beyond her title and badge. She caught the flash of cameras across the street and hoped her detectives were coming up with something useful.

"Tomorrow night I have plans." If she had the courage to explore a new path in her relationship with Deke. She'd been looking forward to the potential with the artist. Now, with a new neighbor bent on hovering, it seemed she might have a choice. Did she want one?

Right now she wanted some quiet. "Thanks for your help, Riley."

He nodded, gracing her with a slow smile she found so much more attractive than his grin. "Be sure to lock your doors."

"I think that's my line."

"Not tonight, Abby. I'm right next door if you need me."

Baffled by the temptation he presented, she escaped into her house, throwing the dead bolt and security chain. She didn't need to look to know he'd waited to be sure she locked up.

In the kitchen, she checked the lock on the back door and pulled the curtains. As she cleaned up dinner, her thoughts wandered between Deke and Riley and she told herself it was an exercise in distraction. It would be years before that horrible image of Calder under the ladder faded from her memory.

Ruthlessly, she forced her mind to lighter issues. As much as she enjoyed Deke, Riley stirred some new, previously undefined feminine flutter. Her girlfriends would blame it on the tool belt, and they might have a point. He had good hands, too, broad and strong.

And warm, she remembered, thinking of how he'd touched her when the ambulance arrived.

She was smart enough to know better, wise enough to look past the handsome face and sexy features to the man underneath. Yet she entertained a purely physical fantasy as she headed upstairs to bed.

What in the world was going on with her? The man was a stranger....

And, with an unknown enemy haunting her, a stranger was the last thing she needed in her life right now.

Chapter Six

"Sir, a call."

Deke set aside his novel. The sitting room where he chatted weekly with Abby had become his favorite place to plan and strategize. He watched the fire in the hearth, waiting until his assistant had pulled the door closed before dealing with the caller, "Yes?"

"I went by, but she had company."

"Explain," Deke replied. The news startled him at first. Abby never had company. He knew her habits as well as his own.

"I drove by with the channel open and I heard voices."

This was no cause for alarm. Her company was likely just a brief visit with her neighbor. The older woman played mother to the entire block. She would have heard about the vandalism and come by to offer moral support.

It couldn't be allowed to continue. Deke needed Abby to come to him. He'd been waiting for hours for her to show up and cry on his shoulder—or in the manner more suitable to Abby—ask his advice. With the fear he'd incited among the citizens of her beloved town, he'd made himself her only friend in this dumpy, godforsaken place and his patience was growing thin.

"I waited and then came in closer," his employee continued. "Looks like the guy from one of those setup teams.

The one who's been working at the department. They looked pretty cozy."

The guy? Cozy? Deke's hand clutched the upholstered arm of his chair. That couldn't be possible. She wouldn't take the risk. He'd thoughtfully and carefully nurtured her paranoia to the point that she didn't trust anyone.

"Find out who he is. I want everything you can find on him."

"I'm on it."

What could she be thinking? The idea of his trophy, his *reward,* spending her time with one of the temporary workers passing through town, set his temper blazing. He didn't fight it, letting it burn, vaporizing the haze of his misplaced esteem and affection for Abigail Jensen. She was now his enemy with no potential for redemption.

"Updates every hour. I want pictures, as well."

"Already handled."

"Really?" Deke knew better than to ask how. It was satisfying to have something going right. The people he hired quickly learned about his zero tolerance for failure. He supposed he owed the man some encouragement. "This afternoon's vandalism was good work."

"Thank you."

"You can trust them to keep quiet?" Deke wondered about the misfits the man had hired to deface the town's historic welcome sign.

"I don't trust anyone that much."

"Good." It was the tacit confirmation he wanted that the vandals were dead. Dead men didn't tell tales. "I'll leave you to it."

The call ended and Deke walked to the window that overlooked the water. It was a worthy view of the quaint little town when the moon was full. Tonight it was dull and gray, the sky full of clouds. Mother Nature seemed all too willing to accommodate Belclare's hope for a fresh blanket of picturesque snow to kick off their annual event.

The only good thing about the tourist season was the potential for more victims and even more suspects. The police department would have no rest until the next shipment was safely through. And when he was done with Abigail Jensen, when she was thoroughly ruined and dead at his feet, Deke promised himself he would move from this insipid place. He wanted to find somewhere with more space and more sunshine to go with his anonymity.

With his endgame in mind, he called in his assistant and gave the next orders. Yes, a fresh blanket of snow would fit perfectly into his plan. That way the spilled blood would show up a vivid red.

Chapter Seven

Abby rushed through the back door toward her office, already an hour behind schedule and her mind a jumble of details that needed to be handled swiftly. Checking on her neighbor this morning had taken longer than she'd expected, but it had been necessary. Calder was a friend, and now, a victim. Learning who might have wanted to hurt him to get to her was essential.

Then she'd discovered someone had broken into her garage last night. Nothing appeared to be missing or damaged—except her pride, which was exactly why she had no intention of making a formal report on it. If the chief of police couldn't protect her own home, how was she going to protect the town? She shook her head. The feds would holler again about protection and security. Maybe they had a point. The extra patrols would have to be enough—the people she was responsible for in this community took priority. With any luck they'd catch the troublemaker before a security system could be installed. Maybe she was losing it? Her mind and her ability to get the job done.

No time to debate the latter. This morning's delays had cost her valuable mental prep time going into today's meeting with Mayor Scott and Martin Filmore. Sadly, she couldn't put off this potential minefield. Both men were waiting for her and came to their feet as she walked in. Their easy presence in her office made her want to shoot something.

"Good morning," she offered, not even trying to smile.

"You're fifteen minutes late," Mayor Scott said.

"I hope the sergeant made you comfortable." Based on the two cups of coffee on her desk, it looked as if they were comfortable enough.

She put her coat on the rack and set her purse to the side before taking her seat.

"Have you found the vandals?"

She'd had the entire twenty seconds of walking across the police station to read that report. "Not yet. The team posted last night didn't encounter any more trouble." She shifted her full attention to Martin. "Have you come up with plan of action for restoring the welcome sign?"

"I met with the decorating company, yes. They agreed to create a temporary sign while the original is removed and sent for restoration."

Mayor Scott cleared his throat. "The town council released the appropriate funds."

"That is good news," Abby said. "My officers have reorganized their schedules and patrol routes to—"

"Is that absolutely necessary?" Martin interrupted.

"Yes, Mr. Filmore," Abby replied, struggling for control. "As I explained yesterday, based on recent events, I believe the extra patrols are imperative to keeping this city safe. In fact, I was about to ask—" she glanced at the mayor "—for a small slice of the emergency funds to hire a few extra officers from Baltimore for the opening weekend."

"No."

She blinked at the mayor's stern response. "Excuse me?"

"We've had enough public attention of the wrong kind. The media has painted a target on Belclare. We'll be lucky if we aren't facing a ghost town this weekend. Are you trying to bankrupt our city, Chief?"

Abby clamped her mouth shut, startled by this one-hundred-eighty degree turnaround from the man who didn't believe in the concept of bad publicity. How had everything and everyone around her changed so suddenly? The answer followed hot on the heels of that question. *Fear.* The kind of fear her actions had brought to the citizens of Belclare changed people.

Nothing she could do about that. Protecting the citizens was her job. Appeasing them—if it got in the way—was not.

"I concur," Mr. Filmore added with an arrogant tilt of his chin.

Of course he concurred. These guys were the drama twins, each with a slightly differing agenda. She laced her fingers together, wishing for her own cup of coffee, but that would have to wait. "The town council will approve the overtime expenses for my officers." It wasn't a question. Fortunately for the mayor, he seemed to understand that, as well. A vague dip of his head showed acknowledgment even if he would never say as much out loud. She moved on. "My officers are not on patrol to threaten or interfere with anyone, but in our experience a vigilant, visible presence is its own deterrent."

"It didn't deter more trouble on your street last night," Filmore blurted out, his face turning red with frustration. "You all but sent out engraved invitations for every criminal to come test you. Belclare will pay the ultimate price."

She bit back the sharp retort dancing on the tip of her tongue. "What would you have me do differently, Mr. Filmore?"

His mouth flapped like a fish for several seconds. "I'm not qualified to say, but I have gumption enough to know what you've done so far isn't working." He turned to the mayor. "All I know is that what you're doing is ruining the most important time of year for our town."

Gutless wonders, both of them, she thought. Their support for her success with the drug bust had shifted with the arrival of the very first federal agent. The instant the first threat hit the airwaves she was public enemy number one with these two men.

"Well, I must admit the generous promotional spots Deke Maynard provided should go a long way to salvaging opening weekend," Mayor Scott allowed, smoothing a hand over his glaring holiday-plaid tie.

Ghost town or a decent turnout? She wished he'd pick a theory and stick with it.

On the short drive into the office, she'd only caught a teaser about Deke's upcoming call-in interview on the radio. The man rarely bothered with publicity and she knew it made him uncomfortable, but if he was in her corner, urging people to attend the Christmas Village, she owed him a big thank-you.

"Will you at least decorate the police cars?" the historic society's president asked.

"That's a favorite tradition around here, Mr. Filmore," Abby agreed. "I'll make sure someone takes care of that right away." She'd already assigned Danny to follow up on that detail, but she didn't see the need to let Filmore know she'd had the idea first. Maybe appeasing was necessary at this point.

"Thank you," he allowed.

Never an easy person to be around, Filmore fidgeted more than usual today. She chalked it up to distress over the ruination of the heirloom welcome sign on top of his disapproval of her new patrol protocol.

Both men stood. Finally. With handshakes and an exchange of "Merry Christmas," they left her alone in her office.

Turning to her computer, she found websites for the local television and radio stations. The impromptu media junket Deke had managed this morning was getting an outpouring of positive responses. The man had single-handedly muted the negative press regarding the crime wave in Belclare. Offering an additional painting for the silent auction that benefitted the Belclare Food Bank was a lure that would bring in serious tourist traffic. Maynard rarely sold his original paintings, though he displayed new work in the local gallery and occasionally chose pieces for limited commercial print runs. Abby was overwhelmed with gratitude for the man who seemed to be her only ally in town. She picked up her cell phone and dialed his number.

His assistant answered in his typical muted monotone and, moments later, Deke's voice filled her ear.

"Darling, how are you today?"

Better than Calder, she thought with no small measure of guilt. While the officers who'd taken over the search had found tracks in the snow behind the house, they'd lost the trail at the next street. "At the moment I'm out of the mayor's doghouse," she replied. "Thanks to you."

"Anything for a friend. We can't let something as silly and petty as vandals get in the way of a good tourist season."

She wished petty and silly crimes were all she had to think about. "Well, once more you've put your support into action and I'm immensely grateful."

"Does that mean you'll skip your meeting and join me this evening?"

She hesitated. Was that what she wanted it to mean? Sharing dinner with Deke would be a marvelous escape from a typical evening. She indulged in the fantasy, imagining the balm of excellent food paired with the perfect wine and intelligent conversation in front of the fireplace in his dining room. Would anything be better?

An image of those threats on the welcome sign and then on her neighbor's house blotted out her fantasy. She tried to shake it off, but the memory of Calder pinned under the ladder shivered through her.

"Abby? Are you there?"

"Yes, of course." Her palms went clammy. Calder was a good neighbor. He'd made minor repairs around her house, sometimes in exchange for only a six-pack of beer. It helped to have a neighbor like him when she didn't have time for a man in her life otherwise. Was time really the problem or was it just another excuse? She pushed the thought away and answered Deke's question. "Yes. Sorry, I'm here. As much as I'd like to join you, I'm afraid I will have to pass on dinner."

She pressed her thumb to the point between her eyebrows, hoping to ease another wave of tension. Putting off Deke after he'd done so much for her felt like an insult. At the very least it felt like she was taking him for granted. She didn't want to visit him in the hospital, either. Someone out there had made a public vow to hurt her and the people she cared about. The threats weren't going away and the problem was escalating. Whoever put the vandals and assailants in motion knew how to get under her skin. Injuring her neighbor and going through her garage were way too close for comfort. She didn't dare consider what might be next.

"Are you sure?" he pressed.

She'd offended him. "I value you, Deke," she confessed,

hoping he'd understand. "As a citizen and as a friend. Whoever wants me out of here is willing to hurt those around me to make a point. I don't want them to hurt you."

"I'm quite capable of watching out for myself," he assured her.

The tension in his voice had given way to something gentler. She could picture that barely there smile on his face. "You've done a fine job." Abby rocked back in her chair. "Will you give me a rain check on dinner?"

He sighed. "Tonight, tomorrow, next week. Whatever best suits your crime-fighting schedule. Consider the invitation open."

"Thank you. That means a great deal." And when this was behind her, she'd make up for lost time.

"Is that just the chief of police talking?"

"No." Was he flirting with her? "True friends seem hard to find under the current circumstances."

"I'm here for you, Abby."

She felt her cheeks heat with his steady reassurance. Thank goodness, they weren't having this talk in person. What was it about this man that made her waffle so much? One minute she wanted him to be more than a friend, the next she wasn't so sure. "I'll be in touch, Deke. Thank you again for going above and beyond for opening weekend. Please be careful and call in if you need any assistance."

"Always. You do the same."

"Definitely." She was smiling when the call disconnected and it felt genuine for the first time in ages. This nonsense in the media and with whomever had decided to terrify her town had only started a little over a week ago, but she couldn't deny the stress was taking a toll.

She checked the time. It was too soon to expect any news from the officers who'd come by when she'd found her garage door hanging open. With little more than half an hour before the hardware store opened for business, she decided to check her email. Buying a new lock for the garage wouldn't be a high point of her day, but she needed it secure for her peace of mind. And a new snow shovel to deal with the fresh snow predicted for this evening. Hers had been taken to the crime lab to analyze what had appeared to be dried blood on the blade. The idea that someone had *borrowed* her snow shovel and used it for something untoward was a little out there, as theories went, but considering the other strange happenings around here lately she wasn't taking any chances.

Half an hour would be enough time to review the overflowing email in-box and send any threat with a clear target up the line to the feds.

Braced for more hateful messages, she set to work.

RILEY TURNED DOWN the volume on the radio clipped to his ladder. All of Belclare was enamored with Deke Maynard and his unflinching support of Chief Jensen. It was the third time this morning he'd heard the new ad for the Christmas Village opening weekend.

The artist—in his mind he added a sneer to the word—made him edgy. There was more going on behind the sparkling windows of the man's perfectly restored home. A great deal more than the sketches and scenic oils on canvas displayed with such care in the gallery window down the street evoked.

Riley knew his role here. He understood that he couldn't jump at every shadow while he was learning the landscape. This wasn't a short game Casey had him playing.

That didn't necessarily rule out the immediate trouble closing in on Chief Jensen. Filmore, the uptight snob who wanted to lift the added patrols, particularly the foot patrols, was near the top of Riley's list. The man's priorities were way off. Being passionate about architecture and history was fine. But what kind of person preferred historical accuracy over the safety of the general public?

A man with something to hide, in Riley's opinion. Or something more to gain.

In less than two days, the Christmas Village would be hosting the first major rush of tourists for the season. So far, he hadn't pinpointed a clear threat, but someone was ramping up the effort against the chief.

According to Danny, Chief Jensen was spending an inordinate amount of time behind closed doors since the drug bust, sorting out the loonies from the more substantial threats that were flooding the station's snail mail and email every day. Chief Jensen sent high-level threats to the feds for further analysis. Anything Director Casey could tie to Belclare, he sent back to Riley, but so far, no hard intel had come his way.

He'd overheard people whispering about the vandalism and the attack on Calder; however, there weren't any leads beyond wild speculation and fingers pointing at him and the other temporary workers in town. The easy theory wasn't close to accurate when it came to him and he didn't suspect any of his co-workers. But in a community as close as Belclare it was far more comfortable and convenient to blame outsiders.

Whoever was behind the trouble was using human nature to their advantage. Surely a cop as smart as Jensen wouldn't have settled for that lousy, easy explanation. But Riley wondered why the person or group behind all this thought she would.

He took his assignment for the day—the hardware store on Main Street—and knocked it out in record time with the help of two other guys from the crew.

While they tested lights and put the final touches on

the displays, Riley casually observed the people watching them. There was decent foot traffic in the business center of town and for the most part people were cautiously friendly. He might have a lifetime assignment here, but it wouldn't be a hardship. It wasn't as if he had family or a significant other waiting somewhere else. He could see a place like this being home.

With a few minutes before the next load of decorations from the warehouse was due, he walked into the hardware store to look around. An agent's best asset was a thorough knowledge of the situation.

"Welcome, welcome," an older woman behind the counter greeted him. "You look like a man who needs a new pair of gloves."

He pulled his cold, red hands from the pockets of his vest and blew on them a little. "I don't use gloves with close work like this."

"Well, that's understandable," she allowed. "Take your time and warm up some anyway."

"That wind can be a bear," he said, hoping he sounded friendly. He wanted to get her talking. Listening to the chatter among the locals was another excellent tool for assignments like this one.

"Part of the charm this close to the water," she replied with a twinkle in her bright blue eyes. "Only the tough ones stick it out. Will you be moving on soon?"

He hesitated at the aisle with bins of nails and fasteners stretched out on either side. "I might be around a while." He shot her a grin. "I'll get used to the charm. And I already have another job lined up in Belclare when the decorations are done."

"That's good news, I suppose."

Riley recognized the curiosity in her voice. She was

interested in his wallet as well as his purpose. He'd happily use that lead-in. "I think so."

"That company you're working for knows your plans?"

He stepped up to the counter, ready to play the gossip game. "They know I earn every penny of what they pay me and that's enough."

"Hmm."

He stuck out his hand. "Riley O'Brien," he said. "Do you handle special orders?"

The older woman's eyes lit up. "Of course. Peg Blackwell, at your service."

"Pleased to meet you, Ms. Blackwell."

"Peg."

Riley acknowledged the correction with a quick nod. "I find myself in need of—"

The bell over the door jingled, interrupting the request he'd been about to make. He found himself in need, but the context changed at the sight of Chief Jensen. He glanced at Peg, wondering if she'd hit a silent alarm to summon the chief when he'd walked in. Did he look that suspicious?

"Good morning, Peg," Abby called, wiping her feet on the doormat.

"Chief," the lady behind the counter replied.

Riley surveyed his assignment. The chief looked overdressed for a hardware store, in a soft Christmas-red sweater and charcoal slacks with heeled boots far too dressy for the weather. Her cheeks were bright pink from the cold and a wisp of blond hair had escaped from her ponytail and caught in her lip gloss.

He struggled to ignore the feelings she roused in him. Yes, he'd been sent to protect her, but he was taking her safety much too personally—in record time at that.

Behind the counter, Peg's demeanor shifted and she gave off a vibe as cold as the biting wind outside. No love lost between these two, Riley decided, wondering if it was just the recent trouble or if their problems went deeper. Not everyone in town was a potential terrorist, but someone was the ringleader of all the trouble falling on Belclare and the police chief.

"Good morning, Mr. O'Brien."

He corrected her with a slow shake of his head.

She sighed and tucked a wayward lock of hair behind her ear. "Good morning, Riley. Is that your work out front?"

"It sure is," Peg volunteered.

"I had some help along the way," he said.

"It looks good." Abby gifted him with a smile.

"Thanks." He gave her a small bow. "I was about to look over some wood stain options while I wait for the next decorating assignment."

"Aisle three, near the corner," Peg suggested warmly. Her tone dropped several degrees when she spoke to the chief. "What brings you by?"

Riley ambled away, visions in his head of the options for the kitchen while he eavesdropped on the women at the counter.

"I need a new lock set for my garage," Abby said. "And a snow shovel."

Questions rattled through Riley's head and he hoped Peg would ask them. He hadn't spotted any problems at her place before he'd driven in to work.

"Was it frozen?" Peg asked. "You could've asked Calder to have a look. That is, if he wasn't in the hospital."

Ah, so that was the crux of it. Peg and Calder were friends and the lady was blaming the chief for his injury. Wasn't fair. Abby hadn't scrawled that threat on the guy's house and she hadn't pushed over the ladder. None of this was her fault. Whether these people wanted to face it or not, trouble was brewing in their idyllic little town. The only thing Abby was guilty of was drawing it to the surface.

"Not frozen. Just broken. I guess it wasn't as sturdy as it should have been."

He admired Abby's patience with the constant doubt and irritation. Compared to the threats he knew she was receiving, a little grumpiness must feel like a cakewalk. Riley listened as Peg led Abby to the correct aisle for locks.

"Front of the store for the shovel," Peg explained, sounding friendlier in Riley's opinion. "They're calling for a couple of inches tomorrow night."

He couldn't hear Abby's answer as the women walked farther from him, but Peg came to his rescue with a startled explanation that carried through the store.

"Good grief. Are you okay?"

Abby must have answered in the affirmative because suddenly Peg's tone changed again. "I respect what it takes to do your job, young lady, but your mouth has put us all in a world of hurt."

Riley started across the store, ready to leap to Abby's defense. He couldn't be the only person in Belclare who recognized her decisions were rooted in her unflagging dedication.

"What happened?" he demanded, ignoring the way Abby jumped at his interruption. "Did the crime-scene techs find something at Calder's place?"

"No." Abby cleared her throat. "Someone broke the lock on my garage. It's nothing to worry about."

"I don't think so," Riley challenged. "You live right next door to me. If there's some twisted prowler in our neighborhood, I'd like to know how to help you catch him."

Peg's jaw dropped, her expression shifting from disapproval to shock. *Good.* The citizens of Belclare should realize Abby Jensen was doing her job and doing it well. At great personal risk. She might have tossed out an ultimatum in the heat of victory over the drug bust, but he couldn't be the only person around here capable of seeing how she was backing it up. Or trying to.

The email brief he'd read this morning detailed chatter about another drug shipment heading this way. It would likely come through the docks, but there were plenty of vendors descending on the town, as well. In short, the suspect pool was growing instead of shrinking. The situation was overwhelming for a department as small as Abby's.

"I can do it," Abby said.

"That's obvious," Riley agreed, "but we can all use a little help sometimes." She frowned at him so he barreled on with a subject change. "Looks like you're dressed for another press conference. I'll get the lock fixed while you deal with whatever is already on your schedule."

Her frown deepened to a scowl. "What do you know about how I dress?"

"YouTube is everywhere," he said, shooting her a grin. "I keep up with local events. And I heard the ads that artist guy in town put out this morning."

"Deke Maynard?" Her frustration turned to confusion. "What about him?"

"That's the one." He held out his hand. "You'll back up his good publicity with another statement, right?"

She nodded. "Sure. Of course."

"Thought so. Since you have your hands full keeping the peace and chasing the bad guys, give me the lock." When she dropped it into his hand he barely stifled a cheer. "Now, what happened to your snow shovel?"

"We bagged it and sent it to the lab. I don't know that there's anything to officially report as of yet." She shrugged. "For that matter, the material on the blade may not have been blood, but I'll feel better when I've confirmed one way or the other. I'm optimistic since we haven't heard about any victims lying around."

"Give it time," Peg muttered under her breath as she headed back toward the sales counter. "Will that be cash or charge?"

"Cash," Abby said, following her. "Thanks for your help, Peg."

"Anytime." The older woman's demeanor had softened a bit more.

"You're sure you have time for this, Riley?" Abby asked him.

He nodded, hearing the distinct groan of the brakes on the truck he was expecting from the warehouse. "I'll take care of it as soon as I get home."

"The department is running an extra patrol around our street," Abby warned. "Be prepared to let them know you're helping me out."

"Sure thing."

She paid for her purchases, but he carried them out to his truck after she left. Knowing she hadn't assaulted anyone, he wondered who wanted her out of the way so badly they'd resort to planting evidence in her garage. And why hadn't she wanted to file an official report about it?

The bigger question remained: What else could he do to stay close enough to protect her?

Chapter Eight

Frustrated after her security meeting with the Christmas Village vendors, Abby drove home, the hard-rock music pumped as high as she dared. Just as she'd been walking out of her office, the crime lab had called. They identified the tissue on the blade of her snow shovel as human, but it was too early to have any results back on DNA that might match up with evidence in the various databases. The relevant concern was the traces of spray paint in the hair fibers.

She'd vowed to keep this town safe no matter the cost. It wouldn't take much media speculation to convince people she'd taken justice into her own hands. She would never kill someone over graffiti, but just the rumor of it could ruin her career. There was no way to keep the incident off the record now. In fact, her hasty decision could work against her.

God, she was tired.

Gadsden had taken her report, but they both knew being at home in bed alone wasn't enough of an alibi even for a police chief. She'd earned a bit of sympathy and leeway because of the threats raining down on her head, but at some point last night or early this morning, someone with evil intent had been close enough to break in and plant evidence on her snow shovel. Damn it, this was exactly why she needed a dog. But what dog wanted a home with a human who was rarely there?

Her emotions had run the gamut from shock to vengeance as she'd waded through the rest of her crappy day. Someone was screwing with her and she vowed to get to the bottom of it.

Her press conference had gone well, thanks to the unexpected personal appearance of their resident celebrity. Deke hadn't said anything, but he certainly was going out of his way to help her weather the storm. She appreciated that, but siding with her so publicly put him right in the line of fire. As much as she appreciated his support, she worried he would regret giving it. On some level, she understood this was his way of showing he cared. She suspected he didn't do that often. Whether that made her special or not, she wasn't clear on just yet. Her and Deke's relationship— friendship, whatever it was—was complicated.

The worst part was that other than a few reporters she didn't recognize, most of the folks who'd showed up to watch the press conference in person were lifelong residents of Belclare.

In the days following the drug bust, she found herself looking twice at people she'd known for years. Wondering what was going on behind closed doors—or worse—closed minds. It didn't help that she saw the same dark curiosity in the community as people looked at each other. And at her.

It seemed common sense and yet support was too much to ask for these days. Even Peg had been nearly hostile about the recent problems and potential economic fallout. The department received more calls every day from concerned citizens sure the various outsiders helping with the Christmas Village were causing the trouble. Soothing those worries was only dragging down morale at the station, but she didn't know how to turn things around.

Abby had to admit, in the quiet of her car, that she wasn't very accepting of the few people who were offering support to her and her department. It seemed business owners like Peg were siding with Mayor Scott's opinion that she'd gone too far and put everyone's livelihood in jeopardy. Deke had probably saved opening weekend, but that didn't get her off the hook. The mayor clearly wanted her to do more to smooth the ruffled feathers.

At the light, she debated driving up and thanking Deke personally. But knowing how much he valued his privacy, she headed home instead. No sense alienating him, too, just because she wanted a shoulder to lean on. And though he'd invited her to dinner once more when the media had dispersed, he'd done enough for her today.

Thoughts of Deke's shoulder slipped right out of her mind as she turned onto her street. Her neighbors had been busy while she'd been sorting through threats, suspects and a frightening lack of witnesses. Christmas lights outlined roofs and shrubs; lawn ornaments featuring scenes from reindeer pulling sleighs to gentle nativities glowed on snow-dusted lawns.

But the gas lamp posts in each yard… Wow! Who had managed to get all of the neighbors to do that? Parking in her driveway, she got out of her car and admired the effect of wide red and white ribbons that turned each lamp post into a candy cane. Even hers. Happiness washed over her that whoever had come up with the idea had automatically included her. The effect was unifying yet neutral enough that it didn't fight with the individual displays each family preferred. Belatedly, she noticed that even the tall generic streetlights at each end of the block were similarly decorated.

With the heart of Belclare becoming a Christmas Village each year, the residential areas joined in, too. It was a friendly competition within each neighborhood. Exhausted or not, she needed to get her own yard decorated before her neighbors gave up on her.

It had been smart to avoid dinner with Deke, and not just for his protection. She needed a hefty dose of something normal. With a smile for her decorated lamppost, she turned to face her house, thinking about what she could get done tonight. Deep down, part of her was still turning over the puzzle of who had broken into her garage and planted evidence.

The troubling thought had her whipping back around to have another look at Calder's house. The lights were up across the roofline and draped over the shrubs. While many homes on her street went with white lights, for the past three seasons Calder and Libby deferred to their young daughter and created a colorful display. The inflatable snow globe was new, as was the Santa Stop Here sign on the chimney.

Calder couldn't have done that. She'd visited with him in the hospital at lunchtime and the doctors didn't plan to release him before tomorrow. Libby was pregnant. Abby sighed. She supposed another neighbor had stepped in. Not surprising.

"You like it? I thought the stop sign was a nice touch."

Riley O'Brien had rounded the front corner of Calder's house. He gestured to the tiny white icicle lights dripping prettily from the roofline. He'd wrapped the front windows with wide ribbon as if they were packages. That trademark grin spread across his face. The sleeves of his flannel shirt were rolled up. He held a tape measure in his hands and his tool belt slung low across his lean hips. He looked exactly like the carpenter he claimed to be.

Realization dawned on her. "This is all your doing, isn't it?"

He shrugged one shoulder. "I finished work early. I was bored."

She surveyed Calder's house again. The view was safer than staring with fascinated interest at her new neighbor. "Tell me you had help." After last night, she didn't like the idea of anyone working on a ladder alone. Not so close to where she lived anyway.

"Peg and Danny helped. Plus a few of the kids after the school bus dropped them off. It was a team effort."

Danny wasn't much more than a kid himself, so that made sense. "Peg?" Abby felt her jaw drop. "You're kidding." After the deep freeze she'd given Abby today, she was surprised the woman came anywhere near here. But, then, Calder was her friend, too.

"Not at all," Riley assured her. "Peg came over to take a look at the kitchen and talk flooring. She did all the gas lamps. I think she got a kick out of pitching in."

"Peg," Abby repeated dumbly. It seemed impossible that the woman had decorated anywhere near Abby's house rather than pummel it with eggs. "You're like the Pied Piper," Abby said with a shake of her head, "the way you get people to cooperate."

"The nuns said Tom Sawyer, but it's about the same, I guess." He gave another careless hitch of his shoulder.

"Nuns?" Now she was really confused.

His gaze shifted to Calder's place and back to her. "My teachers. Irish parents, remember? Catholic school's practically a requirement. Our school did a lot of community outreach like repair work and local theater. We learned early that jobs were easier when more people got involved."

"Well, it doesn't matter what they said then, I'm grateful to you now. It looks beautiful."

"I thought the street could use a mood lifter."

"You thought right."

He walked over and held up a shiny brass key. "Your

lock is repaired and the new snow shovel is right inside the door."

"Thanks," she said, pulling out her key ring. Anything to keep her from gawking at the man making such a positive impact around her town. All evidence pointed to him as an asset, one of the good guys, but she couldn't help wondering if she was being a fool to trust him so easily.

He tucked his hands into his pockets. "Any leads?"

"On which case?"

He shrugged. "Any or all of them."

"No leads on anything. At this point, I'm lucky I still have a job."

"It's not your fault Belclare is under siege."

She shook her head, tired of making zip for progress. "Under siege feels about right." Abby indulged in a heartfelt sigh. "Unfortunately."

As she'd gone through her day, his words had been in the back of her mind. Who would gain the most if she was gone or if she even backed down? There was no clear answer, but she knew he was right. The question had her considering almost everyone in town as a threat again. A position that danced on the edge of paranoia.

"How's Calder?"

She turned, feeling her lips curve in a relieved smile. "Healing quickly enough to give the nursing staff a hard time." She pulled out her phone to take a picture of his house. "He'll be thrilled when he sees this."

"Peg already did that," Riley said.

"Oh." She lowered her phone, feeling silly. "Of course she did."

"I'm sure he wouldn't mind another one. All lit up at night it's even better."

"True." She snapped the picture and sent it to Calder.

"Well, I'd better get busy with my own yard or I'll get the Grinch award."

"Seriously? They give those out?"

"Well, it's not an official thing." She raised her arms wide, indicating the whole block. "But it's real enough and I'm obviously way behind. When you live in Belclare, holiday spirit is kind of required."

"Let me help."

She waved an arm, indicating the entire block. "You've done plenty."

He looked at her house, his eyes crinkling at the corners. "You'll need a ladder."

She clenched her teeth against the memory of last night. "There are other options." She could just string lights over the bushes and around the doorway. A couple wreaths on the shutters would help. It wouldn't be an award-winning display, but it would be enough. Maybe she'd pick up an inflatable ornament this year.

"I don't think so. Whatever you have planned, you're not working out here alone. Come with me."

She automatically fell into step behind him, before she caught herself. "Wait. Who made you boss of the evening?"

When he turned, his mouth was twitching. "Which one of us is current on holiday decorating skills?"

"I have plenty of experience."

"Great. Tell me what you want done and where the decorations are stored and I'll do it for you. Even my boss says I'm the fastest guy on the team this year."

No surprise. She'd heard nothing but praise when she'd called the company and checked up on him. "Congratulations, but helping me isn't necessary."

He stopped short right in the middle of their driveways and she nearly barreled into his chest. She sort of wished she had.

"Necessary or not, that's how it's going to be, Abby."

The way he said her name made her feel like a completely different person. It made her want to step away from official roles and just be…herself. At least a slightly more relaxed version of herself. More like the person she'd been before the fallout from the drug bust.

"I wouldn't do anything differently," she said.

"Do you have a picture of how you did things before?"

"Yes, but I didn't mean the decorations," she clarified. "I was thinking about the drug bust."

He rocked back on his heels and crossed his arms. She didn't understand how he could look so comfortable in the chill of the evening in only his thermal and flannel shirts, jeans and boots. Maybe the tool belt had a heater built in. The thought that maybe *he* was the heater made her shiver.

Every time she saw him, he reinforced her growing opinion that he was a friendly, competent and kind man. The type of man a woman would be lucky to know. And that was the crux. Knowing her, being around her, could prove extremely unlucky for him. "You should just go on inside and take a break. I can handle it."

"No." He shook his head resolutely.

"Riley, please."

He leaned down into her face until they were nearly nose to nose. "You're stuck with my help. Deal with it."

She could see the flecks of gold in his brown eyes. Her gaze drifted lower, to his mouth. His lips tipped up at one corner and she forced her eyes back to his before he could tease her with that wicked grin. It didn't help. He was staring at her mouth. She licked her lips, wondering how he would kiss. Slow and easy? Quick and hard? She'd be happy with either. Both even.

She stepped back before she gave in and found out. She didn't want him to get hurt because some unidentified terrorist wanted to make her suffer. But he wasn't backing down. Did that make him foolish or her careless for appreciating it?

"Okay. Fine."

He straightened. "Glad you understand. Now, will you show me where you store the decorations?"

She tipped her head back toward the garage. "In the loft."

"All right." He walked to the bed of his truck and unlocked the storage bin on one side. "I'm grabbing a couple of work lights."

"Good idea." It would be dark as pitch in that garage loft.

She walked on back to the garage and tested out the key he'd given her for the new lock. It felt solid and worked smoothly. She expected nothing less. Everywhere he'd been in Belclare, people commented on his friendliness as well as his expertise with all kinds of odd jobs.

Inside, she flipped the switch, grateful for the light. The narrow space was big enough for her car, but she rarely parked in here, thinking it offered her neighbors a sense of security when she left the official sedan out in the driveway. After what happened to Calder, her neighbors probably felt differently now.

"Thinking about this morning?"

She wanted to kick something but checked the urge. "I don't understand why anyone would so obviously plant evidence like that."

"To get under your skin."

"Well, it's working. But I'm not letting these scumbags make me doubt what's right."

"Good." He walked past her and reached for her stepladder, carrying it over to access the loft.

The clatter of the aluminum as he opened it and the legs settling securely on the cement floor made her swear.

"You okay?"

"I'm angry." She drew in a big, deep breath. Didn't help. "Calder's an innocent bystander. Why don't they just come at me?"

"A broken lock and planted evidence sounds to me like they are," Riley said, climbing up a few rungs of the ladder until he could read the labels on the plastic boxes stored there. "Which ones do you want me to bring down?"

"The red box of wreaths and the green box of lights should do it."

"You're sure?"

"I can always add more when things settle down."

His laughter bounced around the garage. "All things considered, I wouldn't count on that happening anytime soon."

She took the red box he handed down and set it on the floor. "Meaning?"

"Don't jump all over me for stating the obvious." He propped the green box on his shoulder as he came down the ladder. "Someone wants to get even with you or at least make a point that they're above your attempts to enforce the law."

If only she could figure out who. "We've been over all the evidence in the drug bust, interviewed all the employees and anyone resembling a witness." As he replaced the ladder on the hooks, she picked up the red box and led the way out to the front yard. Riley followed with the heavier bin full of lights. "And we're no closer to unraveling who's really behind it all."

She opened the bins and pulled out the pictures she'd taken of last year's display while he plugged in the work lights.

He peered over her shoulder at the pictures, looked back at her house and then laughed.

"It looks that bad to your expert eye?" she asked, annoyed just a little.

"Not at all," he said, taking a step back. "I've just never seen anyone so—" he shrugged "—organized."

"Your dad taught you to swing a hammer—mine taught me to plan and document." His face clouded over, but before she could ask him anything, he motioned for the paper and pictures.

"You want the same setup?" He glanced from the pictures to the bins at their feet to the front of her house.

"It's simple, but pretty. No one complains." She'd thought the wreaths on the shutters had framed her Christmas tree in the front window rather nicely last year. And the lit evergreen garland around her front door tied it all together.

"All right. Give me an hour."

"I don't believe in double standards. We're doing this together." The teamwork wasn't just about safety.

"Want me to wait while you change clothes?"

"I'll just get my boots from the back door. Give me a second."

As they worked, she discovered she liked the company of the new guy in town. Give him time, she bemoaned, and he'd learn to hate her, too. Irritated with her uncharacteristic self-pity, she pulled out the garland for the door and its extension cord. She plugged it in, confirmed the lights were working and then handed the garland to him. "You should be able to reach this without the ladder."

He arched an eyebrow but followed her over and, as she'd said, centered the garland on the hook above the door frame. When it was positioned to his satisfaction, she plugged it in again and smiled. "Perfect."

"Thanks." He took a theater-worthy bow. "What's next?"

"I'll start lighting the shrubs if you hang the wreaths on the shutters."

"Deal."

Under the glare of the work lights they finished transforming her home in record time. He made a few little changes and she liked the improved overall effect. "You are good at this," she said as he packed up the work lights.

"I've had plenty of practice these past few days."

She stacked the empty bins together and returned them to the garage.

"I drove down Main Street this afternoon," she said when she found him waiting for her in the driveway. "It looks amazing, a step up from last year."

"That's what the boss asked for. I bet it's even prettier when it's lit up at night," he said. "Want to go for a drive?"

She did. Desperately. The intensity scared her. "Aren't you tired of Christmas lights and holiday displays by now?"

"Aren't you tired of police work?"

"A little," she confessed, startling a laugh out of both of them.

"Take a drive with me. I'll buy you a drink."

"Didn't you offer to fix me dinner?"

He unhooked his tool belt and stowed it in the truck. "Maybe I'll let a professional handle it tonight. I wouldn't want to overwhelm you with all my talents at once."

"You're a terrible flirt."

"So I've been told." He winked, opening the passenger door of his truck for her.

"No, I mean you're really bad at it."

"You want me to up my game?"

Yes. No. Uncertain, she pulled the door shut. When he slid into the driver's seat she said, "I don't want any games. I want you to be yourself."

"Easy enough." He stared at her for a moment that went on and on and she realized she was holding her breath. "What you see is what you get, Abby."

How did he do that? How did he make her feel so wanted

and alive with just a few words? She tried to analyze it, to view him as she might a suspect, searching for motive, but she couldn't quite pin him down. His body language screamed sincere interest, she knew that much. And yet he was utterly unflappable about the attraction sparking between them.

"I heard you had an inside tip on the shipment," he asked as they left the serenity of their street behind.

"That's the popular rumor."

"It isn't true?"

She shook her head. Telling him the truth would be stupid, but the one thing they didn't have was a fresh perspective. The man had serious people skills.

"You've met quite a few people in Belclare," she said.

"Are you saying I've met your informant?"

"I just told you there wasn't one. Why are you so curious about it?"

He outlined the steering wheel with his fingertips as they waited for a red light to change. "I'm more curious about how you operate. You're obviously dedicated to the job and that's good for the community. These threats are affecting everyone and that doesn't sit right with me. Cowards who use the innocent irritate me."

"Right there with you on that one."

"You must have some ideas on suspects."

"After what happened to Calder, I suspect the worst. Of everyone," she clarified. "It's problematic."

He turned onto Main and she seized on the distraction, admiring an elaborate new sleigh full of gifts, towed by reindeer in brilliant harnesses and flanked by decorated trees. "Wow," she whispered. "The tourists are going to eat this up."

"Wait until you see how the park turned out."

"Let's go look." She twisted around in the seat, hoping to catch a glimpse as they passed the intersection.

"Right after we eat. The decorations will be there all month."

RILEY WAS A little surprised Abby didn't argue more as he found an open parking space in the lot behind the pub he'd checked out a couple of nights ago. He shut off the truck's engine and pulled the key from the ignition. Before he could reach for his door, she stopped him, her hand light on his arm. He frowned. "What's wrong?"

"Just think it through," she answered. "You've said you want to stay in Belclare."

He nodded. "Right. I showed you the signed lease."

"That's my point, Riley. Having dinner with me could create long-term problems for you."

His thoughts turned dark at the implication. A woman with her stellar record and dedication shouldn't have to put up with this kind of crap. Not from the community and not from the lowlifes who wanted to exploit her concern for that community. "Are you hungry?"

"Yes," she said, her mouth curving into a soft smile. "But I have plenty of food at home."

He wondered what she'd do if he just kissed her the way he wanted to. His feelings were unexpected and unprofessional, but that didn't lessen the desire. Thinking about the way she'd looked at him earlier, he considered capitalizing on a relationship to stay close to her, but if she ever discovered his real identity and purpose it would hurt her. He didn't know her well, but he could tell she put stock in honesty and even his secrets were lies.

Tell her the truth, a voice echoed in the back of his mind. He wished it were that simple.

She didn't deserve the shock and pain of discovering

what he was. Or rather, what he wasn't. He didn't want to give her any more reasons to second-guess her instincts. He didn't want to be one more source of anxiety and disappointment.

"Well, too bad," he said resolutely. "We're here now. It's not my business what other people think any more than it's theirs what I think or do."

"It's not just what they think—"

"It's what the people behind the threats will do. I get it."

"And you don't care?"

"Oh, I care." It surprised him how much he cared. About his job, her, even Belclare as a whole. "I've been in stressful situations before."

"Care to elaborate?"

"Not out here." He shot her another grin, the one he'd learned distracted her. It worked again, as her eyes landed like a caress on his lips. "I'll be fine, Abby, no matter the fallout."

She was right. Heads turned as they entered the pub and found a small table near the scarred oak bar. "That thing could use some attention," he said.

"I think they call it character."

"Yeah, well, sometimes people forget the 'care' part of character."

A smile bloomed on her face. "Are you set on remodeling the whole town?" she asked after the waitress took their drink order.

"Of course not. Fixing things is just in my blood."

She seemed to mull over that statement for a moment before firing the next question. "Will your parents visit? I'm sure they'd be thrilled with what you've done."

He was granted a short reprieve as their drinks and a basket of the pub's hand-cut potato chips arrived. Lying was critical to his success here. It was absolutely essential to keeping her safe and finding the culprits behind the threats. So why was he fighting it so hard?

He steered the conversation to simpler topics while he stewed over his predictable nature. This need for attachment and approval had been a problem for as long as he could remember.

He understood it was a product of being an orphan with no clear understanding of his real past. Making up his history had been amusing and no one knew enough to correct his theories. Some days he'd been the son of humble farmers, other days he had superhero blood in his veins.

In no small measure, he'd found a working solution as one of Director Casey's Specialists. He'd become part of a professional family where the past didn't matter. Together, learning from the best operatives and support techs, they'd been able to accomplish tasks other law enforcement teams couldn't.

Now he was out here on his own. An island once more. Casey had asked him to think this through. Riley wondered if his mentor had anticipated this sort of emotional blowback.

"What's bothering you?"

He looked up from his plate into Abby's concerned face. "Just thinking about my parents," he said. It was true enough. Being an adult didn't change his curiosity about where he'd come from. "You're right. They would be proud of the work I've done here."

She smiled. "Will you invite them?"

"You just want more tourist traffic," he teased. "I've sent pictures. They don't travel much this time of year." Riley didn't want to think about the kind of failure that would bring his professional parent, Thomas Casey, to Belclare.

"You'll have to let me know what they think."

"Sure."

From her purse, he heard her phone chime. "Do you have them send those 24/7?"

"Right now I do. Just a traffic dispatch." She leaned forward, lowering her voice. "I'm worried about this weekend. We received threats against specific targets today."

"They damn well better not mess with our display in the park. I worked hard on that."

Her smile didn't quite reach her eyes. "The park. The police station. The docks. Homeland Security called me again, but I don't have anything new to tell them."

"If they're so worried, they should send you some manpower."

Her eyes went wide and her head bobbed up and down. "That's what I said. Belclare citizens check out. I know it has to be someone close, but I've turned over every stone and double-checked every rumor. We aren't getting closer."

"You will."

"After what happened to Calder...well, I can't help but think of worst-case scenarios."

"That's natural."

"I know. Deke's publicity efforts likely saved opening weekend, but I don't want some sick group turning the happy crowds into victims and ruining everything."

He reached over and caught her hand. "People are resilient. Even if the worst happens, the town will rally behind you."

"More likely they'll rally with cheers and confetti at my going-away party."

"I don't believe that. Everyone I talk to likes you."

She narrowed her gaze, assessed him. "You're lying."

He cleared his throat. "I didn't say they liked your victory speech."

"Nice," she said, pulling her hand away as if she just realized they were touching. *In public.*

"I don't know much about your line of work, but if you ever need someone to bounce theories off, I can listen."

"Thanks."

He heard the sincerity in that single word and wished he could offer her more assurances. His own searches into the backgrounds of those who were most outspoken hadn't turned up any clear connection to known terrorists.

Everyone at the top said this was a sleeper cell. If it was true, whoever they'd planted here in Belclare had been provided with a rock-solid cover. He didn't care for the grim parallel that made to his situation. The food arrived and he decided to forget work long enough for them to actually enjoy what they'd come here for—dinner.

"Great." She stared at her phone, looking like someone had sucker punched her.

"More trouble?" His senses went on alert.

"You could say that. They found a match for the DNA on my snow shovel."

"Can you talk about it?"

"I probably shouldn't." She swiped at her phone, then raised her blue eyes to meet his. "It appears to have been used against a guy with a long and impressive rap sheet."

"Someone in Belclare has an impressive rap sheet?"

"No." She scowled at her phone another minute or two while he wolfed down more of his burger. "This guy's current address is a morgue in Baltimore. Preliminary cause of death is head trauma."

Alarms went off in Riley's mind. The implications of that were pretty dangerous for her.

"I should get to the office." She looked longingly at her plate, clearly irritated by the idea of leaving her dinner unfinished. "I love these burgers, but my appetite is gone." She grimaced and tossed her phone back into her purse.

"It won't wait until morning?"

She shook her head. "I need to head this off with the Baltimore P.D."

He agreed 100 percent. Someone was trying to set her up for murder. The why was an easy guess. If she was in legal trouble it would get her out of the way. But who needed her out of the way and what did they have planned when they succeeded? Planting evidence of a crime was a potential goal of its own. Make the chief look guilty and muddy her reputation, lessen the *good* and the impact of her big takedown.

That effort would prove impotent. Abby was one of the most recognized and respected people in town. Unless time of death was the middle of the night, it was likely someone in Belclare could offer her an alibi. As her neighbor, he could easily vouch for the times that her car came and went from the driveway between their houses.

"Are you worried?"

Her blue eyes narrowed at him. "Are you asking if I did it?"

He snorted. "I know you didn't do it."

She leaned back and crossed her arms over her chest. "Care to explain how it is you're so certain? I haven't even given you any details."

"I don't need them. You live next door and I'm a light sleeper." He leaned closer. "I'm using the bedroom on that side of the house. Your car didn't go anywhere last night."

"You didn't happen to hear anyone busting open my garage and stealing my shovel, did you?"

"No," he confessed with a shake of his head. "They managed that sometime after I left for work."

"You think they wanted me to find it."

He shrugged. "Sure. It was a hassle for you, this morning, right?"

"It was a violation," she said, her voice hard. "Something like this could cost me my job, whether or not I'm innocent."

"Just proves my point. Whoever did it got to you, threw a wrench in your schedule, and now that you have a body to go along with the bloody shovel you have a serious, ongoing distraction from your responsibilities in Belclare."

"For a guy who's just passing through you seem to have your finger on the pulse around here."

He grinned at her. "I keep telling you I like your town. When will you believe me?"

She winced. "It may not be my town much longer."

"That's doubtful. You don't strike me as the type to go down without a fight." He winked at her. "I've seen the video that proves it."

Those bright blue eyes rolled up to the ceiling. "If I could go back in time and tell myself to shut up, I would."

He laughed. "And miss all this fun?"

A fire truck went roaring past the pub and her phone rang again.

She pulled it out of her bag, but when she read the message, all the blood drained from her face. "The police station's on fire."

He caught the waitress's attention and signaled for the check. "Let's get you over there."

"I can walk."

"Absolutely not." It might be the opening her enemies were looking for. Tossing cash onto the table, he escorted her through the pub with a hand at the small of her back.

Her poise and self-control impressed him. She carried her head high, her stride easy, but he felt the tension in her rigid posture and the tight muscles under his fingertips. Any more stressful surprises would break another person, but he didn't think Abby would snap. Not now, not ever. While he admired her fortitude, he worried that her unyielding nature would only push the culprits behind this threat to up the ante. His concerns were justified as they reached the police station and found the end of the building closest to the employee parking area engulfed in flames.

"Some days I long for a world without YouTube," she said as he parked across the street, well away from the responding firefighters.

"If the problem is a terrorist cell within Belclare, YouTube is irrelevant," he pointed out. He turned, feeling her intense gaze on him. "What?"

"Again, not sounding like a typical construction worker."

He shrugged that off. "I can read and I listen to the news. Besides, between the sign, the internet and your mention of Homeland Security, I'd have to be an ostrich not to come to that conclusion."

"Of course."

He'd made her wary again. Damn it. She was a smart woman and she must be picking up on more than his ability to connect a few dots between the details she had started to confide. "If you have questions for me I'll answer them." With the cover story, of course. This entire operation was about keeping her safe. To do that, he had to gain her trust.

She tore her gaze from the fire to study him. "I believe you would." She opened the door. "But those questions will have to wait."

He tagged along as she marched toward the fire chief supervising the process of dousing the flames. The fire chief kept her at a safe distance and, after a brief exchange, urged her toward the other cops who'd been unwillingly evicted from the police station. But she didn't move, remaining apart and scowling at the blaze lapping along the roof.

"Did he tell you anything?"

"Only that they'll have it contained shortly."

"Good to know."

Her fury was obvious. What she intended to do about it, not so much. She didn't need speculation or suggestions from the new guy in town. He couldn't decide what to do, other than his job. "I'll take you home when you're ready."

"I'm not going anywhere until the building is secure."

"I figured as much."

She finally pulled her gaze away from the fire. "You don't have to wait. One of the officers can take me home."

"Waiting isn't a problem."

After another minute or two, she stalked over to the officers who'd been ousted from their building. Riley stayed put, having a pretty good idea of how that conversation would go. Instead of following her, which felt a little clingy and intrusive, he scanned the bystanders, looking for anything remotely suspicious. Spotting Mr. Filmore standing on the other side of the fire trucks, he headed that way.

"Hello, Mr. Filmore," he said, hand extended.

The man squinted at him from behind his glasses. "Who—? Oh. You're that decorator fellow."

"That's me." Riley pushed his hands into his pockets, not surprised that Mr. Filmore refused to shake hands. People didn't come wound any tighter than the man who obsessed about the historic accuracy of every snowflake in Belclare.

"Why are you here?"

Riley wanted to ask him the same question. "I was grabbing dinner at the pub and heard the commotion." No sense giving him any ammunition to use against Abby later.

"Were you in the building?"

"Yes, of course," Filmore said, wringing his hands. "I had another issue to discuss with Chief Jensen."

"Is everything settled with the welcome sign?" It had been on the project board for this afternoon, but Riley had been with a different team at the park.

"As much as can be expected," Filmore groused. "She

has to *do* something!" He turned abruptly, the fire and emergency lights casting grim shadows across his pinched features. "This eyesore is intolerable."

Exactly what did the man think Abby should do? Apologize to the criminals and terrorists? Grab a fire hose? "You'll be surprised how fast we can clean things up. I'll pitch in. Will you?"

Filmore ignored him. "This season is doomed to fail. Belclare may never recover."

"The rest of the town looks fantastic," Riley said. "I bet Chief Jensen is already planning how to keep everyone safe for Saturday's opening."

"I know your type," Filmore said, shifting to put himself toe-to-toe with Riley. "Every year it takes more of you than last year. You say the right things, but you don't care."

Riley opened his mouth, but Filmore was on a roll.

"That building is eighty years old. I've personally overseen every so-called improvement of the past twenty-some years." The garish lights emphasized Filmore's wild eyes. "This is an unmitigated disaster all because of her!" He flung his arm in Abby's direction. "She talks safety but she's a hypocrite. That building does not deserve to suffer."

The man was starting to sound a little warped to Riley. "Take it easy, Mr. Filmore."

"Take it easy? She is single-handedly destroying this town."

Riley fought the urge to put the man out of everyone's misery. Two quiet punches and Mr. Filmore could rethink his priorities while his body learned how to function again.

Moving Filmore up on his list of potential suspects, Riley muttered some soothing nonsense in an attempt to calm the man down. Just when he thought he was making progress, Filmore launched into another tirade.

Before Riley could steer her away, Abby walked right

into Filmore's outburst. He pushed Riley aside and start-ing shouting at her.

"This is *your* fault!"

"Mr. Filmore—" she put a hand on his shoulder "—are you okay?"

He shrugged her off. "Absolutely not!"

"Would you like me to call over a paramedic?" She gave Riley a look to do it anyway.

Incensed, Mr. Filmore put himself right in her face and it took all of Riley's self-control to abide by Abby's signal to step back and let the man blow. He didn't know how Abby put up with Filmore's increasingly outrageous accusations.

"Mr. Filmore," she said when he paused for air. "I am sorry for your distress. I know how much Belclare means to you."

"You are a failure! This city has never been more un-safe. Opening weekend is ruined! The people of this town deserve better than you."

Riley moved to intervene, ready to protect either Filmore or Abby. He wasn't sure which one would need him more. The last thing he expected was for Abby to slip her arm through Mr. Filmore's as if they were the best of friends. "I understand your concern. Have you seen the park yet?"

"Of course."

"I think the decorating crew outdid themselves. Were you pleased?"

"Yes. But at this rate it will all go up in smoke tomor-row."

Riley trailed after them, unwilling to leave her alone with a nut like Filmore. Riley might suggest she keep a few of the guys he'd been working with in town as extra security. He couldn't be sure she'd accept the idea, but it could resolve part of her manpower issue. For two blocks, he considered ideas and solutions and what he had to share in his next report for Director Casey, and then they rounded the corner and all three of them stopped.

Memorial Park sat like a jewel in the heart of Belclare. The scent of fresh greenery laced the cold air and out here, the burning police station might as well be on a different planet. Logically, he knew it was the breeze from the water blowing the acrid smoke in the opposite direction, but the effect was stunning.

"Isn't this lovely, Mr. Filmore? It looks just like those pictures from the 1940s."

"It does," he allowed, his voice tight. "The decorators did well here."

Riley kept his mouth shut so he wouldn't blow the progress Abby was making.

"I agree." Abby's voice was steady and calm in the brittle air. "Tourists will love this, they'll flock here, taking pictures and making memories. Belclare will be fine."

"But the burned-out station is an eyesore," he moaned.

"You know what I didn't see at the station?"

"What?"

"I didn't see any flames on the front of the building."

Riley realized she was right. The roof had been burning as well as the back, but the facade hadn't been on fire. In fact the displays in front of the building were mostly intact.

"The police department may have to take up temporary residence at Sadie's for a few days," Abby offered, "but at first glance the tourists won't know the difference."

"You sound so sure," Filmore mumbled.

"I am. The buildings you protect so well, the structures you speak for, were here long before either of us. Thanks to your dedication, they will be here long after we're gone. Tonight's setback notwithstanding."

"You're right. I'm sorry I lost my temper."

Riley was sure he heard tears in Filmore's voice.

"These have been trying times," she added graciously, "but we'll get through it. Together."

Filmore stopped short in the middle of the sidewalk and Riley braced for trouble.

"Yes, it will take both of us to get this done," Filmore agreed. He reached over and covered her gloved hand with his. "Belclare means so much to me, Chief Jensen. My apologies."

Riley didn't like the tone and his mind ran off in conspiratorial directions over Filmore's phrasing.

But Abby just smiled at the older man. "Sometimes those things that mean the most drive us to do things we never dreamed ourselves capable of doing," she said.

"There are times for extreme measures."

"Yes." She turned them back toward Main Street, back toward the mess and destruction of the fire.

Riley noticed how the Belclare police officers had managed to spread out at even intervals, on both sides of the street.

"Sometimes when we care so much about a cause, we're willing to hurt the people and places we love," she continued.

Filmore flinched and tried to pull free of Abby's grip, but she held firm. "I don't know what you mean," he protested. "Release me."

"Mr. Filmore, I can't do that." With her free hand, she motioned to one of the men across the street. "Martin Filmore, you are under arrest for arson."

She started to read him his rights, but he interrupted. "Stop this at once. This is absurd." He rubbed his gloved hands together. "I—I was in the police station when the fire started."

"So I've been told," she said, and then continued reading his rights.

"Chief Jensen, I love that old building. You know I could never do such a heinous thing."

Riley noticed tears rolling down the older man's cheeks as he was crying in earnest now. The denials were tumbling free. If Filmore was guilty, he did a fine job portraying an emotionally distraught innocent bystander. He would have to send this up the line to Director Casey immediately.

"I know you'd never want to." Abby let him ramble as another officer stepped up to cuff him and help him gently into the back of a cruiser. With the police station on fire, where they would question him was anyone's guess.

When Filmore was gone and the firefighters finished a final walk-through, Abby returned to the truck. "You stayed."

He opened the passenger door for her. "Said I would."

"I appreciate it."

"No problem." He closed her door and walked around the hood, slid in behind the steering wheel. Throughout the ordeal, she hadn't shown any of the weariness she clearly felt now. "Why did you arrest him?"

"The officers on duty said he was squirrely and he kept eyeing my office where they believe the fire started."

Riley's jaw clenched. Everyone in town knew she frequently worked late. Did she realize Filmore might've killed her? And if she hadn't been in the office, starting the fire there would reflect badly on her, further damaging her reputation.

"On top of those circumstantial points," she continued, "he'd been at the station this morning for a meeting about the graffiti. He had access to the office and he doesn't usually bother me twice in one week, much less in a day."

Riley thought about the detonators. "Did you see him plant anything in your office?"

"No, but I was effectively distracted by a few other issues."

"Filmore strikes me as a high-maintenance kind of guy."

"If he did set the fire, and that seems likely, that makes him the kind of guy who's managed to deceive me for years." He heard the sorrow in her voice, knew she was wondering who else was fooling her. "While I'm happy to remove a problem, it's hard to wrap my head around the idea that Filmore was arranging drug deals and hurling those other threats at me."

"I can't see him toppling Calder's ladder," Riley said.

"Agreed."

"What's next?" She looked so tired he wished he could take her home.

"First a warrant for Filmore's house," she explained, her voice weary. "Then, as soon as we have any real evidence, I'll have to write up something for the feds."

"Do you want me to take you to Filmore's?"

"No. They don't need me hovering. My officers are good at what they do." She sighed and leaned her head back against the seat. "Right now I just want to get home and sink into a tub full of bubbles."

Well, there was an image that would be haunting him all night. Developments and reports could only offer so much distraction from the thought of Abby's naked body covered only by fragile bubbles. Right next door. At least, she was calling it a night. A good night's sleep would go a long way. Not that he'd be getting any shut-eye.

There were other questions he could ask, but he kept them to himself. He didn't want to pile on any more than he already had, even in the role of curious neighbor. He would leave the nosing around to Mrs. Wilks. For tonight anyway.

Arresting Filmore, admitting Homeland Security might be right about a homegrown terrorist cell operating in Belclare wouldn't be easy developments for Abby to accept. This was her town, after all. No one wanted to believe they didn't recognize evil when they saw it.

But Riley knew for certain that evil was sometimes the last suspect on the list.

Chapter Nine

The comfortable silence on the drive home soothed Abby, offering a blissful relief after the noise of the firefighters, the concerns of her officers and the erratic ramblings of Filmore. She hoped the search warrant turned up something conclusive and useful. As much as she hated the idea that Martin Filmore had fooled her all these years, it would be news to celebrate and reassure her town, as well as the tourists they hoped would come out for the weekend.

As a police officer, and now as a chief, nothing felt worse than knowing the community questioned their general safety. Sure, life involved some measure of risk, but when people doubted the ability of their law enforcement, things had a tendency to spiral out of control.

"Want to talk about it?"

She looked across the seat to her new neighbor who'd made himself her chauffeur for the evening. "I'd rather not."

"If that changes, you know where to find me."

Did she ever. Last night had been bad enough with images of him following her into sleep and all through her dreams. Had she ever been so infatuated? Not as an adult.

Waking with Riley O'Brien on her mind had been a delicious start to the day. She could tell from the way her pulse skipped and danced when she saw him that the situation wasn't likely to resolve anytime soon. Not without some sort of acknowledgment or action. But this was the worst time to entertain the idea of a new relationship or even friends with benefits.

When he pulled into the driveway, Abby tried to summon the strength to get out of the car. She wanted a shower first to get the smoke out of her hair, then a long soak in a bubble bath. She might leave her coat on the rail outside the kitchen door so it could air out. Mr. Filmore had attacked her police station. Specifically her office. She didn't need spray paint and graffiti to understand the significance and potential deadly consequences.

At least he'd failed on that count, she thought as another wave of relief washed over her. No one had been injured. That was one positive point in this mess.

But something had pushed Filmore to act against what he held most dear and set fire to a piece of history. Hopefully, the interrogation and search would provide a solid direction. Her gut said Filmore was simply a cog in a wheel, but if that was true, who was calling the shots? Who had the leverage to push Filmore over the edge?

It seemed impossible that she was considering people she had known for years.

What she needed was a better lead, but neither the evidence nor her instincts were cooperating at the moment.

"Hey." Riley snagged her attention with a soft tap on her shoulder. "Are you the fake or real type?"

With all that had happened, somehow the question grated on her last nerve. She glared at him. "What kind of question is that?"

He leaned back, lifting his hand from her shoulder. "Ease up, Abby. I was referring to Christmas trees."

"Oh!" She wanted to laugh and shake free of the constant edginess plaguing her, but she couldn't quite pull it off. "I have a fake one in the attic that I'll pull down when

I get a chance. The idea of wandering through a Christmas tree lot…" Her voice trailed off.

"You've received threats about shopping for Christmas trees?"

She reached for the door handle, immediately regretting the careless words. Overtired, she wouldn't be any good to anyone. Based on the muttering, Riley was offended by the idea of that kind of threat. "Not exactly." She shouldn't tell him anything and yet she suddenly wanted to talk about all of it. She wanted to unburden herself, even if he was basically a stranger.

Maybe *because* he was a stranger. He wouldn't have any preconceived notions about what should and shouldn't bother her.

There had been ridiculous, silly threats that were obviously from lunatics piling on to her sudden notoriety. And there had been the more direct threats from people who either knew firsthand or had researched Belclare's annual traditions. "It's not a big deal."

"No? I think I'd disagree if you told me the truth."

She forced her lips into a reassuring smile. "It was a silly one," she managed. Why could she be so strong for the people in her department and hold her ground with the likes of Mayor Scott and Mr. Filmore but not with Riley?

With Riley she was too ready to confess her weaknesses and worries. Though she wouldn't change a thing about her decisions, she had the irrational urge to discuss those decisions with him. He triggered some tiny, long-forgotten part of her that trusted people. The part of her she'd shut down in favor of navigating the boys' club that was law enforcement. Taking over as chief in Belclare had been a step up the career ladder, but the welcoming people here had given her a significant measure of relief, as well. Her officers and support staff served Belclare with pride, accepting her easily enough. That didn't mean she burdened them with the thoughts or concerns that fell on her shoulders.

Until the drug bust, she hadn't needed to. Her role as police chief came with a burden of responsibility that she carried willingly and easily. Previously, the most serious crime in Belclare had been the occasional petty theft or bar fight. She wouldn't allow that reputation for safety to change. Not on her watch and especially not during the tourist season that buoyed the town from year to year.

Riley had been kind and supportive, but she would do well to remember she didn't really know him.

"You're thinking too deeply again."

She blinked. He was in front of her—he had, in fact, left the driver's seat and come around to open her door while her mind had been skipping around. She glanced at the empty driver's seat and back to where he stood now.

"Come on." He held out a hand to help her. "I'll walk you in."

Did he think she'd get lost between the drive and the door? Was he worried she'd turn into his kitchen rather than her own? Now, that was a tempting thought. She put her hand in his, knowing before they touched that his skin would be warm, his palm rough from work. "I was going to tell you." She just hadn't decided if she'd tell him her professional troubles or her intimate, personal desires.

"So tell me." He gave her fingers a gentle squeeze, encouraging her to move, but she stayed in the seat.

The view was striking, the moment weighted with significance as her heart pounded in her chest. Surely he could hear it, too. She reached out, wiping away the smudge of soot near his hairline. Filled with need and raw awareness, she wanted to simultaneously rush forward and stop time as she leaned close and pressed her lips to his.

He didn't respond. His hand, fingers warm around hers, didn't even twitch.

Stupid. Idiot. The internal reprimand continued as she pulled back, searching for the right words. There had to be some lighthearted phrase that could explain away her unwelcome blunder into his personal space. She might have to move. Out of the neighborhood. She'd go find a hotel if he'd just let her go.

Hysterical laughter bubbled in her chest, but she smothered it. This kiss might just succeed where all of the criminal threats and fallout from the drug bust had failed. The impetuous kiss might drive her right out of Belclare. "Excuse me." She didn't know where to go. He remained rooted in place, blocking the logical way out of the truck.

She tried to decide if she could slide across the bench seat and out the driver's door and still maintain her dignity. Of course her dignity had taken flight during that brief one-sided kiss. She'd misinterpreted his kindness as a reflection of her attraction. How…totally stupid. She was too weary to come up with a better word. Good grief, she was a fool. How had her intuition failed her so badly?

Why didn't he say anything? She frowned at their joined hands. Why wouldn't he let go of her?

"Excuse me," she repeated, shocked that it was even possible for her to feel increasingly humiliated with every passing second. She shifted, trying to scoot away from that strange, bewildered expression on his face. Trying to escape the mortifying moment.

"Wait." The single word he uttered sounded strained.

She froze, too embarrassed to look at him.

"Abby."

"Mmm-hmm?"

"You surprised me."

"Okay. Sorry." She winced as the apology tumbled from

her lips. This wasn't like her. None of this was like her. "Thanks for your help. Have a nice—"

She gasped as he tugged her back to the edge of the seat. He pulled her knees to either side of his trim hips and linked his hands at the small of her back. His breath fanned softly against her skin, mingling with her own as he leaned close enough that his lips were on hers. Light at first, then a claiming that sent her pulse into overdrive.

Her hands fisted in the front of his vest and she hung on for dear life. The kiss spun out, sweeping her away as his tongue stroked into her mouth. She tasted the smoky air, the lingering pepper of the fries and the unique flavor of him. She wrapped her legs around him, her heart racing. Relief and desire were a heady mix as the embarrassment of moments ago was blasted away by this passionate flare.

"You surprised me," he repeated, this time against her cheek.

"Remind me to do it more often," she said, nipping gently at his jaw. "You have an interesting response."

He chuckled, pulling her close enough to feel his arousal. His brown eyes glinted in the weak light cast by the lamp in the cab.

"Oh." She dropped her head to his shoulder. "Anyone might see us out here." Obviously she'd lost all of her powers of common sense when it came to Riley O'Brien.

"So come inside with me." His wide palms cruised up and down her back, his fingers sliding under the clasp of her bra. "I have cookies."

"I can't do that," she replied, though she'd be hard-pressed to come up with a logical excuse right this second.

"Then your place. We'll skip the cookies."

She laughed. "No. Not there, either."

He kissed her again and she nearly relented. "All right."

He reached up and flicked the switch, plunging the truck into darkness. "It's a challenge, but I can make it work here."

She should've found that offensive, but all she could do was laugh. She couldn't remember anyone in her past who made her laugh, who made her feel as lighthearted as Riley did. "You really don't waste time."

His mouth was warm and tender as he trailed kisses across her cheek to her ear. "You knew that," he murmured.

She let the words shiver through her, let her head fall back, granting him full access to her throat. A warm feeling bloomed in her chest, something more than the passion he stoked with his sensual touches. Yes, she did know that about him. At the moment, she appreciated it.

Not enough people were willing to be so honest about what they wanted. He wanted her—the physical evidence was clear on that. She wanted him, too, but she couldn't bring herself to satisfy this rush of lust in his truck in full view of her neighbors or the patrol car assigned to the neighborhood. Mayor Scott would have a field day using a public indecency ticket against her in the next town council meeting.

She pushed at his shoulders. "Hey, are you trying to kill my career?"

"What?"

"There's a morality clause in my contract." He fluttered kisses along the sensitive skin of her neck and she giggled. "Stop." She pushed at him again, taking every millimeter of space he reluctantly gave her to gather herself. "Seriously. Stop."

"I have to?"

"Yes. For the moment."

He grumbled but eased back. The cold air was bracing, but it wouldn't cool down the all-consuming heat she felt deep inside. That unquenchable fire could only be satisfied by the man in front of her.

"I'm not teasing you," she said, wanting to be as direct and clear as he'd been with her.

His brow furrowed. "I didn't say you were."

"Good. I just, um, wanted to get that out in the open. I, *ah*—" she pushed at her hair "—want this to happen. Just not tonight. Not out here."

"I'm all for a warmer venue." He put his hands to her waist and boosted her out of the truck, letting her body slide down his in a slow, delicious caress. "I'll walk you to the door."

He nearly destroyed her resolve with that smoldering gaze and hot, strong body so ready for her. "You're a walking temptation," she accused.

"Same goes." He paused, one boot on the bottom step, his hand catching her coat sleeve. "I'm right next door."

She felt her lips curve. "Trust me, I'm aware."

"I don't like the idea of you being alone tonight."

"There are certain disadvantages," she said, dragging a fingertip along the rough stubble of his jaw. "But I'll manage."

He cupped her palm to his lips. "Lock your doors."

She almost gave in. "You, too." But he didn't let her go at that.

RILEY STARED INTO those wide blue eyes, his blood running hot, but it wasn't all about those kisses. He was furious about the fire and more than a little concerned about the evidence on the shovel. The more he thought about it, the more likely he decided it had been an attempt on her life—at the very least on her freedom.

It was hard to believe Filmore had taken that leap on his own. Was one person planning all of these stunts? Or were they up against more than one threat? And how long before this nebulous enemy tried again?

The smart thing was to take a step back and be clear about the situation, despite what his body wanted. This was a razor's edge he was dancing on and he didn't want to ever give her cause to doubt him or his motives toward her.

He didn't expect to be drawn so strongly to Abby on a personal level, but she captivated him. From her consistent strength and determination through the adversity to her passionate kisses.

"How will emergencies get handled tonight?" With the police station closed, it was the perfect opportunity for someone to strike. His gaze roamed the shadows, searching for threats.

"Everything's handled, Riley. I'll be fine."

He wanted to believe her. "Let me sleep on your couch."

"No. The couch isn't big enough for both of us." Her smile was as loaded as her words. "I need quiet more than…"

He stepped back. It was easy enough to fill in the blanks. Tonight had left him with plenty of business to take care of before morning. "Give me your phone."

That sultry smile still teasing her lips, she pulled it out of her pocket and placed it in his palm. He added his name and number to her contacts and returned it.

"Keep your phone close."

She nodded her agreement before pulling away from his touch. He waited while she went inside. Walking backward, watching her at the window, he crossed over to his back door. Every gut instinct he had said leaving her alone was the wrong thing to do.

Whatever was happening, whoever was behind all this, it felt as if they were getting closer to the goal of destroying her with every passing hour.

She gave a little wave as she locked her back door. He returned it just before she dropped the curtain back in place. He noticed she'd left her coat on the back step to air out. Following her example, he removed his vest and slung it over the handrail.

But when he went to pull his screen door shut, it wouldn't latch. Something was caught under the door near the hinges.

Squeezing through the narrowed opening, he used his phone as a flashlight and saw the problem: a wool scarf.

It looked familiar, but it didn't smell like Abby's bright citrus fragrance and he'd never seen her wear anything in the soft pastel colors. Mrs. Wilks would know who it belonged to, she had the pulse of the whole neighborhood, but Riley didn't want to disturb her at this hour. He had more pressing matters to deal with.

He grabbed a beer, sipping at it slowly while he waited for his laptop to warm up. As much as he wanted to stare out of the side windows toward Abby's house, he resisted. Director Casey had tasked him with protecting her and Riley wasn't convinced Filmore was the end of the threat. The violent messages on the sign had promised a more expansive fallout for Abby as well as the citizens of Belclare. A few acts of vandalism, he suspected, were only the beginning.

While they would certainly be affected if their police chief was injured, killed or simply removed, most people of Belclare wouldn't suffer specifically. What in the hell was the ultimate plan and who was so damned determined to make Abby pay?

AT ELEVEN HE WENT OUT and turned off the Christmas lights. The patrol car drove by on the cross street as he lingered at the front door, watching as the displays winked into darkness up and down the street.

Only Abby's lights stayed on. He thought of her upstairs in her bathtub, her skin warm and rosy under the layer of bubbles. A quick rush of troubling what-if scenarios flashed through his mind and just when he'd decided to grab his pistol from the kitchen, her door opened and she stepped out into the cold night air to turn off her lights.

She was cute as all get out in a thick robe, her hair piled high on her head. It was too easy to imagine how she'd emerged from the tub, dried off that amazing body and tucked herself into that warm robe. Only his training kept him in place when every fiber of his being longed to race across the short distance, scoop her into his arms and carry her up to bed—hers or his, didn't matter.

That would be one way to be sure no one hurt her tonight. He needed to protect her. Protect the city. Better not to blow the long game with a shortsighted leap that could backfire and hurt them both. Between her trust issues and his lies, the odds were stacked against them, even without the people trying to oust her or murder her.

After she'd gone back in, Riley did the same and finished his report, bringing Director Casey up to speed. Feeling like a slacker for not making more progress identifying targets, he ended the email with a recommendation to take a closer look into Filmore's past. His sources in Belclare hadn't given him much to go on, though that might change as news spread of the man's arrest.

On the den floor, Riley laid out maps of the city given to him by the decorating company. What value did Belclare offer terrorists? It was a friendly community. Small and close-knit. Putting a sleeper cell here didn't make sense.

There was the proximity to Baltimore and even Washington, D.C. The docks on the Chesapeake Bay offered easy access up and down the Eastern Seaboard, but that only explained the drug traffic.

"Why plant terrorists here?" Riley laced his fingers behind his head. "What's the attraction?"

The docks? The Christmas Village? Other than those two things, the only claim to fame was the recluse artist who'd been devoted enough to Belclare to speak out on the morning shows urging people to visit the Christmas Village.

Riley let out a frustrated groan. He was going in circles. His best guesses were getting him nowhere. He considered Filmore nothing more than a whiny snob, but the man had set fire to an historical landmark.

"What am I missing?" He mulled over the question as he put away the maps and tossed the beer bottle into the recycling bin. His best hope at this hour was a revelation in his sleep. The boss wanted him down at the warehouse early tomorrow and showing up sluggish would do more harm than good. For both of his jobs.

He might not have identified the threat, but he could feel it, just out of sight, waiting to strike.

Chapter Ten

Friday, December 2, 8:45 a.m.

Abby's gaze drifted from the laptop to her cell phone. She'd called in at six to check on things and decided both she and her officers would be more effective if she worked from home today. With the reporters dogging her every step, it was best if she stayed out of the way.

Besides, she didn't want any witnesses to her persistent daydreams. Even with an in-box full of more dire and personal threats, she couldn't get her mind off Riley's kisses.

The man had skills that went far beyond hanging garland and looking hot in a tool belt. The first thing she'd done this morning was check the driveway, hoping for a glimpse of him, but his truck was gone.

So she'd called in and tried to focus on being chief of police—a job which, according to today's overwhelmed in-box, she was failing miserably. In the meetings following the drug bust, both FBI and Homeland Security agents had told her to hand the bulk of this off to someone in her department. They'd had good reasons and she didn't doubt their experience. But she'd taken a look at her small department and just couldn't saddle any of her officers with this kind of mess.

She'd been at it long enough now that she recognized

the spam and lunatics, easily weeding them out before she forwarded messages she thought were valid on up to the federal analysts. Belclare didn't have the cyber forensic experts to follow the bread crumbs to something helpful.

She was making her second pot of coffee when her doorbell rang. Hoping it might be Mrs. Wilks with cookies, she hurried to the door. Flowers filled her peephole, an arrangement large enough that it hid the face of the deliveryman.

Mrs. Wilks would've come to the back. Cautious now, she opened the door. "Yes?"

"Delivery for Chief Jensen."

She smiled, recognizing Deke's cultured voice behind the green floral tissue paper. "What are you doing?" She opened the door wider and invited him in.

"I thought you deserved something beautiful after the recent trouble," he said, handing her the vase.

The scent of lilies and roses filled her front room as she set the arrangement on her coffee table. She unwrapped the protective tissue and marveled at the flowers and the crystal vase.

"For a shy, artistic celebrity, you're spending a great deal of time out and about," she said.

"For a police chief you seem to be spending a great deal of time in the field," he countered.

Fair point. "Would you like coffee?"

"No, thank you. I can't stay long." He removed his cap and gloves and settled into the wing chair facing her. "How bad is the station?"

"It's not destroyed, which is a plus. And they tell me it's possible that no one will know the difference from the front."

"Clever arsonist. Are you sure you have the right man?"

She nodded sadly. "I've seen the video. Filmore cried throughout his confession."

"He does love all of this old architecture."

"He does," she agreed. "We're still trying to sort out what drove him over the edge."

"How fortunate you were nearby to get him off the streets."

She rubbed her palms together as she gathered her thoughts. Guilt nipped at her for skipping dinner with Deke only to wind up at the pub with Riley. She and Deke didn't have anything officially personal beyond their weekly coffee, yet she sensed he wanted something more from her. Something more that she'd thought she was interested in, as well, despite her reluctance to cross that line.

Well, she thought as her cheeks heated, she'd certainly leaped over that line with both lips and most of her body last night with Riley. Which meant it was time to clear the air with Deke. Hopefully, she was just misinterpreting his signals. Braced for embarrassment, she tried to explain.

She cleared her throat. "I was close to the station, though I didn't intend to be. After I called you, I came home to find my neighbors had been decorating like crazy. My yard looked stark in comparison." She couldn't stop babbling. "One of my neighbors helped me get caught up in record time. The least I could do was buy him a burger at the pub."

"Of course. Your passion for this community is what makes you stand out. It's what makes them love you so," Deke said, waving off her concern with a flick of his hand. "Think nothing of it, my dear. Our plans were tentative at best. I only came out today to see a friend and offer a bit of encouragement during this ordeal."

Ordeal felt a little strong, but Deke enjoyed formality and drama. It showed in his work as well as every other facet of his life, including impersonating a floral delivery driver. And she wasn't about to quibble over semantics with a friend.

"Thank you. The flowers are gorgeous and definitely brightened my day."

His gaze roamed around the room and she was afraid to ask what he thought. Compared to the grand expanse of his home, hers must be a laughable disappointment. But none of those reactions showed on his face.

"I heard you had a little trouble yourself."

"Someone broke into my garage and tried to tie me to a murder."

"That's absurd. Do you need a lawyer?"

She was sure he could afford the best. "No. I cleared it up with the Baltimore P.D. first thing this morning. While no one knows how my shovel got involved, it wasn't the murder weapon."

"What a relief. For all of us." His smile was kind and friendly as he pushed to his feet and donned the ball cap and gloves. "Tomorrow's opening day will be a resounding success," he declared. "I'm sure of it." He gave her a quick hug. "And the city will have you to thank."

"Not just me," she said, uncomfortable with his effusive praise. "Everyone has worked together to make this the best season ever. Thanks for everything, Deke."

"It's my pleasure."

She locked the door when he returned to his car. On her way back to the kitchen she paused to enjoy the flowers. It was a thoughtful gesture, a bit over the top, but thoughtful. The arrangement was too big for her small kitchen table, but she felt too exposed working in the front room.

If this was her worst dilemma today, things were looking up.

Chapter Eleven

Home from his errand, Deke tapped an impatient rhythm on the cold pane of the window. He was surrounded by idiots. The man on the ladder hadn't had the decency to die. Somehow no one had put Chief Jensen into cuffs for bashing a repeat offender over the head with her shovel, despite her lack of a believable alibi. And now, rather than inciting fear, the fire had seemingly fueled the woman's determination to maintain her hard stance against the attacks on her town.

He cursed the skills that had put him in this precarious position. It wasn't his job to micromanage something as pedestrian as the crime-versus-law balance in Belclare and yet those who kept him in business insisted he clean it up. Fools. They were wasting his talent.

His job was creating the strategies that furthered the cause. Tempted to ignore his orders in favor of more effective strikes elsewhere, he soothed himself with the small progress he'd made with the police chief.

The only other consolation was that revenue from the Christmas Village would surely be down in light of the current violence. No amount of greenery and twinkling lights could hide the stain on Belclare, and the shopkeepers who needed the financial infusion would force their once-beloved chief of police out of the way long enough for him to take a giant leap forward in making reparations.

The latest drug shipment was half the size of the one Abby had discovered. Thanks to the distraction of the fire, it had come and gone already with no one the wiser. Now, with his superiors slightly at ease, he could focus on vengeance. He picked up the phone and relayed his next orders.

Waiting for the fun to start, he contemplated all the ways things could go right. And wrong.

If he couldn't bring Chief Jensen to him with the promise of a friendship, he could certainly prey on her need to defend and protect. Either way, he would be thrilled when she finally came running right into his trap.

Her new neighbor was no match for Deke. If he got in the way he would be just another casualty of this war.

Chapter Twelve

Riley spent the morning much as he'd spent the night: thinking of Abby. Not just the kiss, but the serious threat chasing her around town. Personally and professionally, the woman and her predicament consumed his attention.

His arms full of plastic wrapping and cardboard boxes, he headed out to the Dumpsters and recycling bins. He pulled out his knife and sliced through the tape, breaking down the boxes for recycling. The decorating team was nearly done setting up and not a moment too soon. A light snow was predicted for this evening, which would surely make tomorrow's opening day perfect for all the expected visitors.

As he walked back into the warehouse, he spotted a black wallet caught between the Dumpster and the warehouse. He pulled out the tri-folded leather, only to realize it was a woman's wallet. Looking around, he didn't see any of the women who were part of the crew. Figuring someone would come forward soon, he walked on into the supervisor's office. "Anyone looking for this?" he asked, holding it up.

His boss removed his reading glasses. "No one's said anything to me."

"I found it behind the Dumpster and thought I'd rather have a witness when I open it."

His boss nodded. "Go for it. Then I need you to make sure the welcome sign is done right."

With a nod, Riley popped the snap and stared, dumbfounded by the image of Mrs. Wilks on the driver's license. "What the hell?"

"You know her?"

"She lives down the street from the house I'm renting."

His boss checked the clock on the wall. "Take it over to her, grab some lunch then swing by and check on the welcome sign. The pair on that is more likely to build a snowman than finish the job in a timely manner."

"Sure thing."

Fifteen minutes later, Riley was across town and parked in his driveway next to Abby's car. After the fire he knew she'd be working from home and he had to squash the urge to knock on her door just to say hello.

If he played his cards right, maybe he could get a repeat performance of last night's kisses. Which was not exactly why Director Casey had planted him here. Denying himself the satisfaction of admiring the work they'd done on her yard, he fixed his attention forward and kept on walking down the sidewalk.

"Riley?"

Abby.

He turned back to greet her. "Hey." She was dressed in a sweater and jeans. He had yet to decide which wardrobe he preferred, the professional one or her more casual side. She looked so temping in everything she wore.

"Are you already done for the day?"

He wanted to believe that was hope he heard in her voice. "No." He held up the wallet.

"What's that?"

"Mrs. Wilks's wallet. I'm returning it."

It didn't matter that he was on the sidewalk and she was

standing in her doorway—he could see doubt stamped all over her face.

"Where did you find it?" She stepped outside and pulled her door closed behind her.

"Near the Dumpster behind the warehouse."

"When?"

He looked at his watch. "About an hour ago."

"And you walked all the way over here."

"No." He pointed to his truck. "It's my lunch break. I drove over here to return it. I'm guessing she doesn't realize she lost it. Or that someone nabbed it."

"Do you not hear how odd that sounds?"

"Maybe," he admitted. "Are you accusing me of something?"

She hesitated, then shook her head. "No." She came down the walk to join him. "Can I take a look?"

"If you'd rather be the one to give it back to her, be my guest." Irritated with the way she twisted him up, he handed the wallet over and started back for his house.

"Hang on." She reached out and caught him lightly at the waist. The heat and strength of her fingers startled him almost as much as the sizzle that shot through his system at the contact. After last night, he should have expected it. "I don't mean to be overprotective of the people I care about."

He nodded. "It's probably habit by now."

"Even if she wasn't a friend," Abby said, "her safety is my responsibility."

He covered her hands with his. "I understand. You take it over and I'll head back to work." He wasn't sure what to do next. He wanted to kiss her but knew she'd rather not have anyone on the street see that kind of display. And he didn't trust his control around her. When she didn't move, he frowned. "What's wrong? You look upset." Had something else happened?

"I'm not upset."

Her pale face and rapid breath offered a decent impersonation of pretty-damn-scared, but he took the safe route and didn't share his thoughts. "I get it. She matters to you. This worries you. Go." He jerked his head toward the street. "Make sure she's okay."

"It's just that…" Abby cleared her throat, but she wouldn't meet his gaze. "Lately I…imagine the worst in every situation. Come on, let's take it to her together."

Her admission showed him just how far they'd come so very quickly. She trusted him to some degree. That meant a great deal to him on more levels than one.

When they reached Mrs. Wilks's door, Abby pressed the doorbell and they listened to the happy chime beyond the closed door. Once the familiar tune had faded, silence filled the air.

Several seconds passed then Riley asked, "Does she nap in the afternoons?"

"She's too busy to nap," Abby said, turning to walk around to the back of the house.

"Then she's out. Without her wallet," he observed. "Her car's not in the driveway."

Ignoring him, Abby knocked at the back door and called out. When no one answered, she tried the knob, but even with a little jiggle, it remained locked.

"Turn around," she said. "I know where she keeps a key."

Trying not to laugh, he did as ordered while she retrieved the spare key. She probably didn't want to know that he'd already identified the hiding place under the second step near the handrail. It was the cleanest spot on the stairs.

Hadn't he just decided that Abby was beginning to trust him? *Ha!*

"All right." Abby reached for the door. "Let's go in and check on her."

They really didn't have any evidence that something was wrong. Except the wallet in his hand. He didn't know her well, but Mrs. Wilks didn't strike him as the sort to toss her wallet out by mistake. Not to mention he couldn't imagine what business she had at the docks. The same things were probably running through Abby's mind.

"Mrs. Wilks?" Abby's voice carried through the kitchen.

As Riley followed her inside, he noticed the only light came from the window over the sink and the door they'd opened. The coffeepot on the counter was full, but the warmer light was off. A programmable model, he realized as Abby called out again. He tried not to jump to conclusions, but this wasn't adding up to anything good.

"Does she have family nearby?"

"Her son lives in Baltimore," Abby answered. "Mrs. Wilks? It's Abby and—crap."

Abby had flipped on the hallway light. Crap didn't begin to define the mess. From his position behind her he could see the overturned umbrella stand, smashed pictures of grandchildren and other bits and pieces of Mrs. Wilks's decor broken and scattered across the floor.

Clearly, whoever had broken into her house wasn't worried about leaving a mess. A rush through the house confirmed Mrs. Wilks was not at home.

Abby turned on him. "When was the last time you saw her?"

He studied her, recognized her cop persona. "Is this another interrogation?"

"No. Maybe." She clenched her fists. "Just answer me. I need a time frame."

He thought about it. "I haven't seen her since Calder got hurt."

Abby's shoulders slumped. "Damn it. I was afraid you'd say that. She didn't help with the decorating yesterday?"

He shook his head. "When did you see her last?"

Her lips quivered. "I checked with her yesterday morning after discovering the damaged lock on my garage, but she said she didn't hear anything." She shook her head. "How did I go an entire day and not miss her?"

Riley could rattle off the reasons but figured it would only add to her misplaced guilt. "We can ask around the block, see if anyone saw anything."

"That's a good idea." She held out her hand for the wallet. "I'll hang on to this and call in someone to start a report and a search for her car."

Riley wanted to hold her and give her some comfort but knew she'd resist. She'd switched over to police chief mode and all he could do was try to help.

He'd seen her face when Calder had been hurt, when the station was on fire, and thought he knew her pained expression. Neither incident had anything on the torment haunting her vivid blue eyes right now. She blamed herself and he didn't have the words to reassure her.

"I'm sorry I pulled it away from the Dumpster." He wanted to take some of the burden, but she didn't let it go.

Abby caught her lower lip between her teeth. "I doubt that will make any difference. I'll send a team over there to look around just in case."

He heard her muttering oaths and violent promises as she called for backup. By the time he exited the back door, two of Belclare's finest were emerging from cruisers, guns drawn.

"Hold it right there."

Riley stopped, raised his hands. "Take it easy, officers. Chief Jensen is inside."

"What have you done with her?"

"Abby," he called over his shoulder.

"No," snapped the officer closest to the steps. "What have you done with Mrs. Wilks?"

"I haven't done anything with her."

"Riley?" Abby walked out the side door. She swore when she saw her officers. "Gadsden, what's going on?"

He wished her first request had been for them to lower their weapons, but he could wait it out. He hoped.

"We found Mrs. Wilks's car down by the docks. Evidence inside the vehicle led us to the Hamilton place. There we found a scarf belonging to Mrs. Wilks on the rail by the back door. Since that's where O'Brien is living, makes sense that he knows something about her sudden disappearance."

"Riley?"

He hated the doubt he heard in Abby's voice. More, he hated the person orchestrating this mess. Riley had already vetted everyone on the Belclare police force and come up empty. He'd yet to find anyone who had a beef with Calder, which confirmed his suspicion that someone was using the community to torture Abby. It wasn't a stretch to see the deadly potential here and Riley had to find a way to head it off.

"I found a scarf last night when I got home," Riley said, his eyes still on the weapons aimed at him. "It was caught in the door, so I picked it up, looped it over the rail," he explained. "I don't have a clue where it came from."

"You need to come with us, Mr. O'Brien."

"Wait a second," Abby said in her no-nonsense chief's voice. "Put away your weapons."

Finally. Riley lowered his hands but kept them in plain view. "Thanks," he murmured to her as the officers complied.

"What evidence led you to Riley's—the Hamilton house?"

"A tool with O'Brien's name on it. Everyone in town knows he moved in there."

"Never tried to hide it," Riley tossed out.

"Hush," Abby said. "What kind of tool?"

Gadsden clearly preferred that Riley implicate himself, but he relented. "A hammer."

With a tight nod, Riley silently vowed that he'd get even with the bastard behind this. "I haven't kidnapped anyone. I have at least three hammers in the truck. There's always one on my tool belt. I used one yesterday when we set up the park display and again when we decorated the street. You can check with my coworkers or any of the neighbors."

"We'll need to check your story. Let's take a walk," Gadsden suggested. "I have a few more questions for you."

"No." Abby denied that request. "Do you have any sort of timeline yet?"

"The dock workers who reported the car don't recall seeing it parked out there before this morning."

"So you're thinking this all happened last night."

Gadsden nodded. "It's possible the fire was a diversion."

"I'm starting to agree," Abby said, giving voice to one of Riley's developing theories.

He could not afford to waste time in a holding cell. He didn't think she could afford to be without his protection, even though she didn't realize that was his real purpose here. Once more he toyed with the idea of telling her the truth, but he wasn't about to admit anything in front of her officers.

"I found the scarf when I came home for the night." He just managed to avoid Abby's gaze. "Around eleven."

"Did you see him arrive home, Chief?"

"Yes." She gestured to the door she'd exited. "We have a crime scene inside that needs to be processed. From what I can see—the bed hasn't been slept in and the coffee that brewed automatically this morning is still waiting in the carafe—Mrs. Wilks was attacked and taken from her home late last night."

"You didn't see anyone hanging around before that?" Gadsden pressed.

"No," Abby said resolutely.

Riley kept studying the policemen. Between the crowd at the pub and the bystanders at the fire, surely they'd heard he'd driven Abby home. What were they tiptoeing around?

"We'd like to take him in for questioning."

"No," Abby repeated. "He was with me," she said with a resigned sigh. "I drove home from the station and Riley met me out front to help me decorate my house. Before that, Danny and Peg can vouch for his contribution to decorating the rest of the street."

"Yes, ma'am. But after that?"

"After, I took Mr. O'Brien to the pub for dinner. It was a dinner we never finished because Martin Filmore went off the deep end and set our police station on fire."

Gadsden rocked back on his heels. "And after that?"

In Gadsden's place, Riley would've ducked from the laser glare Abby aimed at him. "I watched him walk over to his house."

"Did you watch him go inside?"

"No."

"So you can't verify his story about the scarf."

"I can verify everything else, including his character, Officer Gadsden," she said pointedly.

Riley muted his shock over that statement. She must trust him more than he thought. Well, she had kissed him first. And she'd let him keep kissing her once he'd recovered from the unexpected surprise.

"Yes, ma'am." Gadsden rubbed his palm over his holstered weapon. "But why frame him?"

"Good question," she countered. "Why don't you start figuring it out?"

Riley gave the officer credit for persistence.

"Based on the evidence of a struggle inside and everything you've found we need to assume the worst," Abby relented. "But Riley was not involved in her disappearance."

"All right." Gadsden acquiesced.

"Give me the address for the car," Abby instructed. "I'll head that way. You two can take over here."

"Yes, ma'am."

"Come on," she said to Riley. "We'll take my car. Give them your keys."

He raised his eyebrows but pulled them out of his pocket.

"When you're done with this scene, process his truck. Thoroughly," she instructed. "I'll make sure his prints get into the system so you can rule them out."

He told himself the cover story established by the Specialists would hold up under the scrutiny of the Belclare police department and he fell into step beside her. She darted into her house, returned seconds later with her purse and then rushed for her car.

"How are they going to process anything without a police station?"

Abby unclipped her keys from her purse strap. "Filmore was kind enough to leave us with half of a police station."

"Just not the half your office was in."

"Exactly." She nodded, pulling open her car door. "We're wasting time. Get in."

She barely waited for him to buckle his seat belt before she hit the sirens and went barreling out of the neighborhood.

"You're angry," he observed.

Abby thought about that as she negotiated the light traffic. Moving to a smaller town was the best thing she'd ever done. For herself and her career. She wasn't going to let some sick bastard ruin that by picking off her friends. "Yes."

"About being my alibi?"

"Only a little," she admitted.

"Your officers are protective and loyal. That's a good thing."

He had a valid point, which only emphasized how any of the men and women on the Belclare force could become targets at any time. Had, in fact, if she considered last night's fire.

She slowed for the congestion on Main Street and it gave her time to glance at him. In profile his face was stern, his eyes on the road. The clean-shaved jaw was set with a determination that mirrored hers. He'd been so calm and steady with Calder and again at the fire. He'd barely flinched when Gadsden and Miller had been ready to haul him in. Somehow it made her feel better about taking a civilian to another crime scene. For the briefest of seconds, she wondered again if she was a fool to let him so close. She'd certainly misread Filmore, but she couldn't dwell on that mistake.

"I'm angry that some maladjusted perp is yanking me around and messing with my friends." She stomped on the accelerator once she was clear of the traffic. "More than that, I'm worried about Mrs. Wilks."

"We'll find her."

"We damn well better find her alive. If he's killed her—"

"He?"

She focused on the road. At this speed she had to or she'd be risking their lives, too. And she wasn't letting the person responsible for all of this off that easily. "A generic term at this point."

"But?"

How did he know there was a "but"? She supposed it

was obvious. "Some of the more recent emails, the more personal threats, feel like they've been written by one person. Male. Thanks to technology they might be coming in from all across the globe, but I think one man is leading this vendetta against me."

"That's a big leap, Abby. The video was a smash hit."

She swore, taking the fork toward the docks. "It's Chief Jensen when we're on scene."

"Yes, ma'am."

He sounded like Gadsden. She didn't have time to decide how she felt about that. As they approached the scene, she left her lights on but turned off the siren. "I know you didn't do this. When we get there feel free to verify that's your hammer."

"Unless it isn't."

"Unless it isn't," she echoed. She couldn't picture Riley kidnapping Mrs. Wilks with a hammer or anything else. Maybe he'd hold her hostage for more cookies. The idea made her want to smile. But first she had to find her neighbor...and friend.

She parked the car and prepared herself for the worst. If Mrs. Wilks had been found, they would've radioed that information to her en route.

"Chief Jensen."

"Yes?" She faced Riley, startled by the intensity in his golden brown eyes.

"I *didn't* do this."

"I know." Her instincts wouldn't be that skewed by a few hot kisses and helpful deeds. Looking away from him, she let her gaze wander across the docks. A time-worn industrial scene on the best of days, the mismatched collection of warehouses, cranes and container yard weren't any more inviting with the dusting of snow.

"We have to find her," she said to herself. "I won't let

some faceless terrorists win." She exited the car, grateful she'd opted for sturdy denim trousers and a thick sweater for working at home today.

The grim expressions on the responding officers' faces told her they hadn't come up with anything positive, but she asked for the status anyway.

"Nothing new." Detective Calloway slid a dark look toward Riley. "What's he doing here?"

She found it interesting that Gadsden hadn't called ahead with a warning that Riley was with her. "He's not responsible for this," she said in an unyielding tone. "He can also verify if the item that implicates him is in fact his."

Calloway scowled at Riley. "Come on then. It's over here."

She watched every nuance of Riley's body language for stress and found none. He was either very good at hiding his reactions, or absolutely oblivious to the risks. Despite her belief in his innocence, they had to follow the evidence.

The detective held the hammer, enveloped in an evidence bag, in front of Riley's face. "It has your name on it, O'Brien."

Abby continued to watch for an indicator that Riley was lying about any of this. He didn't even flinch as he manipulated the hammer inside the bag until his name showed. "Every temp worker in town has used one like this at some point this week. It's company issue." He handed it back. "Name or not, that isn't mine."

He didn't need to start lying now. "Your name is right there on the handle," she argued.

"Sure is," he agreed. "But that isn't how I write my name."

"What?" She and the detective took a closer look at the same time.

"Compare it to the tools in my truck and you'll see. Someone else wrote my name there."

She nodded at Calloway. He called over to Gadsden for a quick picture and count of the hammers in Riley's truck. When the picture proved Riley was correct, she sighed, relieved and frustrated. She appreciated the confirmation of his innocence, but they weren't any closer to finding Mrs. Wilks.

"What now?" Calloway wanted to know.

"We talk to the folks who reported the abandoned vehicle."

With a nod to Riley, she invited him to tag along as she posed her questions to the workers on-site. No one had been spotted coming or going from the vehicle. There were a few cameras on the docks, which had helped her bust the drug runners, but Mrs. Wilks's car had been placed in a blind spot.

"On purpose," Riley observed as they walked around the area. "They did a sloppy job trying to frame me," he added.

She looked down the docks. The company he worked for was renting space in the warehouse farthest from the water. It was the largest but also offered better security and more parking. "What are the cameras like at your warehouse?"

"Are you kidding?" Riley pushed his hands into his pockets. "With all the negative attention, the boss added his own closed-circuit system. Says it's the first time he felt like he had to."

"Does everyone on the team know that?"

Riley shrugged. "I think so, but can't say for sure."

She walked back to where Calloway was overseeing the arrival of the tow truck for Mrs. Wilks's car. "Let's get the video from the warehouse where Riley works. Maybe we'll identify who tossed the wallet at the Dumpster."

Calloway hustled off to do as she requested. The only

thing left to do was examine the car and she wanted to get that done before it was towed to the impound lot. Abby's gut twisted, but she couldn't avoid the inevitable. She told herself the odds of finding anything her officers had overlooked were slim to none, but she had to try. She owed it to her neighbor.

"Come on," she said to Riley, handing him latex gloves. She had no desire to do this alone. Let the department—hell, the entire town—speculate, but she needed his support right now on a very personal level.

Mrs. Wilks was more than a neighbor, she'd become a dear friend. Based on the latest trash in Abby's in-box, the man tormenting her had targeted and kidnapped Mrs. Wilks solely because she and Abby were friends. With every step, the burdens got heavier. The symbolic vandalism. Calder. Her shovel used against one of the vandals. Filmore and the fire.

She paused at the driver's side, gazing across the top of the car at Riley. "I'm done playing catch-up here. We find Mrs. Wilks and then I'm doing whatever it takes to put this to rest."

"Sounds like a plan."

Abby didn't quite know how she'd do it, but she knew it was past time. There had to be some way to connect the dots and put a stop to this. Belclare was her town and she wouldn't cower in a corner while terrorists dealt out fear. She put on the gloves to preserve any evidence and opened the driver's door.

The driver's seat was pushed back much too far for Mrs. Wilks's smaller frame. "She didn't drive herself," she noted.

"Which might mean two perps. One to drive, one to control the hostage."

Abby nodded, bending down for a closer look at the

floor mats. "She's feisty. It might have required two perps just to subdue her."

"When does she prepare her coffeemaker?"

"Huh?"

"She has a programmable pot. It was full and turned off when we were in the house. She had to have set it at some point."

"Typically, she does that during the commercial break before the news. At least, that's what I've seen her do on the rare occasions I was there at that time of night."

"All right. Neither of us saw any strange cars on the street when we got home from the fire."

Abby's face heated as she recalled those steamy kisses. "We weren't exactly looking for anything out of place."

He shot her a wicked grin, the one full of sexy promises that made her pulse kick in hopeful anticipation. She ruthlessly reminded herself they were at a crime scene.

"Look at that." He pointed to the floor cushion in the backseat closest to her side.

She opened the back door and shifted, letting the bright sunlight fall on a pink smudge on the upholstery. She sniffed at it, recognizing the cosmetic fragrance. "Lipstick. Damn it."

Abby stood up, pulling the crisp air deep into her lungs, willing her stomach to settle down.

"Well, it's confirmation she or someone wearing lipstick was in the car," Riley said, coming over to her side so they could speak without being overheard. "Unless she typically kissed her backseat."

She opened her mouth to say they'd known that already, but he was right—without an eyewitness, they'd been assuming Mrs. Wilks had been a passenger in the car.

"Okay." Abby took another deep breath. "You and I arrived in the neighborhood just after eleven. Mrs. Wilks would have made her coffee before that. Assuming the altercation was limited to the hallway, one or two men grabbed her from her house before the evening news wrapped up.

Abby might have heard something if she hadn't been in the shower wishing she had the guts to invite Riley over to wash her back. A weak laugh slipped out at the thought. If she'd done that, bringing him out of his house, he might actually have seen or heard something.

"This isn't your fault, Chief Jensen," he said.

She cursed herself for allowing him to see the uncertainties nagging at her. "Not quite what I was thinking, but close enough." She pointed to the tires. "I'm not seeing anything on the tread or wheel wells that I wouldn't expect to find in Belclare."

"So what did they do in between grabbing her and dumping the car?"

Refusing to let her emotions run amok down that path, Abby regained a small measure of control. Planting her hands on her hips, she said, "Let's check the trunk."

"No one's done that?"

"They said it was empty, but I want to look anyway."

"Fresh eyes?"

"Exactly." She went around to the passenger side and popped open the glove box to hit the trunk release. The car shifted when the trunk lid opened. "There has to be some clue about what they've done with her."

"Stop." Riley held up a hand, his gaze locked on the interior of the trunk.

"What?"

"Back away and pull back the others, too."

"Tell me why," she insisted.

"Bomb."

The single word, delivered so calmly, jolted her system.

"The trunk was empty when they found the car. No one could have planted a bomb since my guys got here."

"Abby," he warned. "Listen to me. Please."

What could he possibly know about bombs? But his face was pale and now his body was rigid with tension. "I'm not leaving without taking a look."

He shook his head, sending her a ferocious scowl, but she didn't care. He had to be wrong. Her people had already popped the trunk and declared it empty and void of evidence.

"Fine. But call in a bomb squad while you look."

Belclare didn't have a bomb squad. She couldn't recall for sure, but one of the firefighters might have had military experience with disarming explosives. The closest fully trained team was in Baltimore. "Is there a timer?"

"I don't know yet."

She stepped up next to him, but all she saw was the coarse fabric lining the trunk. "Riley, what am I missing here?"

"Too many wires into the brake lights." He pointed out the difference between the right and left sides. "Call someone, *now.*"

"There's no one local," she whispered, even as she entered the number for the state police. "If we're lucky they can have someone here in half an hour." *Lucky* being the operative word.

No sooner had she'd ended the call than the sound of heavy engines jerked her attention to the parking lot behind them. She swore when two media vans stopped at the perimeter, as she'd requested. "Great. Now we'll have an audience."

"Someone tipped them off."

"Possibly, but anyone can listen to the police radio," she replied, equally irritated. "Tell me what to do."

"Any chance you'll back off while I take a closer look?"

"No."

She watched as he looked around the docks.

"You felt the car shift when you hit the button, right?"

"Yes." She'd definitely felt it.

"I'm going to look for some kind of timer."

She held her breath when he leaned into the trunk, pulling a knife from his pocket. She appreciated his concern, but if the terrorists wanted her dead, they could detonate the bomb at any time—an assessment that assumed they were watching this play out.

Riley's back blocked her view, so she used her cell to update the officers behind them. There was no way to be subtle about clearing the area, especially when she didn't know how big a threat they were dealing with.

Finally, she couldn't take it anymore. "Riley?"

"It's counting down, Abby. Please get to safety."

Fear trickled into her veins. "Only if you're coming with me."

"I'll be right behind you."

"I don't believe you." She actually laughed a little when he swore. "Can you disarm it?"

"Not sure," he said.

Every second seemed to tick by with individual clarity. "How much time?"

"Enough."

"Good."

"No. Weird. Ask yourself who benefits from blowing this up while you stand by helplessly?"

She cast a glance over her shoulder at the media. "I know who it hurts. All of Belclare. Is there anything resembling evidence?"

"Probably, but the explosion will destroy it," he countered. "Get me the keys."

"Why?"

"Do it, Chief Jensen. The sooner this is resolved, the sooner we can find Mrs. Wilks."

She darted back to Calloway. He found the right evidence bag and tossed it to her. But when she turned back, she realized Riley had tricked her into leaving him.

Somehow he'd started the car without the key and was steering Mrs. Wilks sedan toward the water.

Understanding dawned slowly. He intended to put the car in the water to save the surrounding area from the explosion. What had he seen on that bomb and why hadn't he been honest about it? For that matter, why didn't the terrorists behind this throw the switch? She didn't want Riley in any more danger, but the tactics didn't make sense. None of this made sense.

His words echoed in her mind and she prayed they weren't the last ones she'd hear him speak. *Who gains?* The phrase consumed her as she alternately watched the sedan's progress and the people gathered around watching with her. Any one of them could have a thumb on a detonator ready to make this a spectacular tragedy.

Who gains? She couldn't come up with an answer, not while she watched a civilian, a stranger who'd so quickly slipped through her defenses, sacrifice himself. If he lived, she might have to beat him senseless for putting her through this.

The sedan's engine revved suddenly and she waited for the explosion, but Riley jumped out of the driver's seat and the car rolled off the dock and into the water.

Riley hadn't even gained his feet when the explosion sent water spouting into the air like a fountain.

Heedless of the media and public opinion, she raced down the dock to check on him. "What the hell were you thinking?" she shouted in his face even as she looked him up and down.

"I'm fine, thanks for asking."

"That was stupid."

"Would you rather the thing blew up the dock? Imagine the fallout. The lost revenue. The cleanup."

"Stop using logic. You could've been killed."

"I don't think so."

"What does that mean?" She wanted to hug him and punch him at the same time. "I should have you arrested."

"On what grounds?"

"You're a danger to yourself."

"But not to others?"

She didn't have time to dignify that. They'd reached the area where the police had been holding people back and everyone burst into applause and cheers.

"Smile," she instructed, although she knew he was already doing so. "You're a hero."

"An hour ago I was a suspect."

"Not in my book," she said.

She answered a few questions posed by the reporters of the local station and let Mayor Scott, who'd caught the scent of a good public relations opportunity, handle the rest. Once she'd given instructions to the officers on the scene, she pulled Riley away from the noise and chaos.

"Even with the bomb neutralized, it will be a wonder if anyone comes out tomorrow," she grumbled.

"It will probably be the biggest opening day ever."

"That's not funny," she said. "We still have to find Mrs. Wilks."

"I have an idea, but you're not going to like it."

"Try me. She's my number-one priority." Once she found her neighbor, then Abby would take the time to ask how Riley had developed such a thorough recognition of bombs.

She was sure there was a reasonable explanation, but she wanted to hear it from him.

The Belclare police force wasn't comprised of idiots, but they hadn't noticed the threat when they'd searched the trunk. Unless one of them was in on it.

She jerked herself back from that slippery slope. Paranoia would not resolve this any sooner for her lost neighbor.

"Here." Riley handed her a rolled-up piece of paper.

"What's this?" She opened it, startled to see a line sketch of the Belclare shore. Three different points were marked with different numbers.

"It was wrapped around the primary wire."

"Dear Lord," she whispered. "That's why they left her car out here. It's a countdown game."

He nodded. "One sick scavenger hunt. If it's counting from the explosion in the car, that only gives us ten more minutes to reach the first point."

"She won't be at that one."

"You can't be sure," he said gently. "And someone else might be."

He was right. Her stomach pitched and rolled. Anger and fear fought for dominance, but neither would help save Mrs. Wilks or anyone else.

"She's an innocent old lady," Abby said through clenched teeth. It infuriated her that people she cared about were suffering because she knew how to do her job. Because she'd vowed to keep Belclare crime-free. "She might already be dead of exposure."

Riley rubbed her arms, chasing away the chill that threatened to drag her under. "You have to stay positive."

Positive was becoming exhausting. "But be prepared for the worst."

He acknowledged her comment with a bob of his head. "I can get started while you organize a search party."

"No. This is personal and I'm done taking risks with the lives of those who trust me."

"Abby, if you ditch protocol and rules now, every effort you've made is for nothing. Stick with your system. It works."

He was right and Mrs. Wilks needed Abby at the top of her game.

"I'm heading to the first point. Get a team together and do this the right way."

"Fine. I'll be right behind you," she said, echoing his words from earlier.

"I believe you," he said, smiling.

She longed to give him a kiss, but that would make him more of a target than he already was.

As she shared the map with Calloway and issued orders, pairing off available troops in different directions, her mind mulled over the question of *who gains*.

Today's events only confirmed her worst suspicions. This wasn't simply a matter of random thugs descending on her town to prove a point. No, the problems were being meticulously planned and carried out from right inside Belclare.

The feds had warned her that the drugs might be funding a sleeper cell. But she hadn't wanted to believe anyone in her town was capable of fooling the entire community that way. She hadn't wanted to admit she'd been fooled.

By their nature sleeper cells blended in, participated and carried on as valuable members of a community. Until called to action.

The drug bust had not been a random event. The vandals, Calder's attacker, Filmore. Mrs. Wilks's kidnapper. The evidence planted to implicate both her and Riley in different crimes. None of it had been random.

As the search teams set off, Abby jogged along in Riley's wake. She wasn't about to let her newest ally face her enemies alone.

Chapter Thirteen

Riley didn't hold out much hope that Mrs. Wilks would be at the first marker as he rushed down to the rocky shoreline. That would be too easy. He pulled his cell phone from his pocket, checked the reception and entered Director Casey's personal number.

"This is unexpected," Casey answered.

"Yes, sir. Things are escalating rapidly. Do you have anything connecting the names I sent?"

"Not yet."

Riley paused, picking his way around an outcropping of sharp slate-colored stones. "Calder is clean." He'd thought Calder's accident might have been staged to disguise his link to the terrorist cell, but not anymore. The man had no ties to the drug runners and while Calder knew Filmore, their association had been strictly professional. "It's like ghosts taking potshots around here."

"Stay on it," Casey said. "Belclare needs you. We picked up the call to the state police for backup. FYI, they have a bomb squad but it likely won't arrive in time."

On that sour news the call ended. Riley put his phone away and checked his watch. He had to be getting close to the first marker.

He looked over his shoulder at the docks. The search teams Abby had put into play were combing other parts of the shoreline. Riley gazed out across the water. One of the tugboats was motoring out into the bay. Hopefully the team on board was working for their side and not the terrorists. Checking his watch, he had less than three minutes to find the marker or, if the map and timing were accurate, there would be another explosion.

"Mrs. Wilks!" he called out, praying there wasn't another victim to rescue...or recover.

He chose his steps with more care, alert for a glimpse of a trip wire or any sign someone had been here. He saw it then, a rounded cache of stones that wasn't quite as natural as the rest of the area. He approached with extreme caution despite the dwindling time, unwilling to rush and set something off prematurely.

A bullet whistled past his head, knocking the top stone from the cache. Riley had jerked back, seeking cover, when he heard the soft whimper.

"Mrs. Wilks?"

Another muffled response came from closer to the scruffy, wind-sculpted trees to his left. Rocks and twigs skittered down the slope toward him.

He took that as an affirmative.

The small cascade revealed red and green wires running from the cache of rocks up into the trees. Definitely a bomb, he thought grimly. "Hold still," he called out to the woman. God help them both if she did something to set it off.

He peered up but couldn't pick out the armed guard. The shooter could be anywhere, in a tree or undercover on the ground.

In the back of his mind, a clock seemed to tick off the seconds. He wondered about the twisted strategist who'd gone to such lengths just to get even with Abby. Whatever the goal, he had to deal with this first.

Stretched out on his belly, he inched closer to the wiring. Another bullet bit into the rock-strewn ground milli-meters from his fingertips. Splintered rocks bit at his face. Even if he'd had a weapon it wouldn't have done him much good at the moment. There was no time for him to stop and return fire.

Both he and the guard were equally determined to suc-ceed, with Mrs. Wilks's life in the balance. Riley shifted as fast as he dared up the slope and the radio at his belt crackled.

"At your back," Abby's voice came through the device.

Despite his precarious position, Riley smiled. Of course she had his back. Thinking about how the bomb in the car had been wired, he went for the cache of explosives closer to the water. He couldn't afford to waste precious seconds with a panicked hostage.

This time when the sniper fired, another weapon re-turned fire. Out of habit, Riley kept track of the bullets from Abby. The Belclare P.D. used 9mm handguns with a fifteen-round clip. Whatever Abby was firing was beefier than that, the sound too deep for a standard 9mm.

His attention on the bomb, he ignored the shouting, knowing Abby would follow protocol and ask for a sur-render. The timer was inside twenty seconds when Riley disconnected the detonator. He followed the wires up the bank, another volley of gunfire flying over his head.

"Mrs. Wilks!" Relief at finding her alive washed over him and he wanted to shout in victory when he saw the timer on the device strapped to her waist frozen at twelve seconds. "You're fine. It's over," he said, cutting through the tape and sliding the explosives away from her.

Her round face was pale under the dirt and her eyes were shining with tears. "This might hurt," he warned, gently peeling away the duct tape covering her mouth. He looked at the adhesive side, noting the smudge of pink lipstick.

"Thank you!" She threw herself into him and he caught her, letting her cling.

"Are you hurt?"

"My pride," she said, tears flowing freely now. "The bruises will heal faster, I'm sure, but I'm so cold."

"Nothing broken?" He pulled the radio from his belt and called for paramedics. "Nothing bleeding?"

"I'm fine," she insisted. "My word. They were shooting at you."

He decided the woman had an ironclad fortitude to be more worried about him than herself. "It wasn't as close as it looked. Did you see who did this to you? Can you give us a description?" Then he noticed something missing. "You aren't wearing your glasses."

"Young man, my distance vision is still perfect."

Which meant she might or might not be able to describe the person or persons who had done this to her.

Tree limbs popped and snapped as something crashed down nearly on top of them.

"Get down!" He didn't hesitate at Abby's command, pushing Mrs. Wilks back into the shallow hollow that might well have been her grave.

He heard one more deep shot from Abby's gun, followed by a terrible sound that split the air in two. The concussion wave from the explosion threw him down and a blast of heat kept him there while pieces of trees and rock and ash fell all around them like dirty rain.

Two more loud explosions sounded too close for comfort, shaking the earth and rocks under them. It reminded him of the day he'd watched a crew take down an old building two blocks from the orphanage. He hoped that meant the other caches were blown and this trial was over.

The eerie silence that followed swallowed him up, surrounding him and Mrs. Wilks. He peered out at the shore and spotted the grisly debris of what had surely been the sniper.

"Where is Abby?" Mrs. Wilks cried. "Is she all right?"

Riley twisted around to check the place he'd last heard her, smiling when she stood tall, leaning into the slope, her gun down and just behind her leg. "I'm right here, Mrs. Wilks," she called out. Her chest heaved as she gulped in air. "Don't worry about me."

Riley moved a bit so the older woman could see her friend and neighbor.

"Oh, thank heaven. Thank heaven for both of you." She clasped her hands over her heart, then let Riley help her to her feet. He kept her turned from the mess closer to the shore as Abby stepped forward to wrap her in a warm hug. "Help will be here shortly. You don't have to walk."

"I will walk out of here. Lord only knows how they got me into this predicament to start."

Abby shot a look at Riley. "They?"

"Yes. I made the coffee and started up to bed and there they were, right in my living room."

"You saw their faces?"

"No," she said, shaking her head. The gesture threw her off balance, but Riley steadied her. "They had black ski masks on."

"We saw the mess in your house," Abby said. "You put up quite a fight."

"I clocked one of them in the knee with that hickory stick I keep in the umbrella stand."

Riley made a mental note to watch for someone with a fresh limp. He could tell by the way Abby's eyebrows arched that she was thinking the same thing and would pass that detail on to every shift and the extra patrols.

The radios he and Abby were wearing crackled as verification came from other teams that the other bombs were neutralized without any casualties. No sign of additional hostages. That was something anyway. Even without a bomb squad on-site they'd managed to clear the area and ensure that the explosions intended to kill and maim had harmed no one.

As the paramedics met them, Riley caught Abby's hand. "Thanks for the cover fire."

"Least I could do," she said.

"What do you carry?" She showed him the .40 caliber gun. "Nice," he said with a smile.

Abby shrugged, her attention darting all around.

"What's wrong?"

"He blew himself up, I think," she said quietly. She clamped her lips together, breathing deep through her nose. "I fired at his feet. A warning shot. But he…"

Riley didn't want her thinking about that gruesome blood smear on the rocks. "Did you recognize him? Was he limping?"

"No." She shook her head. "His face was painted with camouflage and he wore green patterned gear. I didn't recognize anything about him. As for the limp, who could tell on this terrain?"

True. "The feds will be all over this."

"I know." Her shoulders hitched and she rubbed at her arms. "I never thought I'd be grateful for their help. This is one crime scene I'm happy to turn over."

"It's over." Hopefully for good, but at least for the moment.

She nodded. "We'll have to give statements. I have all kinds of paperwork." She swore. "And a press conference."

"Then we'd best get at it." He gestured for her to lead the way to the docks.

"I'm a mess," she complained, picking a twig from her sleeve. "This sweater isn't worth giving away."

He reached out and pulled a leaf from her hair. "You're beautiful." He wanted to kiss her, to reassure himself she was safe and in one piece.

"You're just saying that to make me feel better."

"I'm saying it because it's the truth." He waited, cradling her hands in his until she finally looked at him. Her eyes went wide, then she smiled and looked away. "Your department, hell, the whole town, should throw you a parade. You're a hero, Abby."

"You did the hard part," she argued.

"Don't dodge the compliment."

"Fine." She took a big breath and looked out over the water one last time. "But I'm a hero with a ton of paperwork to do."

He was damn happy that they were all alive to do that paperwork. Today had been too close.

ABBY TURNED FROM the podium and the crush of questions, letting Mayor Scott finish things up. During this press conference, she'd been more careful with her words without compromising her determination. She would not allow this nonsense to continue in her town. Having Mrs. Wilks home safe had done just the opposite of what her enemies wanted. The rescue boosted her popularity. Even if he'd wanted to, the mayor wouldn't be able to oust her now.

It should give her comfort, but instead she worried over how things could get worse. Who might end up a victim next? She couldn't afford to think about that here, where the cameras might capture the worry on her face. Most of the reporters were still asking questions about the man who'd driven Mrs. Wilks's car into the bay.

They weren't alone. She had more than a few questions for Riley O'Brien, too. Though she would be forever grateful for what he'd done, how had a construction worker turned Christmas-decorating guru known how to disarm a bomb?

The mayor deflected the hard questions and tailored his answers to suit his purposes. He'd dubbed Riley the hero of Belclare, telling everyone Riley had gone to the hospital simply as a precaution, and the mayor would be stopping there next. Yes, of course the mayor and town council would be looking into honoring Belclare's newest hero in the coming days.

It went on and on. Abby listened enough to applaud or nod stoically in the right places. The most she would get out of this was a lesson in managing the press. At last they were done and she retreated into the station while the mayor's team cleaned up the podium.

"Nicely done, Jensen." Mayor Scott shook her hand, adding a pat on her shoulder.

Despite having taken a shower and changed into a clean suit, she felt weary and frustrated. The last thing she needed was a political shadow. "It was a group effort," she replied. Right now, she wanted that group scouring security footage. Two men had attacked Mrs. Wilks, but only one was dead. She needed to find the other man to help her break up what she now felt confident was a local terrorist cell.

When the mayor was done shaking hands, she and her officers were able to get busy. Abby settled behind a spare desk, her gaze drifting over the plastic sheeting that blocked off the burned side of the building. The cleaning crew claimed they would finish today, but fresh paint and new equipment was only the first part. The emotional impact would stay with her and the department for weeks, if not longer. In her gut, she knew that was the real motivation behind the fire.

She slipped the flash drive into her computer and

started another search through Filmore's life. Who—local or otherwise—could have compelled him to set that fire?

Her gaze skimmed from her laptop screen and out across the bullpen. It took a concerted effort to resist the tug of paranoia and go back to the facts in front of her.

"Chief!" She looked up again as Gadsden waved her over. "I've got the wallet getting tossed at the warehouse Dumpster."

With a fresh surge of energy, she hurried over to Gadsden. "Praise God for detail-oriented people."

Gadsden pointed out the wallet sailing through the air.

"Great. Now we back it up. There has to be something that shows us a bit more," she said, praying it was true.

"This gives us a timeline," he replied, pointing at the date and time in the corner of the video. "The car and Mrs. Wilks had to have been staged before this point."

Abby nodded. As leads went, she'd seen stronger, but it was a starting point. "And that looks like a blatant attempt to implicate Ri—Mr. O'Brien or one of his coworkers."

"Yeah," Gadsden agreed. "Good bet the scarf was planted rather than an accident. Who would've guessed you'd be his alibi."

She pointedly ignored that comment. "See if there are other views or angles around the docks in this time frame." She wanted the second assailant. Her hands fisted at her sides. "I want faces. No one should feel that comfortable causing havoc in this town."

"You know, it's possible Mr. O'Brien knew what to do with those bombs because he *is* involved."

"Show me more evidence and we'll follow it," she said. Just because Gadsden was right didn't mean she had to like it. During the crisis, she'd led by example as they'd followed and eliminated the evidence already planted against Riley.

She would continue to do her job, no matter how sticky or uncomfortable things got.

Gadsden was right, however. Riley had shown awareness and expertise that only came from training and experience. He owed her answers. Now she just had to smother her feelings and find the objectivity and courage to ask the right questions.

The calm professionalism that had earned her this post was crumbling to pieces inside her, though she refused to let it show. She wanted to slam doors. Throw things. Shoot something. Declare a police emergency and conduct a door-to-door search. She nearly laughed, thinking about how the mayor would spin that.

Their best lead had blown himself up, a fanatic so dedicated he preferred suicide over capture. It wasn't a good sign of things to come. And yet, to the best of her knowledge no one in Belclare was missing.

The other caches of explosives along the shoreline had blown within a minute of the sniper. That detail alone strongly indicated a supervisor with an impatient trigger finger. Her instincts wouldn't let her chalk it up to blind luck. It was a miracle no one on the search teams had been seriously injured. Only Riley's quick work and the note he'd salvaged had saved no telling how many lives.

Was his finding that note part of the plan, too?

She shook off the thought and looked around the station. The men and women who served the Belclare police department were top-notch, but there simply weren't enough of them to patrol every high-risk area every hour of the day. The docks were a valuable target. Main Street, packed with tourists, would certainly make the news if something bad happened. She forced herself to imagine the worst-case scenario if this cell launched an attack when the park was full of families.

She'd appealed to the community to keep watch and report anything suspicious, praising the dock workers and giving them much of the credit for today's rescue operation. Without that kind of vigilance and action, she'd said, Mrs. Wilks might have died.

"We'll track 'em down, Chief."

Gadsden's assurance snapped her from her thoughts, but it would be a long time before she relaxed. "Yes," she agreed. "We will track down every last one of them."

Returning to her temporary desk, she noticed a new email in-box alert flashing on her screen. Sinking into the chair, anticipating the worst, she clicked on it.

Congratulations, Chief Jensen. You win today's skirmish but this war isn't over.

There was an attachment. Against her better judgment, she opened it. A three-panel cartoon strip filled the screen. First a caricature of the bandstand in the park, then that picture overlaid with animated flames. The last panel was a sad little pile of ash topped with an oversize police shield sporting her badge number.

They'd do it. She felt it in her gut. This opening weekend or not, they had the will and resources to make her worst nightmare come true.

"Cowards," she whispered to herself. "Bring it on." She sent the file up the line to the federal agencies that were supposedly doing something helpful behind the scenes to break up the sleeper cell they had suspected from the beginning was in Belclare. While she was grateful the federal teams were taking care of all the bomb evidence out by the water, anytime they wanted to step in with some real, boots-on-the-ground help, that would be fine by her.

She leaned back, the springs on the worn-out chair

squeaking in protest. Her department was crammed into half of their normal working space. Filmore had protected the building's facade but wreaked havoc inside. Her officers were tired and more than a little edgy with all of the reacting they'd been doing.

They were stretched too thin with the extra patrols, and asking them to maintain that level indefinitely was unacceptable. She needed a new play, something offensive that would bring this war to a head. For her department, as well as for the community at large.

If the terrorist cell could create chaos using people from petty criminals to snipers to historical society presidents, she could sure as hell plan a resounding victory with the people on her side. Assuming there were people on her side.

That list seemed terribly short. Maybe it was better to use a neutral party.

For the potentially crazy idea that popped into her mind, a neutral party, one well versed in personal defense, was her best option. Her only option. She ran her fingertips along on the edge of the desk. She shouldn't do it, shouldn't put any civilians in the line of fire for any reason. Except the terrorists had done that for her and they didn't show the first inclination of stopping.

The Lewiston family lived outside Belclare town limits and took advantage of the fact at every opportunity. Since becoming the Belclare police chief she'd tossed out more than one citation for an illegal whiskey still. The Lewistons just didn't buy into the concept of law enforcement on private property. They were all excellent game hunters, blessed with perfect aim, and her officers knew firsthand they were always armed.

But each December the family got their legal act together and assembled the proper permits because the ideal place for their Christmas tree sales lot straddled a narrow smidge of the town line. Their reputation for offering the finest trees in three counties drew record numbers of buyers every year. Alongside the Christmas Village, it had become a symbiotic partnership benefiting both the Lewiston family and Belclare.

She flipped back through her file of threatening emails, finding the one she'd mentioned to Riley about the Christmas tree lot. No, it hadn't been anything overt or direct, but the threat was phrased by someone who knew the Lewiston reputation for trouble the other eleven months of the year.

Damn it.

She should have considered that before, but now she would use it to her advantage. Resting her hands lightly on her keyboard, she measured her words carefully. If she could draw out the person planning all of this chaos, she could bring this to an end before anyone else—tourist or resident—got hurt.

There was no way to know for sure that the email would be read by the right person in time, but she had to try. When she was absolutely certain her invitation presented the perfect combination of bravado and temptation, she hit Send. As the message crossed cyberspace to the three most frequent addresses used on her hate mail, she murmured a prayer.

It was possible the feds would also catch wind of her idea, but it was a risk she had to take. To do nothing, to let this terrorist cell keep chipping away at her friends, her town and her confidence was intolerable. At least the Lewiston family could aptly defend themselves.

"Let's have our own merry Christmas," she muttered. "I'll bring a one-size-fits-all ticket to prison for you." She gathered her computer, cell phone and purse and said goodbye to everyone for the evening, but she didn't go straight home.

Taking her time, she drove out to see the welcome sign, admiring the creative display that set the mood for the tourists she hoped would arrive en masse tomorrow.

Coming back through the center of town, she felt like a little kid as she passed each display. Transformed, each street had an individual holiday theme, ranging from fanciful to elegant. The decorating teams had delivered yet again. Because they were outsiders it would be so easy to blame the vendors and temporary workers for the trouble, but she knew better. Her instincts told her the root of this crime wave was local.

Filmore would be impressed and pleased with the end results and, for a moment, she entertained the idea of snapping a picture of Main Street to take to him. She drove out to the park instead. The ironwork at the park entrance had been lit with white lights and the garland wound with sparkling ribbon, much like the lampposts on her neighborhood street.

Thoughts of Riley followed her as she slowly moved through the park. He'd shown both heroism and expertise today at the dock. He'd revealed an interest and awareness of her work most men didn't possess.

Maybe, as he'd said, he was just in the right place at the right time. Maybe he did plan to stay in Belclare because he liked the town. And when pigs started flying maybe she would believe him just because he kissed her so well.

There was more to the man and his story. As her pulse sped up, she realized exactly how eager she was to have some answers. Not only for the Wilks case, but for herself.

Snow started falling as Abby reached the bandstand and this time she did pull over and park. Vendor booths were scattered around behind the sloped green where Belclare residents enjoyed concerts and performances by the community theater. Santa Claus and his elves would take requests from ten to four. The Ferris wheel would run all day and into the night for the next three weeks, its colorful lights a beacon of holiday happiness.

She would not let anyone wreck that for the citizens she protected or for the tourists.

Getting out of her car, she enjoyed the utter quiet as big fat flakes caught in her hair and eyelashes. After soaking up the peaceful moment and letting it restore her battered nerves, she used her phone to take a few pictures. But she already knew the truth. The sick little cartoon from her email had been drawn up based on this year's bandstand display.

Provided the tourists were brave enough to come out despite the troubles in Belclare, tomorrow this area of the park would be crowded with people enjoying the carnival atmosphere in this winter wonderland. And if everything went according to plan at the Christmas tree lot, they would safely enjoy the experience and have happy memories to cherish.

Satisfied she could pull off her plans, she drove home. Turning into her neighborhood, she passed house after house with decorated Christmas trees in the windows. She really needed to put up her tree.

It seemed every front window on her street sported a decorated tree. Calder's window had a tree blooming with colorful lights and, without taking a closer look, Abby knew it would be sporting lengths of paper chains and macaroni garlands made by the excited hands of a happy child.

She pulled into her driveway and stopped her car next to Riley's truck. He'd plugged in the lights for her outdoor display, but her empty window looked like the Grinch had come by. Even Mrs. Wilks and Riley had managed to decorate their trees today despite bombs, hospital visits and police reports.

There was nothing more she could do tonight to net the terrorist cell. She might as well get busy and pull down the artificial tree from the attic.

The light came on over Riley's back door and she watched, mesmerized with the way his body moved as he stomped into his boots and slipped his arms through the red vest he always wore.

He walked up to her car and reached for the door handle. She hit the unlock button and let him open the door for her. "Such service," she said, stepping into the cold air.

"I've been watching for you," he said, a wide smile on his face. "You looked great at the press conference."

The snow fell on his hair and shoulders, sparkling before melting.

"Thanks. Weren't you at the hospital?"

"Sure, but they released me right away." He held out his hands for her inspection, but she was looking at the scrapes on his face. "Just a few scratches."

The criminals had called this a skirmish, but Riley's face had taken a beating. She reached out, not quite touching the butterfly closures across one lean cheekbone. It was a miracle his eyes had been spared.

Riley turned his face and brushed his lips across her palm. "I have a surprise for you." He walked backward toward his house, as if he couldn't stand to take his eyes off her.

Feeling inordinately flattered by that, she felt herself smiling back at him. Until an echo of Gadsden's voice intruded with the reminder that Riley might be working for the terrorists, too. "Why?"

"I need a reason?"

Everyone had reasons and agendas for the things they did. She didn't want to cloud the moment with work and worry, but she didn't want to be a fool if his handsome face hid a sinister purpose. "I guess not."

"Wow. You must be tired."

"Why do you say that?" She stepped forward, hopelessly drawn to him despite the risk. Maybe because of it. She told herself she was just anticipating the surprise.

"You gave up the questioning too quickly." His eyebrows bobbed up and down. "I was kind of expecting an interrogation."

"All right." He'd opened the door and she had to follow through. "What are you up to?" *Way to start strong, Abby.*

He grinned. "Wait right there. Don't move."

"Uh-huh." She folded her arms across her chest, hoping she wasn't being a complete idiot.

He disappeared behind the house and worry clogged her throat when she heard a scrape and rustle. "Are you okay?" Should she go for her gun or just dive in to provide backup for whatever he'd encountered?

"I'm fine," he called. "Stay put."

Fine. "I saw Mrs. Wilks got her tree up and…" She lost her train of thought as Riley came back into view. Or rather, as an enormous, fresh fir tree came into view, propelled by Riley's untied boots. "What's that?"

He leaned around the tree. "It's a *real* Christmas tree." His smile chased away every question and doubt hanging over her. No one harboring ill intent could look so happy over something as sentimental as a Christmas tree. Completely weak as rationalizations went, she let instinct have its way. That single expression changed her whole evening, erasing the turmoil of the criminal element plaguing her town.

The rich scent of the fresh-cut evergreen rolled over her, renewing her in the quiet snowfall. "It's huge."

"Mrs. Wilks helped me pick out all three of them at the Lewiston farm. She said they always have the best trees."

She swallowed down a resurgence of fresh doubt at the coincidence. "Three?"

"Yeah. One for her, one for me, and this one for you."

"I saw the windows when I pulled in," she said.

"We've probably been almost as busy as you." He set the tree down between them. "Of course, we've definitely had more fun. If you don't want it I'll find it another home."

"I want it," she said quickly. "It's perfect." She returned to her car for her purse to hide the unexpected nerves flooding her system. It had been such a long day and this was the perfect way to wrap it up. Or maybe she was losing her mind and had surrendered to the inevitable.

He looked the tree up and down. "I picked up a new tree stand since I couldn't be sure where yours was."

"Sounds like you thought of everything."

He hitched a shoulder. "I'm a detail guy."

"Yes. I've noticed." She unlocked her back door and let him wrestle the tree inside.

"Which way?"

"Down the hall and to the left."

She was impressed when he didn't knock anything over or off the walls as he maneuvered down the narrow hallway. It brought back an unwelcome reminder of the mess they'd found at Mrs. Wilks's house.

Another realization struck her, but she waited until he had the tree safely leaning between a chair and the wall. "You took her tree-shopping and helped her decorate to keep an eye on her, didn't you?"

He slipped his hands into his pockets. "Guilty as charged."

"I bet you even helped her clean up the mess in her house."

He shrugged. "Is that a problem?"

"No." It was thoughtful. Kind.

"She's one tough lady," he said. "But no one should deal with that alone. Besides, she gave me more cookies."

"Lucky man," Abby said, laughing. She was enjoying the normalcy of this moment. Standing here with him, she had the strangest sensation things might be okay. Who'd have guessed a stranger could make her feel this safe and stable in the midst of such a violent assault on Belclare?

"I'll just go get the tree stand."

"How does leftover lasagna sound?"

His gaze locked with hers, then drifted slowly to her mouth. She hoped it meant he wanted to kiss her as much as she wanted to kiss him.

"Delicious."

"Okay. I'll—" she hitched her thumb over her shoulder to the kitchen "—just get started on that while you put the tree in water."

Riley didn't move right away. He looked around the room. "You want it centered in the window, right?"

"Please."

"I can do that." He looked at her ceiling, then her furniture. Then his eyes landed on the flowers from Deke on her coffee table. His eyebrows snapped together in a hard scowl. "An admirer?" He tipped his head to the lavish arrangement.

"Not even close," she said. Her warm mood burst like a bubble. "It was a friendly gesture from Deke Maynard."

"Sure."

She slipped out of her coat and hooked it on the hall tree at the front door. Deke was the furthest thing from her mind with Riley filling up her front room. "It was meant as encouragement."

"That's some serious encouragement," he said softly. "You know, if I'm poaching here—"

"Poaching?" She cut him off, bristling at the archaic choice of words. "I'm not endangered wildlife, Riley."

"You know that's not what I meant."

She planted her hands on her hips. "One minute you're buying me a Christmas tree—with a stand—and the next you think I'm playing around or something."

He stepped forward but stopped when she held out a hand. "That is not what I meant."

"Then clear it up right now," she demanded.

"I like you." He took another step, stopping just as his chest brushed her fingers. "I want you," he added, his gaze hot on her. "I go after what I want, what I like. Sometimes I come on a little strong."

Her mind reeled at his speech. Her indignation faded. She was more surprised her knees didn't buckle. He was an arm's length away and her imagination leaped into overdrive, her mind on how his hands and mouth would feel if he closed the distance and kissed her. Did men come any hotter than this one? "I kissed you first," she muttered. "That should have been a clue."

His mouth twitched. "I remember. But I'm new in town and I don't know all the dynamics. What I do know is that I don't like sharing."

Where this was coming from dawned on her then. "Danny told you I meet with Deke every week."

Riley bobbed his head, but his eyes didn't leave hers.

"It's coffee. As friends." She reached back and pulled out the pins holding her hair up in a bun. Slipping the pins into her pocket, she raked her hands through her hair. It didn't escape her notice how Riley's eyes tracked every move. "He's talented, and very shy. He's also extremely influential."

"I heard the ads."

"Precisely my point. He's been very supportive. The flowers were a nice surprise from a friend."

"He delivered them personally?"

It seemed an odd thing for him to latch on to. "You just delivered a tree," she pointed out. "Deke is only a friend." She might have briefly hoped for more, but in the presence of Riley she understood exactly how lonely she'd been. Deke might have eventually been more, but not now. "It was important to me to maintain that friendship for Belclare."

"Got it."

"Do you?"

"Yes." He raised her hand from his chest to his lips. "You are a brave, gorgeous woman. Can you blame me for assuming there was competition?"

She rolled her eyes, though the compliment warmed her from head to toe. She pulled her hands free. Giving in to temptation, she leaned forward and kissed his cheek. "Go get the stand. I'll get dinner."

"Yes, ma'am."

"You don't ever have to say that to me again," she said, leading him back down the hall to the kitchen.

She found an apron to protect her skirt and kept herself on task, starting the oven and prepping a salad to go with the leftover lasagna. It was a comfortable time as Riley worked, bringing in the tree stand and a handsaw. A prepared man was a treasure, she thought absently as she slid the lasagna into the oven.

Riley called her to the front room for an opinion. "Well?"

"It's beautiful." She wasn't sure how, but he'd managed to find the perfect tree. It fit the space beautifully. "You sure don't waste any time."

"The present is all we're guaranteed."

The pragmatic philosophy reminded her that she'd likely

stirred up a brand-new hornets' nest before she'd left the station. Tomorrow could very well be her professional downfall if she'd overplayed her hand in that email.

"How much time before dinner's ready?"

She checked her watch. "Fifteen more minutes."

"Great. Point me to your decorations and I'll pull down the boxes."

"I can do that tomorrow," she protested. "You've really done enough."

"I'm on a roll here," he said with that dead-sexy grin. "If Mrs. Wilks and I can decorate two trees—"

"She helped you decorate your tree?" He really had been keeping an eye on the older woman. His kindness created a warmth inside Abby that had been missing in recent weeks.

"The cookies went to my head," he replied.

"Right." Abby started up the stairs. "I keep the boxes of decorations in the attic."

She tried not to think about how close he was as his boots sounded on the steps behind her. The man sent her system into overdrive with just a look. *The present is all we're guaranteed.* His words echoed in her head, mocking her, tempting her. If leaving the lasagna wasn't risking a fire, she might have taken him on an immediate and *present* detour to her bedroom.

She pulled down the access door in the ceiling and unfolded the steps. "Christmas boxes are just to the right."

Squeezing around him, she headed back downstairs. "Riley?" He paused on the steps. "Thanks."

"Your lasagna is well worth it."

There he went, lightening the mood and putting her at ease.

She returned to the kitchen with a smile on her face and had a quick debate over which table to set. The kitchen felt too casual and the dining room felt like too much pressure.

She split the difference with green place mats and a votive centered on a bright red napkin on the kitchen table. It felt like something out of a magazine from the 1950s, but she heard Riley in the hallway and knew she didn't have time to start over.

"THAT'S QUITE A VIGNETTE," Riley said, pausing in the doorway and taking it all in. It was a significant part of his job in Belclare to keep an eye on her, but it was a major perk, too. He'd told her the truth: he liked her. In uniform. In a firefight on the shore. Looking elegant in the ivory shirt, black skirt and heels that she wore right now.

He liked kissing her. And talking with her. Even arguing over bombs or flowers. "Smells even better the second time around," he said, searching for a way to get his mind back on the matter at hand. He needed to know if she'd learned anything about the dead sniper or the men who'd kidnapped Mrs. Wilks.

With the Christmas Village officially opening tomorrow, it would be easier if they could narrow the search parameters beyond ruling out Calder and Mrs. Wilks. He probably shouldn't have spent so many hours babysitting Mrs. Wilks, but he'd learned a lot just from listening to the woman chatter.

"Thanks. Have a seat," Abby said. "Do you want wine?"

"No, thanks." He watched her pour a generous glass for herself. He peered around her to the oven timer. Six minutes was enough time. "Do you mind if I grab a beer from my place?"

"Not at all."

He went next door as fast as he could without running until he got inside. Then he pounded up the stairs and changed into khakis and a button-down. He'd cleaned up after the ordeal on the shore, of course, but he'd been dealing with fresh pine trees and dusty boxes the rest of the day. Dressed the way she was, she deserved to share the meal with a man wearing something better than his work jeans and thermal shirt. It was the excuse he was sticking with anyway. He was too rushed to review his sudden urge to impress her. He brushed the dust out of his hair and then found his socks and deck shoes.

When he returned to her kitchen door, beer in hand, she was pulling the casserole dish out of the oven. She set it on the table and looked up, her jaw dropping. "What… You didn't have to…get all dressed up."

"Yeah, I did," he replied. The way she looked at him proved it a hundred times over. He came around and pulled out her chair, noticing the level in the wineglass was the same, but the lipstick print at the rim was new.

So he wasn't the only one dealing with a few nerves. Nice. The big question remained—were her nerves a residual from the tumultuous day or somehow related to him? He decided he could deal with the combination as long as he was a contributing factor.

She started the small talk as they filled their plates and he kept the conversation light, as well. While he wanted to know about the issues with the case, he respected that she needed a little distance.

"You look great," she said as she assembled a small bite of salad on her fork.

"Thanks." He'd noticed she wasn't eating, just sort of moving her food around on her plate, but he didn't think his wardrobe change was the cause. "What's distracting you?"

"Nothing. Everything." She poked at another piece of romaine lettuce and rolled a cherry tomato on top, but she didn't put it in her mouth.

"I'm a good listener."

"I've noticed." She looked up, smiling. "But this isn't the time."

He took a sip of beer. "Offer stands. You know where to find me."

"True."

He cast around for a better distraction. "Are you picky about stringing lights?"

Her gaze narrowed at him. "Define picky."

"Well." He pushed his plate back and leaned forward a bit. "In my experience there are three kinds of people when it comes to Christmas lights."

"Do tell."

"There are those who don't care how the job gets done. Then there are those who are picky about something. Either the amount of wiring that shows or starting at the top versus the bottom. You get the idea."

She nodded, her mouth full of salad.

Progress. "Then there are the insane types who are morally opposed to anything less than their personal definition of lighting perfection. A precise balance across every branch, the cords all arranged out of sight and connected at the back of the tree... Well, you get the idea."

"Yes." She paused, filling her mouth with a big bite of lasagna.

"Mrs. Wilks is picky in a sweet, traditional way. She likes white lights that go from the bottom to the top, casting her angel tree topper in a halo of light."

"Well said." She raised her glass to him. "You like colored lights."

"To be fair, those were left over from one of the displays. No time to shop, so I bought them from my boss yesterday."

"What will you do for ornaments?"

"Peg had a decent selection at the hardware store. Thought I'd go by tomorrow." That put the tension right back in her face. Damn. He mentally scrambled. "When I was a kid, each grade level took turns decorating the big Christmas tree in the narthex each year."

"Based on what you've done to Belclare you must have loved it."

"Not when Sister Mary Catherine was in charge. She was one of the insane types when it came to stringing lights. For the sake of the children I hope someone eventually donates a pre-lit fake tree to the church."

She relaxed enough to chuckle at the story and he was relieved to share something real about his past with her. "Are you going to answer the question?"

She pushed her chair back from the table and carried her wineglass to the counter. Mischief flashed in her eyes as she watched him. "What will you do if I admit I'm an insane sort?"

"I'll let you string them yourself."

"No problem. I've done it before. Every year of my adult life, in fact."

"Sounds like you have a system. Maybe I'll learn something new," he said, matching her teasing tone as he picked up their plates.

She moved forward to take them. "You don't have to clean up."

"I know." In her heels, she was almost eye level with him. He leaned in and kissed her. The contact was just a soft meeting of lips, nothing involved or intense, but it rocked his world all the same. "You cooked. I'll clean."

She shot him a look full of suspicion. "Either your mother raised you well or two trees are too much for you in one day."

"Could be both," he replied, grinning. "And you did mention all that experience."

"I did." She stepped back, raised her hands in surrender. "You clean, I'll string. Just out of pity for you."

He cleaned up the table and dishes in record time. Not only did he want to watch her process, but he remembered too late that the tree would ruin her shirt. When he reached the front room, he found her on her knees by the outlet under the window, the lit string of colored lights in her hands apparently forgotten. She was staring past the tree toward Calder's house, surely reliving her friend's accident.

The snow was coming down a little heavier now and would really set the mood for the Christmas Village in the morning. Belclare couldn't have wished for better weather and he was surprised by how much he hoped the sudden crime spree didn't hurt the event.

This place, after such a short time, felt more like home than anywhere he'd been before. He looked to Abby and knew she was a big part of the reason.

"Hey," he said gently, not wanting to startle her.

She turned and the hard expression in her eyes startled him. This wasn't a woman mourning a friend's pain or struggling with guilt that she might be part of the cause. No, that was sheer determination in her eyes.

"You've done something," he said without thinking.

"What?" She blinked rapidly and her expression cleared. "No. I just don't know where to start."

"Bull." He dropped to his knee beside her. "You barely remember why you're in here."

"That's rude."

"Rude might just be the beginning," he corrected. "Hand over the lights before you ruin your shirt."

"I can do it."

"I know, Abby." She could do whatever she set her mind to. Which worried him considering what she was up against. He wanted her to tell him, but why would she?

As far as she knew he was only a carpenter with some life experience. "But I bet you don't normally string lights dressed like that. Test the next string."

"Riley."

"What? There's no shame in accepting a little help." He couldn't look at her. He was too close to offering her more truth than she needed. More than he was allowed to share.

Eyeing the distance from the tree to the outlet, he started weaving lights through the lower branches at record speed. His hands knew what to do, which was nice considering he had no idea how to proceed with Abby.

"Riley?"

He adjusted the cord so the connector would be hidden. "Next string." He held out his free hand, but nothing landed in it.

"Look at me."

He sat back on his heels. "My pleasure." He tried to focus on her, just her, not his irrational fear for her safety. She'd kicked off her shoes and her feet were tucked under her, the skirt riding just above her knees.

"I was thinking about what you said, that we only have the present."

"Okay." He didn't know what to do with his empty hands. Was that a veiled invitation to demand professional answers or personal pleasure? There was nothing in her gaze or body language to clue him in. "I can work on the tree lights in the present."

"You can." Her smile was slow and lovely in the soft light of the lamp in the corner. She put the next strand of lights in his hand.

Grateful for the distraction, he went back to the task.

"You're a man of many talents," she said carefully. "Can you tell me where you learned about bombs?"

Officially, the answer was no. "I learned about explosives on the job," he said, choosing not to specify which job.

"But we didn't open that trunk and find explosives. You found wires. And the note."

"Wires that didn't belong. Wires that led to explosives. The note was meant to be found. If not by me, then by you or another officer." He risked a look over his shoulder, catching the thoughtful crease between her brows. Someone had made her doubt him when she didn't really want to. He resumed stringing each branch with lights. "Explosives are used in a number of construction situations. I've had my share of experience handling those situations. Truth is, I know a little something about a lot of things, Abby. Cars, flooring, garland. It's why I took the job here." Another nugget of truth, though he doubted she'd ever willingly forgive him for the omission. "It's why I took on the Hamilton house."

"Okay."

He finished with that strand and plugged it into the previous one. "Plug it in," he said, nodding to the outlet. "Let's see if you're happy so far."

On hands and knees, she gave his resolve one hell of a test as she plugged it in. He turned his gaze to the tree before she caught him lusting after the sweet, ripe curve of her backside.

"Wow," she whispered. "It's lovely."

Man of many talents, he thought. "I'm thinking you're less picky and more the easygoing type."

"You wish," she said. "Forgive the interrogation. You were just cucumber-cool with everything today, I thought maybe you'd spent time as a cop or…"

"A criminal?"

"They are known to wander."

"Would a criminal have helped Mrs. Wilks?"

"No, but a con man might."

He'd walked right into that one. "Well, she does make a chocolate-chip cookie worth reforming for, but I'm neither criminal nor con man."

"No. According to Mayor Scott, you're the hero of Belclare."

He choked on that moniker. "I could go the rest of my life without having those words aimed at me," he said. "You can trust me, Abby." If anyone in Belclare was on her side, it was him. "Let's finish this." He was referring to more than the tree.

"Maybe I don't trust myself," she admitted, handing him more lights. "Every time I turn around something else is damaged or someone else is in jeopardy."

"You got the win today."

She snorted and started pacing across the room behind him. "No one to question is hardly a victory. They didn't recover any helpful prints at Mrs. Wilks's house."

"Has Filmore offered anything more?"

"No."

Her impatience was disconcerting. He'd bet his fake cover story family and their shepherd's pie that she'd done something drastic. "I trust you," he said. "So do Mrs. Wilks, Calder, Peg, your department. They aren't idiots, Abby, and you don't have to be a lifelong resident of Belclare to see they rely on you because they know they can."

He wrestled his way through the middle section of the tree, grateful that it kept him from reaching for her. She had to bring him a stepladder to finish the top, but he could tell she was pleased when the job was done.

"I hate stringing lights," she said.

"Happy to help."

"Whether I start at the top or the bottom," she continued, "I always get irritated and careless before the job is done."

"That sounds really out of character for you."

"It's one place patience fails me." Laughing at herself, she handed him a star for the top of the tree.

"Don't you want to put it on?"

She shook her head. "You're already there."

"All right." He secured the star to the top and stepped down, setting the ladder to the side so it would be there when she put on the ornaments. "Looks good, if I do say so myself."

She pulled the drapes across the window. "I agree." But she was staring at him, not the tree. "You have sap on your shirt." She came closer and pointed to the offending spot.

"It'll wash."

"It's not your only good shirt?"

"No." Though most of his clothes were in storage while he sorted out where he'd live in Belclare.

"That's good." She reached out and yanked his shirt open, sending buttons flying.

"Abby?"

"I'm living in the present," she said. "I've always wanted to do that, but until you, I haven't been inspired." Her hands, warm and soft, flattened against his bare chest. "Tell me you're surprised. Please?" She pressed up on her toes, her lips brushing fleetingly against his.

"Surprised?" Then he remembered her words last night in the truck. "Oh, yeah." He wrapped her in his arms and pulled her close, the silk of her shirt an enticing, filmy barrier against his skin. Slowly, taking his time instead of just taking, he lowered his mouth to meet hers.

Her lips were soft and needy, and when her tongue stroked against his it was sweeter than it had been last night. She tasted of the deep red wine she'd had at dinner, a dark, sultry counterbalance to the crisp pine and sweet roses scenting the air.

She pushed the shirt over his shoulders and down his arms. Reluctantly, he released her to shake free of the binding fabric. He was nearly ready to beg, desperately eager to learn everything about her body, about how well it would fit with his. He wanted to discover what she liked and more, what made her absolutely crazy with passion.

Her hands molded and caressed his arms while he feathered kisses along the side of her neck, nipping gently at the warm curve of her shoulder.

She tempted him to rush with her kisses, her touch and her soft sighs. "Abby," he whispered against her skin. His blood pounded through his veins. If there had ever been another woman, he couldn't remember it.

There was only her, here and now in this moment. He skimmed his hand up her ribs to cup her full breast. With a moan, she arched into his touch and he felt her nipple pebble against his palm. He couldn't wait to taste her.

He heard the soft purr of a zipper followed by the rustle of fabric as her skirt fell to the floor. Ready to protest as she stepped away from him, the view stole his breath and he couldn't form the words. Lace-topped stockings caressed each thigh and the creamy skin above invited a thorough exploration.

She came back to him and wound her arms around his neck. He hitched her up until those long thighs circled his hips. He turned, bracing her back against the wall. Happily, he'd take her right here, or on the couch—hell, even the steps looked good.

All of the above. All in good time.

He carried her to the couch and sank into the cushions, her legs straddling his thighs, all of her open to his touch. He peeled away her shirt and trailed his fingers along the straps of her bra. When he unhooked it and let the lingerie fall away, he held her, learning how she wanted to be touched.

He set out to show her how beautiful she was to him. How she made him feel so wanted. Skimming his hands over every inch of her flesh, he showed her what she meant. He pulled her close, taking first one breast then the other into his mouth, teasing her soft flesh with tongue and teeth. Her palms were braced on his shoulders, and her little moans were sweet encouragement.

She shifted away, bringing her mouth down to his. The kiss turned into a sensual dual as her tongue slid across his. Her hands cruised over his chest and lower until he was rocking his erection into her delicious touch.

As she opened his slacks, taking him in hand, he slipped a finger under that lace and found her wet, hot and ready. Need surged through him. "Abby." He raised up, stripping away his clothing. The only remaining barrier was her panties. With a wink, he reached out and tore them away.

Wearing only her thigh-highs, she came over him, gliding down slowly until she'd taken him fully inside her. He waited, holding back by some miracle, while she set the pace. It was worth the wait—when she moved it was heaven. Gripping her hips, he met her body with each stroke, until her climax shuddered through her and around him, her fingertips digging into his shoulders.

His release came a moment later and she dropped her head against his shoulder, panting and snuggling close as they floated back to reality.

After a few minutes she shifted again. "Told you the couch is too small." She stood up, keeping his hands in hers. "Come share my bed."

He didn't know it was possible to go from completely sated to all-out need in the span of one staircase, but it happened.

When they reached her bedroom her tender kiss ignited an encore performance that stole his breath. Spent, her body felt as pliable as butter sprawled across his chest. He heard her whispering softly against his skin but couldn't make out the words. "What was that?" he asked.

She raised her head, propping her chin on her hands to meet his gaze. "'Soul meets soul on lovers' lips.'"

He ran a finger down her spine. "You're quoting Shelley?"

"It seems to fit." Her smile was nothing short of radiant. "You know the quote."

"I do."

"You consistently surprise me, Riley."

He combed his hand through her hair. "Same goes, Abby."

She pulled the covers over them and snuggled next to him. "I'm glad you're here."

"Me, too." He pressed a kiss to her hair and listened to the simple perfection of her breath until she fell asleep.

Chapter Fourteen

Saturday, December 3, 6:40 a.m.

Abby slipped from the bed, careful not to disturb Riley. He was sprawled facedown across the mattress, the tangled sheets leaving him more exposed than covered. Of all her recent challenges, exiting the bed proved the most difficult.

With a wistful sigh, she kept moving. She'd make it up to him later. Tonight, after they had the terrorist in custody, they could celebrate. They could even go down to the park and join the fun of a successful opening day of the Christmas Village.

She found dark jeans and a sweater and dressed in the guest room so she wouldn't wake him. Then she wrote him a note and left it on her pillow. If she was lucky, this would all be over before he realized she was gone.

Optimism was a good thing.

WHEN RILEY HEARD Abby leave the house he opened his eyes. Rolling over, he stared at her bedroom ceiling, only moving after he heard the low rumble of her car engine. Still he waited until the noise faded before he rolled out of the bed.

He supposed he should be flattered she trusted him enough to leave him alone in her house. This was, after all, the opportunity he'd wanted since arriving in Belclare. He reclaimed his clothing and dressed quickly, pausing just long enough to read the apologetic note that said she'd been called to the station on an emergency.

Yes, he'd been sleeping deeply with her supple body in his arms, but he knew her phone hadn't made any of the obnoxious sounds she'd programmed for police business. In between rounds of lovemaking, she'd made a point of putting it on the charger next to the bed.

So, if not official business, where had she run off to so early? He didn't like the answers that immediately came to mind. Last night he'd suspected she had made a move of some sort in hopes of thwarting the enemy. Now, he was certain she was up to something she didn't want anyone else to know about. Fastening his watch, he checked the time. Two hours before the official opening of the Christmas Village.

He did a quick search on his way out. In the kitchen he found another note inviting him to help himself to coffee and whatever else he wanted and asking him to lock up as he left. Eggs and toast weren't his primary concern. He wanted her to tell him what she was up to.

He suppressed the sinking feeling in his gut as he violated her privacy and opened the laptop she'd left on the kitchen table, but it had to be done. Keeping her safely in her post as Belclare's police chief was his first order of business.

Finding the email requesting a meeting with the sleeper cell leader landed like a punch to the gut and his breath stalled in his chest. Irrational as it was, temper and a strange hurt surged through him. He knew she didn't trust him completely, and he even understood why. But to take this step without any backup was desperate. The terrorist leader would cut her down without a second thought and use her death as a cautionary tale to others who would try to prevent further operations.

He closed her computer and locked up her house, darting across the driveway to his place. He fought his first instinct to don the tactical gear and weapons stashed behind the wall in the bedroom closet—that wasn't the answer.

Instead, mustering his operational calm, he changed into jeans and a thermal shirt. He shrugged into a shoulder holster and checked the load on his 9mm. Covering the gun with a thick chamois shirt, he headed downstairs for his boots and down vest. He'd think of a reason to explain his return visit to the Christmas tree lot on the way.

Chapter Fifteen

Abby chose a spot close to the entrance of the Lewiston tree lot, not surprised her car was the only one in the parking area. She'd decided on this location because of the family and because it gave her enemy the illusion of several ways in and out.

The chicken-wire fencing didn't offer much in the way of a challenge or a deterrent to trespassers. Though they'd never suffered a threat or lost property, the Lewiston family maintained an armed watch on the lot 24/7. One of them would be around, watching.

"Welcome to your last day in my town," Abby murmured, as she checked her weapon and slid the extra clips of ammunition into her coat pockets. Provided her email had made it through to the right party and her challenge had been accepted, the terrorist grip on Belclare was about to end.

With her badge in plain view on her jacket and her Glock in hand, she stepped out of the car. The sun was bright in the sky, but the air was bitter cold. The wind nipped at her cheeks and chilled the denim of her jeans. Her boots crunched on the snow-covered gravel of the parking area. Alternately stepping and pausing to listen, her gun lowered but ready, she cautiously entered the forest of Christmas trees neatly organized by size and type.

She felt eyes on her and knew she'd drawn the attention of at least one member of the Lewiston family. Based on the increased patrols, she knew her officers could be on-site within three minutes of an emergency call. Three minutes gave her plenty of time to draw out a confession or at least identify a viable suspect.

Her radio crackled. "Mornin', Chief," a voice rasped. "One trespasser in the northeast corner. No visible weapon."

Of course the Lewistons would know the police channels. She nodded, appreciating the tip as much as the automatic cooperation. She'd just started moving with more confidence to that position when the same voice sounded off again.

"Second contact directly east of your position has a shoulder holster. Don't know what you're up to but seems like you've got some interest."

A quick prickle of fear skittered down her spine. She hadn't expected this to be easy. With a bit of clever maneuvering she could still pull this off. Failure wasn't an option.

Keeping rows of trees between her and the east side of the lot, she moved closer to the corner, eager to find who was waiting.

The sound of a shotgun rang out, sending birds into flight. The lower branches of a tree splintered on her right. Fresh pine filled the air. The tree slumped to the side and she caught sight of a familiar red vest diving for cover.

The terrorist could *not* be Riley. The words bounced around in her head. No, the jackass terrorist was messing with her. She couldn't have been so wrong as to sleep with her enemy.

"Show yourself!" She dropped to her belly, looking for boots and listening for movement. "I thought you came to negotiate."

"I believe he came to kill you."

Where was that voice coming from? And what the hell was Deke doing out here? He'd never spent so much time away from his house. Feet appeared in her line of sight but no boots. The high shine on the shoes and the dark slacks warned that it was in fact the artist who'd come to meet her. Could she have so badly misjudged the man?

She measured the distance to the man and stayed low. "What brings you out this morning, Deke?"

"I've wanted to tell you for ages, darling," he replied, not moving from his position. "I do so much more than paint."

It was him! She'd been a fool! So grateful for his help to the town's well-being—to her well-being, she hadn't seen the forest for the trees. Now, with Christmas trees surrounding her, she saw exactly what she'd been missing.

"No time like the present," Abby offered, checking Deke's position again and spotting boots moving closer to him. Tied this time, there was no mistaking Riley's footwear. If it was him, why wasn't he defending himself? And her? Her heart turned as cold as the ground beneath her chest. Tears stung her eyes. She would cry later. Right now, she had a confession to gain and an arrest to make. Maybe two.

"I'm not sure you can handle the truth, sweet Abby," Deke taunted.

Fury tightened her lips. "Your being here says it all. That email only went to my haters. That tells me a hell of a lot."

"Are you sure, Abby? More than one federal agency has been watching Belclare. I was sent to keep an eye on things…to protect you." He sounded as calm as he did over coffee in his parlor. "Do stand up and let's discuss this rationally. You know me, Abby. Why would you hide from me? If I'd wanted you dead, I could have easily made that happen on any number of occasions."

At least that last part was the truth. "Yes," she said, pushing to her feet. She'd had enough. She wanted the truth. "Why don't we all three discuss this right now."

"Agreed." Riley stepped clear of the trees he was using for cover, holding a gun aimed at Deke's chest.

Deke's gloved hands were raised and empty, palms facing out.

As if seeing him for the first time, she could tell by Riley's stance that carpentry wasn't his primary vocation. Questions ripped through her, not one of them relevant to this particular moment and all too painful. "Lower your weapon," she ordered, her voice quavering.

"No." He didn't flinch. "Deke Maynard is a killer, the mastermind behind all of this. We just got confirmation."

"The convenient lies of an expert assassin," Deke countered, shaking his head as if the accusations were nothing more serious than the ranting of an unhappy child. "I saw the media footage of him with that poor woman's car. Quite a heroic feat, designed to impress you, Abby. He's been lying to you all along. I've been doing some research of my own and Riley O'Brien is not who he claims he is."

"You know damn good and well I didn't have anything to do with any of this, Abby," Riley argued, fury darkening his face.

Deke made a disapproving *tsk-tsk*. "He got that close? You mustn't blame yourself. His specific…*ah*…skills are well-known in unsavory circles."

Abby tried to summon her voice but it wasn't happening. All she could do was watch the two men who had fooled her so completely. Maybe she didn't deserve to be Belclare's chief of police after all.

"Deke is a terrorist," Riley accused. "The dump of Filmore's phone records shows a connection."

"The man and I chatted frequently about what was best

for the town," Deke explained. "You know how obsessed he is with preservation."

Abby struggled with the decision. They were both so convincing. She searched for a defining question, one that would expose the liar. "Someone convinced Filmore to set that fire."

"A search of his home turned up nothing of consequence," Deke said, dropping his hands to his pockets with a new measure of confidence that no one was going to shoot him. "I believe he thought he could save the town by making you look bad."

Deke glanced beyond her, to her left. What was he looking for? She risked a glance in that direction, but she didn't see any movement. If someone was closing in on them, the Lewiston guard would fire or, at the very least, warn her.

"Think, Abby," Riley challenged, bringing her attention back on point. His gun was still trained on Deke.

"Lower the gun," she repeated, the mixture of hurt and anger building in her chest making it hard to breathe.

Riley shot her a disappointed look but did as she asked this time. Abby looked from Deke to Riley and back again. Her heart screamed for her to make the right choice, her temper told her to drag them both to jail.

"Yes, do think carefully," Deke said, his voice steady and smooth as silk while she wrestled with her indecision. "This man, this *stranger,* has used you to further a terrible cause."

"How long are you going to listen to this crap?" Riley demanded. "How well do you really know him, Abby?"

Deke was the eccentric artist, the local recluse who only came down from his studio to grace the people with enough wisdom and charm to keep them satisfied. And perpetually curious. Beyond weekly coffee and the occasional canvas displayed in the gallery window, what did she know about how he spent his time or where his assets came from?

She didn't want to believe he was the bad guy, but she couldn't quite believe he was a federal agent.

A wave of guilt rushed over her. She'd enjoyed his attentions, believing his interest and supportive friendship had been genuine. Had his flattery made her blind to the facts of his true nature?

"Finish this, Abby," Riley urged. "Don't make a mistake that will get us both killed."

His voice slid low and rough across her senses, much as those working hands of his had slipped over her body last night. If he was the assassin Deke claimed, Riley had certainly been close enough to take her out any number of times, as well.

It was the worst kind of standoff. She was staring at a hero and a killer. She only had to decide which one was which. Being wrong could very well cost her her life. Being right could cost her the love of her life. She nearly laughed at herself for ever thinking she enjoyed making the tough calls.

Sirens approached and brakes squealed, making the turn from the paved road into the gravel parking lot. Here was her backup—who would she send back in cuffs?

"Abby," Deke coaxed. "You know me."

"He's a liar, Abby," Riley insisted.

Her gaze locked with Riley's and suddenly she knew. Heart and gut instinct aligned in one perfect moment of clarity. Riley had warned her there was more to this situation and he'd repeatedly asked her who stood to gain. She couldn't prove it in legal terms, but she wouldn't have to. *Unless she was wrong.*

Her backup rushed into position next to her.

"Arrest Mr. Maynard," she announced. She kept her gun trained on Deke until Officer Gadsden had him handcuffed. "I'll notify Homeland Security." She risked a look at Riley. "Mr. O'Brien?"

"Yes?"

"I'll need you to come in and make a formal statement." A statement that better include a thorough explanation of that confirmation he'd mentioned, as well as his surprise appearance out here.

He arched an eyebrow. Whether that silent, subtle gesture was about her official tone or something else, she didn't care to analyze right now.

"I can do that. Anything else?"

Oh, there was a lot more, but this wasn't the place to get into the other issues. "The city of Belclare thanks you." She turned her back on him before she broke down entirely. The chief of police did not dissolve into a puddle of mush in front of terrorists and curious citizens.

"Hey, Chief!"

She looked over at Jerry Lewiston, the head of the Lewiston family. He was standing near the area Deke had been looking at. "Yes?"

"Can we keep the bomb?"

"I beg your pardon?" The shock of his words cleared away the emotional cobwebs. Thankfully.

"Way I figure, it's a fair exchange for the damaged tree."

"I'd have to disagree," she said, striding over to see what the hell he was talking about. "It's evidence."

"But it was my boy who helped your friend in the red vest disarm it and save your life."

She looked down, her knees wobbling. It had been a close call. Lewiston was right. If this had gone off… "You saw who planted it."

"I did." He lifted his chin toward Deke. "That fancy one. Probably thought we were all asleep. I guess he don't know us Lewistons too well."

The confirmation that she'd made the right choice should have been more satisfying, but all she could think about were how foolish she'd been to ever trust Deke Maynard and how many lies Riley had told her. "Just the one?"

"Yes, ma'am."

"It has to come with me."

Lewiston was clearly disappointed. She motioned him to move closer, away from the bomb. "You realize this puts me in your debt."

The man smiled, understanding. "All right then, guess that's a fair trade."

She relayed the details to the feds and assigned the appropriate instructions. When she finally settled behind the wheel of her car, she risked one more glance at Riley, who stood at the entrance watching her.

He would put Belclare behind him as soon as his statement was signed. Why wouldn't he? He had obviously been sent here.

Fine. It was for the best. Amazing sex wasn't enough reason for him to stay. Not when she couldn't trust him. Obviously, she didn't know him at all. If she were any other woman under normal circumstances, she would run straight to Riley and rest easy in the illusion of security she found in his embrace. Good grief, if she were any other woman, she wouldn't have been stuck in this impossible dilemma to start with.

If she'd been any other woman, men like Deke Maynard and Riley O'Brien might easily have overlooked her. Power, duty and responsibility were as much a part of her as her blond hair and preference for candy-apple-red toenail polish.

Apparently Deke was the only person who sensed there was any lingering naïveté to exploit. She couldn't wrap her head around how *that* revelation made her feel.

Well, she'd just have to count this a hard lesson learned. This incident marked the last time she trusted first and asked questions later—particularly when it came to men. No one else would ever be allowed close enough to hurt her.

She put the car in gear and followed the officers transporting Deke to the station.

It was over.

IN HIS TRUCK, Riley fumed every second of the short trip to the police station. "The city of Belclare thanks me, my ass."

The only thanks he wanted was a paycheck for a good day's work. He didn't want any gratitude from Belclare or the chief of police.

Well, at least the latter was partly true. What he wanted was the woman behind the badge. He needed her. More, he needed her to understand what they'd shared was real, not another facet of the game that bastard Maynard had been playing with her.

Why couldn't she tell the difference?

His hand flexed and released around the leather-wrapped steering wheel. He supposed if she couldn't tell the difference to some degree he'd be listening to one of Belclare's finest rattle off his Miranda rights about now. Her face danced across his vision. Not the lovely, poetry-quoting face of last night, but the accusing expression, full of doubt as she decided which man to believe and which to haul in.

He might be new in town, but she could hardly call him a stranger. Not after last night. Not after all that they'd shared before that. He had to find a way to make her listen. *Soul meets soul on lovers' lips.* She'd been the one to quote Shelley as her body had been draped over his like a sensual blanket last night.

She'd said those words while he'd been thinking about the ramifications of his lifelong assignment to Belclare. To her. And he'd felt the truth of her words sink deep into his system. Accepted. Known. In that moment he understood to the bone who he was: *hers*.

Nothing in his life had ever felt more perfect or so full of promise and potential than that moment. Damned if he was going to just give in and let her walk away from what they'd started. If the tables were reversed, she wouldn't let him hide.

Riley stalked into the station, his irritation with her hovering like a dark cloud over his head. He gave his statement and accepted the thank-yous for saving her life and helping to solve the mystery. It seemed he wasn't a stranger to anyone but her. He didn't need a shrink to tell him why that stung so much.

His official task complete, he lingered at the station, knowing he had to talk this out with her now rather than later. They processed the artist-terrorist, though the man showed no signs of cooperating despite Gadsden finding a remote detonator for the bomb in his pocket.

While Abby remained locked in the conference room with the mayor and some suit from Homeland Security, Riley used his phone to check email.

She had no idea how good he was at the waiting game.

Chapter Sixteen

Abby closed the door, clinging to the last thread of her control. "You've been lying to me." She pulled the cord on the blinds at the conference room window, blocking the curious gazes from her department. "About everything."

"Not everything," Riley countered.

"The only reason you aren't in cuffs is because you saved Mrs. Wilks."

"And you."

Her breath stuttered at his audacity. She hated that he was right. That she'd been duped. "And me," she agreed through clenched teeth. "Though I would have managed without you. My plan to draw out the terrorist worked."

"Apparently, but you were up against—"

"What? Who?" She was shouting. Clamping her lips together, she stopped until she could regain control. "Sit down and tell me everything you think you know about the threats against me." As he took a seat, she settled into her chair and carefully removed her .40 caliber Glock, placing it on the table. "Convince me you aren't one of those threats."

He glanced at the weapon before meeting her gaze. "I think you know better."

She didn't. Not now. She wanted to believe him, desperately, but that was thinking with her heart. Here, under these circumstances, being a cop trumped being a woman.

Homeland Security had briefed her about a new task force that placed agents in suspect, high-risk areas.

Apparently Riley was a one-man task force. And though that didn't make him the enemy, it made him the man who'd lied to her…used her. "You said you had confirmation of Deke's involvement." The feds had denied that claim. They were executing a search of his house now.

When this was resolved, when she knew what he was really doing in her town, then she could berate herself for sleeping with him, for falling for the lies—spoken and un-spoken.

"Abby," he began.

"Chief Jensen," she corrected.

"Chief Jensen," he echoed, tension in his tone. "You re-ally don't have the cl—"

"If you finish that sentence with 'clearance' I will shoot you on principle."

"A stunt like that means a lot of paperwork."

"Accidents happen. Firearms are dangerous."

So ARE YOU, Riley thought, deciding maybe he shouldn't twitch a muscle. "So put it away," he suggested. He didn't think the weapon was nearly as deadly as the woman on the other side of the table. "Where are you holding Mr. Maynard?"

"That isn't your concern."

He should have told her last night, security clearances be damned. He'd wanted to tell her she wasn't in this alone the night one of Maynard's lackeys had pushed Calder off the ladder.

Now it was too late. Her gorgeous blue gaze had turned icy. She felt betrayed and he could hardly blame her. Ironic really, that when he knew just who he wanted to be and why, when his identity felt more real and true than any other time in his life, the woman he wanted to be real for wouldn't believe in him.

"Mr. O'Brien?"

"Riley," he said, frustrated by her insistence on reverting to these formalities. He couldn't leave town even if he wanted to. Director Casey had planted him here for a reason. Belclare was still a ripe target. Whatever she believed, this wasn't over yet.

"Start talking or I'm dumping you in a holding cell."

"On what charge?" He jerked a thumb over his shoulder. "All of Belclare thinks I'm a hero."

"I suppose that was your plan. Waltz into my town, win over the locals and seduce the little-lady police chief."

No one thought of her that way. "Last night was no one-sided seduction," he said, leaning forward, ignoring the damned gun on the desk.

"Let's stick with today," she snapped, color flooding her cheeks. "Who are you? Start with your real name."

He gripped the arms of the chair. Might as well spill it all—he doubted she would grant him another chance to clear the air. "I have no idea what my real name is. Riley O'Brien is what the teachers and staff in the orphanage called me. When I graduated, I traded a few years in the military for college tuition. Now I'm here."

"No Irish parents?"

"Your guess is as good as mine." He shook his head. His childhood fantasies of home and hearth felt silly now. The fragile new hope she'd kindled sputtered out beneath her unrelenting blue gaze.

"There seems to be a significant gap in your personal history."

"I agree." He refused to elaborate, even if it was possible. Whether or not she hated him for what they shared on a personal level, Belclare was his post and he wouldn't jeopardize that. If he was exposed or ousted, who would protect her?

Let her hate him for lying about his past, but she'd come to mean too much in such a short time for him to walk away and leave her safety to someone else.

"Who sent you here?" Her eyes flared as something else occurred to her. "What in the hell did you do to the Hamiltons?"

He rolled his eyes, aggravated by her suddenly over-active imagination. "Call the Realtor, check in on them. I showed you the paperwork. You know I came by the house honestly when I was decorating the realty office storefront."

She scoffed at that, her fingertips dancing along the grip of her gun.

This really couldn't get any worse. Unless she shot him. "Call. Verify my story. I'm not going anywhere."

"Oh, yes, you are. Tell me the truth and then get out of my town."

"I told you the truth." At least as much as he dared to explain right now. Deke was in custody, but were the men who did his dirty work planning to follow through on what-ever orders he'd already issued? It was too soon to tell. If he could get Abby to calm down, he had a feeling she'd agree with his assessment.

He was furious that Deke had managed to expose him and kill her trust. From Riley's vantage point, exposing him gave anyone a clear shot at Abby.

"The *whole* truth."

The only truth that mattered to Riley was sitting on the other side of the desk. Abby had started as an assignment, but she was so much more now. He didn't think she wanted to hear that. She wouldn't want to hear how he admired this side of her. Even with her substantial fury leveled at him, he admired her. Wanted her. He shook his head. "The truth that matters is I am here to protect you and your town from a very real terrorist threat. Your success this morning notwithstanding, my orders have not changed. You don't have the authority to send me anywhere." Not professionally anyway, but he left that unsaid.

She swore, impressing him with her colorful vocabulary. "The explosives are secure. The man using the docks and this town as his personal criminal playground is in custody. Belclare is safe again. You can go."

But the threat against her personally, the promise to make her an example, still loomed over her head. "I have to stay." He pushed to his feet. "I'm sorry that makes you uncomfortable, Abby."

His heart clutched when she picked up her gun, but she returned it carefully to her purse as she pushed to her feet, as well.

"Mr. O'Brien, I don't want to see you. Not next door, not in my station, not at the pub. Stick to your so-called orders if you must, but stay out of my sight."

"On one condition."

"You don't get to name conditions here!" She trembled with the fury she obviously felt.

He wasn't leaving until he'd warned her. "Keep someone with you. I don't think this is over."

"Is that a threat?"

"Of course not," he said. It felt like one of those shipping containers was sitting on his chest. This might be the last time he was this close to her—he couldn't let fear ruin it.

"I'll stay out of your sight, but I'm next door if you ever need me."

"I won't."

He believed her. He paused with one hand on the door-knob and turned back to face her. "Last night—"

"Don't you dare say it."

"—was everything to me," he finished.

"Get out." Her hands fisted at her sides and he knew she wanted to throw something.

"You asked for the truth." He left the room and walked out of the station, wishing the back door was still an option. He kept his gaze straight ahead, avoiding eye contact with everyone.

When Danny called out, Riley just raised a hand, unwilling to pause for a conversation. Tomorrow would be a better day. The sting of embarrassment would ease and she'd calm down. She might never forgive him, but out of sight or not, he was determined to keep her safe enough to enjoy a long life of hating him.

He was backing out of his parking space when his cell phone rang. The caller ID showed a blocked number and Riley flinched as he pulled back into the parking space to take the call.

"That takedown looks good," Director Casey said in his ear.

"News travels fast."

"You don't sound happy. Is there more?"

"I think so. She arrested Deke Maynard, but it was too easy," Riley said, finally able to articulate what bothered him most. "The bomb he'd planted was elementary. Anyone could have disarmed it."

"You expected someone with more tactical experience?"

"If a threat is serious enough to incite this much concern across federal agencies, then yes, I expect to encounter experienced people on the ground, too."

"Sleeper cells are often populated with civilians. It's the definition."

"Soft is one thing. Ignorant is another. You can't pull me out yet."

"I wasn't planning to. Long-term and indefinite, remember?"

Riley took a deep, relieved breath. "Thanks."

"Got a theory?"

"Deke Maynard has his eye on Chief Jensen. He might be a master strategist with all the crap he's managed here, but I think somewhere along the line it became personal."

"Artists can be twitchy."

"Sure," Riley admitted, though he had little experience. "They're searching his place and squeezing the butler for info."

"The analysts will sort it out."

"Thank you."

"One more thing," Casey said. "A new version of her speech on YouTube surfaced an hour ago. We've blocked it and we're tracing the party who loaded it."

"How was it modified?"

"Red crosshairs over her face and different scenery. The analysts haven't sorted out the background yet, but the landscape is covered with snow. We can't tell if the images are current or older. So it appears your hunch is correct. Stay close to her."

"No problem," Riley lied. "Can you send it to me?"

"Already done."

"Thank you, sir."

"If you need backup, just say the word. We can get someone into place now, before any more trouble hits."

"Yes, sir. I'll let you know."

The kind of backup he really needed, Director Casey couldn't provide. No amount of tactical expertise would fix the mess he'd made here.

He pulled up the video on his phone and his blood ran

cold. The new images in the background ranged from the current display in the park to the podium in front of the scorched police station where Abby had given her latest press conference.

But it was the angle of the photos that told Riley all he needed to know. He sent the request for backup, knowing the assassin was about to make his move. Regardless of how Abby felt about him personally, he would implement protective measures. No detail was too small, no request too big if it meant keeping her alive.

Chapter Seventeen

For the first time since the fire, Abby was grateful her office had been charred. She wasn't even upset the cleanup was taking longer than promised. Working at home would be for the best. Despite the proximity to Riley, at home behind closed doors and drawn curtains she could cry. Scream into a pillow. Her mascara could streak down her face and her nose could turn Rudolph-red. At home, no one could watch her fall apart.

She couldn't believe Maynard had gotten bail. Evidently he owned at least one judge—a man Abby thought she knew. Of course, Maynard had been forced to surrender his passport. So what? The man could have twenty for all anyone knew.

This day could not suck any worse.

She pulled all the way into her garage this time, unwilling to risk even a glimpse of Riley. Hurrying to the house, she dropped her purse on the table and drew the curtains in her kitchen and den.

But nothing blotted out the scent of her Christmas tree. A day ago it had been the best scent ever. Now, she felt nauseous. Reluctantly, she walked down the hallway. Like ripping off a bandage, she had to get this over with and find a way to rid him from her system. Her knees quivering, she turned into the front room.

And stalled.

"Welcome home, my dear." Deke, standing in the middle of the room, revealed a gun, raising it until the barrel was even with her chest.

Abby saw the cold death in his eyes, knew making a run was futile. How could she have been so wrong about him? "You'll never get away with this."

"Darling, I already have. Reliable witnesses are ready to testify they saw me at my attorney's office during the time of your tragic death."

His hand was too steady. She was out of time and options. Her gun was in her purse where she'd left it in the kitchen.

She sidestepped around the coffee table.

Deke wagged a finger. "No, no. Just take a seat. This will all be over shortly."

"What?" She stayed on her feet. "You're going to make this look like a suicide?" She had to keep him talking. "People know me better than that." She had to think of something.

He tipped his head to the side. "It was a thought. But you're right. And the damage lasts longer if your killer might be roaming free in Belclare."

"You're a monster. You worked Filmore into a frenzy."

"No," he snapped, stepping forward. "Filmore was his own worst enemy. The man was a small cog in a large machine. I am much more valuable. You might have been an asset, but instead you became an impediment. Now you must go. And don't worry, my attorneys will prove your pathetic police work was all wrong. You can die knowing you didn't stop me."

He was insane. Unfortunately, he'd focused all of that insanity on her. There was no babbling remorse over what he'd done or what he was about to do. His confidence unnerved her, but she refused to give in without a fight.

He'd moved drugs through her town, nearly killed two of her neighbors, three if she counted Riley, and burned down her police station. No, she would not give in while she still had an ounce of breath in her lungs.

"Why don't you just go?" she whispered. She needed him to believe she was completely beaten. "I'll let you walk away. I'll tell the world I was wrong." She forced herself to sit on the edge of the couch and reached out to trace the soft petal of a rose in the flowers he'd brought her yesterday.

Deke laughed, the sound harsh and laced with violent intent. "Oh, you might give me a head start, but you'd never give up or lie. You have far too much integrity. I sincerely regret to say that is your downfall."

"You'd be the white whale, too big for me to ever catch."

"How you tempt me." He came around the coffee table and sat beside her with that elegant grace she used to admire and now detested. "Unfortunately for you, I am a greedy white whale and the bounty on your head has become more than I can resist. You see, bigger fish than I want you gone."

He reached out, taking a lock of her hair and winding it around his fingers. "I did have hopes for you. For us."

"Tell me," she whispered, trying to hide how he made her skin crawl. She had to disarm him, it was her only hope.

There was a creak on the stairs and everything in him shifted. His eyes darted in that direction and then back to her, his features twisting into an evil snarl. His hand fisted in her hair and he yanked her head back. The muzzle of the gun was cold against the tender skin under her jaw. "Come out or I'll blow off her head!" he shouted.

Abby went still, fighting the instinct to squirm. "Who are you talking to?"

"Your lover, I'm sure. I cannot believe you took up with him. You don't even know him. He's lied to you every bit as much as I have!"

She hated that Deke was right, but then again, she'd known Deke for years and had never seen this darkness in him.

Maybe she was a fool.

"No one is here, Deke," she said. Everyone thought the bad guy was caught. She'd pushed Riley away after learning the truth. If she didn't think of some way out of this, she'd never have the chance to apologize. Intense regret swamped her. She squeezed her eyes shut against a sudden rush of tears, but one escaped, trickling back into her hair.

"Who are you crying for, darling?"

The endearment, so ugly in Deke's elitist tones, snapped her out of her self-pity.

"Kill me or run," she said, gathering her courage. "But make a damned decision already." She elbowed him in the gut and stomped on his foot. It wasn't an effective strike at this angle, but it forced the gun from her face and the distraction bought her precious seconds. He still had her by the hair. She pulled her knees to her chest and kicked out, hitting him in the chest and forcing the air from his lungs.

His fingers released her. A wild shot exploded from the weapon and breezed by her head. He shouted more threats as she rolled to the floor, but she ignored them all, searching for any kind of weapon. Her coffee table splintered and the vase toppled, spilling water all over her.

Deke swore, lunging for her again. She grabbed the vase and bashed him over the head.

Another gunshot rang out, and Deke's body went limp, crushing hers.

The coppery smell of fresh blood mixed with the clean

pine and sweet roses and lilies that had brightened the room so cheerfully just a day ago.

She pushed at Deke's shoulders, not sure if he was dead or merely unconscious. The floor shook as people pounded into her house.

Then she was surrounded by people dressed in black tactical SWAT gear. She only knew they weren't from Belclare, or even Baltimore. The team lifted Deke's body off her, carrying him and his gun out of her house. She asked if he was dead, but no one answered her.

"Are you injured?"

She shook her head. Only her coffee table and a wall or two. The raw wounds she suffered wouldn't benefit from a bandage.

"Someone will contact you for a statement," one of the team said, and then he walked away.

The sudden quiet in their absence was nearly as shocking as their entrance had been.

She pushed up to the couch, but it felt slimy. Contaminated by Deke's deception and violence. Raking her hair back from her face, her knees wobbled as she tried to walk away from the destroyed room. She just couldn't face the mess and destruction right now. Couldn't cope with all that it signified.

The bathroom upstairs was too far. She might as well climb Mount Everest. She stepped out of her shoes and stumbled along to the kitchen.

A man clad in black tactical gear filled the room, his back to her. He didn't have a helmet and she recognized the sandy-brown hair as well as the spread of his shoulders. Shoulders she'd leaned on more than once in past days. Shoulders she'd clung to last night with part of him deep inside her. "Riley?"

Her hand covered her lips. Was that even his name?

"Have a seat, Abby."

"You…" She looked back toward the hallway. "You're here to take my statement?"

"Eventually. Right now I just want to take care of you."

"I'm fine."

He stripped off his bulletproof vest and set it on the floor by the back door. "You're in shock."

"On a few levels," she confessed. "You saved my life." He'd said that was his job, his real purpose in Belclare.

"I had a little help."

"But I said…" She had to clear away the emotion clogging her throat. "I said awful things at the station."

"I might have deserved them." He shrugged. "I hurt you." He ran warm water over a paper towel, then squeezed out the excess. Pulling another chair closer, he started cleaning her face.

"I can do that," she protested, abruptly annoyed by his tenderness. He should be angry with her. She should still be angry with him. What did it mean that he was here? Was he just doing his job again or was there more to it?

It scared her how much she wanted there to be more to it.

He washed her face and sat back, staring at her. There were questions in his soft brown gaze that echoed the ones chasing through her mind.

"You handled yourself well," he said.

"Is he dead?"

"Don't know," Riley answered. "Does it matter?"

"Only if he causes more trouble."

"Well, dead or alive, I can assure you Deke Maynard is done causing trouble."

"You're sure about that?"

He nodded. "No lawyer will get him off or out on bail now."

She believed him. She should ask for proof, but it was

there in his steady, golden-brown gaze. He was telling her the truth.

"I want a new couch," she blurted.

"That's reasonable."

"This time I want it bigger."

One of his dark eyebrows arched and his lips twitched at the corner. "Big enough for two?"

She nodded. "Maybe a sectional."

He laughed and pulled her to her feet, wrapping his arms around her. "Now we have two houses needing repair work."

Abby spread her hands flat across his chest, stroking up and over his shoulders, following the firm muscles under the black ribbed sweater down to his hands. "I know a guy who's good with his hands." She lifted his hands to her lips, kissing each finger in turn.

"You do?"

She looked up into his warm brown eyes and felt the weight of the world simply fall away. "I do."

"Took you long enough to decide between us today."

She wondered if he could forgive her hesitation or if it would be the end of them after all. "I was wrong but there were mitigating circumstances."

"Let's talk about those circumstances."

"You know," she said, trying not to look at him, "you're free to go now. You got the bad guy. Saved my life—again."

"I wish that was true."

"What does that mean?" Did she even want to know?

She slumped against him, too tired for games. Riley had proved himself a jack-of-all-trades, from hanging garland to making her feel treasured *in* bed as well as out of it. Here, behind closed doors, no one was watching; she could lean in and steal a kiss and no one could call her weak. No one could judge her momentary lapse from police chief to normal woman.

Before temptation got the better of her, Riley came to her rescue again. He gently cradled her face in his palms, holding her steady for his kiss. She watched him close the distance, her eyes drifting shut as his lips met hers. But the kiss was fleeting, not deep as she'd hoped and his breath whispered across her face.

"I'm not free."

She opened her eyes, caught in the tender, golden-brown gaze assessing her. "What?"

"You have me well and truly caught, Abby Jensen."

She was so confused, so worried he might have to go— or want to go. "What do you want from me?"

"What I've never had." He smoothed a hand over her hair, his eyes searching hers. "I want roots. A home and family. *You,* forever."

It was mutual. *It was so mutual.* How did he pack so much intensity and intention into those few words? Her heart stuttered. She'd never really understood that a stuttering heart was possible until now. Forever was monumental. Wasn't it? She barely knew him. But forever was plenty of time to get to know him. There she went, arguing with herself!

"Think about it," he said, the words soft and warm against her lips. "I'm not leaving Belclare. I'm here to stay."

"Why?" She wanted him to kiss her the way he had last night when the world and all its problems had simply vanished. She wanted a kiss that blanked her mind and didn't leave room for questions about the past or present. A kiss that didn't carry any worries for the future.

"You know why," he murmured as his lips landed warm and soft on hers.

What started gently escalated as she wound her arms

around his waist, drawing him closer and pouring her heart into it. She wanted him to feel what she was too afraid to say. Too afraid to ask. How strange when her heart felt so safe that the rest of her trembled with fear.

Her career, her life's work, meant facing fear potentially every day. But here, with Riley, she knew there was more at stake and none of it was within her control.

Well, not much of it anyway.

He broke the kiss and studied her face. "You're thinking."

She couldn't deny it. "About you. Me. Us."

"*Us* works."

"Yes, I think it does." She took a deep breath and blurted out what neither of them could afford to overlook. "Homeland made it clear I'm still a target."

Riley rolled his eyes, but he didn't step away. "Tell me Mayor Scott didn't hear them."

"He did," she said with a smile, "but this is about you. I can handle the mayor."

"I'm not leaving." He drew her body up tight against his. "Not leaving town." He kissed her nose. "Not leaving you." He kissed her lips. "Not leaving us."

"Because of your assignment?" She hated the way her voice wobbled on the question.

"Because of *you*. I love you. Get used to it."

She pushed up on her toes and kissed him again. "I can do that."

"And?"

"And what?" she teased, trailing a fingertip along his full lower lip. He caught her finger in his teeth and growled just a little. "Oh. I have to say it?"

Another low rumble sounded in his throat.

"But I thought you knew."

He bit down a smidge harder and she laughed. "All right.

I love you, too." She tugged her finger away. "Whether you're a carpenter or a bodyguard or just the hunk next door, I love you, too. *Forever.*"

Epilogue

Thomas Casey read the report from Specialist O'Brien,
pleased with the reduced threat rating for Belclare. Chief
Jensen wasn't exactly in the clear—she might never be—
but at least she had the best possible protection in place.

Thomas stared at the mountain of folders on his desk.
Belclare was only the beginning.

* * * * *

MILLS & BOON®

'Tis the season to be daring…

The perfect books for all your glamorous Christmas needs come complete with gorgeous billionaire bad-boy heroes and are overflowing with champagne!

These fantastic 3-in-1s are must-have reads for all Modern™, Desire™ and Modern Tempted™ fans.

Get your copies today at
www.millsandboon.co.uk/Xmasmod

MILLS & BOON®

Want to get more from Mills & Boon?

Here's what's available to you if you join the
exclusive **Mills & Boon eBook Club** today:

- ✦ *Convenience – choose your books each month*
- ✦ *Exclusive – receive your books a month before
  anywhere else*
- ✦ *Flexibility – change your subscription at any time*
- ✦ *Variety – gain access to eBook-only series*
- ✦ *Value – subscriptions from just £1.99 a month*

So visit **www.millsandboon.co.uk/esubs** today
to be a part of this exclusive eBook Club!